BETRAYAL ON THE BOWERY

Also available by Kate Belli

Gilded Gotham Mysteries
Deception by Gaslight

BETRAYAL ON THE BOWERY

A GILDED GOTHAM MYSTERY

Kate Belli

NEW YORK

Copyright © 2021 by Kate Belli

Published in the United States by Crooked Lane Books, an imprint of The Quick Brown Fox & Company LLC.

Crooked Lane Books and its logo are trademarks of The Quick Brown Fox & Company LLC.

Library of Congress Catalog-in-Publication data available upon request.

ISBN (hardcover): 978-1-64385-758-9
ISBN (ebook): 978-1-64385-759-6

Cover design by Nicole Lecht

Printed in the United States.

www.crookedlanebooks.com

Crooked Lane Books
34 West 27th St., 10th Floor
New York, NY 10001

First Edition: October 2021

10 9 8 7 6 5 4 3 2 1

For Marc, who also bided his time.
I'm eternally grateful.

CHAPTER 1

Milton-Bradley Nuptials End in Chaos; Disgraceful Behavior from New York City's Citizenry

Polly Palmer, *New York City Globe*

May 27, 1889

The wedding of Rupert Milton, sixth Earl of Umberland, Viscount of Heath, to Montana-born copper heiress Esmerelda Bradley took place at ten in the morning this past Saturday at Grace Church in Manhattan. This author understands readers are anticipating an exhaustive chronicle detailing the beauty of the bride, the color of the bridesmaids' dresses, and a precise inventory of lavish gifts.

Regretfully, I am unable to accommodate readers' expectations.

This is not to say that the bride's beauty was unremarkable. Quite the opposite. Indeed, Esmerelda Bradley, or "Esmie" as she is known to her intimates, emerged from an elaborately decorated carriage appearing serene and resplendent in beaded ice-blue silk trimmed with Belgian lace. Unfortunately, the bride was unable to present an untroubled countenance for long, as on her short journey to the church's doors, she was forced to pass through what amounted to a veritable gauntlet of uninvited, gawking spectators, each more determined than the last to shout lewd remarks, either about the bride herself, her intended, or her late mother.

It is this author's understanding that crowds began to gather in the streets surrounding Grace Church in the dim predawn hours, wanting to position themselves in a good spot to view the arrival of the wedding party. By eight in the morning, their number had swelled to the thousands. Police officers brought in to manage the crowds were completely overwhelmed.

It was no better inside the church. Though police had been stationed at the front doors to vet the guests, there arose a brisk trade in forged invitations, and many of the uninvited curious simply waved a similar-looking card at the officers and marched in. Unlucky invitees who arrived too close to the start time of ten o'clock were understandably disgruntled to discover completely full pews. Many were forced to stand in the side aisles and gather in the back, including the venerable Mrs. Astor, who affected the sour look of one having swallowed a lemon.

It is public knowledge that Elmira Bradley, the late mother of the bride, was brutally murdered last year. Other so-called journalistic organizations in this city have continually reminded the public of this fact in the weeks leading up to the wedding, stoking a macabre curiosity and intrigue surrounding the event. While such choices are highly unethical and these news outlets ought to be ashamed, the real fault lies squarely at the feet of the general public.

You, my fellow New Yorkers, behaved disgracefully. The noise of the gathered crowd outside was so voluminous, it was difficult inside for the priest to be heard. You disrupted and attempted to ruin what should have been a happy, peaceful moment for a bride and groom who have suffered a terrible time and an insurmountable loss. Upon the newly wedded couple's departing the church, I was shocked to observe a near frenzy among the onlookers, many of whom tore at the bride's dress in an effort to gain a souvenir of the event. So dangerous was the situation, and so frightened the bride, the groom was compelled to sweep her into his arms and carry her to their waiting carriage.

Indeed, several well-timed blows from the best man were all, I fear, that kept the couple from becoming overwhelmed and possibly trampled to death on the very steps of the church in which they had just been wed.

I have never witnessed such barbaric actions. I urge each and every one of you present to reflect deeply on your behavior, and to seek forgiveness from your maker. Shame.

★ ★ ★

Genevieve folded her arms and waited.

Her editor, Arthur Horace, put down the draft of her article and leaned back in his chair. He regarded her with weary resignation.

She lifted her chin a notch, still waiting.

"Genevieve, I can't print this."

And there it is. She had expected nothing less, but her heart still plunged with disappointment and anger.

"Do you disagree with a word I wrote?"

"No," Arthur admitted, removing his glasses and polishing them on the lapel of his rumpled jacket. It was a tactic she recognized, one Arthur used to buy time to think.

"The public behaved abominably," Genevieve pressed, sensing her editor's indecision. "Poor Esmie was scared out of her wits."

Arthur sighed, replacing his glasses. "I understand and share your outrage, Genevieve. The public *did* behave quite terribly, and I'm sure poor Miss Bradley—erm, Countess Umberland now, I suppose—was terrified. But I can't print this"—he held up his hand to stop her half-voiced protest—"as it stands," he finished, voice firm.

An impatient noise escaped her before she could stop it. Arthur's furry gray eyebrows shot to the top of his forehead.

He shook the draft of the article at her. "Mrs. Astor swallowed a lemon? *So-called* journalistic outlets? Genevieve, much of this is simply inflammatory. I have no interest in antagonizing our competition, let alone the Astors." The piece of paper fluttered across his desk and landed on the edge close to Genevieve, who snatched it back.

"Clean it up," Arthur ordered, turning his attention to what he had been writing before she entered. "But keep the part about the groom carrying Esmie down the steps," he added, not looking up from the page in front of him. "Romance, Genevieve. That's what people want in a story about a wedding."

Genevieve looked down at the words she had written, frustration welling in her chest. "If you don't want the kind of story I write, Mr. Horace, perhaps you should assign someone else to the society column," she said in as polite a tone as she could manage through clenched teeth. Which was not terribly polite.

Arthur's eyebrows rose again as he put down his pencil. His look had shifted from one of resignation to irritation. "You hounded me for years to write something more substantive, Genevieve. I've given it to you. You've done well with the column these last few months." He bent over his desk again, clearly signaling the conversation was over.

Genevieve's anger, which had been bubbling along at a nice low simmer, now burst forth before she could help it. "How scintillating can I make endless garden parties in Newport and weddings in Grace Church sound?" she exploded, shaking the paper back at Arthur, who blinked in surprise. "It's all the same, over and over. Let me write *real* stories, Arthur. You know I can do it."

Her editor leaned back again and eyed her over his glasses. "And who says the society column isn't comprised of real stories? There's meat on those bones, Genevieve, if you'll find it. Your predecessor did."

If anything, the mention of the late Jackson Waglie, *The Globe*'s prior society columnist, set her teeth even more on edge. Yes, fine, the overbearing, pompous man had managed to write a column that had kept the Astor 400 on the edge of their collective seat every week. Waglie had somehow had the ability to turn a routine story about a late Friday night society supper into a dramatic tale of Shakespearean proportions, complete with Machiavellian twists and turns, heroes and villains. Reputations were made and had crumbled based on his words; debutantes fled in fear at the mere sight of him; and even the staunchest society matron and the most hardened of robber barons had tried to stay on his good side.

Bad press could make or break a family's standing, and Waglie had exploited his power to the hilt.

"He was mean," Genevieve grumbled. She keenly recalled being on the receiving end of some of Waglie's more barbed comments. "I have no wish to be unkind."

"I don't believe you have to be unkind. There is drama in the daily, Genevieve. Nobody has to die to make a compelling story," Arthur said meaningfully before turning his attention back to his scribbling.

Genevieve huffed a breath in response and irritably gathered her papers. She plopped herself at her desk and stared at her list of upcoming assignments in annoyance: a luncheon at the Stiltons', the engagement of Trudy Barlow to Ralph Nestor. Her eyes glazed over just thinking about writing the pieces.

If only someone would *die,* she thought savagely. Things were far more exciting when there was a murder to investigate.

Later, in the small, dark hours of the night when she couldn't sleep, she would wonder if her scandalous thoughts had somehow set the whole terrifying affair in motion. Genevieve was not prone to superstition, but on a deep, primal level, she would never be able to shake the yoke of responsibility she secretly felt for the rash of murders that followed.

Genevieve had wished for someone to die, and death, conveniently, had obliged.

★   ★   ★

It began on one of the prettiest days New York City had seen all year. A warm, soft breeze caressed Genevieve's face, ruffling her skirt and carrying with it a fresh summery scent, remarkable for anywhere in the city, even more so considering she was at the harbor, which typically smelled of rotting fish.

Esmie and Rupert were on their way. Genevieve had watched their ascent up the gangplank and into the ship's luxurious confines some ten minutes prior, after a team of porters had successfully wrangled the couple's vast piles of luggage.

She squinted from underneath her pale green parasol, searching for Esmie's slim, lavender-clad form on the upper deck, but knew it was probably too soon for her friends to appear. Settling into a state room took time.

A transatlantic voyage always felt exciting to Genevieve, even if she wasn't the one departing. There was something hopeful and energetic about it, and today, with its perfect weather, epitomized the feeling: the docks were bustling, full of sailors shouting instructions, families counting their children, porters giving orders, all against the jaunty sound of waves lapping against pilings. Seagulls swooped and screeched, darting high against the clouds before diving back toward brackish waters, only to soar upward again. The ship's massive, lemony-colored funnels and jovial masts were so perfectly set against the brilliant azure sky they nearly resembled a painted backdrop at the theater.

Genevieve inhaled and twirled her parasol, content to soak in the atmosphere and wait to wave her friends off toward their new life.

She sensed, rather than saw, Daniel's hesitant presence, a cautious figure whose footsteps slowed as he approached.

Her heart began to accelerate. Taking a deep breath, she turned and extended her hand.

"Mr. McCaffrey." He looked as dashing as ever in a light summer suit: tall and strong-jawed, the sun picking up a hint of red in his dark hair, with eyes that almost matched the day's luminous sky. Those eyes regarded her with a hint of surprise, perhaps that she was using his family name.

It was better, though, to keep their relations formal.

Safer.

"Miss Stewart," Daniel replied, taking both her cue and her hand. His grip was firm, and the warmth of his palm seared through her fine mesh glove. "I did not get a chance to say, but you looked beautiful at the wedding," he continued. She and Daniel had both been members of the wedding party; indeed, Daniel had been Rupert's best man.

The compliment suffused her with unexpected pleasure, and she felt a slight flush stain her cheeks. "Really? I don't think peach is quite my color, but it is nice for a June wedding."

She detected a hint of shyness around Daniel's answering smile. "The bride certainly looked beautiful," he politely replied. "I hear from Rupert she has you to thank for it."

Genevieve smiled back. "Some time ago, she asked for my help in choosing new clothes. We've spent quite a bit of time at the dressmaker's this past year." She didn't voice the painful circumstances surrounding these outings. Of course, Daniel already knew about the horrific murder of Esmie's mother the previous year; the late Elmira Bradley had insisted on dressing her only daughter in garish, unflattering ensembles, leaving the poor girl quite uninformed when it came to choosing clothing. Upon Mrs. Bradley's demise, Esmie had asked Genevieve to help her select a new wardrobe, a task Genevieve had accepted with reluctance. She had been surprised at how pleasurable the visits had become, and at the deeper friendship she and Esmie had formed.

What Daniel likely didn't know was that Genevieve's newly sprung relationship with Esmie had helped fill the awful, gaping hole left by the veritable disappearance of one of her oldest and dearest friends in the world. Callie Maple's only living family, her grandmother, had passed on the previous autumn, leaving Callie with nothing. Well, almost nothing. She had inherited an insurmountable pile of debts and a set of nearly priceless family diamonds she adamantly refused to sell.

Genevieve blinked twice, quickly, to prevent unbidden tears from spilling. Callie had kindly but firmly refused offers of assistance from all quarters, and there had been many. Come the holiday season, Callie had taken things a step further, and kindly but firmly cut herself off from her previous life.

Genevieve had no idea where her dear friend was these days. She hadn't seen Callie in five months. While she was reasonably sure she could find Callie if she looked hard enough, Callie had made it very clear she didn't want to be found.

"Please, let me be for a while," Callie had said to her and Eliza at their last meeting, the three of them shivering under the lonely, bare branches of the trees in Washington Square Park. It was soon after Callie had sold the townhouse that had been her grandmother's, using the funds to pay off as many debts as she could. "I need time to myself."

"Callie, we just want to help. Where will you sleep? Live? How will you eat? Please come live with me, or Genevieve," Eliza had pleaded, tears in her eyes. It was an offer they had both made countless times.

Callie had looked across the desolate, empty park toward her former home and shaken her head, pale but resolute. "This isn't my world anymore. I love you both, but if you love me, you'll let me go. Please don't look for me."

Genevieve could still feel the pain lodged in her chest as she had watched Callie walk away, she and Eliza gripping each other and openly weeping. She had considered trying to find Callie in the intervening months, many times, but the memory of the look on Callie's face as she had asked to be left alone held her back.

For now.

Daniel seemed to sense her shift in mood and changed the topic. "I quite liked your recent article as well," he said.

Genevieve's teeth clenched, her automatic reaction to the reminder of Arthur's editorial changes to her piece, and made an effort to relax her jaw. "The behavior of this city was a disgrace," she said. "It was the least I could do." The much-abridged form of her original article had appeared in Monday's paper, minus any reference to Mrs. Astor and lemons. She noticed Daniel didn't bring up the bit that mentioned him. Her mind flashed to the frightening moment on the stairs of the church: the frantic crowds closing in on their group, snatching at the lace on Esmie's dress; the claustrophobic, panicked feeling of being trapped; the fury on Daniel's face as he physically repelled frenzied onlookers, allowing herself and the other bridesmaids to descend to their waiting carriages.

"I quite agree," Daniel answered gravely. "You handled it well. I suppose it's for the best they're off to the continent now, though I will miss Rupert. Do you plan to visit once they're settled in England?"

Genevieve forced her mind back to the present moment. Rupert and Esmie would honeymoon on the continent for the summer and then make their home—for now, at least—at Rupert's apparently decrepit, ancestral estate in Sussex, which Esmie's fortune was meant to help repair.

Would she go? It was impossible to say. Everything felt so unsettled at present; the summer was shaping up to be a rather odd, disjointed season. She still had inroads to make in her career. Callie was missing. She and her family weren't even relocating to their Newport home until later this summer, once her brother, Gavin, returned from Egypt.

"Perhaps," she said. "In time. I hope Esmie likes England. She deserves some happiness."

"Rupert will be good to her."

"He'd better be." Genevieve was rather fond of Rupert, as everyone was. It was impossible *not* to be fond of Rupert.

But she didn't quite trust him.

"I daresay she'll enjoy Italy," Daniel said.

"Everyone enjoys Italy," she agreed.

"Yes," he replied shortly.

An awkward silence ensued. Genevieve idly twirled her parasol again and stifled a sigh. She couldn't blame Daniel for being a bit uncomfortable in her presence. She had, after all, rejected his proposal of marriage the previous year. She remained convinced the proposal had not been made in earnest, but rather as a knee-jerk solution to a perceived problem. Regardless, she had rejected him.

Rejected him, and then spent the following year avoiding him, and memories of that proposal, as best she could.

Luckily, she spotted Rupert and Esmie leaning against the railing of the upper deck of the ship. "There they are," she said with relief, happy to remove her mind from that dark winter moment, pointing the couple out to Daniel and waving.

Daniel followed the line of her finger and waved his straw hat in Rupert and Esmie's direction. "I think they're pleased to be leaving," he said, more to himself than to her.

Genevieve guessed he was correct. Between the murder of Esmie's mother, the death of several of the culprits responsible, and the mayhem at their own wedding, she was sure Rupert and Esmie were ready to take a long, perhaps permanent break from New York.

Rupert made some exaggerated gestures toward them, indicating he and Esmie were heading below deck but would return momentarily. The awkward silence between her and Daniel returned.

Genevieve closed her parasol, mostly to give her hands something to do, and turned her face briefly toward the sun, closing her eyes against its heat. Pangs of regret radiated from her chest and into her very limbs, making them feel heavy, at odds with the lightness in the day's air: regret at the time that had passed, regret that she and Daniel seemed to have lost something precious and ineffable, regret that on that cold March night, over a year ago, the word *no* instead of *yes* had sprung from her lips.

What if you had said yes? her own mind whispered persuasively. She shoved the thought away with force, as she had every other time it had popped into her brain, unbidden and unwelcome, over the past year.

"Genevieve," Daniel said. The hesitancy in his voice caused her to open her eyes. She suddenly found she wanted, very much, to hear what he had to say next.

A shrill, loud woman's scream erupted from the ship, cutting off all thoughts of what Daniel might have been about to say.

Somehow, she knew. She had never heard Esmie scream before, but she knew.

"I think that was Esmie." Rational disbelief warred with her gut instinct. Genevieve stared at Daniel, willing him to contradict her, but he looked as stunned as she felt.

"Daniel!" The hoarse shout came from the boat as well. Rupert had reappeared on a lower deck and was gesturing frantically. "Come quickly!"

Barely glancing at her, Daniel grabbed her hand and began to sprint toward the gangplank. Fear and exhilaration rushed to Genevieve's head as she hitched up her skirts and raced along with him, weaving between startled bystanders, most of whom had stopped in their tracks at the first sound of the scream. Up the gangplank they went, Daniel shoving aside a sailor on his way. He slowed momentarily and looked back at her, his eyes questioning.

Why is he stopping? "What are you waiting for?" she snapped. "Go!" Genevieve tilted her head up the gangplank.

Daniel led her straight into what appeared to be the first-class lounge, abruptly halting as some sailors rushed past them toward the exit. Genevieve crashed into Daniel's back, nearly knocking him over, panting.

She gaped at the interior. Skylights of stained glass transformed the brilliant June sun outside into a kaleidoscope of softly colored lights, illuminating mahogany paneled walls. Comfortable armchairs covered in a rich, floral brocade were arranged around low tables, and a beautifully patterned carpet stretched across the vast room's floor, punctuated by the occasional potted palm tree.

Genevieve had heard the *Sophia Victoria* was elegant, a veritable floating hotel, and truly, she had never seen such opulence on an ocean liner before.

"That way." Daniel pointed in the direction from which the sailors had come, and hurried through the vast room and down an equally elegant passageway, still holding Genevieve's hand. "Rupert said they were in the royal port suite—if this boat is like other liners, that should be in the stern."

They brushed past a pair of maids, bustling down the passageway with their arms full of linens and whispering furiously. At one point a white-bearded gentleman poked his head out of his stateroom door and demanded to know what was happening as they rushed by.

Finally they came to an open door and burst into a sitting room, decorated in white and gold, with gilded cherubs holding wall sconces aloft. Daniel pulled her toward one of the bedrooms, and only then, once they had entered and surveyed the scene in front of them, did he drop her hand.

A chill swept over Genevieve despite the warm air wafting in through the open porthole. She wasn't sure if it was due to the loss of warmth of Daniel's hand, which had felt so reassuring in hers, or to what she was witnessing.

Esmie stood at the far end of the room, pressed against a wall, her complexion ashen. A shaky hand covered her mouth, and she was staring down with wide eyes. On the floor, Rupert, her husband of exactly one week, was kneeling over the body of a man. The man's glassy eyes sightlessly pointed toward the plastered rococo ceiling. Traces of vomit were crusted around his mouth and down his shirt, which was soaked through with sweat.

Genevieve recognized the dead man instantly, even as Rupert reached forward to gently close the man's eyes.

"Oh Rupert," she breathed. "What have you done?"

CHAPTER 2

"Done?" Rupert stared at Genevieve with wild eyes, his tone incredulous. "I haven't *done* anything. He was in *our* stateroom when Esmie and I came down to get her parasol. Vomited all over the floor, yelled some crazy things, then promptly fell over and *died*." He looked from Genevieve to Daniel, to Esmie, then back at the dead man on the floor. "In *my* bedroom, no less."

Daniel swiftly knelt next to Rupert and shoved his hands into the dead man's jacket pockets. If he wasn't mistaken, there was little time to lose. He heard Esmie gasp.

"Daniel, is that quite necessary?" Genevieve asked in a warning voice.

A corner of his mouth twitched; so, he was back to being "Daniel" as opposed to "Mr. McCaffrey." Well, that was one handy thing about death, he supposed: it did bring people together.

"I'm trying to find out who this is," Daniel murmured. His fingers closed on a small, round metal object buried within the dead man's interior pocket. The body under Daniel's hand was still unnervingly warm, as if the man had simply lain down on the suite's floor for a nap. But the stillness of the man's chest—no heartbeat, no rise and fall of breath—told a different story. "Those sailors we saw running—they were on their way to fetch the authorities, yes?" Rupert nodded.

"But we know who it is," Genevieve protested.

Daniel stopped short. "You do?"

"Yes," Esmie said in a strangled voice. "It's Marcus Dalrymple." Her hand moved from her mouth to close around her own throat, as if trying to contain another scream building there.

"Agnes and Houston Dalrymple's son?" Daniel puzzled, studying the dead man's face more closely. He knew the parents socially. Houston's father had been great friends with Jacob Van Joost, whose fortune Daniel had inherited. Now he could see the resemblance, in both the long nose and the red hair. He cast a wary glance at Esmie, praying she wouldn't scream again.

"We were friends," Esmie said, in a small, shocked voice.

Genevieve gingerly skirted around the body, moving to stand by Esmie and put an arm around her shoulders. Daniel noticed, for the first time, that vomit was splattered across the front of Esmie's dark lavender dress.

"More than friends, I'd say," Rupert added, leaning back to sit on his heels and pushing a fall of blond hair out of his eyes. He slid his eyes toward Daniel. "Marcus was my competition for Esmie's hand."

Everyone looked toward Esmie, who shook her head bewilderedly. "It was never serious," she said sadly. "Marcus and I were both rather odd ducks in society. He had a stammer, you know. We both enjoyed books. I think he only proposed because I was kind to him." Tears began to slide down her pale cheeks, and she sagged into Genevieve's side.

"Why did you turn him down?" Daniel asked. He absentmindedly shoved the metal coin into his own pocket and moved his search to Marcus's trousers.

"Daniel, we've told you who the man is, must you keep rummaging through his clothing?" Genevieve asked angrily. "It's obscene."

He ignored her. "Esmie?"

"Rupert came along," she answered simply. Rupert's head jerked up. He rose and gently peeled Esmie away from Genevieve, gathering her into his arms.

Daniel's search yielded nothing useful: a handkerchief smeared with the man's sick, a wallet containing a few bills, a few other stray coins. Nothing that would indicate why Marcus had stumbled, unwell, into Rupert and Esmie's stateroom on an ocean liner about to set sail.

"Was he scheduled to make the crossing?" Daniel asked, sitting back on his heels now. The sheer alarm of Rupert's call and his mad dash with Genevieve through the ship was slowly being replaced by a heavy, brooding feeling, resting square in his chest. Something was very, very wrong here.

Nobody had an answer. "Most families are preparing to head to their summer homes," Genevieve said hesitantly. "The Dalrymples are not perhaps the most active family in society, but they do tend to follow tradition." She shrugged. "It's possible they decided to tour the continent instead this year."

"No," Esmie said, lifting her tear-stained face from where it had been buried in Rupert's shoulder. "He was here for me."

Rupert nodded solemnly. "It did seem that way. He fell right on Esmie, clutching at her dress and trying to say her name." He pulled Esmie closer as she shuddered.

Daniel digested this, still puzzled. "But you married another man just last Saturday," he mused. "A bit late for the boy to be confessing his feelings."

Esmie shook her head. "He wasn't here to win me over. I think he was trying to warn me."

Alarm bells began to fire off in Daniel's head. "Warn you? Against what?"

She turned to look at Rupert, who tried to explain. "He said, 'Esmie . . . danger . . . demon . . . red eyes.' Then he"—here Rupert gestured to the front of Esmie's dress, indicating Marcus's sick—"and collapsed."

"Demon red eyes?" Daniel repeated, baffled. He scrubbed his hand across his face absentmindedly, trying to sort this out. "Does that mean anything to either of you?" Rupert and Esmie both shook their heads.

"Rupert," Daniel said, standing up and wiping his hands on his own handkerchief, "I need to ask you, quickly. Did you have anything to do with this?"

"*Me?*" Rupert drew himself to his full height, pulling away from Esmie. "How can you ask such a thing? I've told you what happened—the man was clearly in love with *my wife*, came here to talk her out of leaving on our honeymoon with some deranged tale about demons, and perished. On my *bedroom floor*. He was obviously ill." A look of alarm crossed Rupert's face. "You don't think it's catching, do you? Another cholera outbreak?" He took a cautious step farther away from the corpse.

"He was slurring his words, Daniel," Esmie said gently. Her tears had dried, but she regarded Marcus's body with sadness. "I believe he was under the influence of drink."

"I have to ask, Rupert. Given what transpired last year," Daniel lowered his voice and cast a swift glance toward the open bedroom door. The previous winter, Rupert had engaged in a series of audacious jewel thefts under the alias of Robin Hood, driven by financial desperation and a compulsion he found impossible to control. An unscrupulous group of investors, led by the gangster Tommy Meade, had murdered several people, including Esmie's mother, and attempted to frame Rupert and Daniel for the killings.

If anything, Rupert managed to look more outraged. "And as I thought we established last year"—he also lowered his voice, the words coming out in a seething hiss— "I'm no killer and never have been."

"I know that—" Daniel began, but Rupert cut him off.

"I haven't even stolen anything in over a year," he whispered furiously. "Nearly being blamed for murders I didn't commit rather knocked the urge to thieve out of me. Besides," he said, glancing toward his wife, "I promised Esmie."

Sharp frustration cut through Daniel. "Stop," he bit out. "I know that. But the police may find it suspicious that your new bride's only other suitor conveniently expired on the floor of your suite. Given *last year*, you are in a precarious position." Daniel and Genevieve had discovered who was responsible for the murders and had managed to have the jewel thefts blamed on men who were dead.

There were still some alive, though, beyond the four of them, who knew Rupert was the true thief.

Uneasy silence descended over the room, but it was short-lived. The heavy pounding of footsteps soon sounded, and three panting sailors burst into the bedroom, followed closely by two uniformed police officers and a short, powerfully built man, in a drab brown suit, sporting a large moustache.

Daniel tamped down an internal curse of frustration at the sight of the mustached man. He had crossed paths with

Detective Aloysius Longstreet many times, mostly when he was attempting to help those from his former neighborhood of Five Points who found themselves on the wrong side of the law. The man was a veritable pit bull terrier; once he had a suspect in his teeth, he wouldn't let go until they were vanquished.

Moving away from the body, Daniel edged past Longstreet, who gave him a short nod of recognition. The officers hustled him, Rupert, Esmie, and Genevieve into the suite's adjacent sitting room. The policemen were trying and failing to appear nonchalant about the room's luxurious interior; they kept glancing around with wide eyes until Longstreet barked for their return. The officers gave stern orders not to leave the suite and returned to the bedroom, trading places with the sailors, two of whom rushed out of the suite, presumably to tell their officers that the ship's departure would now be delayed. The other lingered in the open bedroom door, keeping one eye on the detective and the other on Daniel's group.

Daniel resisted the urge to pace the room. The appearance of Longstreet made him uneasy, but it wouldn't do to let that show. A black-jacketed porter hovered solicitously in the doorway and offered, in German-accented but impeccable English, to bring all of them some cold water or lemonade.

"That would be most kind," Rupert answered in a low voice. He too was standing, and he moved from staring out the porthole of the sitting room to behind Esmie's chair, resting a hand on her shoulder. They both looked exhausted and disheveled. She motioned for him to lean down, and whispered into his ear. He nodded in reply.

"Might the countess change her clothing?" he inquired of the detective through the open bedroom door. "She has some things in her bedroom next door."

The porter returned, bearing a silver tray laden with tall crystal glasses, each glistening with pearly drops of condensation. Daniel hadn't realized how thirsty he had become until the cool, icy water slid down his parched throat. He almost wished he could rub the cold glass over his forehead, now sticky with dried sweat.

Longstreet strolled in from the bedroom and eyed the front of Esmie's dress, the porter, the gilded cherubs, all with a slight sneer. The ostentatiousness of the room seemed to rankle him.

He nodded at Esmie, once. "You may change, but I'll be wanting that dress," he said, adding a curt "No" to the porter at the offer of a drink.

"My maid is still seeing to some of the other luggage below," Esmie replied, her voice weary.

"I can help," Genevieve offered.

Longstreet gave Genevieve an assessing glance but again nodded once before returning to the bedroom where the dead body lay.

Genevieve cast Daniel a swift, questioning look. He understood instantly: Was there anything she needed to discuss in whispers with Esmie behind closed doors? His mind raced through probable scenarios, but in the end he gave her a miniscule head shake. Frankly, Esmie didn't appear as though she could handle much more today.

The silent exchange with Genevieve was familiar, and comforting.

The ladies retreated to the suite's second bedroom and shut the door. Daniel finally sat, crossing an ankle over the opposite knee, and tapped his finger against his chin. He strained to make out the low murmurs of the detective and officers in the other room, but it was useless. Rupert slumped into a chair himself, taking a long pull on his glass of lemonade.

They sat, silent and waiting. Daniel listened to a glided clock tick the seconds away and took the occasional sip from his water glass. Rupert closed his eyes. In the silence, Daniel allowed his mind to gingerly probe the mute conversation he had briefly shared with Genevieve; they'd had many such exchanges the previous year when they were embroiled in a murder investigation together.

Perhaps they could regain some of their old familiarity.

Perhaps they could be friends again.

It was surprising how much the thought made him ache.

The ladies emerged from Esmie's bedroom, Genevieve holding the stained lavender dress bundled in her arms. Esmie had changed into a swiss-dotted, dove-gray cotton day dress, and, Daniel thought approvingly, looked much more composed than before. He was not surprised, though, knowing from past experience that she was made of sterner stuff than she seemed. Both he and Rupert stood upon the ladies' entrance.

Longstreet bustled in, followed by one of the officers. "Take that," he ordered the policeman, gesturing toward the dress Genevieve held. He motioned for the ladies to sit, hooked his thumbs in his belt loops and rocked back on his heels. The other officer emerged and stood in the doorway, with a pad and pencil to take notes, displacing the sailor, who scuttled to the main doorway of the suite.

"Well then," Longstreet began, once Esmie and Genevieve were settled. His manner was briskly genial, but Daniel saw steel in the man's dark eyes. "Tell me what you know."

Rupert told the tale: the attempted retrieval of Esmie's parasol, Marcus's unexpected presence, the slurred speech and stumbling. The officer with the pad scratched it all down.

"He said Esmie's name," Rupert reported, "and clutched at her dress. Then he keeled over."

Longstreet's sharp eyes bored into Rupert. "Nothing else?"

Daniel kept his expression neutral as Rupert shook his head and lied. "Nothing."

"I screamed," Esmie added softly, "and some of the sailors came running. We had seen our friends below on the dock, there to wave us off, and Rupert yelled he was going to get help. This man kindly stayed with me"—she gestured toward the remaining sailor—"until Rupert returned."

Nobody said anything about demons.

"I tried to help him, I did," the sailor said in a thick cockney accent, sliding his eyes toward the bedroom where the dead body lay. Longstreet fixed the sailor in his gaze. The poor man removed his hat and began turning it over in his hands, around and around. He looked traumatized. "I held his hand and told him to hang on, but he just kept gasping. Then his lordship returned and told me to fetch the police, so off I ran."

Longstreet eyed them all in turn, his gaze finally settling on Daniel. "Mr. McCaffrey," he said in a cold tone. There was no love lost between them. "And how do you know these people?"

"The earl and I have been friends since school," Daniel replied. Longstreet's eyebrows raised; Daniel was deliberately needling the detective by using Rupert's title, but didn't care. "I was the best man at their wedding last week."

"And is this your wife?" Longstreet asked, tilting his head toward Genevieve.

"No," Genevieve cut in. "Genevieve Stewart. Also a friend of the couple, here to see them off on their honeymoon."

"Honeymoon, eh?" Longstreet cast another disdainful glance around the richly appointed suite before turning his attention back to Esmie. "And how did you know the deceased, ma'am?"

"Your ladyship," Rupert corrected the detective sharply.

Longstreet narrowed his eyes. "We're in America, sir."

Esmie cut in, giving Rupert a quelling look, and repeated the same story she had told Daniel and Genevieve, about Marcus's attempt to woo her, her refusal of his proposal, how they were friends.

Longstreet remained silent once Esmie had finished, and allowed the moment to stretch, long and uncomfortable. Rupert shifted a little in his chair. Daniel cast a quick warning glance at his friends: he knew this tactic. Longstreet was betting someone would feel the need to fill that silence and keep talking, perhaps reveal something they shouldn't.

Luckily, it was the cockney sailor who piped up first.

"Some of the other lads were saying there was a drunk down on the docks earlier. A tall red-headed fellow, they said. That he was weaving, had already puked all over the place. They were hoping he wasn't coming aboard." The sailor looked nervously between Longstreet and Rupert, seemingly torn between wanting to stay in both men's good graces.

Daniel saw Rupert's shoulders sag a tiny bit in relief before he straightened up and resumed his expression of haughty British aristocrat.

Longstreet's shrewd eyes assessed the sailor, who twisted uncomfortably under their weight.

"Seems cut and dry, doesn't it?" Longstreet said. "Our young man was rejected, spends the week following the wedding getting good and drunk—was he a guest, by the way?" Following Esmie's miserable nod, Longstreet's expression tightened into something Daniel couldn't quite read. "Spends the next week tying one on, then comes here in a misguided, last-ditch effort to win the lady back." He paused, seeming to want to assess the effect of his words on those assembled. Nobody moved a muscle.

"The poor lad must have got a bad batch of rotgut in there somewhere," Longstreet continued, "or maybe he had a weak heart. The coroner will have a look and answer what he can." His gaze slid toward Esmie, gauging her reaction to the idea of an autopsy. She remained still and pale as a statue.

Daniel tried to calculate the likelihood of Longstreet actually believing the tale he'd spun, and letting the matter rest.

The odds were not high.

Longstreet regarded Rupert and Esmie with mock regret. "I apologize that you cannot leave on your honeymoon." He annunciated the last word with a touch of wryness. "But none of you may leave the city until this is resolved. I'm off to summon the coroner's office now. Officer Markle here will take your relevant information, and after that you are free to leave. Except you," he said, pointing at the sailor, who stood at attention, "I'll need to speak to those others you mentioned, who saw the drunken man on the dock. The rest of you, I'll be in touch." With a nod toward the officer with the pad, Longstreet gave them all a final warning glance and left the suite.

Daniel released a soft breath as Officer Markle began taking down their names and addresses. He stood when it was his turn, then stepped out of the way and idly thrust his hands into his pockets as the policeman moved on to Genevieve.

A round, solid object under his fingertips brought the memory of absentmindedly pocketing Dalrymple's coin rushing back. *Dammit*. His annoyance with himself was instantly tempered by relief; at least Longstreet had already left. The sharp-eyed detective surely would have spotted the guilty look he now undoubtedly wore.

Daniel swore again in his head. He hadn't meant to steal a dead man's loose change, but couldn't very well return it now. Resolving to pop the coin into the collection box of the first church he passed, if he could ever get off this bloody boat, Daniel's fingers turned the smooth metal disk around in his pocket.

An hour later, the group stood on the dock, blinking in the bright sunshine. Daniel and Genevieve had stayed to help Rupert and Esmie organize all the luggage so recently deposited on the boat; it had been quite an ordeal, tracking down the correct pieces, arranging for their transport back to Esmie's father's mansion, where the couple would stay until Detective Longstreet allowed them to leave.

"We may have to postpone until September," Rupert said mournfully, gazing with regret at the stately ocean liner. "We had planned to be out of Italy by August, to avoid the worst of the heat," he complained.

"Rupert, let's go," Esmie urged, gesturing toward a cab that was disembarking passengers. "You don't mind, do you?" she asked Genevieve.

Genevieve hugged her friend. "Of course not. Go home and rest. I'll send a note tomorrow to see if you're up for a visitor."

"I'm sure I shall be." Esmie climbed into the cab, with a hand from Rupert.

Daniel clasped his friend's hand in his and looked warningly into Rupert's brown eyes. "Be careful," he said quietly. "Lay low until this is settled." A worried expression settled on Rupert's features, and he nodded in agreement.

"Pay us a call, will you? Amos is going to be none too pleased to see us on his doorstep again so soon," Rupert said, referring to Esmie's father. "He was pretty shaken by what happened at the wedding. I think he was looking forward to being on his own for a bit."

"I am sure he'll be happy to have you both under his roof," Daniel replied, though he wondered if Rupert was right. The match between Esmie and Rupert had largely been orchestrated by Esmie's late mother, who had desperately wanted her only daughter to marry a titled aristocrat. Amos cared little for Rupert but had agreed to keep Elmira happy. And after his wife's death, to keep Esmie happy.

Daniel stood next to Genevieve and watched the cab clatter away down a cobblestone street, heading uptown. He could hear a man's voice exploding in anger, and a stern but calm voice answering in measured, practiced tones. Daniel grimaced. Word was spreading both that the ship's departure was going to be delayed and that a death onboard was the cause. The sun was shining as brightly as ever, but the mood surrounding him on the docks was turning suspicious and angry as passengers wondered how long they would be inconvenienced.

Plus, a death onboard prior to the ship's departure would surely spook the sailors, a superstitious lot under the best of circumstances.

"What now?" Genevieve's clear voice asked. She was looking around warily, seeming also to sense the mingled undercurrents of fear and displeasure rippling around them.

What now, indeed? He hadn't felt this wrung out since last year. Since the last time they had spent more than a polite five minutes in each other's company.

But he relished the feeling all the same. He had allowed himself the comfort of numbness for a year, of work and routine and, frankly, boredom.

Whatever was happening now, whatever the death of Marcus Dalrymple meant, god forgive him, but he was no longer bored.

Daniel breathed in a deep lungful of sea air. Right before the eruption of Esmie's scream, he had been on the cusp of asking Genevieve to join him for a drink. It suddenly seemed like the most appealing idea, to sit and rest in a garden café, to drink in Genevieve's beauty while sipping a glass of wine. The seal that had existed between them over the past year seemed to have broken, and now he was eager for more, and wanted to hear everything: how she was liking writing the society pages, what her plans for the summer were.

The dark, brooding feeling that had overtaken him in the *Sophia Victoria*'s lavish suite was easing slightly.

What if the tale Detective Longstreet had spun was the truth? What if Marcus's death was not untoward, not sinister, and just what had been suggested: a desperate, drunken, unfortunate move by a troubled young man?

It was possible. He wanted to believe it was possible.

"Would you care to join me for an early dinner?" he ventured.

Genevieve regarded him with wide, surprised eyes. She bit her lip and stared in the direction Rupert and Esmie's carriage had gone, and he could see indecision playing across her face.

Disappointment welled, quickly followed by resignation. Too much time had passed; the circumstances of their friendship last year were too strained to overcome. He took a breath to tell her it was fine, she needn't worry, and he would not make such an overture again.

"I would like that," she replied. And smiled.

A pang of something hot and hopeful blossomed in his chest, and he couldn't help but smile back. For a moment they stood on the busy docks, grinning at each other like imbeciles.

"I'll find us a cab," Daniel said, still smiling. He saw one approaching the docks and raised a hand to flag it down, thrusting the other in his pocket without thinking. Again, his fingers found the coin he had accidentally purloined from Marcus Dalrymple's pocket. He pulled it out to show Genevieve and apologize—she had been angry at his rifling through the dead man's clothing, and perhaps she had been correct in her reticence.

The late afternoon sun glinted off the shining surface of the coin as Daniel held it aloft, pinched between his left thumb and forefinger. Only it wasn't a coin, he realized with a start, or at least not one with any legal tender. It appeared to be cast in a baser metal than any currency he'd encountered, for starters, and there was no numerical value.

Curious, Daniel dropped the coin into his palm to get a better look.

His insides instantly plummeted and a chill overtook him despite the warm temperature. Daniel almost laughed. To think, just a moment ago, he'd actually entertained the notion that Marcus's death could be straightforward. That he and Genevieve could have a simple drink and start over.

That they could interact in a circumstance that didn't involve tragedy.

That didn't involve murder.

Because the simple medallion in his hand suggested all those things, and more, were not true.

"Daniel?" Genevieve was by his side, puzzling at the medallion in his palm. "What is that?"

She smelled like she always had, like springtime. Like freshly cut grass and lilacs. The scent was light and airy and cut through all the other scents at the docks, and straight through to his core.

"This, Genevieve"—the light, cheap metal in his hand suddenly seemed to weigh a ton—"this is trouble."

CHAPTER 3

As the sun-warmed day wound its way toward a perfectly sultry dusk, late golden light streamed through a ceiling made of curved linden branches, dappling long rows of tables beneath. High arches of sparkling lights were placed among the trees, and the air was filled with the friendly chatter of voices, mostly speaking German.

After the day she'd had, it was almost like entering an enchanted fairyland.

"Where are we?" Genevieve asked Daniel, awe-struck.

"Liszt Beer Garden," he said with some hesitancy. "We don't have to stay here. Would you prefer to go to Sherry's?" He began to turn his body back toward the door, but Genevieve stopped him with a hand to his arm.

"No," she said. "Let's stay. This is lovely."

And it *was* lovely. Genevieve had been so distracted and upset by the events of the afternoon that when Daniel had offered to take them to a place he knew, she had simply agreed and spent the entire cab ride mindlessly watching the buildings pass, her mind racing. She had been puzzled when the cab stopped on Avenue A in Dutchtown, but was utterly charmed by where Daniel had brought her.

Daniel led them to open seats at the far end of one of the tables. A nearby family smiled in their direction as they sat, and Genevieve was surprised to hear Daniel exchange a few words in German with the parents, who laughed heartily at something he said and nodded their encouragement. A little girl with a head full of blonde ringlets, who appeared to be about five, shyly waved at Genevieve. She waved back, causing the girl to bury her head under her mother's arm in a fit of delight.

Genevieve grinned at the group, then raised a brow at Daniel.

"You're full of surprises."

He gave an amused huff in response. "My German isn't that good, actually. But it was useful to learn a few key phrases when I was growing up."

Of course. Daniel had grown up in Five Points, but Germans accounted for a large percentage of the population of the Lower East Side.

"What did you say to them?"

"Just that it had been a long day, and I was ready for a beer."

Genevieve looked around. The garden was beginning to fill, mostly with families like the one sitting nearby. "I'm surprised to see so many children here, though I rather like it."

"Most of these people don't see their children all day, so on a Saturday night they want to be together. It will get really crowded tomorrow afternoon, when everyone is off work."

Her stomach rumbled rather loudly, though hopefully the general noise of the place drowned it out. "Will someone bring a menu?"

Daniel looked thoughtful. "I don't think there is a menu. What sounds good? Oysters? Have you had beer before?"

Genevieve felt her nose wrinkle. "Once at Newport, I had a sip from my brother's bottle. I didn't quite care for it," she confessed, lowering her voice.

His mouth quirked up in a half smile. "My guess is you didn't try anything particularly good. Are you willing to give it another go?"

A band struck up lively music from the other end of the garden, and the crowd cheered its approval. The little girl with the blonde curls hopped off her bench and began twirling, gravel crunching under her feet, her family applauding. The atmosphere of genial good cheer and merriment was infectious, and Genevieve felt the day's woes not exactly disappear—not entirely—but concede a fraction of the space they had been occupying in her mind.

It was enough, for now.

"I am," she answered. Pleasure lit Daniel's face in response.

A red-cheeked woman in a green dress bustled toward their table, and Daniel rattled off a few more phrases in German. Genevieve leaned back in her chair and allowed the unknown words to wash over her, soothing her as much as the soft orange light of the setting sun.

"Why did you choose this restaurant?" she asked Daniel once the waitress had gone.

Darkness crept back into Daniel's face, which had lightened as he, too, watched the little girl dancing. "I wanted the most cheerful place I could think of," he said. He sat back and ran a hand through his hair. "I have a bad feeling about what happened today, Genevieve."

Genevieve frowned, instantly yanked back to the day's events. "Of course," she said quietly. "A man died. Somehow our friends got wrapped up in it."

"And now there's this," Daniel opened his palm, revealing the small metal medallion.

Annoyance flared within her. "I told you not to rum-mage through poor Marcus's pockets," she complained. Genevieve snatched the coin out of Daniel's hand and squinted at it closely. It was a plain, small brass circle, about the size of a penny, with no ornamentation save a man's face in profile on both sides. "Who is that?" she wondered.

Daniel gently plucked the coin from her fingers and placed it back in his inside pocket.

"That," he answered, leaning forward, "is John Boyle."

Genevieve frowned, wracking her brain to make a con-nection. "Am I supposed to know who that is?"

"Of Boyle's Suicide Tavern."

She could feel her eyebrows raise. "*Suicide?* What a dreadful name."

Daniel nodded somberly but managed a smile for the waitress as she returned with two frosty mugs topped with foam and a large plate of oysters glistening on a bed of ice. He waited for her retreat before speaking again, as Genevieve tried a cautious sip of her lager. The creaminess of the foam was followed by a bubbly, slightly bitter rush of cool liquid down her throat. She stared at the mug in surprise.

"This is good," Genevieve said. It was nothing like the watery, tepid beverage she had sipped from her brother Charles's bottle all those years ago. Daniel laughed and ges-tured toward her upper lip, and she felt a blush rise as she wiped foam away from her mouth.

"I'm glad you like it," he said, offering her an oyster, loosened from its shell. Here was familiarity; Genevieve loved oysters. The comforting, briny taste exploded in her mouth, pairing perfectly with the strong flavor of the beer. She allowed the food and drink to act as a slight balm while Daniel spun a grisly tale.

"Boyle's is a dive on the Bowery, near Houston." At Genevieve's raised brows, he nodded. "That's right, it's not too terribly far from here, distance-wise. But it might as well be a world away." She watched as his eyes roamed over the beer hall, taking in the dangling lights, the cheerful music, the children playing under their parents' indulgent gazes. "It's a horrendous place," he continued, "mostly full of sailors, with, um, rooms for women to rent upstairs." He peered at her, and Genevieve nodded to show she understood. "Women only wind up there if they've truly nowhere else to go," Daniel continued. "In recent years, some of these unfortunate souls have begun to take their own lives, and the bar began to develop a reputation. Boyle is a thug, but he's also a fairly keen businessman—he seized on the name and capitalized on it. If you can spend the night at Boyle's and come out alive"—Daniel patted his breast pocket, the medallion nestled somewhere in its depths—"you get one of these."

Genevieve took a long swallow of her beer, considering. "So you think Marcus's death had something to do with this bar? Perhaps he started there, took something to kill himself, and it didn't take effect until he reached the boat?"

"I don't know," Daniel admitted. He chose an oyster and used a small, blunt knife to carefully extract it from its shell, a thoughtful frown on his face. "It's mostly the women who end their lives there."

"You heard that sailor, and Rupert and Esmie. It does sound as if poor Marcus had perhaps been given a bad bottle of something. Would this bar actually give a man tainted drink?" she wondered.

Genevieve watched the slight rise of Daniel's Adam's apple as the oyster slid down his throat. The sight made her swallow herself, and she took a hasty drink.

Perhaps the lager was going to her head.

"Absolutely," Daniel replied once he'd finished swallowing. "Hot whiskey mixed with camphor and cocaine, rum laced with benzene, all kinds of concoctions that promise oblivion but that could easily kill a man. Such drinks are often given to marks—those who appear easy to rob."

"Well, then. It seems this medallion rather proves the sailor's theory, doesn't it? Marcus spent the night at this place and ordered or was given something he shouldn't have drunk." Genevieve pondered this sadly. "We should give that to the authorities." She pointed toward his pocket.

"Here's what I don't understand, Genevieve." Daniel leaned forward, close enough that she caught a whiff of his piney aftershave, still pungent even after the long day they'd had. "Why would someone like Marcus Dalrymple be at Boyle's Suicide Tavern?"

Genevieve ran her finger around the bumpy edge of an empty oyster shell. "He was drinking away his sorrows," she suggested. "Upset that Esmie had married Rupert."

Daniel shook his head in frustration. "Rupert and Esmie were engaged for over a year, a long engagement because of Elmira Bradley's death. They were courting for at least six months before the announcement. I didn't know Marcus, but do you really think he spent two years pining over Esmie? And that a man like him would do so at one of the worst dives in town? Esmie said he was shy."

"He was." Genevieve nodded slowly. "And as she noted, he had a stammer. He was a rather bookish young man, I believe. He was quite young when he proposed to Esmie, only eighteen I think."

"I recall his parents as solid, decent folks. It sounds as though young Marcus would have to have undergone quite a transformation to find himself at a place like Boyle's. It doesn't add up, Genevieve."

"No, I suppose it doesn't," she admitted. "Though when it comes to love, who knows?"

A small, pregnant pause rose between them. Daniel blinked a few times, then noisily cleared his throat and took a long drink of lager. Genevieve busied herself with rearranging the few remaining oysters on their platter. She could feel another blush rising, which was silly.

He had never said he loved her, nor she him.

It was, in fact, why she had not accepted when he proposed.

And yet that moment clearly popped into her head as soon as the word "love" left her mouth. A moment she had taken great pains to avoid thinking about for months now, unfolding like an elaborate theatrical tableau within her head not once, but twice today.

Genevieve watched over the rim of her glass as Daniel flagged down the waitress and ordered two more glasses after sending a questioning look her way. It was full twilight now, with stars just beginning to peek through a deepening indigo sky. A warm breeze rattled the leaves overhead.

"Well, it sounds as though this Boyle's is someplace we ought to investigate," she said, anxious to shift the conversation back to safer ground. Funny that talk of death was safer than talk of love, between them.

A look of absolute alarm crossed Daniel's face. "There is no way you are going to Boyle's Suicide Tavern."

The smallest bit of foam sloshed to the table as the smiling waitress set down their fresh drinks. Genevieve picked hers up and slurped a bit of the foam from the top. This was a familiar argument, and one she knew she could win.

"You know I can take care of myself," she reminded him.

"That I do," Daniel replied wryly, taking his own glass. "I distinctly recall a pistol being aimed squarely at my forehead."

Genevieve smiled at the memory. "I am an excellent shot," she allowed.

"I've no doubt."

"So that's settled."

"Your skill with a firearm is settled. Having you accompany me to one of the most dangerous bars in the city is not."

"How bad can it be in broad daylight?"

Daniel gave her a grim look over the top of his own foam. "Bad."

"We'll be careful," Genevieve insisted. "Besides, you know I'll lurk in the shrubbery and simply follow you if we don't go together."

Daniel groaned, and Genevieve grinned, knowing she had won.

"Fine," Daniel groused. "Tomorrow—let's say noon. Where shall I get you? I've a morning appointment uptown."

"I have a morning appointment as well," she informed him smartly. "Can we meet in front of your house at noon? Does that work?"

"It does," he agreed, and she allowed herself a small internal moment of triumph. He frowned at her for a moment and appeared to be on the verge of arguing again. Genevieve sat straighter and steeled herself to fight, but then Daniel blew out a breath and leaned back in his chair, sending an enchanting, lazy smile her way instead.

"How do you like your new role at the paper?" he asked, abandoning whatever protest he'd been about to make.

Genevieve could feel another flush rising in response to that smile. A pretty young woman with flaxen hair, two tables over, caught sight of Daniel and did a quick double take, earning her a sharp elbow from her mother.

"Well, it's better than writing about 'ladies' interests," she admitted. The flaxen-haired girl kept stealing glances their way when her mother wasn't looking. She appeared younger than Genevieve.

Daniel added a raised brow to his smile and took a healthy swallow of his beer. "What are those meant to be?"

"Child-rearing. Perfume. This season's cut for skirts." She shrugged, then chose her next words carefully. "I appreciate Arthur's faith in me but can't help thinking he should have more. After what we uncovered last year . . ." She glanced around, but other than the continual peeks from the young girl, nobody seemed to be paying them any special attention. "And what I was able to write about, I'd have thought he'd allow me to pursue real stories. Investigations."

Daniel looked thoughtful. "I would think society is full of things to investigate."

His words were so close to what Arthur had said, it gave Genevieve pause.

"Well, we can start with tomorrow," she finally replied, raising her glass in Daniel's direction. He seemed surprised but followed suit.

"Tomorrow," he agreed. Daniel gently clinked his glass to hers, but his expression was troubled.

Genevieve took a deep drink and sighed. Despite the delightful frothiness of the lager, the gentle summer breeze, and the magic of twilight, the mood at their corner of the long table had turned.

It was time to depart and see what tomorrow would bring.

★ ★ ★

The next morning, Genevieve stopped short at the sight that greeted her in front of Frank Westwood's Fifth Avenue mansion.

"Are you following me?" she asked irritably. Why was Daniel on the front steps of the home where she had an appointment? "I thought we were meeting at your house at noon."

"I should ask you the same question." Daniel appeared as annoyed as she felt. "You were the one who threatened to lurk in the bushes and trail after me. An activity with which you have a history, I might add."

"Why would I follow you?" she asked, ignoring the barb about having followed him before. She had, true, but only because she'd thought he was Robin Hood. "I have a meeting here."

"As do I."

Genevieve's tired brain attempted to sort out what was occurring. The strain of the previous day's activities—finding Rupert bent over Marcus's corpse, being questioned by the authorities—had caught up to her last night, and try as she might, she hadn't slept terribly well.

Daniel didn't look as though he'd rested much either. He was clean-shaven and well dressed as always, but his eyes were a bit red-rimmed, and he seemed pale.

She tried again. "I don't think you understand. I have an invitation. It asks me to pay a call about an investigative matter at nine o'clock."

Affront and bewilderment mingled on Daniel's face. "I have the same note," he said, pulling a creamy card from his pocket and passing it to her.

Genevieve snatched the paper from Daniel's hand and was chagrined to read the exact same words addressed to him as had been written to her.

She huffed, embarrassment now joining her exasperation, and checked the timepiece pinned to her dress: it was exactly two minutes before nine.

"Well." Genevieve could feel her lips pursing in displeasure as she handed the note back. She had been flattered to receive the invitation, pleased that someone recalled her investigative work of the previous year. The note didn't seem as special now. She peered down Fifth Avenue. "Are we the only two? Or can we expect a hoard of potential investigators to join us?"

The front door opened, and rather than the butler or maid Genevieve expected to see, Mr. Westwood himself stood in its frame.

"Come in, come in," he urged them. "No need to linger on the street like salesmen. Come in." He didn't smile, but opened the door wider and gestured for them to enter.

Genevieve caught herself exchanging a dubious look with Daniel as he politely stepped back and allowed her to mount the front steps first.

"I apologize that it is so early, and on a Sunday to boot. My staff has the morning off for church, you see, and I wanted some privacy," Mr. Westwood explained as he took Daniel's hat and Genevieve's parasol. He was of average height and possessed the same neatly trimmed, brown beard laced with gray and the same comfortable stomach as so many of the wealthy men of the city. "Come this way."

Daniel raised his brows at her as she passed, following their host into a sitting room, and she resisted the urge to stick her tongue out at him like a child.

At Mr. Westwood's direction, Genevieve settled herself into a comfortable leather club chair, with Daniel in the chair next to her. Decorative inlaid paneling lined the walls, interspersed with large, arched mirrors. The room's curtains had been thrown back to let in the morning sun, she noticed, but the windows were not cracked to let in any fresh air, and despite the warm temperatures,

Mr. Westwood had a fire crackling away in the grate. The room was quite large, but what could have been an open and breezy space felt oppressive and stifling with the closed windows and added heat.

A coffee service was laid out on a table between the chairs and the sofa on which their host had settled himself.

"Would you mind, Miss Stewart?" Mr. Westwood asked, gesturing toward the coffee. "I'm sure I'd make a hash of it."

Genevieve sighed internally at being expected to play the hostess—not that she minded serving coffee or felt it was beneath her—but why did men feel they couldn't perform the simplest of domestic tasks? How challenging was it to pour coffee from a pot to a cup and ask if someone took cream or sugar?

"Thank you." Mr. Westwood smiled at her as she handed him his cup, and Genevieve noticed the smile didn't quite reach his eyes. Daniel nodded his thanks as well as he accepted his cup, and she saw the corners of his mouth twitch, as if he were trying to hold back a laugh. She jostled the saucer a tiny bit, splashing hot liquid onto his hand.

"Ow." Daniel shot her a look that clearly read, *What did I do?* Genevieve smiled sweetly in return and took her seat with her own cup, affecting a look of pure innocence.

"And thank you both for coming," Mr. Westwood said when she was settled. "I'm sure you're wondering why I've asked you both to come. I'm afraid it's not pleasant and has to do with my daughter, Nora. She's missing, you see. And I'd like you both to help me find her."

CHAPTER 4

Daniel carefully set his cup down on the table beside him. He wasn't quite sure what he'd expected to hear this morning, but it wasn't this.

"I'm afraid there's been a mistake, Mr. Westwood," he answered politely. "You should contact the authorities. I confess I assumed you wanted my help with a legal matter, and while normally I would ask that you come to my offices, I felt with you I could make an exception and honor your wishes to meet here." He and Frank Westwood were members of the same club, and while he barely knew the man, when he'd received the invitation, he'd decided to take the meeting as a courtesy.

"No," Frank replied sharply. "No police. Now, if I am mistaken in your ability to help me, then I apologize. But perhaps you would at least listen? A young lady's life might be at stake."

Daniel glanced at Genevieve, who blanched slightly at the mention of a potential death. "I don't understand, Mr. Westwood," she said cautiously. "Why do you think we can help you?"

Their host looked between the two of them. "Because you two solved the case of Robin Hood last year," he said simply. "And exposed that crime ring led by Huffington."

Genevieve's eyes went wide.

"That was Miss Stewart's doing, Frank," Daniel said. "She was the one who uncovered the jewel thief and the criminal behavior of those led by Andrew Huffington. She wrote the articles exposing the entire affair." Daniel's real involvement with unmasking the sham investing group that had been profiting from the construction of slums, as well as committing murder to cover their crimes, was not public knowledge.

Or so he'd thought.

Frank cast a shrewd eye in his direction. "It's not only the women who gossip, Daniel. People talk."

Daniel exchanged another glance with Genevieve and expected the startled look on her face mirrored his own. An unfamiliar uneasiness prickled within him. Although he was used to being the subject of gossip, it unnerved him a bit to think that the work he and Genevieve had done, the secrets they had uncovered, were being discussed behind closed doors. He quickly rearranged his features into a more neutral expression.

"I know the two of you did it together," Frank pressed. "I don't want the police involved, and I want to find my daughter. I need discretion, and I need someone who understands how we work." At this, Frank looked toward Genevieve. "Our kind of people," he stressed. "The police sometimes lack the appropriate background for this kind of matter."

It was obvious what Frank meant; he was talking about class. About money. Genevieve came from it, and Daniel didn't. While he had inherited a vast pile of money, enough that his fortune, which he managed carefully, probably equaled Frank's own, he was often still considered an outsider because of his roots in Manhattan's notorious Five Points neighborhood.

Frank turned his attention toward Daniel. "You are part of this world now," he said gruffly, gesturing around the room, indicating its grandness. "And also you're not." If anything, Daniel felt more shocked. His origins in poverty were well known, but the mere fact of his money typically acted as a kind of insulation against this type of bluntness. "Which, I think, allows you some distance from all the nonsense that often accompanies this life. I hope you'll forgive me for speaking plainly."

"You want it both ways," Daniel said quietly.

Frank grunted slightly, eyebrows raising. "Perhaps I do."

Genevieve, who had been following this exchange with a worried expression, put her own coffee down with a clink. Daniel didn't blame her; it was almost stiflingly hot in the room, far too warm for a hot beverage to be appealing.

"Mr. Westwood," she said, and Daniel recognized the pique in her voice. He held in a small smile; Westwood was about to get an earful. "You're coming dangerously close to being insulting. Perhaps you should tell us what you wish from us, and quickly, or I do believe we will thank you for the refreshment and leave."

Daniel was heartily tempted to leave anyway. He could see the bright summer sunshine glittering off the facades of Fifth Avenue just outside the closed window. It was shaping up to be another perfect day, and the thought of bolting from this oppressive room and inhaling a deep lungful of the sweet June air was overwhelmingly appealing.

Frank leaned back and eyed Genevieve appraisingly. "I apologize, then, if I've given offense. To either of you. But

I am desperate, and sometimes desperate men act in ways unbecoming to a gentleman."

Genevieve slid her eyes toward Daniel with a look that plainly said she was leaving the decision up to him. He allowed the moment to stretch and pondered what he knew about Frank Westwood.

It was precious little, he realized. Frank's fortune came from inherited sugar plantations, he knew, and as far as Daniel was aware, Frank continued to run the business well. He also suspected the sugar plantations were why Frank had joined the Union League Club, which during the Civil War had broken away from the original Union Club in protest over the latter's Southern sympathies. While he couldn't recall exactly where the plantations were—somewhere in the Caribbean, certainly—much of the sugar business had been dependent on the slave trade, just as the prewar plantations of the American South. Frank wanted his loyalties to the Union to be unquestioned.

What else? Daniel hadn't heard any whispers at the club about any particular vices. Frank was older than Daniel, probably in his early fifties, and Daniel knew Frank's wife had passed away nearly a decade ago. How old was this missing daughter? He realized with a start he had no idea.

Genevieve raised a slight brow in his direction. The look was asking, *Well?*

Frank was sitting calmly enough, slowly stirring his coffee, but Daniel could detect a slight tightness around the older man's mouth as he awaited their verdict. The stifling heat from the room was starting to feel overwhelming, but Daniel felt he couldn't walk away yet. He knew the pain of a missing loved one.

He offered Genevieve a tiny shrug and a head tilt in response. *Let's hear more.*

"Why don't you tell us what you know, Frank," Daniel said. The older man's shoulders came down an infinitesimal amount in apparent relief. He recrossed his legs and relaxed slightly into his chair.

"What do you know of my daughter, Daniel?" Frank began.

"Almost nothing," Daniel confessed. "You used the term 'young lady,' so I assume—I hope—we're not talking of a small child?" He didn't care what Frank wanted. If a child was involved, he would go straight to the authorities himself.

Frank shifted a bit. "No, no. Nora is eighteen. I daresay Miss Stewart knows her."

Both men turned to Genevieve, who colored a little. "Nora and I have not been formally introduced, but I am aware of who she is, yes." Daniel was perplexed; why did she sound uncomfortable?

"What Miss Stewart is too kind to say is that, even though Nora made her debut only last year, she has already acquired a bit of a reputation," Frank said. "I'm sure your paper would have encouraged you to cover her antics sooner or later."

Genevieve blushed a bit more deeply. "I do not believe it is my job to repeat unfounded rumors in my column, Mr. Westwood," she said carefully. "Nor to cast aspersions about young ladies, in particular, without firm evidence."

"That's kind of you, but business is business, and I understand papers have to sell. You wouldn't have been able to ignore her for long," Frank grumbled. Daniel turned a curious eye toward Genevieve. "I'm sure Miss Stewart can fill you in on the gossip, Daniel," Frank continued. "I'm only glad her mother isn't alive to witness her daughter's behavior." For a moment, Frank's gaze dropped toward his coffee, but when he raised it his look was hard.

"I'm more concerned with a young man she claims to be in love with." Frank's sarcastic tone made it clear exactly what he thought of this sentiment. "I'm afraid she's run off with him. You see why I don't want the police involved. This is a personal matter."

"Exactly how long has Nora been missing, Frank?" Daniel inquired.

There was a slight pause. "Three days," Frank admitted.

Genevieve and Daniel shared a quick, astonished glance.

"I know," Frank said, seeming sheepish. "But I thought she'd come back on her own. This young fellow, he comes from nothing. He has nothing to offer a young lady of Nora's position. And Nora . . . well, like many young ladies of her station, she enjoys certain niceties."

"Who is this young man?" Genevieve asked.

It was Frank's turn to color slightly. "I don't know," he admitted. "Nora refused to tell me. We were arguing one night, late, after one of her . . . escapades. I was preparing to send her abroad with her Aunt Celine, my late wife's sister, who had agreed to come and act as a chaperone to Nora. I was trying to explain how she was rendering herself unmarriageable with her wild behavior, and she told me she didn't care, that she was in love with someone already, someone I wouldn't approve of, and they would elope if they must." Frank shifted again, uncomfortably it seemed. "I threatened to cut her off financially, and she claimed not to care, that their love was all they needed." Frank met Daniel's eyes directly. "I'm not sorry to say I would have locked her in her room if I could have. But her aunt was arriving from Cleveland within days, and they would set sail. I foolishly thought I could contain Nora myself until then. The next morning, she was gone. I sent a cable to her aunt, fabricated an illness. But I can't pretend she's unwell forever. And I am beginning to worry."

Beginning to worry? Daniel didn't have any children, but if he had, he sure as hell wouldn't wait three days to begin the search were one missing. Genevieve shot him a concerned look, and Daniel knew she was thinking, as was he, of Daniel's long-lost younger siblings, who had been snatched from the streets of the Lower East Side and sent god knows where on the orphan trains, part of the movement to send orphaned, homeless children to foster families, mostly in the Midwest. Of course, his siblings hadn't been homeless, or unwanted. Just poor. That had been over twenty-five years ago, and he'd never stopped looking for them.

Daniel suppressed the urge to sigh. Sweat was beginning to bead between his shoulder blades, prickle the undersides of his arms. It wasn't only the close, hot air of the room that was causing discomfort, though he now wondered if the fire was a deliberate tactic to make them uneasy. Something felt disingenuous about this whole affair; he just couldn't put his finger on exactly what.

Were they to agree to help, there was little with which to work. Once again, he glanced Genevieve's way. She gave him the smallest of nods and an encouraging look, and he understood she wanted to help. Tamping down the feeling that getting involved with whatever was happening here was a mistake, he answered with another head tilt.

The desire to appease Genevieve was winning out over his common sense, it seemed.

Interesting, that. He shoved the thought aside but internally vowed to pick it up to examine later.

"We'll help you, Mr. Westwood," she said, sounding satisfied and turning her attention back to Frank.

"But," Daniel interjected, cutting short the look of relief that had begun to cross the older man's face, "if at any point we feel we need to approach the police, we shall do so." Daniel cut his eyes slightly toward Genevieve, hoping Frank would understand: he wasn't going to endanger her.

Frank assessed him again, and Daniel could tell the older man was weighing whether he really meant it. Finally grunting his assent, Frank rose to shake both their hands.

"Thank you," he said. "Please keep me appraised of your progress. I just want Nora home and safe." He reached into his inner breast pocket and pulled out a carte de visite, handing it to Daniel. "This may come in handy. It's recent, from this past winter."

The young woman in the photograph beamed at Daniel with an impish smile, her fair hair piled high, with a small frizz of bangs gracing her forehead. Daniel didn't know the specifics of ladies' fashion, but he knew enough to recognize she was dressed for a ball, in a pale gown gathered at the shoulders and nipped in at the waist, posed with what appeared to be complete unselfconsciousness in a photographer's studio.

"From one of the parties last season," Frank murmured. Daniel nodded; debutantes often had their photograph taken on the occasion of the larger events of the social year.

"The Blodgett Ball?" Genevieve guessed, peering over his shoulder at the photograph. "The fur trimming her hem and neckline . . . it was a winter-themed ball, and I seem to recall Nora outfitted as a snow princess." Her finger grazed the image's surface, directing his attention to a tiara buried in the subject's curls.

"Could be." Frank smiled slightly and shrugged. "I confess I can't keep up with the themes of this party or that one."

Now that he had seen the girl's face, Daniel was glad they had decided to help, despite his earlier misgivings. Nora looked so young. He passed the photograph to Genevieve for safekeeping, and promised they would do what they could.

★　★　★

Resisting the urge to take off his jacket once outside, Daniel settled instead for fanning his face with his straw hat and taking a series of deep, cleansing breaths. It was cooler standing in the early summer sunshine than it had been inside Frank Westwood's drawing room.

"Well, as we're already together, we might as well go to Boyle's now," Daniel mused. His heart sank at the thought of entering the depressing tavern on this bright morning. But he had promised, and it was probably better to get it over with. "Shall I hail a cab?"

"Heavens, no!" Genevieve exclaimed. Sneaking a quick look over her shoulder toward the house from which they'd emerged, she took Daniel's arm and led him half-way down the block before speaking again. "I couldn't bear to be in an enclosed space again quite so soon," she confessed in a quieter voice. "It was truly awful in there. What could Mr. Westwood have been thinking, lighting a fire on a gorgeous summer day? I'm sure I appear quite damp, do I not?"

She did have a slight sheen to her face, but Daniel knew better than to answer that question honestly. "You look perfect," he reassured her.

Which was not, in fact, a lie.

"Are you fine with walking a bit?" Genevieve asked, opening her pale blue parasol to shield herself from the climbing sun. "I could do with the fresh air."

"Me as well," Daniel agreed, surprised at how relieved he was to put off the errand. "We're in no rush. Though I must ask again: Are you sure you wish to accompany me to Boyle's?"

Genevieve wrinkled her nose at him. "Don't start *again*. It's a sunny Sunday morning. Surely it won't be too dangerous at this time of day?" She gave him a worried look.

Daniel sighed. "It may be less crowded, simply because it is early still. For the types that frequent such establishments, that is. But Boyle's is never *not* dangerous." He lowered his voice as a well-heeled family came up the sidewalk toward them, surely returning from church, the young mother pushing a pram while the father held the hand of a little boy who appeared to be about three.

"I have come prepared," Genevieve confided in a low voice once they passed the group.

"You brought a gun?" He had one as well, a revolver safely holstered near the small of his back, hidden under his jacket.

"A new one, a Remington derringer." Genevieve held up a small reticule decorated with beaded roses in the same pale blue as her dress. "Much easier to carry."

A bubble of laughter gathered in his chest and burst out before he could stifle it. This was what he had missed about Genevieve over the past year—that unique mix of humor and boldness. She reminded him of the sassy, daring girls he had grown up with, new to the country and full of ambitious plans.

Now that they were out of Frank Westwood's stuffy mansion, he was enjoying the heck out of this morning. Birds were chirping in the bright green trees that lined Fifth Avenue, and more and more families, dressed in their Sunday best, were beginning to populate the sidewalk, some perhaps emerging from church, some perhaps out for a stroll or on their way to the park. A soft breeze was blowing the scent of hawthorn blossoms, and he was strolling leisurely with one of the most fascinating women he had ever met.

Headed toward a hellish destination. But until they arrived, he was determined to relish the day.

"Tell me more about Nora Westwood," he asked, turning the conversation away from firearms. "What has she done to earn such censure from her father?"

Genevieve pursed her lips, thinking. "There's always a wild crowd in the younger set," she began. "I suppose you weren't in town when you were that age." She was referring to the younger members of society, those in their late teens and early twenties.

"I was," Daniel said. "For part of it. I apprenticed with Phelps and Rochester law firm, learning the trade. I went abroad in '78, when I was twenty-four."

"Oh!" Genevieve flashed him a wide, surprised smile. "I was sixteen then, not quite out in society yet. Were you . . .?" She paused, seeming unsure about how to phrase what she wanted to ask.

"Did I participate in society?" Daniel asked wryly. "Not that much, no. I was still fairly unsure about whether I wanted to. I learned the law, and made some friends." He shrugged, remembering the throbs of loneliness he had felt in those years. "It helped once Rupert settled in New York for good. But then, of course, he and I traded places, and I went to the continent. That's when I began to experiment with being a part of high society: in London and Paris. And eventually when I would make my visits back to New York."

They paused at the busy intersection of Fifth Avenue and 59th Street. The crowds were getting thicker, with

Sunday promenaders now out in droves. Daniel had begun seeing more and more people he knew, and noticed Genevieve nodding at acquaintances they passed as well.

Given that they had circulated a rumor of courtship last year, walking together on Fifth Avenue on a Sunday was bound to start some gossip.

"Let's head east, and walk down Park Avenue instead," Genevieve suddenly suggested.

"Good idea," he agreed.

Once they were on a quieter street, Daniel continued. "So no, I didn't participate in the social season when I was that age. Exactly how wild does this wild crowd become?"

"Oh, they overly imbibe in drink, flirt too much. That kind of thing. Mostly it's men, sometimes with a young lady or two on the periphery. But the young set right now seems a bit more extreme. There are rumors of them daring each other to engage in increasingly outlandish behavior: midnight horse races in the park, slumming tours, even dabbling in narcotics."

Daniel pondered this, thoughtful. "Do you think Marcus Dalrymple was a part of this group?"

His question brought an astonished laugh from Genevieve. "Heavens, no. Marcus was just as Esmie described: studious, shy. I can't think he would have been involved with those young men."

"But he was their age? They are his peers?"

Genevieve had a troubled expression. "Yes," she confirmed. "That is a good point. They surely all went to school together."

"A visit to Boyle's would certainly fall into the category of outlandish, for young men of their social status," Daniel mused.

"Do you think that's what happened?" Genevieve asked. "Perhaps Marcus was dared to spend the night there by some old friends, and that's how he came by the medallion?"

Daniel paused, taking in the bright sky, the leafy branches overhead, the clean streets of the wealthy. They were delaying the inevitable; the sooner they got this visit to Boyle's out of the way, the better.

"There's only one way to find out," he said, looking for an oncoming cab to hail. "Let's get this over with."

CHAPTER 5

Genevieve flinched as sparks rained down from above. Heat briefly seared her hand as she swatted at her dress, but it was too late. Black marks of charred soot now dotted her left shoulder, marring the pale blue muslin.

With dismay, she tutted over a small hole in the ivory lace trim on the bodice. The woman her mother employed for their laundry might be able to get out the black stains, but there was no fixing that hole.

"Might we *not* walk under the train?" Out of extreme caution, Daniel had had the cab drop them a few blocks from the tavern, asking if she minded walking. She hadn't, but now she wished she'd insisted the cab take them straight to the bar's front door. Genevieve could hear the peevishness of her own voice, which added to her aggravation. She sounded like the stereotypical society lady afraid to sully her dress. She knew Daniel was aware that she was more than willing to get dirty, but this *was* a new dress.

It had been difficult to know what to wear when one started the day with an appointment with a wealthy sugar baron on Fifth Avenue, immediately followed by a visit to what was apparently the most disreputable bar in the city.

Without waiting for Daniel to answer, Genevieve took advantage of a break in the Bowery traffic and darted across the street.

Daniel joined her and walked by her side in silence for a few moments.

"You're an intelligent woman, but I must point out there is a train track on this side of the street as well," he finally said. She noticed he eyed the marks on her dress, but chose—wisely, she felt—not to comment on them.

Of course she knew there were elevated tracks on both sides of the street. It was impossible to miss, as the Bowery was cloaked in deep shadows from the tracks, despite the bright midday sun.

Genevieve huffed and walked faster.

"We can walk down a different block," Daniel continued, "and cut back when we reach the cross street. It's just a few more blocks."

"It's fine," she said through gritted teeth.

"We can't keep crossing the street every time a train comes. Let's walk down a different block—come on." Daniel gestured toward an upcoming intersection and began to lead her around the corner.

"That's ridiculous," she snapped. "Why would we cross to a different street when the establishment we're to visit is on this street?"

"To get out from under the tracks and not further soil your dress?" he suggested mildly enough, but his suggestion only enraged her further. She hoisted her skirts slightly and increased her pace.

"Genevieve." Daniel trotted a few steps to catch up. He put a hand on her arm, and it took a great amount of willpower not to swat it away. "Stop."

Genevieve came to a halt, and her indignation was palpable even to her. Daniel was eyeing her incredulously.

"What has come over you?" he wondered aloud. "You seemed fine on the cab ride here. Is it your dress? I am sorry, I should have known to avoid Bowery. It's frankly not the safest of streets, even in the middle of the day."

Daniel looked so worried that Genevieve could feel her ill temper abating somewhat.

"It's not my dress, though I am sorry about it." She frowned momentarily at the burned lace. "If you must know the truth, I'm *famished*."

Puzzlement replaced worry on Daniel's face. "You're hungry? That's why you're in such a snit?"

"This is not a snit," Genevieve warned. "And yes. Being hungry makes me quite irritable," she confessed. Daniel simply blinked at her for a moment. "It is almost lunchtime," she pointed out.

"Fair enough." He took off his hat to briefly run a hand through his hair, a gesture she had come to learn meant he was thinking.

"It's fine. I'll get something at the bar," she said, gesturing down the street.

"The bar? You think to order a snack at Boyle's?" Now it was his tone that was incredulous.

"They don't serve food?" Hunger began to gnaw at her belly more fiercely at the thought of it not being satiated soon.

Daniel heaved a mighty sigh, irritating her further. "No, Genevieve. They serve watered-down whiskey if you're a man who can pay five cents, or very strong rum for free to pretty young women." He maneuvered her closer to the storefronts along the sidewalk as a train now passed above on their side of the street, raining sparks. "This is foolish," he muttered, once the train and its noise had paused. A man ran by them, pounding up the nearby stairs to reach the train, fighting against the descending crowd of recently debarked passengers. "You have no business going to a place like Boyle's."

The train above began to move with a noisy lurch, and with it rose an aggrieved cry. The running man must not have made it in time.

"It *is* my business," Genevieve insisted, raising her voice over the din of the departing train. "Rupert and Esmie are my friends as well, and you didn't even know Marcus Dalrymple." She angrily brushed aside more sparks as they fell, no longer caring if her dress was singed. "Do I have to remind you how we met?"

Daniel snorted. "As if I could forget. And it was just as foolhardy for you to follow us into Bottle Alley as it is for me to take you to Boyle's."

"But you'll be with me. And I have this," she dangled her beaded reticule at him. "And you know I'll just—"

"Go by yourself if we don't go together," Daniel finished her sentence for her. "*Christ*, woman, you are determined to get yourself killed."

"I am not. But I am determined not to be excluded from investigating whatever is ailing our friends simply because of my sex!"

Daniel seemed on the cusp of protesting again, then exhaled in apparent acquiescence. "Fine. But you are to do as I say, without question. I already got an earful from Charles last summer about how I endangered you."

This delighted Genevieve. "Really? Charles laid into you?" The younger of her two older brothers was usually the quiet one.

Peering at a nearby sign to check their cross street, Daniel cut left and gestured for her to follow. "He did. One of the few times I made it to Newport last summer. Cornered me at a picnic after a sailing race and made his opinion of me abundantly clear. It wasn't flattering."

Genevieve grinned. "Good old Charles. He taught me to shoot, you know."

"I recall."

"You're lucky Gavin was still abroad," she observed. "He likely would have expressed his opinion with his fists, and verbally sometime after."

Daniel gave her an astonished look. "Are all you Stewarts so violent?"

"Yes, indeed."

"Then I consider myself fortunate Gavin remains overseas."

"Not for long. He is coming home later this summer."

"Lucky me," Daniel muttered. He turned right again, then grabbed her hand and pulled her across Houston Street as an omnibus rattled past.

"Where are we going?" Genevieve asked once they were safely across. "I thought you said Boyle's was on the Bowery."

"We are getting you something to eat. I'm not taking you someplace like Boyle's when you're volatile from hunger."

They crossed to another block, lined with tenement buildings. Children played in the streets, and vendors crowded the sidewalks. Residents were calling to each other in a language that sounded somewhat like German, but she could tell it wasn't. Daniel stopped in front of a man with a long beard and twinkling eyes who carried a long pole festooned with what looked like rolls with a hole in the center. Daniel handed the man some money, who slid two of the rolls off the pole, wrapped each in a bit of paper and handed them over.

Daniel gave one to her. It smelled delicious, and from the gentle warmth seeping through its thin wrapping it was clearly freshly baked.

"Shall I just . . . bite it?" she asked. The outer crust was shiny and smooth.

In response, Daniel bit into his own, and raised a brow in her direction, chewing.

Genevieve took a cautious bite, the crust breaking and the chewy, tangy bread filling her mouth.

"This is wonderful," she managed after she swallowed, before taking another bite.

"I know. It's called a bagel, a type of Jewish bread." They began walking uptown again, but more slowly this time.

"Did you grow up with these?" It felt very freeing to be walking in the sunshine, munching on a fragrant roll in the middle of the street.

"No," he said. "These came mostly with the Polish communities that have arrived in the past twenty years or so. My cousin Kathleen introduced me to the bagel."

Genevieve swallowed a particularly large mouthful. "Is that your cousin who runs . . . um . . ." She gave him a questioning look, not wanting to voice the word out loud.

"Yes, Kathleen owns a brothel. Quite a successful one too." His mouth tipped into a half smile.

"Right." Genevieve could feel herself coloring.

Daniel took the empty paper from her hand and balled it with his own, thrusting it deep into his pocket. "Are you feeling better?" he asked.

"Much. Thank you."

"Do you feel ready to head to Boyle's?"

Genevieve reopened the parasol she had closed to eat her bagel, and twirled it jauntily. Everything felt better when one's stomach was full. "Let's go."

★ ★ ★

The exterior of Boyle's Suicide Tavern was both unassuming and unimpressive. A dull brick, four-story tenement building, the ground floor had large windows typical of most bars in the area. The inscription on the door, though, sent chills up Genevieve's spine: "Better Dead."

The interior was no better. A small, dusty room with a bar running along one end, gloomy despite the large windows and copious exterior sunshine, there was not a single piece of furniture in the entire space. The overpowering smell of stale beer assaulted Genevieve's nostrils.

"Has it closed for good?" she puzzled in a whisper. The clearly unused room was unsettling.

Daniel glanced over his shoulder at her, then tilted his head toward a small, modest-looking door set almost behind the bar.

"Remember what I said," he warned in a low voice. "Do as I say, and please don't ask questions." The unsettled feeling intensified, and Genevieve nodded.

The door opened to reveal a much larger, almost cavernous back room. There was a stage at the far end from where they had entered—empty at present—as well as tables and chairs, and barstools lined up along a second, longer bar. There were few customers on an early Sunday afternoon, but the place wasn't empty. Two tables were occupied by sullen-looking men, both of whom glanced up and scowled at her and Daniel. A sailor was hunched over, presumably asleep, at a third table. A young woman in what could best be described as a nightgown was leaning over one of the sullen men, speaking to him in low, soothing tones while another young woman—though girl was really a more appropriate descriptor—halfheartedly swiped at an empty table with a filthy-looking rag.

"What do you want?" The voice made Genevieve jump slightly. She hadn't noticed the man behind the bar before, though wasn't sure how one could miss him. He was easily as large as Daniel's secretary, Asher, who had been a boxer in his younger days. This man set a glass down on the bar and eyed them with distrust.

"We're hoping for some information," Daniel said as he approached, Genevieve trailing in his wake. She noticed Daniel's speech had become rougher, the "r's" subtly dropping.

"We don't serve that here," the large man said in a voice that brooked no argument. His rolled-up shirtsleeves revealed the most massive forearms Genevieve had ever seen. "I can give you whiskey, or you can leave."

Daniel pulled the medallion from his pocket. "This was found on the body of a young man, tall, slender, red hair. Goes by Marcus. Sound familiar?"

The man eyed the medallion. "Nope."

"But these ain't given out unless someone successfully spends the night here, yeah?"

A shrug roiled the bartender's giant shoulders. "Those things get passed around. The kids like to brag they've survived Boyle's. Most of 'em never set foot in the joint. Now order or get out." He placed his meaty arms on the bar and leaned forward, his large forehead furrowing in menace.

Genevieve inched closer to Daniel's side. One of the men at a nearby table had swiveled in his seat and was watching the exchange through narrowed eyes. The woman who had been speaking with him had disappeared.

That didn't bode well. "Let's go," she whispered in Daniel's ear.

Daniel shifted his eyes toward the man in the chair, who stood and casually leaned against his table; then his gaze went back to the bartender.

"John here?" he asked casually.

The barkeep's eyebrows rose. "No. I heard your pretty lady friend say she wants to leave, so why don't you do that. Don't make me come out from behind this bar."

But Daniel was already backing up a few steps toward the door, keeping Genevieve close. "We're going, Eddie. Sorry to trouble you." She shot a startled look Daniel's way; did he *know* this man?

Once they were through the door and back in the bare front room, Daniel heaved a breath of relief and pulled Genevieve to the street. "Come on," he muttered, leading her toward the corner. They paused once they reached Houston Street.

"I didn't realize you *knew* this John Boyle fellow. And you called that man by name—Eddie—do you know him too?" The sounds of traffic, the bustling of people on the streets, were comforting after the eerie silence and claustrophobic feeling of being inside Boyle's. Her body involuntarily shuddered at the memory of the bartender's threatening demeanor.

"I know John slightly, through my former . . . uh . . . associates." He slid her a meaningful glance, then peered back up the street, frowning. Genevieve understood: Daniel meant his ties to the Bayard Toughs, one of Five Point's notorious gangs.

"Same with Knockout Eddie. Haven't seen him in forever, but everyone knows him by reputation. He's the most feared bouncer in the entire Lower East Side. Used to box against Asher," Daniel continued, still looking distractedly down the street. "Come with me."

"What's a bouncer?" she asked, following Daniel across the Bowery.

"Someone who guards the door, kicks out anyone unwelcome." On the opposite corner Daniel paused, gesturing for her to wait, and lowered his voice. "He's been arrested for murder multiple times, but any witnesses found, of course, eventually claim they saw nothing. And just guess who else Eddie knows well?"

Genevieve's breath caught. "Tommy Meade?" The gangster's thugs had attempted to kill Genevieve twice the previous year. And nearly succeeded.

"The very same."

The next moment, the girl who had been cleaning tables at Boyle's rounded the corner and nearly bumped into them. She squealed and tried to dart past, but Daniel gently held her arm.

"Miss? Can we speak for a moment?" Daniel slipped a dollar bill into her hand. "Just talk, that's all."

The girl's brown eyes widened at the sight of the dollar, which she managed to disappear under the folds of her tattered gray shawl. Glancing once over her shoulder, she stepped closer to the side of the building and produced a cigarette from under the same shawl.

"Make it quick," she said, accepting a light from Daniel. She was a beautiful girl, with big, round, dark eyes framed by thick lashes. The girl pushed a lock of brown hair behind an ear with one hand and held her cigarette up for a drag with the other, shivering despite the warm temperatures.

"Did the man I described to Knockout Eddie sound familiar to you?" Daniel asked quietly. "Tall, red-haired, lanky? About twenty?"

The girl exhaled a plume of smoke and shook her head resolutely. "Not me." She pulled her shawl closer and stole another look over her shoulder.

On impulse, Genevieve reached into her reticule and pulled out Nora Westwood's picture. "What about this girl? Have you seen her at the bar?"

The girl recoiled at the sight of the picture. Pressing her lips together, she mutely shook her head and tried to dodge around them again.

Daniel held the girl's arm fast and leaned in close. "What is it? You've seen that girl? Her name is Nora. Does she need help?"

"I can't say," the girl whispered. She sounded terrified. "Please, Mr. Meade would—" With a mighty yank, she managed to pull herself free from Daniel's grasp and ran back in the direction she had come from, leaving her unfinished sentence dangling in the light breeze.

An unbidden rush of fear enveloped Genevieve. She had never thought to cross paths with Tommy Meade again, the very man who'd tried to kill her. But if he was somehow involved in Nora Westwood's disappearance, her worst nightmare might be coming true.

CHAPTER 6

Daniel stood as Genevieve approached the table. She had chosen their meeting spot this time, a rooftop garden in the city's theater district, and he was glad to be in the sultry, early summer air after their earlier visit to the depressing backroom at Boyle's. They had gone to their respective homes to rest and change, Genevieve discarding her soot-marred dress for a yellow silk more appropriate for evening.

"What suits you?" Daniel asked after helping her into her seat. "A gin drink or perhaps some champagne?"

"Champagne, definitely," she replied, settling in and sighing with pleasure. "It is so lovely to be outdoors after the day we had, is it not?"

As Daniel signaled to the waiter and placed their order, he reflected that he should no longer be surprised when he and Genevieve seemed to think in tandem. It had happened often enough when they had been working together the previous year. But his defenses were rusty, and he was unprepared for the jolt of pleasure that shot through him at hearing her verbalize exactly what he had been thinking.

But voicing such feelings would do nobody any good.

"It is," he agreed instead, keeping his response simple.

"I will admit I was a bit shaken by what that girl said," Genevieve confided, lowering her voice, even though the other well-heeled customers were paying them little mind. A year ago it would have been a different story; when he had first returned to New York everyone, it seemed, had wanted to curry his favor. Society was used to his presence now, sporadic as it was, and appearing at the occasional restaurant or party didn't cause the stir it once had.

Despite this, a few sidelong glances were being sent their way, probably because he was sharing a table with the society columnist for one of the city's largest newspapers, and one with whom he had pretended to be romantically involved the previous year. Well, they could all search in vain in tomorrow's paper for some juicy tidbit. One thing he knew and trusted about Genevieve: his secrets were safe with her.

Besides, he had few left at this point.

"I was as well," Daniel confessed in turn. He was not simply placating Genevieve, he *had* been shaken, to use Genevieve's word, to hear the girl from Boyle's invoke Meade's name.

"Do you know what he is doing?" Genevieve asked delicately. Daniel noted that neither of them seemed to want to say Meade's name aloud.

He waited to answer while the waiter brought their champagne, popped the cork, and poured. An orchestra on the far stage, framed by an elaborate set meant to invoke a Swiss mountain village, played light, calming music. The late evening sun was just beginning its descent, and a few stars blinked into view.

"He has gone into partnership with a brewery based out of Wisconsin and is working to open an operation for them here," Daniel said.

"So, a pivot from a mayoral candidacy," Genevieve mused. Tommy Meade had been making a bid for mayor the previous year, and while he was investigated but never charged for the crimes they had uncovered, he had been forced to abandon his campaign.

"One that we ruined," Daniel added quietly. "Yes, he couldn't make it as a politician, so he's trying his hand at successful businessman."

"And is he still involved with his . . . other activities?" Genevieve didn't need to articulate what she meant; Daniel knew she was referring to Meade's position as leader of one of New York's deadliest gangs.

"I'm certain of it," Daniel replied. "Those *activities* are not ones you abandon lightly." He should know. He hadn't been actively involved with his own gang for almost fifteen years but still remained connected to the organization. Gang ties in New York never really broke except by death. "He has maintained a front of legal enterprises for years. I know he's part owner in several bars and businesses on the Lower East Side."

"Including Boyle's?"

"After what that young woman today said, I'd wager money on it," Daniel replied. He picked up his glass and tilted it toward her. Looking pleased, Genevieve followed suit.

"What are we toasting?" she asked.

Daniel weighed his options, then decided to verbalize exactly what he was thinking.

What he was hoping.

"To our renewed partnership," Daniel declared, raising his glass a bit higher. His heart thudded, and he resisted the urge to hold his breath. It wasn't until he voiced the words aloud that he realized how much he wanted them to be true. How much he wanted to work with Genevieve again.

Genevieve looked momentarily thunderstruck, but a wide smile soon spread across her face. "To our partnership," she echoed, the tapping of her glass against his creating a resounding *clink*.

Pleasure suffused him. Not that he was pleased about Marcus Dalrymple's death, or Nora Westwood's disappearance.

But he had *missed* Genevieve. He hadn't known how much until he saw her again and once more felt that uncanny connection they seemed to share.

"We'll get to the bottom of what's going on," he promised. "With Marcus and Nora."

A worried look flitted across her face, there and gone in a flash. "It is troubling that they both seemed to have connection to a place such as Boyle's. It makes no sense."

"And no firm connection to each other, that you know of, other than their ages," Daniel confirmed.

"None of which I am aware, but I don't claim to know every association of every member of society. That crowd is quite a bit younger than I. Perhaps they had a childhood friendship that was maintained, or their parents are intimates."

"Is there a way to find out? Others we can question perhaps?"

Genevieve took a sip of her champagne, looking thoughtful. "I am sure there is. Let me think on it."

Daniel sighed deeply and allowed himself to relax a bit more into his chair. The events of the past two days danced in his mind's eye, but there did not appear to be any more that could be done this evening.

"I can speak to the Dalrymples, if you like," he offered. "They were friendly with Jacob."

"Though should you give them time? They did just lose their son. Maybe my inquiries of their friends can yield something without being intrusive."

"I know how to be discreet."

Genevieve rolled her eyes. "Nobody is questioning your discretion. Indeed, you've been so discreet this past year, many thought you'd left town for good. Where have you been hiding, anyway?"

It was on the tip of Daniel's tongue to tell Genevieve he had been avoiding society to avoid running into *her*, but in the end he held it. He wouldn't be able to bear it if her expression was one of relief. "I've been here and there." He shrugged instead. "Perhaps you aren't attending the right parties."

Her brows shot almost to the top of her forehead. "I attend *all* the parties," Genevieve said. "For work," she added primly.

Daniel leaned so far forward he could inhale her scent. "Not all of them," he said with a significant raise of one brow.

Genevieve looked puzzled for a moment, then swatted his arm playfully. "I am not talking of *gentlemen's* gatherings." She colored slightly at the words but forged ahead gamely. "Is that what you have been up to? You beast, you must know there is a shortage of eligible men at society events."

A bark of laughter escaped before he could help it. "Eligible men? My only purpose in this town is to round out the numbers between the sexes at a ball? Perpetuate the species?"

"Exactly what the young ladies are expected to do," Genevieve shot back, her color rising further. "Why should you be let off the hook?"

"Society can rub along just fine without me, I'm sure," he stated wryly. "The species will survive."

Genevieve opened her mouth to retort, and Daniel grinned, ready to receive whatever she intended to lob his way, when a woman's startled scream pierced the gentle night. He was on his feet before his mind had time to process the sound, his body instinctively reacting.

"What is it?" Genevieve asked, straining to see. A general commotion flared up near the entrance of the restaurant. She stood too, her face suddenly drained of color.

"Beware! It's coming!" yelled a hoarse male voice. The musicians stopped playing and several of them, too, stood to see the cause of the commotion. Yelps and small shrieks rose from the direction of the entrance, and a group of ladies in bright summer colors suddenly scattered like an agitated flock of birds.

"The demon. It's coming!"

A young man staggered into view, disheveled, his jacket hanging open and his shirt unbuttoned halfway. A stout man in evening clothes took a step toward the young man, with his hands outstretched as if to placate him, while a matron in mauve silk hovered behind the stout man's left shoulder, her eyes wide with horror.

"Don't touch me!" the young man screamed, lurching a few steps away and banging into a table with enough force to send cutlery and crystal shattering to the floor. Gasping, the stout man grabbed his wife's hand and pulled her toward the entrance, followed by several other well-heeled couples.

Unnerved, Daniel took a protective step toward Genevieve. "Stand behind me," he ordered in a low voice. Genevieve shot him an annoyed look at his presumption but scooched a few inches closer to him anyway, craning her neck to see what was happening.

Screams erupted as another group darted toward the door, pushing at each other in their haste to leave the restaurant.

"I said it's coming! *Run!*" the man yelled, his voice beginning to break. He had pulled a knife from one of the tables and was now brandishing it toward another well-dressed man who approached to help.

"Daniel," Genevieve gasped.

"It's a butter knife," he muttered back. The band scrambled off the stage as the young man changed course and lunged in their direction, several clutching their instruments to their chests. "Can't do much damage. But still, this could get ugly. Do you recognize him?"

"I've seen his face but can't place the name.." She pursed her lips in frustration.

"You've seen him? Where?"

Genevieve shook her head. "Newport? I can't recall."

Daniel pulled Genevieve a few more steps to their left as the young man lurched closer toward them.

"It's coming." His statement was matter-of-fact, close to a sob. He was in front of their table now.

Daniel took a step toward the young man. He heard Genevieve's sharp intake of breath as the man swiveled in their direction, waving the butter knife wildly. The pungent mixed smells of vomit, stale alcohol, and unwashed flesh wafted toward them, almost as if the young man had been living on the street. But if Genevieve said he looked familiar, the chances of him being a member of the upper class were high.

"Why don't you run? The demon. It's *coming*." The young man's voice was quieter now, almost defeated. Daniel could see his pupils were dilated, and the sharp tang of urine combined with the stain on the front of the man's pants indicated he had soiled himself.

"How can we stop it?" Daniel asked in a soft tone, hoping to calm the youth. "Let us help." Daniel was dimly aware of sounds in the distance, of more patrons rushing from the restaurant, another dish breaking. Of Genevieve's gently restraining hand on his arm. But he centered his focus on the young man and maintained eye contact, the way one would with a startled animal.

"It can't be stopped," the man said hoarsely. "All we can do is run." His shoulders slumped and his head dropped, the knife clattering to the floor from his suddenly lax hands. Daniel quickly kicked it away.

The noise of the knife sliding across the wooden floor snapped the young man's attention back to them. His nostrils flared, and he bared his lips into a snarl.

"I said, *run*," the man screamed and suddenly darted directly toward them. Reacting on pure instinct, Daniel pushed Genevieve to the ground and assumed a defensive stance, bending his knees and holding up his fists to fend off the impending attack.

Adrenaline-fueled fear morphed to horror as the young man rushed not at him, but past him, hurling himself over the low wall framing the edge of the rooftop.

"No!" Lunging forward, Daniel grabbed at the man's coattails, but was left holding only air. A final, barely intelligible cry came from the man as he plunged twelve stories, followed by the sickening thud of his body smacking into the pavement below.

Shrieks and cries of dread filled the air. Daniel stared at the spot where the man had disappeared, willing time to reverse by five seconds, willing his hands to have been faster.

"It's not your fault." Genevieve was beside him, staring at the same empty patch of air.

Daniel nodded mechanically, but the gesture felt hollow. He should have been faster.

She gently tugged him farther from the edge of the rooftop as some of the remaining patrons ventured closer, exclaiming and pressing their hands to their hearts. Genevieve glanced their way with irritation, then pulled him closer to the entrance.

"What did he say?" she asked quietly. "As he . . ." She gestured toward the wall. "I couldn't quite make it out." Daniel shook his head again, still haunted by the sight of the back of the man's jacket flying upward as his body plummeted. It had been lined with light blue silk, a flash of pale color momentarily emblazoned against the darkening sky, then gone.

"Daniel," Genevieve urged. She shook his arm a bit. "I hear bells. The police are surely coming."

The distant clanging jerked Daniel's attention back to the present moment. "We shouldn't be here," he muttered. "Two young men, both yelling about demons, both dead only a day apart." His gaze traveled toward the small edge of roof again, and he willfully yanked it back.

"Exactly," Genevieve said, sounding relieved. "It would appear odd if we were at both scenes. It *is* odd. I don't know if anyone other than sailors heard Marcus, but the police talked to the sailors, and they'll be here soon. Word will get back to Detective Longstreet. We must go, and quickly."

More and more of the remaining patrons were gathering at the edge of the roof. Daniel quickly scanned the restaurant. The painted scene of the Alpine village sported a huge tear, probably courtesy of one of the fleeing guests. Abandoned musical instruments were scattered across the empty stage, along with knocked-over chairs. Broken glassware and dishes littered the floor, dotted with the occasional upended decorative plant.

"This way," Daniel said, taking Genevieve's hand. He wove through the avid press of bodies craning their necks toward the site of the tragedy and pulled her along. He steered clear of the front entrance of the restaurant, which led to a small but elaborate lobby containing the elevator to shepherd guests back to the ground floor, racing instead to an unobtrusive wooden door tucked away behind a large potted pine tree. Slipping inside, he found what he had hoped, a staircase clearly used by staff. They rushed down the twelve flights, happily passing not a soul. A dingy door at the bottom of the stairs resisted opening at first, but Daniel applied his shoulder, and it eventually relented with a rusty squawk, spilling him into an alley at the back of the building.

"Come on," he gestured for Genevieve to follow. She picked up her skirts, and they darted down the alley, past refuse and the occasional startled rat, away from the ever-growing sounds of clanging police bells.

★　★　★

It was no use.

Try as she might, Genevieve could not force herself to concentrate on the piece she was meant to be writing about the upcoming summer season in Newport. She was keeping close tabs on which families were packing up their houses and leaving town—many of the Astor 400 were going to their summer cottages earlier than usual this year, it seemed, and she really ought to be out there herself by now—and yet she couldn't muster the energy to turn that information into an anticipatory column.

All she could think about were the haunted eyes of the young man who had hurled himself from the Metropolitan Rooftop Theater the previous evening.

It had been another night of little sleep for her, despite the exhausting weekend. But regardless, Genevieve felt keyed up, full of anxious energy. She kept glancing from the near-empty page in her typewriter to the elevator doors of the newsroom, tapping her pencil on the surface of her desk, typing another word or two, chewing on the pencil's end, and checking the doors again. Surely, if she stared at the elevator doors long and hard enough, they would open to reveal the person she most wanted to see at present.

NEWPORT'S SOCIAL SEASON; THE FAMED RESORT RAPIDLY FILLING UP

This was as far as she'd gotten. Barely a headline.

Ping chimed the elevator doors.

At long last, her friend Luther Franklin, who covered homicide for the paper, hurried into the newsroom, looking a little sweaty and more than a little cross. He glanced her way, as he always did when he entered the room, and tossed a little wave in her direction. The fact that he didn't make a beeline directly to her desk for a good-natured morning chat signaled he was working under a tight deadline.

Normally Genevieve would offer a return wave and allow Luther to get on with his work, but this morning she frantically gestured for him to come over.

Luther paused, appearing torn, but finally wound his way through the desks until he reached hers.

"What's up, toots? I haven't got much time today," he said, obviously distracted. His normally friendly face was tight and shuttered.

Genevieve jumped right in. "It's about the man who jumped off the roof of the Metropolitan Theater last night, isn't it?"

Heaving a sigh, Luther crossed his arms over his chest and sent what could only be described as a glare in her direction. Genevieve nearly flinched, so unexpected was the look. She and Luther had been friends for years, and even though at times he had hoped they could be more than friends, an offer she had gently rejected, they'd still remained on good terms.

"Look, Genevieve, I know you were there. A society columnist having champagne with a millionaire doesn't go unnoticed in this town. Half the witnesses I interviewed mentioned it." Luther's expression bordered on sulky.

Ah, that explains it. Luther had been furious with her last year when she had partnered with Daniel to solve the case of Robin Hood, believing she was risking her own safety unnecessarily. He also believed she and Daniel had spent the night together in a hotel room, and while technically this was true, she and Daniel had done nothing more than talk.

Plus, what happened or didn't happen in that hotel room was none of Luther's business.

"Yes, I was there." Genevieve deliberately left Daniel's name out of it. "I saw the poor man perish. Do you know who he was? He looked so familiar to me—it's like a word on the tip of my tongue that I can't quite place."

Luther's manner softened somewhat, but he didn't uncross his arms. "I'm sorry you had to see that," he said. He sighed again. "What a messed-up world, right? The deceased is one Paul Riley, society boy."

"Of course." Relief at the mystery of the dead man's identity suffused Genevieve, she *knew* she had recognized him. She didn't know the Riley family terribly well but recalled they had an adult son, presumably the unfortunate Paul, and she believed an older sister who was married, but she

couldn't recall to whom. "May I ask why you were conducting interviews? This death obviously wasn't a homicide."

Luther gave a one-shouldered shrug. "Maybe not, but it's an odd one. All that yelling about demons? Arthur thought I should dig a little."

The memory of Paul's red-rimmed, besieged-looking eyes and his shattered voice sent a shudder down Genevieve's spine. She and Daniel hadn't reconvened since he had put her in a cab for home two blocks from the Metropolitan Theater the night before, but that there was a connection between Marcus Dalrymple's and Paul Riley's deaths seemed unmistakable.

"Luther, are you also investigating the death of Marcus Dalrymple?" Genevieve attempted to keep her voice casual.

A furrow marred Luther's genial brow. "Dalrymple? Heard some chatter about that, but nothing clear. Everyone's being super hush-hush. Why, what do you know?"

Genevieve's pulse quickened slightly. Obviously, somebody was working hard to keep the circumstances around Marcus's death a secret. She chewed her pencil end and pondered. Longstreet, maybe? Daniel would probably know.

"He asked my friend Esmie to marry him some time ago," Genevieve said. "I'd heard he died, but didn't know anything more. Society column, you know," she lied.

Luther nodded but appeared unconvinced. "All right, toots. I need to get back to it." He started to turn, but Genevieve stopped him.

"Wait. One more thing."

Luther turned, impatience written on his face.

Genevieve slid Nora's photograph across her desk. "Seen any Jane Does that look like her lately?" She tapped her pencil next to Nora's face, frozen in its perpetual, impish smile.

Luther's impatience turned to wariness. "Genevieve, what have you got yourself mixed up in this time?"

She shook her head at him. "It's not like that, Luther. This found me, not the other way around."

Her friend sighed again, now causing *her* to feel impatient. Men were constantly sighing with dismay in her presence, and it did get tiresome. But he picked up the photograph and studied it all the same, then gave her a careful look.

"She's dead?"

"Not that I know of."

"But she might be?"

Genevieve nodded. "She might be."

"Well, I haven't seen her. But I'll keep my eyes peeled," he answered before she could even voice the question.

Luther handed the picture back to her. "You swells should be careful," he said, giving her a troubled look. "Seems like a lot of you are dying these days."

"It does, doesn't it?" Genevieve murmured, more to the photograph than to Luther, who was already making his way back to his own desk, shoulders hunched. Nora's playful visage, trapped in emulsion, gazed back implacably, revealing nothing.

CHAPTER 7

Daniel folded his newspaper and stood, ready to head home and rest. He'd put in what he deemed an acceptable day of work, given how hard it had been to concentrate, then decided to head to the Union League Club for a drink and a change of scenery. He'd hoped to distract himself from the recurring image of the flash of light blue silk, flying upward and then plummeting, along with the rest of the young man, to the pavement below.

But it had been little use. The words in the article in front of him kept swimming together; the mahogany paneled walls of the club felt claustrophobic rather than reassuring, and he finally gave it up as a bad job. Perhaps at home he could find better distraction in a favorite novel. Something Russian might suit his brooding mood—*The Brothers Karamazov*? Or maybe it was time to return to sea, join Captain Ahab on his search for the elusive white whale. The thorniness of this current business was perplexing him to the point of wanting to go about with Ishmael, methodically knocking off people's hats.

"McCaffrey?" Daniel snapped his head around, only to see the man who had posed the question infinitesimally flinch at what must be his fierce expression.

Westwood. Daniel willed his face to relax.

"Frank." Daniel shook the other man's hand. It was hard to ignore how worry had begun to etch what were probably permanent lines in Frank's face, it looked as though he had aged years in the span of a day.

"We need to talk," Frank confided in a low tone. "Do you mind?" He gestured toward the hallway, where smaller, more private rooms were available to those who wished to have discreet conversations.

Daniel followed the older man across the hallway, settled into a blue brocade upholstered chair and accepted a second drink from one of the club's equally discreet staff members, who softly closed the door upon his exit.

"I don't have much to report since yesterday, Frank," Daniel began in a gentle tone. There was no way he was telling Frank Westwood that his daughter had potentially visited a place like Boyle's Suicide Tavern. Not until he had firm answers.

"But I do," Frank said, interrupting him. Daniel noticed a slight tremble in the other man's hands as he clutched his heavy crystal glass. "I don't know if you heard, but a young man fell to his death yesterday from the Metropolitan Rooftop Theater."

Something unpleasant lurched in Daniel's stomach. The story of the suicide had been all over the newspapers, of course, as the press had been on the scene mere moments after the police, though as of now they were declining to publicly name the victim. The articles had also left out any specific mention of demons, though they did note the deceased had been incoherent, and appeared intoxicated.

He suspected the police had a hand in withholding that information.

"I have," Daniel answered carefully. Whether or not it was prudent to admit he had been at the theater the night of the death remained to be seen. Something else to keep quiet, for now.

Frank sighed, deeply and unhappily. "That young man was Paul Riley. I had hoped he and Nora would marry."

The unpleasant thing unfurled and spread. There was an even greater connection, then, among these three young people than he had previously suspected. "Though Nora professed to love another?"

Frustration sat heavily on Frank's features. "A youthful infatuation. Paul was a perfect choice from an upstanding family and would have been an excellent match. And I know he and Nora got on well. They had been friends since their youth." Daniel thought Frank was rather missing the point, but knew that to the elite, marriage was often viewed more as a business transaction than a love match. "But now that Paul is gone, and in such a manner, I am obviously even more concerned for my daughter's safety."

"You don't think it is an unfortunate coincidence?" Daniel asked, taking a sip of his excellent whiskey. With this new knowledge, *he* did not think it a coincidence, but wanted to hear what Frank had to say.

"I can't say. But the fact that my daughter should run away, in defiance of my wishes about her marital future, and three days later the very man I wished for her to marry should perish is not a connection I wish to leave unexplored."

"Was Mr. Riley aware of your wishes? And of Nora's reluctance?" He swirled the liquid in his glass, its churning an appropriate mirror for his thoughts.

"He was, yes. Aware of both." Frank withdrew a cigar from his inner breast pocket and studied it, then seemed to rethink the venture and tucked it back in his pocket.

"And you think Paul took the action he did in unhappiness over Nora not wishing to marry him?" Daniel couldn't bring himself to voice the real words around Paul Riley's actions: "jump," "suicide," "fall". The glimmer of light blue silk flashed in his mind again, and he took a deep drink to hide an involuntary clenching of his jaw.

"Paul wanted the match as well. He and Nora were friends, and I think he was quite smitten with her. His parents approved. But my willful daughter . . ." Frank gazed around the small, intimate space as if expecting to see Nora hiding behind one of the elaborately carved credenzas. "It's all this other fellow's fault. The one who has seduced her, this man she claims to love. Find them, Daniel. Please."

The last word was uttered with difficulty, and Frank's eyes had moved from enraged to haunted.

"We will try," Daniel promised, though he had a sinking feeling it might already be too late. If Boyle had somehow gotten his hooks into Nora, though god knows how, she might be lost for good. Unless they could find her mysterious suitor.

He left Frank staring meditatively at his cigar again, and once in the hallway signaled for a staff member to attend to the older man. Daniel was looking forward to emerging into the June evening when he was waylaid by yet another staff member, the club's very proper concierge, Nichols, who detained him with a raised hand and censorious look.

"Mr. McCaffrey, I do hate to be a bother, but you have a guest," Nichols intoned.

"A guest?" This was surprising. Guests were only allowed in rare circumstances at the Union League Club. "I haven't arranged for a guest."

"Perhaps if you'll follow me? The gentleman is most insistent." Nichols's dour expression reveled his distaste for the unknown guest's insistence.

Daniel's surprise intensified. *A gentleman?* His initial thought had been that perhaps Genevieve had ferreted him out. It would be just like her to attempt entry to the men's-only club, demanding to see him. But he couldn't think what gentleman might chase him down at his private club.

Nichols opened the door to the club's elaborate library, revealing Daniel's mystery guest. *Of course.* Aloysius Longstreet stood with his arms crossed, examining one of the high shelves of books, looking damp under a black bowler hat and tweed jacket, both far too heavy for the warm weather.

"Do let me know if you require anything, Mr. McCaffrey," Nichols said with the utmost politeness, though Daniel caught the disapproving gleam in the concierge's eye.

Longstreet marked Nichols's departure with an equally disapproving gaze, which he then turned on Daniel.

"What can I do for you, Detective Longstreet?" Daniel asked.

The detective offered a slight smirk but said nothing, continuing to take in the ornate library with slightly raised brows. Daniel clasped his hands behind his back and waited, fixing his features into an expression of slightly haughty courtesy. While he normally shied away from affecting the snobbery of the moneyed class, he'd spent enough time among their ranks that he could mimic their ways fairly easily when it suited him.

And as doing so seemed to irritate Aloysius Longstreet, at this moment it suited him fine.

"My visit got you in a spot of trouble with your keepers, McCaffrey?" Longstreet asked, voice dripping with disdain.

Daniel affected a look of surprised nonchalance. "Hardly. Nichols works for us members of the club, same as the rest of the staff," he drawled, flicking his eyes toward Longstreet on the word "staff." He wasn't sure it was the smartest move to antagonize the man, but Longstreet had chased him down on *his* turf as a measure of intimidation, and he'd be damned if he'd let it work.

The detective drew himself up and tightened his lips. "I came to see if you had anything further you wished to tell me regarding the events on board the *Sophia Victoria* on Saturday." Longstreet clasped his hands behind his back and stared, mustache bristling.

Daniel regarded the detective impassively and allowed the silence to stretch. He counted a full sixty seconds in his head before answering.

"No."

Longstreet's mustache twitched once, the only signal of his agitation. "Are you sure? Think carefully, McCaffrey."

Nichols entered at that moment and silently handed Daniel a drink. He tilted his head toward Longstreet and murmured, "And for the gentleman?" Daniel shook his head, once, without bothering to ask Longstreet if he would, in fact, like a drink.

Thrusting one hand in his pocket while taking a leisurely sip, Daniel continued to stare back at Longstreet as Nichols silently glided back out of the room. He counted to sixty twice this time.

"Yes," he said.

Another twitch of the mustache. Another full minute passed. It was Longstreet who finally broke.

"Yes, what?" the detective asked.

"Yes, I'm sure I have nothing more to add about the events of Saturday," Daniel answered, taking another sip.

Longstreet gave no visible reaction to this, but the air in the room seemed to shift quickly, from merely tense to outright threatening. Another long moment passed, though Daniel had stopped counting the seconds. He maintained a casual pose, but his shoulders tightened, and he could feel his heart rate accelerate slightly.

Longstreet emanated fury, and furious men often acted rashly.

"You might want to rethink that, McCaffrey," Longstreet said in a quiet voice with more than an undercurrent of menace. "In fact, I'm sure your friend Lord Umberland would appreciate it if you did. The more we know upfront, you see, the more likely we are to press for leniency when we get to court."

Daniel stifled his intake of breath. Was that a *threat* against Rupert?

"I neither understand nor appreciate whatever you're insinuating, Detective, but this meeting is now over," he said. "I'm sure you can find your own way out."

Longstreet's eyes gleamed with satisfaction that he seemed to have gotten under Daniel's skin at last. As he made his way toward the door, he casually remarked, "I don't suppose you know that late Commissioner Simons was my mentor on the force? No, why would you? I'm sure the lives of common police officers are well beneath your notice. But we were close." Longstreet paused with his hand on the knob and turned back to Daniel. "Think carefully, McCaffrey," he said before slipping from the room. The detective's tone had been mild enough, but Daniel knew a warning when he heard one.

★   ★   ★

"Do you really think Simons would have confided in the likes of that detective?" Genevieve asked in a hissed whisper as they made their way up Fifth Avenue the following afternoon. "About the investments and the plot to frame Rupert? About Rupert being"—she glanced around almost theatrically, with wide eyes, making sure they were far from other pedestrians—"*you know.*"

Daniel knew. And no, he wasn't sure at all whether the late police commissioner would have revealed to Aloysius Longstreet that he, the commissioner, was embroiled in a vicious plot with a gangster and several high-ranking members of society to make massive profits on tenement construction, and to frame Rupert, whom they'd figured out was a jewel thief, for several murders.

"I don't know," he answered in an equally low voice, "but we have to warn Rupert and Esmie, regardless. And we need to find out why Marcus Dalrymple was on that ship."

They were on their way to Rupert at that moment, on another impossibly gorgeous June day. New York was outdoing herself this early summer, and Fifth Avenue was awash with plot after plot of bright blooms in every color as verdant trees swayed gently overhead. The avenue was crowded with well-heeled strollers taking in the bright sunshine and easy, late afternoon breeze.

The Bradley mansion came into view, occupying more than half of the entire next block. It still startled Daniel every time he passed it; even among its massive neighbors, it was a behemoth of a house, the exterior sporting turrets and gargoyles, a hodge-podge of styles and materials that surely made the architect lose sleep. But the late Elmira Bradley, Esmie's mother, had wanted the most extravagant private residence in the city and had been willing to pay ungodly sums to see it built. Daniel knew the interior was as lavish as Elmira had hoped, featuring some twenty bedrooms, a gymnasium, not one but two grand ballrooms, one of the largest private libraries he'd ever seen, an underground swimming pool, and a bowling alley.

Daniel rang the front bell, gesturing with his brows toward the crest carved into the front door. Genevieve rolled her eyes in response. Elmira had been thrilled to see her daughter engaged to a member of the British aristocracy and had planned on capitalizing on her new familial ties to advance her own place in New York society. Unfortunately, her throat had been slit before her plans could come to fruition. Yet her late husband, Amos, had honored her desires to have Rupert's family crest emblazoned on their door, for all passing on Fifth Avenue to see.

A maid ushered them into an elaborate sitting room with a frescoed ceiling featuring a trompe l'oeil scene of putti darting among dissolving clouds. Daniel squinted at the painting.

"Is that . . .?" he asked Genevieve, pointing.

"It is," Rupert's voice answered. He walked into the room and gazed up at the impish, naked figures, one half hiding behind a cloud, only its rosy bottom visible, one tossing a handful of flowers, one drawing back an arrow notched in a bow, and one standing on a fluffy cloud in the act of urinating into the room below. "Amos's doing. Elmira apparently pitched a right fit when she saw it, but Amos just laughed and said if he was going to pay for a pack of naked babies to fly around his ceiling, one of them ought to be doing what a naked baby would rightfully do."

"It's true," Esmie added, trailing in after Rupert. "But Mother grew fond of that particular putto over time, and christened him Cletus."

"Why Cletus?" asked Genevieve, sounding mystified.

"Apparently he reminded Mother of a childhood acquaintance."

"And what is happening here?" Daniel asked, gesturing toward what appeared to be a genuine Ming Dynasty ceramic of a judge of hell, snuggled up against a bronze figurine of the goddess Diana.

"That was me," Amos remarked. Daniel hadn't seen him enter, but Esmie's father's sizable frame now filled the doorway to the room, an unlit cigar firmly clenched in his teeth. "Well, not the Chinaman—that was Elmira. She brought that home one day, and I said to her, 'Elmira, why am I paying three hundred American dollars, made with American-mined copper, for that damned thing? He's green, for Lord's sake. If I'm paying that much for a durned statue, I wanna see one of them Greek goddesses baring her titties,' I told her."

Daniel saw Genevieve blink at Amos's choice of words.

"Papa, language," Esmie said mildly. "We have guests." She was blushing, but only slightly. Daniel guessed she was used to her father's way of speaking by now. Amos was from Montana, and while he had made a fortune in copper mining large enough to rival that of the Vanderbilts', he had never quite accustomed himself to New York society.

"So I go out West for a spell to take care of some business, and what do I find when I come back but that?" Amos continued, gesturing toward the pair of sculptures, chuckling. The Chinese figure's impassive gaze was indeed trained on the goddess's enthusiastically bared chest. "Had me laughing for days. Elmira had a fine sense of humor, when she chose to. Not many here knew that about her." Amos moved the cigar to the other side of his mouth, chomping contentedly as he smiled at the sculptures.

"Humorous" was certainly a word Daniel would never have applied to the late Elmira Bradley, but knowing this personal, unexpected detail about her made him even sorrier about her passing. He hadn't particularly cared for the woman, but she hadn't deserved to be murdered, and was clearly missed by those who loved her.

"You two gonna help my son-in-law?" Amos drawled, turning his sharp eyes to Daniel but gesturing with the cigar to encompass Genevieve as well. "Nasty business, that Dalrymple boy turning up dead."

"We're going to try, yes," Genevieve replied. "I actually have some information that may be useful."

Daniel caught Rupert's quick head shake, silently asking that they wait to discuss until Amos was out of the room, but Rupert's worry was needless.

"I don't need the particulars," Amos said, turning to leave. "They'll tell me anything I need to know. Whatever you need, just ask Esmie." Amos shuffled out of the room as a maid popped in, whom Esmie instructed to bring refreshments.

Once they were alone and settled, Rupert fixed Genevieve in his sights. "Come now, out with it," he demanded. "What have you learned?"

Daniel and Genevieve took turns filling in Rupert and Esmie on what they had gleaned about Marcus's possible connection to Boyle's Suicide Tavern, the disappearance of Nora Westwood, and now the death of Paul Riley.

"All that in three days?" Rupert looked thunderstruck. "What on earth is going on? It's *June*, for Pete's sake. Time for summer houses and croquet and sailing, not all this back-alley skullduggery."

"I don't think murder has a season, dear," Esmie murmured.

"*Murder?*" Rupert's outrage shifted to alarm. "We don't know anyone was *murdered*, do we? Dalrymple drank himself to death, this Nora girl likely ran off with her mystery beau, and poor Riley brought his death upon himself. Right, Daniel?"

Daniel wished he could offer his best friend more reassurance, but he simply couldn't. The unease that had danced on his spine ever since Saturday refused to die, instead growing more insistent with every passing hour.

"Those do seem the obvious answers," he said slowly. "But that is what troubles me. They're all too neat. And I might have bought them if I hadn't found that medal on Marcus's body or if the serving girl at Boyle's hadn't started at Nora's photograph."

"Or mentioned Meade's name," Genevieve added darkly. She clamped her lips shut as the maid from earlier returned with a heavily laden tea tray, setting it down and arranging it to Esmie's instructions. Once the maid left, Esmie picked up the pot.

"Shall I pour? Or would everyone prefer something stronger?" she asked.

"Stronger," Daniel, Genevieve, and Rupert said in unison.

As Rupert went to fetch a bottle, Genevieve turned her attention to Esmie.

"Esmie, you were closest to Marcus. Do you know if he had any association with Nora Westwood or Paul Riley?" she asked.

"None that I know of," Esmie replied, looking bewildered. "I don't—or didn't, in Paul's case—know either of them well, but they don't seem like the sorts with whom Marcus would have associated."

"There's more, I'm afraid," Daniel interjected as Rupert returned with both a dusty bottle of red wine and a crystal decanter of what was probably whiskey. "Rupert, I'm sorry to say that Detective Longstreet threatened you yesterday."

Rupert whirled around from where he was gathering glasses. "Threatened me? But why?"

"He didn't say, but the intent was clear. He seems to suspect you were somehow involved in Marcus's death. And he hinted that he knows of your *activities* from last year."

Esmie rose and gently took the glasses from Rupert's hands as he sputtered. "Why is everyone always trying to frame *me* for murders I didn't commit?" he demanded.

"Daniel, I think we've overlooked something," Genevieve said as Esmie made soothing noises to Rupert. Daniel stood up to take over the making of drinks, struggling with the stubborn cork of the wine bottle, but nodded at Genevieve to indicate he was listening.

"When Paul Riley . . . fell," she continued, "he yelled something. I think it was a message. I think he was trying to tell us who is behind all this."

CHAPTER 8

"Genevieve, I don't think that's relevant," Daniel was shaking his head at her. The cork loosened from the bottle with a definitive pop, and Genevieve's temper spiked with it.

"And I *do*," she said firmly. "It wasn't a senseless yell or a scream. It was a *word*."

"Word? What word?" Rupert had stopped fuming and was bouncing his gaze between the two of them. "Could it help me?"

"Rupert," Daniel admonished, cutting his eyes toward Esmie.

"Help *us*," Rupert amended guiltily. "Though nobody is trying to pin a murder on Esmie," he muttered under his breath.

"It sounded like *grazie*," Genevieve interrupted before Rupert could continue and potentially damage his brand-new marriage. She accepted a glass of dark red wine from Daniel but placed it on a small gilded end table, raising her chin slightly.

When said out loud, it did sound rather ridiculous.

"*Grazie?* As in 'thank you' in Italian?" Esmie sounded doubtful.

"That doesn't make any sense," Rupert added. "Who would he be thanking? And why in Italian? From everything you've said, it seems that Riley was half out of his mind. Maybe he'd begun to dabble in narcotics. Cocaine can really play the devil with one's brain, and I know from personal experience."

"Nobody wants to hear about your experiences with cocaine, Rupert," Daniel said, cutting him off.

"I rather do," said Esmie, looking at her husband with wide eyes.

"Do you really?" Rupert seemed pleasantly surprised. "I shall be happy to tell you all about my sordid past," he added suggestively, picking up her hand and kissing it. "Later, in private."

A flush suffused Esmie's cheeks.

"Ahem," Daniel interrupted. He rolled his eyes at Genevieve, but she, for one, was pleased to see the newlyweds getting on so well. It had not been a love match between the two of them, and it was nice to see that there was perhaps some chemistry there.

Maybe love could grow.

But Daniel was right, there was time for that later. "Yes, back to the business at hand," Genevieve added briskly.

"Well I didn't hear *grazie*," Daniel said, staring into his own glass of red wine. Genevieve's heart lurched slightly. Daniel had been closest to Paul as he hurled himself from the roof; indeed, he had tried to stop Paul from jumping and failed. She hoped this wasn't too painful for him to discuss.

"It sounded more like, 'Guards, see ya,'" he continued, glancing up from his wine. At their collective blank stares, he shrugged slightly. "That's what I heard."

"Guards, see ya? As though he were in prison? I don't believe any of the Rileys were ever imprisoned," Genevieve said, trying to recall if there was a distant Riley relative serving time at Sing Sing.

"Maybe he was being held captive at this bar you mentioned, and escaped," Esmie suggested quietly. Daniel cast a startled glance at Esmie, then caught Genevieve's eye and raised a brow. Though less surprised at Esmie's acuity—she was sharper than she looked—Genevieve nodded back at him thoughtfully. Yes, that could fit.

"Was it Garcia?" Rupert said abruptly. "Like the old haunted mansion?" He'd resumed his seat with a hefty pour of whiskey.

Genevieve saw puzzled faces mirroring her own and was comforted to know she wasn't the only one who had no idea what Rupert was talking about.

"A haunted house? Here in New York?" Esmie asked. She looked more doubtful than before.

"Yes, of course," Rupert said. "A mansion, located on the East River a bit north of Harlem—Oak Point, I believe. It's been abandoned for about twenty years or so and has fallen into a state of total disrepair. Apparently quite haunted. Visiting it is rather a rite of passage among those just out in the season, especially the young men. You all never heard of it?"

Genevieve shook her head, mystified. "Nobody I knew ever talked about it, though it sounds like the sort of thing my brother Gavin would do."

"And I was a wallflower," Esmie remarked, sipping a dainty glass of port. "Nobody talked to me at all."

Her words caused a pang of regret in Genevieve's chest, as she had never gone out of her way to include Esmie in activities when she was younger. "I am sorry, Esmie."

Her friend smiled and waved away Genevieve's concern. "I could have been more outgoing myself. I was so shy I could barely stammer two words together. And of course my mother . . ." She let the thought trail off, turning her attention back to her port.

"Well, we were all a pack of damned fools to have ignored you so," Rupert declared, reaching over and taking hold of Esmie's free hand, causing his bride to blush again. "Daniel?" Rupert prompted.

Daniel gave what could only be described as a snort. "Please. You know I kept to the fringes of society at that age."

"And I was back home—er, my previous home." Rupert waved vaguely toward downtown and, presumably, the harbor. "Trying my luck at participating in the London season for a few years. Lord, it was dreadful. So stuffy. I couldn't wait to get back to the States."

A surge of warmth for her friends encompassed Genevieve. "What a band of misfits we were," she mused. "Are?"

"Were," Daniel said firmly, sending a half smile her way.

"Are," Rupert said just as firmly. "But we're all misfits together, so that's all right."

"Tell us more about this haunted mansion," Esmie urged. Genevieve noticed with a smile that the two were still holding hands.

"Well, I was told about it by some of the younger set. I was sharing a bottle with a whole gang of them—oh, it must have been a decade or so ago? Seven, eight years? Can't recall with whom exactly—the young sets rather blur together over time, don't they—and they told me about it.

It sounded like devilishly good fun, so much so I almost joined them the following night. There are levels of dares, you see—touch the gate, then the front door, enter, spend the night—that sort of thing."

Genevieve felt fear begin to prickle her belly. This sounded far too similar to the dares placed on surviving a night at Boyle's Suicide Tavern. She looked to Daniel, whose furrowed brow revealed he was probably thinking the same thing.

"Something more diverting must have come up for the appointed night, as I did not join the lads, but I never quite forgot about it," Rupert continued.

"Why Garcia?" Daniel asked.

Rupert shrugged. "Honestly, I've told you all I know. It's probably the name of a previous owner, wouldn't you think? But that is definitely the name they said. I remember it distinctly."

"And you can't recall who these youths were? Do you know of anyone who has taken part in this dare?" Genevieve pressed.

"I honestly can't recall—we'd had quite a bit to drink, you know," Rupert said defensively. "But as you said, I'm sure your brother Gavin engaged. He's a bit of a daredevil, that one."

Genevieve had to admit Rupert was correct. "But he's in Egypt until later this summer," she pointed out. "A letter would take too long, and it's hard to get a cable to where he is."

"What about Charles, Genevieve?" asked Esmie, pouring herself another measure of port.

"Charles?" Genevieve mulled this over, accepting more red wine for herself when Esmie offered. Would her other brother have taken such a dare? "Maybe," she said thoughtfully. "He's already in Newport, but I can send him a quick note tomorrow and ask."

"There is one person I'm certain has been to the mansion," Rupert said, sounding glum. Genevieve eyed him with irritation; it was just like Rupert to withhold valuable information while the rest of them were spinning their wheels.

"Well, why didn't you say so?" she asked crossly.

"It's nobody we want to interact with," he said with uncharacteristic gravity. Genevieve's breath caught. People who fit that category comprised a limited but significant list.

"Sarah Huffington," Rupert concluded, tossing back the rest of his whiskey in one swallow.

"Absolutely not," Esmie stood abruptly, her voice like ice. "That woman is partially responsible for my mother's murder. She should be behind bars. There is no way any of us in this room is going to her for information." There were flaming patches of color on Esmie's cheeks, but from fury rather than a blush. Rupert, on the other hand, had grown quite pale.

Genevieve and Daniel exchanged a glance. Sarah Huffington had been in league with Tommy Meade the previous year. The sole reason she had not been convicted was because the only people who could offer solid proof of her involvement in the murders were dead.

But as far as Genevieve knew, Sarah was also the only person alive, other than the four of them, who knew for certain that Rupert had been the jewel thief known as Robin Hood.

No, nobody in the room wanted to speak with Sarah Huffington. She had been keeping a low profile for the past year, playing the part of the grieving widow, though

Genevieve suspected Sarah may have had a hand in her late husband's death, as well. And as Genevieve and Rupert had foiled the scheme to frame Robin Hood for the murders Tommy had arranged, she rather doubted Sarah would deign to speak with them either.

"No, we shall not deal with Mrs. Huffington," Genevieve declared, her voice firm. "But Rupert, how do you even know she has been to this mansion? Did she tell you?" Sarah and Rupert had been friendly at one time.

"The lads," he said, grasping Esmie's hand and tugging it gently, encouraging her to sit down. She snapped her head toward him, jaw clenched, but then sat at his reassuring nod. "I never forgot that either, even though I wasn't friends with her then. They were in awe of her, that a young lady had taken the dare. When we did become friends," Rupert continued, with a guilty glance toward Esmie, who returned it stonily, "I did ask her about it once, but she laughed it off, said it was just kid's play. Those young men, though, they were afraid. Boastful and excited, certainly, but afraid."

Genevieve digested this information. "I can ask Charles what he knows, but I don't like to wait. I feel certain Nora Westwood is in danger somehow." She put down her glass and began to pace the room in frustration.

Daniel stood, too, running a hand through his hair. "You're right. We can't wait. Rupert and I ought to at least visit this mansion and ascertain for ourselves that nothing untoward is happening there."

This stopped Genevieve in her tracks. "Excuse me. I'm right here."

She recognized the stubborn set of Daniel's jaw. "We don't know what we're getting into, Genevieve," he said. "It could be quite dangerous, particularly if Tommy Meade is involved again."

Genevieve expected a wash of fury to overwhelm her, but instead she just felt tired. And sad. Why must they have this same conversation repeatedly?

Esmie must have caught her look, for she instantly hustled Rupert out of the room, over his protests, murmuring to him about refilling the whiskey decanter.

"Am I in this with you or not?" Genevieve asked quietly once their friends had left the room. "You said you wanted a renewed partnership, yet you keep trying to shut me out."

A range of emotions played across Daniel's face in quick succession: anger, worry, and the most fleeting moment of regret. He sat heavily in his recently abandoned armchair. He picked up his wineglass and slowly twirled it by its stem, watching the ruby liquid swirl.

"It's been good to see you these past few days," he finally said, keeping his eyes on the revolving glass. Genevieve kept her silence, not sure where Daniel's train of thought was heading.

Finally he raised his gaze, and the intensity in his piercing blue eyes shot straight to her soul. "I've missed you," he said simply.

Her breath caught, so unexpected was the sentiment.

"I've missed you as well," she admitted. Confusion and gladness and something that felt a little like heartache warred within her for dominance. She shoved them all aside and chose righteous indignation instead, never a good look, but the best she felt she could muster at the moment. "But I can't keep arguing with you about whether some aspect of this investigation is too dangerous for me. It's exhausting, and if it continues, I shall have no choice but to consider our partnership dissolved and to continue exploring this matter on my own." Genevieve drew herself up taller and folded her hands in front of her waist, well aware that she likely looked as schoolmarmish as she sounded.

Daniel rubbed his hand over face, suddenly looking exhausted himself. "You're right," he admitted. "I'm not being fair to you. I simply . . . I hate to see you put yourself at risk," he finally concluded.

"You have just as much chance of finding yourself in a potentially harmful scenario as I," Genevieve pointed out in a low tone. "The risk is similar."

"Right again," Daniel conceded. He stood again, and made an oddly formal little bow of the head. "It won't happen again."

It was a victory, but somehow it felt a bit hollow. As though she had lost more than she had gained.

Genevieve shoved that though aside too. "Thank you," she said in a brisk tone, wishing to put the whole unsettling matter behind them. "Now, let's make a plan."

★ ★ ★

The invigorating snap of salt air revived Genevieve, who had been on the verge of being lulled to sleep toward the end of their long ride to Oak Point. Daniel had thought it best if they drove themselves, and the soothing sounds of horse hooves clip-clopping and the gently passing scenery had had a somnolent effect on her, and she glanced around guiltily. Had she, in fact, actually fallen asleep?

"Welcome back, Sleeping Beauty," Daniel said wryly.

Genevieve stretched her arms overhead and blinked at their surroundings. The sun had disappeared while she dozed, low-hanging gray clouds overtaking what had been another glorious June day. They serenely rolled past vast green estates, each snugly set behind low stone walls, their grand houses peeking toward the street.

"Was I asleep long?" In truth, she felt too refreshed to be embarrassed, though she did realize that napping made her a rather poor travel companion.

"Only fifteen minutes or so," Daniel replied. He reached to his feet and handed her a cloth bag. "Have an apple."

Pleasure suffused her that he had been thoughtful enough to bring food. "Thank you," she said in real appreciation, biting into the crisp red fruit. "I didn't think to pack provisions and am quite famished."

"I learned the hard way," he said, grinning at her.

Genevieve smiled back. She couldn't see the water but knew from the distinctive tang in the air that it was close. "Where is the Sound?"

Daniel gestured with his head down the stony road they were traveling. "Up ahead, farther south."

"South?" She looked around, trying to get her bearings.

"We had to come farther north, then loop back to this spot—the only way the roads take us. This Garcia house is right on the shore, directly ahead."

They passed an imposing stone gate to another estate, and Genevieve glimpsed neatly trimmed hedges lining the drive that led up to the mansion.

"Who on earth lives there?" she murmured, marveling at the grand, square-shaped tower rising from between two expansive wings of a honey-colored stone house.

Daniel glanced past the gates as they rolled by. "I've been there," he remarked. "William Niles's home. He's an attorney, like me, and has been instrumental in reserving much of the land up here for parks."

"Of course, I've met him," Genevieve mused. "It seems so far from the city to make one's primary residence."

"Not everyone wants to be in the center of the hustle and bustle of town," Daniel said. "Here one can have a great deal of land, but it's really not that far from Manhattan. We passed one of the Tiffany estates farther back."

"I wonder how such neighbors feel about the Garcia mansion being in such disrepair," Genevieve said. In the intervening days since their appointment with Rupert and Esmie, Genevieve had plundered the newspaper's archives and unearthed a store of information on the house and its previous occupants. Apparently one of the most lavish houses constructed in its time, it had been built by a Southerner, one Frederick Cummings, in the mid-1850s. A Confederate sympathizer during the war, Cummings had eventually lost the fortune he'd accumulated in both real estate and in trading cotton and tobacco. Once he died in the late 1860s, the mansion sat vacant for about a year before being sold by Cummings's solicitors to a Cuban merchant called Pablo Garcia, which is how it had come by its current name.

"And what happened to Garcia?" Daniel had asked when she'd relayed her findings early in their journey. "Does he still own the house?"

Genevieve had shrugged. "I wasn't able to find out. He had a wife and children. Perhaps they all went back to Cuba."

Daniel pulled the horses to a stop in front of an ornate, wrought-iron gate. It was an imposing structure, and would have been quite handsome in its prime, though now it was dotted with flaking paint and pitted with rust. Beyond the gate, large oaks towered toward increasingly gray clouds, but they were tangled with strangling ivy, and what were once probably smartly trimmed hedges had grown wild and unruly. There was no sign of the house through the morass of dense foliage.

Genevieve eyed the plant-choked drive doubtfully. "Could we even get the carriage down the lane?"

"I'm not sure we can even get past that gate," Daniel sighed. "But we'll get closer for a better look." There was a decently sized, arched wooden bridge, another structure that was once probably charming, stretching over a weed-infested ditch on the way to the front gate. He urged the horses forward over the bridge.

A loud, metallic screech rent the sea-laden air, causing Genevieve to start so much that she dropped her apple core and gripped the sides of the leather seat.

"What on earth . . .?"

As if by magic, the rusted gates slowly began to creak open of their own accord, widening to welcome them like two ancient, spectral arms.

CHAPTER 9

Daniel frowned at the open gates and at the overgrown drive beyond. Genevieve had gone pale, and in truth he was more unnerved by the mechanical gates than he wanted to admit.

"How did that happen?" Genevieve asked in a shaky voice.

"Likely there's a hidden mechanism under the bridge, triggered by the horses. I'm surprised it still works after all this time," Daniel said. He briefly considered climbing down and examining the workings of the automatic gate but discarded the idea. The sky was continuing to darken, shifting from merely overcast to an impending gathering of ominous-looking thunderclouds. It was best they get to the house itself.

Urging the horses onward through the gates, Daniel couldn't help but feel as if they were entering an alternate realm. The overgrown bowers and clusters of knotty vines called to mind the fairy stories of his youth, which had been resplendent with abundant greenery, exotic-sounding clusters of hawthorns and country hedgerows unfathomable to a city boy such as himself. Those stories, though beautiful, had always been limned with danger: ripe with tricksters, otherworldly creatures lurking in the shadows, bright-eyed and eager-fingered, ready to spirit a careless or disobedient child away forever.

"We should walk the rest of the way," he said, stopping the horses when a felled tree blocked their path. Genevieve nodded and climbed down as Daniel tied the horses to a stout branch. He held her hand as she lifted her skirts to near knee-length to clamber over the large tree. Once past the barrier, they continued down the leafy drive, and though they didn't hold hands, he was forcibly reminded again of fairy tales, though this time of the Grimm Brothers' story of Hansel and Gretel, two children walking alone through the woods to an uncertain fate.

"Not to worry," Genevieve said stoutly, as though she sensed his disquiet. "I have brought my *new acquisition* again." She patted her hip and looked around furtively, even though there was not a soul about.

She meant her new pistol, Daniel understood. He eyed with distrust the area of her body she had indicated. "You've got it strapped to yourself under there?" he asked, wondering how she would lift her skirts to get to it in time, should the need arise.

"No, silly," Genevieve replied. "This dress has pockets." She patted the place where presumably the gun was hidden, under a layer of light gray cotton printed with tiny yellow and white flowers.

"One would never guess," Daniel mused.

"I know," she replied in a happy voice. "Pockets are so freeing."

Daniel smiled at this but stopped abruptly at the sight before him, Genevieve halting as well, her mouth a small "O" of surprise.

Like emerging from the winding, shadowed streets of Florence into a bright and expansive piazza, all at once the trees and bracken fell away, and they emerged on a wide, unkempt lawn that rose slightly before sloping to a narrow, rocky beach. At the mild summit, looming over the grass, sand, and water, sat the Garcia mansion.

Though Daniel supposed technically they were looking at the East River, the house sat right at the point where the river merged with Long Island Sound, which itself eventually joined the Atlantic Ocean. That the East River was in actuality a tidal estuary, and not a freshwater river, was harder to ignore here than when in Manhattan: the brackish smell of ocean water was unmistakable, seagulls dove and cried, and he spied some dried seagrass embedded in the rocks at the shore's edge.

But the house was what dominated his field of vision, and he suspected the original owners had designed it so any visitors would have the same sensory experience he currently had: the feeling of traversing from dark to light, emerging from the woods to be both welcomed and intimidated by the mansion. It was an enormous honey-colored structure boasting four stories—five if you counted the windows in what was presumably the basement—containing a central section flanked by two wings, each of the three sections topped by its own tall, graceful mansard roof. Rectangular windows lined each floor like orderly soldiers, and their elegant lines would have been quite handsome under different circumstances. In this instance, though, their multitudes gave Daniel the unsettling feeling of being watched by unseen eyes. The front entrance was shielded by a portico, making it impossible to see the doors under its shadows on this cloudy day.

"Do we just try the front door?" Genevieve asked in a small voice.

"It's the best place to start," Daniel agreed.

The sound of water lapping rock was their accompaniment as they walked the remainder of the drive to the path that led to the portico. A particularly strong breeze whipped off the water and threatened to steal Genevieve's beribboned straw hat, causing her to clamp her hand on her head before giving up and removing the hat altogether. Daniel glanced at the sky, disliking the color of the clouds.

In truth, he disliked this whole mission, suddenly, and he stopped just short of the house's front steps, causing Genevieve to look at him curiously.

"We don't have to do this," Daniel said, the words out of his mouth before he could stop them.

Surprise registered in her face, quickly followed by angry frustration, but he continued before she had a chance to speak. "This isn't about my not wanting you to put yourself in harm's way," he said, guessing the reason for her ire. "I just . . ." Daniel gazed at the empty, foreboding facade of the house, trying to verbalize the feeling of disquiet it gave him. "I don't have a good feeling about this," he finished somewhat lamely.

They both looked up at the imposing structure, which appeared to stare back impassively. It was almost as if the house was biding its time. *Come in or not,* it seemed to say. *I've been rooted to this spot for decades and plan to stand for decades more. Come in and see if you can find my secrets.* The wind picked up again, causing the straw hat in Genevieve's hand to flap. Daniel could feel his hair being tousled and made wild, and drove a hand over his head to calm it, only to have it spring back up in the next gust.

"We owe it to Nora Westwood," Genevieve said.

"Boyle's is a better lead for Nora than here," Daniel said, not really arguing with her, but testing the necessity of this particular visit from all angles, probing its soundness. It was ridiculous to do so in an increasing wind in front of the closed doors of the very house they had come to see, but here they were.

He didn't like this place. It didn't feel right.

"We came all this way, Daniel," Genevieve said in a gentle tone. She glanced at the front doors with a worried expression. "We ought to at least finish what we started."

Peeling paint blighted the doors, which were also scarred with pockmarks of missing wood that resembled bullet holes—perhaps the youths had used these doors as target practice? His unease ratcheted up a notch, but he nodded at Genevieve, feeling his mouth set into a grim line. She was right; they had come a long way, and if anything, his feeling of foreboding probably meant there was something here worth investigating.

After a moment of resistance, the doors gave with a slight groan, and Daniel took a cautious peek inside, Genevieve hovering behind his right shoulder. They stepped in, and he was instantly assaulted by the heavy, cloying scent of mold.

"Ugh," Genevieve wrinkled her nose, staying close to his shoulder. There was a large, elaborate staircase directly in front of them that led to a second-floor landing, which then split and continued to the higher floors in both directions. She directed his attention toward the ceiling, where a massive, wrought-iron chandelier hung high above.

"Let's try through here." Daniel gestured toward the open French doors on their right, one of which was half hanging off its hinges. The room was devoid of furniture, but the walls themselves were flayed and exposed, in some places almost to the house's wooden frame, by the ever-encroaching moist air. Wallpaper hung in tattered strips, and mildew dotted the once-elaborate woodwork. The sea breeze wafted down the chimney and through the brick fireplace, and Daniel felt Genevieve, who remained pressed close behind him, shiver slightly in her light summer dress.

They slowly made their way through the vast rooms of the first floor, walking through what had probably once been dining rooms, parlors, sitting rooms, and an elaborate ballroom. Genevieve pointed out the remnants of wall and ceiling paintings, reminding Daniel eerily of the fresco of flying cherubs they had seen only a few days prior at the Bradleys'. The dampness had eroded most of these to almost nothing, but every few rooms a detail could be spotted: an eye under a partial hat here, part of a hand holding a flower there, the truncated bough of a tree on a ceiling. They encountered more wrought-iron chandeliers, and Daniel noticed that in some rooms it appeared as if something that had once covered the walls had been ripped down.

"Marble paneling, would be my guess," he said, showing the spot to Genevieve. "Who knows when somebody stole it."

"Daniel, look at this." Genevieve had peeled herself away from him after the second room, not straying too far ahead, but examining various corners and broken lighting devices on her own. She gestured at a shabby velvet bellpull, inclining her head toward it in query. At his nod, she gave the bellpull a gentle tug. A resounding, surprisingly clear bell sounded out, then reverberated and echoed throughout the empty rooms. It was impossible to tell from whence the sound originated, but Daniel guessed the lower level, where the servants' quarters were probably located.

They found themselves at the foot of the grand staircase again, on which Genevieve had rested her straw hat when they entered.

"We underestimated the size of this place," Genevieve said. "I should have guessed from the records I saw that it was this massive. Do you know it was called Cummings's Folly before he died? He apparently sunk a small fortune into this house, only to lose it all after the war."

"How did he die?" Daniel asked, running his hand along the filthy bannister of the staircase. He gave it an experimental shake; it seemed solid enough.

Genevieve shrugged. "His obituary simply mentioned a brief illness." She eyed the staircase. "We're going to have to split up, aren't we?"

Touring the first floor had done nothing to ease Daniel's apprehension; if anything, it had increased even more. But yes, if they wanted to investigate this house and return to Manhattan before nightfall, they would have to separate and cover more ground.

"We should have brought lanterns," Genevieve complained, peeking out a window at the sky, which continued to darken. The trees through which they had traversed were now swaying wildly in the increasing wind.

"We should have done a lot of things," Daniel agreed. "But rather than make a second trip, let's see what we can while we're here. I haven't seen anything that speaks of actual danger yet." He refrained from mentioning how much he disliked their task, though. The same feeling of being watched that he'd had on their approach to the house had intensified once inside it. He kept catching himself looking over his shoulder, half expecting to see someone there.

Of course, there never was.

"Fine," Genevieve sighed. "Before it gets any darker, and before this storm hits. I daresay we're in for a wet ride home regardless. I'll take the attic and the fourth floor if you'll do the second and the third?"

"That will do," Daniel said. "But let's save belowstairs until we can do so together."

"Agreed," Genevieve said instantly. It seemed neither of them were willing to explore the lower level alone.

Daniel climbed the first flight with her, then watched her ascend to the fourth floor. Her cheerful, summer dress with its lightly puffed short sleeves and decorative bands of lace seemed totally flimsy and inappropriate for this dank place, and he almost called after her to come back down. As if sensing his worry, Genevieve paused on the top step of the fourth floor and looked back at him. She smiled slightly and patted her hip, where he knew her small derringer was nestled.

"If you need me, ring one of those bellpulls," he yelled up. "I may not hear if you call."

"I will," she promised, and the mere fact that she'd agreed to do so without an argument signaled to Daniel that Genevieve was just as disquieted as he was. He followed her progress, craning his neck to see her slip down the west hallway, until she had traversed out of his sight.

★ ★ ★

After the emptiness of the first floor, Genevieve was surprised to find scattered pieces of furniture in some of the upper bedrooms. Not much, but the occasional wooden chair, its fabric seat and armrests gnawed away by mice or other vermin, and once a sodden mattress, left bare under a broken window. Its sordid, dirty presence gave Genevieve an inexplicable shudder, and she hurried out of that particular room after only a cursory look.

She stopped counting the bedrooms, adjacent sitting and dressing rooms, and ancient water closets after twenty. There had to be over a hundred rooms in this house. She guessed it might be larger than even the Bradley mansion.

A continued search of the fourth floor yielded nothing useful, and Genevieve could feel her frustrations mounting, thankfully edging out the fear that had been lingering in the corners of her body ever since the automatic gate had opened. She placed her hands on her hips and glanced up the final set of stairs, these not part of the main, grand staircase, but tucked around a back corner—a modest staircase instead, signaling it likely led to servants' bedrooms on the fifth floor.

Despite her frustration, she couldn't help but think it might not be reasonable to expect their search to deliver anything useful. What had she expected? Nora Westwood to be demurely seated on the front steps, glad of their arrival? A tidy note from Paul Riley, explaining exactly why he had maybe yelled the word "Garcia" as he plunged to his death?

The attic did indeed contain smaller bedrooms, undoubtedly meant for the staff, and significantly fewer water closets (she only counted one). The rooms were still of varying sizes, though, and some had odd corners and steeply angled ceilings because of the sharp slope of the roof. One, in particular, seized her attention.

Like the other rooms on this floor, this one had slanted walls and a ceiling so low that Genevieve, who was quite tall, had to duck her head considerably to move around. It held a narrow mattress similar to the one she'd seen earlier, though curiously this one was on a tarnished brass bedframe, and a dirty, worn quilt was bunched at the foot of the bed. The room's single, tiny dormer window had a broken pane, and though a small puddle of leftover rainwater was gathered in an adjacent corner, the bed itself appeared dry. Frowning, Genevieve bent to get a closer look, carefully keeping her hands clasped behind her back—the mere thought of touching anything in this house made her skin crawl—when a small, sharp gleam of something metallic on the floor caught her eye.

Steeling herself, Genevieve gingerly knelt down and peered under the bed. The metal object winked dully at her in the dim light. Her heart began to race as she grasped the coin, knowing even before she saw it closely what she would find. Sure enough, John Boyle's profile was stamped onto the side of the cheap metal disk.

A thrill raced down her spine, making her further forget her dread of the house and the muck now staining her hands and the skirt of her dress. This was *it*—here was the proof they had been seeking! Paul Riley hadn't yelled insensibly; he *had* said "Garcia." There *was* some connection between this decrepit mansion and Boyle's Suicide Tavern, some connection between the deaths of Marcus Dalrymple, Paul Riley, and the disappearance of Nora Westwood.

She couldn't wait to find Daniel. Whirling toward the door, Genevieve had only taken two steps in its direction when, without a breeze to blow it or a visible person to push it, the door to the tiny, cramped attic bedroom slammed shut with a definitive thud.

CHAPTER 10

Puzzled, Genevieve frowned at the closed door. An odd wind she must not have felt in her excitement over finding the medal had surely slammed the door—it was the only reasonable explanation. Several unreasonable explanations began to jostle in the periphery of her brain, but she firmly shut them out. Entertaining such notions would not be productive.

And yet, the fear that had slipped from her mind when she found the medallion insidiously crept back in, mounting once the door refused to yield to her tug on the cut-glass knob.

Genevieve tugged harder. The door stayed firmly shut.

Alarm joined her fear, edging out reason as her movements became more and more frantic. She pulled and jostled the doorknob every which way, but it was no use. No matter how much of her considerable strength she used to pull on the door, it wouldn't budge.

"Help, Daniel! Help," Genevieve called, banging on the stubborn wooden surface with the flats of her palms. "Daniel! In here!" she yelled, but only silence answered.

Genevieve took a step back and inhaled a deep, shaky breath, trying to calm her racing heart. The room was so small and cramped she couldn't quite stand upright, adding to her ever-building anxiety. She looked around frantically for a bellpull, recalling Daniel's words, but then let out a shuddering half laugh. Of course, there wouldn't be a bell-pull in a servant's room.

The window? Even as Genevieve scooted gingerly around the bed to the room's one deep dormer window, she knew that route was useless. Misty rain dampened her face, blowing in through the single broken pane—the storm had finally broken, and rain was coming down in heavy sheets outside, often being whipped near sideways by the wind. From this high up, she could make out a wide portion of grass edged by a slice of beach, and thrashing, murky waters beyond. There was no way anyone out there would be able to hear her, five stories up, over the wild wind.

Not that anyone was out there.

She hoped.

Would Daniel even be able to hear her? Or was he trapped somewhere in this horror house as well?

Rain steadily pelted the window, the fine spray coming through the small broken section dampening everything. Genevieve could feel the small hairs around her face begin to frizz as the lace on her dress visibly slackened, and she shivered in the encroaching chill. The stench of mildew, already strong in the house, increased considerably, making her empty-again stomach roil with light nausea.

How was she to get out of here? Surely Daniel would come eventually.

What if he doesn't? a sly voice asked. *What if he's already dead, and you waste away in this attic room, like the forgotten wife in a Gothic novel, waiting for help that never arrives?*

Doing her best to ignore the voice and her ever-increasing panic, Genevieve wrapped her arms around herself for warmth and crouched down to examine the doorknob. She gave it an experimental rattle. It didn't *feel* locked—it wasn't as if the knob refused to turn in her hand; it turned, but the door still refused to budge. She spent another solid five minutes or so simultaneously tugging on the knob and pounding on the scratchy door surface, yelling until her voice began to feel scratchy as well.

Genevieve stopped, unable to control the mild tremors that had begun to wrack her body. She wasn't sure if they were from cold, fear, or both, but they frightened her almost more than the situation itself.

Stop it, she told herself firmly. She stood as tall as she could in the confined space, her head brushing the ceiling at its highest point. *Think.*

Perhaps the rain had caused the wood to swell and the door to become stuck? That was a logical explanation, and logic felt familiar and useful. It helped calm the tremors that had been making her teeth chatter. If the door was swollen shut, then perhaps brute force could work. If she could jostle it just loose enough, perhaps it would open.

If that didn't work, she would fire a shot to alert Daniel as to her whereabouts, but she wanted that to be a last resort. For some reason she didn't want to fully explore, the thought of firing a gun in this house made her uneasy.

As if the house wouldn't like it.

Genevieve carefully placed her derringer in a narrow corner of the room, pointed toward the wall. She had been taught early to have a healthy respect for firearms, and knew that such instruments could have a mind of their own when least expected. She took the medallion she had placed in her pocket and considered it, then set it down next to the grip of her gun. She wished there was a more secure place for it but didn't want to risk it falling out of her pocket because of the action she was about to take.

Setting her teeth against the chill in the room, Genevieve lifted her skirts and tied the damp fabric around her waist, then untied her light summer petticoat and let it drop, hastily nudging it toward a corner of the room with her toe. Standing with her dress rucked up and her legs, encased only in delicate silk bloomers that fell to her knees, exposed, Genevieve frowned at her white lace-up boots. She'd chosen them for utility, as they were what she wore to play tennis, and she had thought they might do rather a lot of walking today, but even so, she wasn't sure they were up to the task of kicking down a door.

Genevieve turned her body sideways and pondered the door. The house was old, and the doors seemed sturdy, but this was the servants' area after all, and perhaps slightly less solid materials had been used in its construction. Taking a deep breath, she kicked the door with all her might, causing the wood to reverberate in its frame with a resounding cracking noise. Satisfied—if she didn't break the door, then perhaps Daniel would at least hear—she began to kick steadily. After what seemed like hours but was probably only minutes, her right leg began to tire and she switched sides.

Nobody had ever accused Genevieve of being delicate. She was almost six feet tall, usually taller than most men in the room, and had always excelled at sports. She rode, played tennis, sailed, and had taken fencing lessons with her brothers for a good many years in her youth. They had also taught her to box, though that activity had been kept secret from her parents. Despite the substantial strength of her legs, though, she seemed to be making no further progress, and in truth was tiring rapidly.

Genevieve stopped, panting. Tears of both fear and determination pricked her eyes, and she wiped them away furiously. The light was fading, and desperation was beginning to cloud her judgment.

One more kick, then the gun. She could shoot through the broken pane in the window, rather than inside the room. Even over the storm, Daniel ought to hear a gunshot.

Turning back to her right leg, Genevieve narrowed her eyes at the door and threw all of her might into one final, giant kick, but just as she began, she heard Daniel's voice calling her name. He sounded faint, as though he were very far away, perhaps even out in the storm itself. Still mid-kick, she opened her mouth to call back, but right as her boot connected with the door it fell away, yanked open by Daniel on the opposite side.

Daniel's name in her mouth turned into a small shriek as her foot continued through the newly opened passage and landed squarely in Daniel's midsection. His expression was almost a caricature of surprise as he let out a mighty *oof*, gripping his stomach and curling in on himself, falling to the ground. Genevieve lost her balance and landed on top of him, the two of them tangled in a heap of groaning limbs.

★ ★ ★

He couldn't catch his breath. Daniel tried to fill his lungs, but the excruciating pain in his stomach made it near impossible. He could only clutch at his middle and turn in on himself like a prawn.

Slowly, by incremental degrees, the agony subsided to the point that he could suck in a gasping lungful of air. Even though the rank scent of mold was only increasing, it was among the sweetest breaths he'd ever inhaled.

Daniel was tortuously aware of the ridiculousness of the situation. He'd barely had a moment to register the shocking sight of Genevieve, damply clad only in her undergarments and boots from the waist down—an incongruous pairing that he'd found, in the split second it took his brain to process the information, almost impossibly alluring—hurling a leg in his direction, before the impact of her booted foot had knocked any conscious thought that wasn't connected to pain from his brain. Now that the agony had lessened—not by much, but enough—his overwhelming sensation was one of relief.

Relief that he had found her. Relief that she was safe.

He had been searching for Genevieve for the better part of thirty minutes, once the storm broke and he realized, despite the late sunset of early summer, that if they didn't leave soon they would be traversing backward, through the wooded path toward the mechanized gate, in complete darkness. Rather foolishly, he had left the lanterns in the carriage, and to be honest, he didn't relish continuing their search in the dark.

Daniel had called for Genevieve repeatedly, striding through the vast, meandering corridors of the fourth floor, thrusting his head through door after door, yet she was nowhere to be found. The unease he had felt since they entered the house continued to grow, and at Genevieve's seeming disappearance he felt it edging toward fearful panic. He'd run up the narrow stairs to the attic, yelling her name frantically, and had just flung open one of the few doors when a loud, rhythmic pounding had begun to resonate from down the hall.

He had rushed toward the door and flung it open, half terrified of what he would find inside, yet what transpired next was nothing he could have imagined.

Genevieve had scrambled off him instantly and was now anxiously hovering above. Her hair had come undone from its pins and was half hanging in a long, tangled mass around his face.

"I am so sorry, Daniel. Have I harmed you? Can you breathe? Let me help you sit up," she urged, attempting to slip a hand behind his back. He held up his own hand in response, stilling her. He wasn't quite ready to sit up yet.

"I'll be all right," he managed to gasp. Relief now flooded her face, and she sat back on her heels while untying her skirts from around her waist.

"I'll be right back," Genevieve said, patting his shoulder. She darted back into the room from which she'd come, her skirts falling down and hiding her legs again. He waited, the ability to breathe easily returning with every passing moment, and noticed a sizable dent in the stout wooden door she'd been kicking. Genevieve emerged after a few minutes, adjusting the waist of her dress as she knelt down by his side again.

"Can you sit now? I found something."

Intrigued, Daniel nodded. With Genevieve's help, he managed to sit upright and not wince. His stomach muscles would be sore for days, perhaps even a week, and he knew he'd be sporting a fine bruise there too. "I'm fine," he murmured in response to Genevieve's look of distress.

He wasn't—not fully—but there was no point in upsetting her further.

"Look," Genevieve said, once he was sitting. She unfurled a fist, and his breath, limited as it was, still caught at the sight. The medallion featuring John Boyle's distinctive profile, identical to the one he'd found on Marcus Dalrymple, gleamed dully in the weakening light.

Daniel expected his heart to pound in excitement at the sight, as that tiny, cheap piece of metal confirmed all their wildest suspicions, but instead that particular organ plummeted to what felt like the depths of his aching stomach. He had hoped to avoid entangling with New York's underworld, particularly with Tommy Meade, ever again. He had hoped to shield Genevieve, for all her bravery and ambition, from any further exposure to how awful their fellow humans could behave toward one another. But if they had to deal with Boyle, and the discovery of this medallion made that encounter seem inevitable, then sooner or later they would probably cross paths with Meade.

He could only hope to delay that meeting as long as possible.

"What is this place, then?" Genevieve asked, glancing around the dingy attic hallway in distaste. Daniel struggled to sit up further; Genevieve was shivering, and the light continued to drop. Despite the stormy conditions outside, it was far past time for them to go. "That door slammed shut on its own, I swear it. How did it stay closed?" she continued, gesturing toward the door from which she'd burst.

His midsection groaned in protest, but Daniel managed to stand and examine the door, running his fingers along the jamb and checking the hinges for a mechanized device like the one that had opened the front gates. But it appeared to be an entirely ordinary wooden door.

"I don't know." He stepped away from the door, frustrated. "I don't know what young men like Marcus or Paul were doing here. But I do know that we need to leave." He removed his lightweight jacket and wrapped it around Genevieve's shoulders, readying them both to face the storm.

★ ★ ★

"A gate that opens on its own! Doors shutting by themselves!" Rupert marveled. "I should have come along—you and Genevieve have all the fun."

Daniel slanted a look at his friend. He had not held back from detailing exactly how unsettling his time in the house had been, particularly the seemingly endless minutes when he hadn't been able to find Genevieve. He had also described in depth their long, soaking ride home; both he and Genevieve had been drenched to the skin by the time he deposited her at her home in Washington Square. "Fun" was the last word he would have chosen to describe the whole experience.

Also, three days later, his stomach muscles were still sore if he breathed too deeply. He had not told Rupert that Genevieve had kicked him in the stomach, though. Nor that she had been in her bloomers when she did.

And especially not that the image of her long, barely clad legs inconveniently popped into his brain more often than he was comfortable with.

"Where is Genevieve anyway?" Rupert asked, as if reading his mind. They were strolling along the meandering, tree-lined paths of Prospect Park in Brooklyn, by Esmie's request. She had a surprise for them, she'd said. But so far neither lady had appeared.

"She had to work," Daniel replied, checking the time. "But it's just seven; she should be along any minute."

"Are we in the right spot?" Rupert asked, sounding peevish. "I hardly know Brooklyn. Why couldn't we have gone to Central Park like always? It's right there. Then we could all go to Delmonico's after."

"We can still go to Delmonico's," Daniel pointed out. "As for why we're in Brooklyn, that is a question for your wife, not me." Privately he had wondered the same thing, but Esmie's instructions had been quite specific. Not that he minded the journey. After Saturday's thunderstorm, the weather had returned to its temperate June self, and he and Rupert had chosen to walk over the Brooklyn Bridge on their way to the park. It was a goodly walk, several miles, but it had given Daniel time to fill Rupert in on all that had transpired at the Garcia mansion.

"I think this is it." Rupert gestured toward a lovely brick Italianate house situated on a rise. He squinted at a small brass plaque affixed near the front door. "Yes, the Litchfield Villa. This is where we're meant to meet them." He shoved his hands in his pockets and looked around expectantly.

Daniel removed his straw hat and fanned himself with it, enjoying the view of rolling hills and inviting brick walkways wending their way through leafy trees. It was a beautiful spot, the paths dotted with couples strolling and mothers pushing prams while children cavorted on the wide, open areas of grass. Being the height of early summer, the sun wouldn't set until nearly nine o'clock, but he guessed if those children were allowed to stay up until dusk, they'd be rewarded with a multitude of blinking fireflies. Daniel thought, not for the first time when in one of the city's vast parks, about how much he and his siblings would have been awestruck by such abundant greenery as children. There had been precious little of it in his neighborhood.

"There they are," Rupert exclaimed. "Oh, hell's bells. She *hasn't*."

Over the crest of a low ridge came Esmie, Genevieve at her side. Daniel gaped in surprise.

Genevieve waved. She was wearing a pale green dress— she favored green, he had noticed, and it favored her back— and a simply enormous smile. Esmie, on the other hand, sported an anxious yet determined expression as she pushed along a sleek black bicycle.

"Blimey," Rupert said, running his hands over the gleaming metal frame. "Where did you find this, Es? I've not seen its like." Daniel nodded in agreement, taking in the contraption. Rather than the high front wheel of the penny-farthing bicycle, this model had two wheels of equal size.

"I ordered it special from Boston," Esmie said shyly, blushing lightly. "It's among the first they've manufactured, called a safety bicycle. I saw it advertised some months ago, and . . . I've wanted to try riding a bicycle for some time." She raised her chin slightly, as if daring any of the others to laugh.

Genevieve beamed at Esmie proudly. "Show them the rest, Esmie."

"You knew about this?" Rupert asked, sounding affronted. "When she didn't even tell her own husband?"

"You weren't her husband yet, Rupert," Genevieve returned mildly. "Go on—show them."

Blushing harder, Esmie grasped the sides of her navy blue skirts and pulled, as if she were about to drop into a curtsey. But instead, a split was revealed, as if she were wearing a pair of very wide trousers. Topped with a rather mannish white shirt and a jaunty straw hat adorned with a red ribbon, it made a fetching yet practical ensemble.

"All those trips to the dressmaker's with Genevieve this past winter," Rupert accused. "This is what you two have been plotting?"

"And my very large trousseau, I'll have you recall," Esmie retorted, still blushing. "I didn't think I'd have a chance to use the bicycle here. I was planning on having it sent on to us in England."

"Oh lord, the look on my mother's face at the sight of you in those trousers would have been worth it," Rupert grinned, clapping once in glee at the thought. "But this is fantastic, and now I must have one as well. Go on—give it a try."

Esmie's blush deepened, but, Daniel surmised, with pleasure rather than embarrassment.

"I apologize for the skullduggery," Esmie said as Genevieve helped her straddle the bicycle and arrange the wide skirt-trousers so they wouldn't get caught in the spokes. "But I didn't want to risk being seen by anyone we know, in case I fall and make an utter fool of myself. Plus, they allow bicycling here only from seven at night until ten in the morning on most paths, so as not to interfere with pedestrians."

"Quite smart of them," Daniel remarked. He was delighted that the mysterious errand for which Esmie had called them together was the simple purchase of a bicycle, that it had nothing to do with death or a possibly haunted mansion or a missing young woman. He watched with real joy as Rupert held the back of the bicycle while Esmie took her first unsteady ride, Genevieve walking quickly at her side; then as Esmie began to pedal faster and find her balance; and finally as Rupert released his hold and, with a joyful cry, Esmie began to pedal down the path, Genevieve running by her side, Rupert whooping and clapping.

He ran to Rupert, savoring the entire moment: the sun that was just starting its descent, the sweet smell of mown grass and early summer leaves, the joy of his friends.

"Can you believe that? Never been on one before today," Rupert marveled, watching Esmie's figure grow smaller as she continued to pedal away.

"It's going well, then, the marriage?" Daniel asked.

Rupert gave an enigmatic smile. "Well enough. It's difficult starting out under her father's nose—that's what the honeymoon was meant to be for, avoiding that situation. But yes, it's well. Marriage is . . . surprising."

Esmie either figured out how to turn or dismounted and turned around, as the pair were now coming back their direction, both looking breathless with laughter. Esmie rang a bell on the handlebar at a pair of builders who happened to be crossing the path at the wrong moment; the men scurried out of the way, yelling, just as Esmie swerved into the grass to avoid them, toppling off the bike.

Daniel and Rupert raced to where she'd fallen, but Esmie was already being lifted up by Genevieve, both laughing as Esmie pushed strands of pale blonde hair off her face. "See? This is why I wanted to avoid Central Park," she said breathlessly. Daniel retrieved her hat from where it had rolled at the base of a nearby tree.

"Daniel, Genevieve," Esmie began as Rupert righted the bicycle, "I did want to ask you, though. Might we be of help, Rupert and I?" Her tone remained lighthearted, but her expression had turned serious. "This does affect us, after all. And it looks as though we won't be going abroad for some months now. We could help. Rupert has . . . skills, as I'm sure you know."

Daniel and Genevieve looked to Rupert, who shrugged. "You don't get in and out of people's houses without picking up a few tricks," he allowed. "Say you need to get into a locked place. Or out of one. Or you need to have in your possession a particular item that does not belong to you. These are some particular skills I could offer."

"And people talk to me," Esmie said quietly. "They say all sorts of things to me because . . . because I think they don't really *see* me. Or they think I've nobody to tell. That may have changed now that I'm a countess." She shared a quick glance with Rupert, and Daniel suddenly wondered how much they had discussed this beforehand. "But old habits, old perceptions of people, die hard. We'd like to try to help, at least if you'll allow it."

Daniel sighed, his joy in the warm evening not vanished, but diminished. It had been nice to pretend, even if just for a few minutes, that there was no investigation to chase.

Genevieve was looking at him quizzically. He raised a brow at her, and she gave a tiny head jiggle. A silent conversation: him asking her opinion, she declaring her uncertainty.

"It's dangerous," Genevieve said quietly. "I learned tonight, for example, that Paul Riley was indeed seen at Boyle's in the nights before he fell." Daniel felt her quick, shuttered glance in his direction and kept his face impassive.

He still had dreams about that light blue silk lining, flying up and then plummeting, his hands a fraction of a second too late.

Daniel frowned at Genevieve. "Luther," she said in answer to his unspoken question.

Ah, Luther Franklin, the homicide reporter. A good source of information, but the other man's obvious feelings for Genevieve were often more of a hindrance than a help.

And so Riley's death was being treated by Genevieve's paper, at least, as a homicide . . . interesting.

"Genevieve is right," he said. "It is dangerous. But," he continued when Rupert opened his mouth, clearly intending to protest, "you may be right also. There may be some way to use both of your unique . . . talents to help with this. Let's find something to eat and see what we can come up with."

Now Genevieve looked ready to protest, but Daniel stilled her with a slight shake of his head. They didn't really know who, or what, they were up against, and they could use all the help they could get.

CHAPTER 11

"I still don't think it was right to involve them," Genevieve fretted, taking a quick sidestep to avoid the sudden shower of sparks that rained from the tracks above. She had learned her lesson well after their last visit to the Bowery.

"It was a risk," Daniel conceded, "but we do need information. We need to know about the circle of friends around Nora and Paul—who exactly are they? Which of these young people was involved, and what were they doing? It does seem as though they—whoever they are—were visiting the Garcia mansion, but was it a simple lark or a dare, and what does Boyle's have to do with it? Esmie and Rupert may be able to find out at least some of that information."

"Don't forget the demons," Genevieve murmured. Even though they were walking down a noisy, crowded street, she was careful to keep her voice low. "What on earth could Marcus and Paul have meant by such a thing? There was no evidence of anything demonic at the mansion." Though she had no idea what, of course, such evidence could entail.

Frankly, walking down the Bowery at night seemed as close to a demonic experience as any a person might experience on earth. Daniel hadn't been exaggerating when he said it would be rough; the notorious street in the darkness was far more threatening than it had been during the day. She had known by the set of his jaw, earlier, that he had not wanted her to accompany him to Boyle's Suicide Tavern at nighttime, but he had clenched his teeth and nodded once when she insisted on accompanying him. She now wondered if that insistence had been a mistake, but refused to turn back. She had demanded to come, and she would see the visit through.

So here she was, keeping her chin high and her expression uninviting, her arm casually linked through Daniel's as if they were a couple, but her hand gripped his forearm tightly.

The scene was ghastly. Groups of drunken men reeled and yelled obscenities, one unfortunate soul being actively sick on the sidewalk so close to her that she was barely able to twitch her skirts out of the way in time. The women appeared to be just as inebriated, with brightly rouged cheeks and low-plunging, cheap bodices, yelling back at the men and often lifting their skirts to their waists to entice a customer. Young men and boys dressed in women's clothing stayed closer to the shadows, though she spied plenty of men linking arms with their choice and entering one of the rows of boarding houses or taverns that lined the street.

Bright flashes of orange sparks continually fell as trains passed, making the surrounding tableau feel even more hellish. Not that she was particularly offended by the fact that some men preferred their own sex or that adults of either gender were sometimes reduced to the point where their bodies were their sole commodity; her mother, an ardent advocate for women's rights, had taught her well and frankly about the range of different sexual impulses in her fellow humans, as well as how not to judge those who felt it necessary to sell themselves. What was heartbreaking was the youth of so many of those doing so, several she saw being little more than children. That and the casual, accompanying violence that broke out seemingly at random: a sudden fistfight at the intersection of Stanton Street, one woman crashing a bottle over the head of another as they neared Houston.

It was hard to believe the magical German beer garden they had visited just two weeks ago was only a few short blocks away. It seemed like another world.

"Walk a little faster, but not too fast," muttered Daniel. Genevieve picked up her pace. She had her trusty derringer in her pocket again, and she thrust the hand not holding Daniel's arm deep into the pocket's confines, comforted by the firearm's slight heft.

She'd dressed more suitably for their visit to Boyle's Suicide Tavern this time. It had been a tough decision, as so many of her summer dresses seemed too light and airy for such an occasion. In the end she'd chosen a rather buttoned-up affair, a black and white, thinly striped skirt topped by a lightweight black jacket with just enough frills on the collar. A black hat with curling white feathers completed the ensemble.

"I should think Nora and Paul's crowd would talk to a society reporter," she said, still keeping her voice low. "I could have spoken with them."

"You wanted to come with me," Daniel reminded her, casting a wry look from the corner of his eye. "Time is of the essence, we agreed. Besides, they're hardly likely to brag about their exploits to a reporter, and risk having their mother and father read something untoward about them in the papers. Esmie's right: they'll talk to her. She's a newly minted countess, after all. It's an evening garden party, perfectly safe. And Rupert will be Rupert. Give the boys some drink. Charm the ladies."

"He oughtn't charm the ladies too much, now he's married," Genevieve remarked. "Aren't we almost there? Everything looks so different at night."

"Yes, halfway up this block. Again, let me do the talking. Agreed?"

Genevieve nodded, already feeling as though she were in over her head. "Agreed."

She swallowed as they again made their way under the ominous inscription above the door: "Better Dead." The interior of the front room looked the same as last time, empty, but the din coming from the larger back room was nearly overwhelming.

Slipping into the space behind Daniel, it was instantly obvious as to why. The bar was completely packed with patrons. A small band played on the back stage, but their efforts were barely audible over the raucous noise of the crowd. At every table, men and women played cards, drank, or openly embraced. Genevieve was not prudish but still felt a blush stain her cheeks at the sight of a man openly nuzzling a woman's bare breasts. She quickly averted her gaze, only to have it be met by the same enormous bouncer that had been so displeased with them on their previous visit, the one Daniel had referred to as Knockout Eddie.

He scowled at them from behind the bar. "We still don't have no information here."

"Whiskey, then," Daniel said easily, sliding a nickel across the grimy surface. Eddie eyed the nickel suspiciously, as if it were a trick of some kind, then, with a grudging look, poured a measure of liquid into a dirty glass.

A slightly cleaner glass of cloudy liquid was plunked in front of Genevieve. "Rum for the lady." Eddie said. He rested his meaty palms on the bar and stared balefully at them.

Genevieve's glass was halfway to her lips when Daniel's foot nudged her ankle, hard. She set it back on the bar again, untouched. Daniel took a swig of his whiskey, his expression remaining bland, and returned Eddie's stare with one of his own. Several minutes ticked by, the ruckus in the bar swirling around their group, indifferent to the ever-growing tension between Daniel and Eddie.

They were like two stray cats, bristling at each other in an alley, each not quite willing to make the first move.

Genevieve wondered how long the stand-off could last. She slipped a hand toward her pocket, felt again the weight of the revolver hidden there.

"McCaffrey," came a voice. Not from behind the bar, but from their backs. Genevieve flinched, looking over her shoulder, but Daniel kept his body casual, slowly turning to face the main room. He propped his elbows on the bar behind him and offered a lazy half smile.

"John," Daniel answered. Genevieve noticed neither man offered to shake hands. "Good to see you."

It was undoubtedly John Boyle, the proprietor of the bar. The sloped line of his forehead, so like his profile stamped on metal, was unmistakable.

John tipped his head in acknowledgment but didn't return the sentiment. "And this is . . .?" he flashed a smile at Genevieve that didn't quite meet his eyes.

"A friend," Daniel said before Genevieve could answer. She nodded at the man, glad she wasn't expected to speak. He looked rather ordinary, if somewhat ostentatiously dressed. A plain face with a wide mouth and heavy eyebrows set under slicked-back dark brown hair. If you passed him on the street, you would be forgiven for assuming he was a grocer who had done well for himself, or the successful proprietor of a shop. Never that he was the overlord of a bar where young women became so desperate they apparently took their own lives.

Despite his stolid, middle-class appearance and grocer's face, menace roiled off the man in waves. He had said or done nothing threatening, but Genevieve instantly sensed he was displeased with their presence.

John's eyes slid back to Daniel, assessing, but in the end he seemed to decide not to press the issue of Genevieve's identity.

"Eddie mentioned you'd come by," John said. "I unfortunately know nothing of the young man you asked after. Now, you want to finish that"—he nodded at the whiskey in Daniel's hand—"and leave."

"Maybe don't bring a lady, if you do come back," Eddie added from behind the bar. "Maybe Asher comes next time," he continued, referring to Daniel's secretary, a former boxer. As with John, the words were said in a perfectly neutral voice, but Genevieve could hear the threat behind them. Her heart began to race, and the hairs on the back of her neck stood up straight. She nudged Daniel's foot back, her meaning clear: *Let's go.*

John's plain face broke into a wide grin at this suggestion. "Yeah, like the good old days. A rematch. Maybe Eddie here can break his nose again."

Daniel's half smile quirked again. "Asher gave as good as he got. Your nose was broken more than once too, Eddie," he said, tossing the remark over his shoulder. "It just got set better." He threw back the rest of his whiskey and set the glass on the counter. Genevieve followed his example and straightened her body to leave, relief beginning to course through her.

"I'm not trying to start anything, John," Daniel said quietly. "Just trying to help a friend. I ever done you wrong?"

John titled his head and eyed Daniel in a considering way. Even though not directed at her, the look still made Genevieve's skin crawl.

She slipped her hand into her pocket.

"Not me," John finally said. "You understand?" A long, hard look passed between them.

Even Genevieve understood: John was referring to Tommy Meade.

Daniel raised his brows slightly and nodded. "Yeah, I get it. Didn't think you the type to sit in anybody's pocket, though."

The air between the two men suddenly frizzled with more than tension, and several things happened at once. From behind the bar, Knockout Eddie's huge arm lifted a bottle, clearly intending to crack it over the top of Daniel's head. Genevieve whipped out her gun and yelled, "Stop!" at Eddie. And, clear as a bell, a scream erupted from the upper floors of the tavern, carrying down the stairs and briefly shocking the cacophonous crowd into a moment of silence.

"The demons! They're coming!" shrieked the woman's voice. *"Ruuuuuuuun!"*

★   ★   ★

Daniel didn't waste a second. He simultaneously pushed Genevieve aside and grabbed her gun, raising it up and firing at the ceiling, just as the bottle meant for his head smashed onto the bar. He closed his eyes against the flying shards of glass as more screams instantly echoed throughout the room in response to the noise of the shot. Firearms were drawn from all quarters, and a fight broke out near the stage. Within seconds, the entire room was brawling.

Daniel grabbed Genevieve's hand and pulled her through the melee, away from Eddie's giant fists and toward the stairs. He ducked as a wild punch came his way and saw Genevieve flinch back in time, sending a quick prayer of gratitude to whoever was listening for her quick reflexes.

"Up the stairs," he yelled over the ever-increasing racket. "It could be Nora." She picked up her skirts and began to run up the narrow staircase and Daniel stayed close, hot on her heels, only to be chased back down as two thugs came barreling toward her.

He spotted an open door that led to the long corridor of the ladies' entrance to their left, and pulled her in that direction. This time he wasn't so lucky dodging blows, and a stray fist caught the edge of his cheekbone.

"Daniel," Genevieve stopped and hovered, trying to keep bodies from knocking him over.

"Go, keep going," he shouted, pushing her toward the corridor and stumbling after her. The flare of pain in his cheek made his vision a trifle blurry, but he pressed them forward. Genevieve's hat went flying and was instantly trampled.

A shot rang out just as they reached the door, causing more screams, and he realized through the haze of tumult that the shot had been meant for one of them.

Glancing back, he saw Eddie in full pursuit, a smoking pistol in one of his large hands and a look of absolute fury on his face. Behind him, standing still and unsullied in the midst of what was quickly becoming carnage, John Boyle watched their progress with the cold eyes of a snake.

"Run, Genevieve. Run!" Daniel gasped hoarsely. His last sight within the wild fracas of the barroom before they were encased in the long hallway was of Eddie, casually picking up clashing patrons and physically tossing them aside.

To get to them.

Daniel shoved Genevieve through the doorway. She picked up her skirts and sprinted down the hallway. His still-sore stomach muscles voiced their protest at being made to work so vigorously as he, too, ran with all his might. They were sitting ducks in the corridor, until they reached the exterior door on the far end.

Just as he and Genevieve burst past a startled doorman, who had been peering down the hallway toward the raucous sounds of the fight, and tumbled out a side door onto Houston Street, the crack of another shot echoed through the corridor, followed closely by the yelp of the doorman as he dove to the ground.

"Keep running," Daniel heaved, gesturing west. They flew down the crowded street, dodging pedestrians with varying levels of success. At some point Daniel realized he still had Genevieve's derringer firmly clasped in his hand, and shoved it into his pocket lest he cause a fatal accident there on the street.

"This way." He grabbed Genevieve's hand again, her other hand lifting her dress high so she could dash with all her might. Her hair had come partially unbound and flew behind her like a long, dark golden flag.

The pop of another gunshot told him Eddie was still in pursuit. He heard Genevieve gasp as startled cries of pedestrians sounded all around them. People ducked and looked around frantically for the sound of the shot, but Daniel didn't dare waste a second to see how close Eddie was. Their one hope was to outrun him and get to safety. Eddie was strong but had never been swift.

Daniel added a burst of speed and pulled up next to Genevieve, eyes darting left and right, frantically gauging the wild, hurling traffic. Spotting a small opening, he once again grabbed Genevieve's hand and led her across the busy street. A terrified-sounding laugh burst from her as they barely skirted an oncoming carriage, dodging four flailing front hooves as the carriage's horses were sharply reined in, the driver screaming obscenities in their wake.

They had made it to the other side of the street, but they weren't safe yet. Keeping hold of Genevieve's hand, together they sprinted past Mott, then Mulberry, both their breaths coming in short, sharp rasps. Daniel turned sharply down Lafayette, pulling Genevieve in his wake, his desperation to reach their destination spurring him faster still.

There it was: the high back garden wall he sought. Though he knew it would be locked, Daniel gave the back gate a strong, experimental tug, but as he expected, the gate held fast.

"I'll be right back," he muttered, eyeing his task. Luckily, the wall was made of stone, and there were convenient footholds. He began to scramble up the ten-foot edifice, digging his fingers and shoving his toes into tiny crevices.

Almost there, almost there.

Reaching the top, he risked a glance down the alley and breathed a sigh of relief. A stroke of luck: there was no sign of Eddie. But he knew the ex–prize fighter could round the corner any moment.

"Daniel," Genevieve hissed, looking up at him with eyes widened by both fear and fury, "don't you dare leave me here!"

"Stay right there," he said in a shouted whisper. Making sure the ground below was clear, Daniel leapt into a lush, private garden, then instantly unbolted the gate and yanked Genevieve inside.

As he relocked the gate, a woman in a bright pink negligee and flowered silk kimono popped out from behind some shrubbery and began running into the building to which this garden belonged. A man in his shirtsleeves emerged after her, hastily shoving his shirttails into his trousers.

"What is the meaning of this?" the man demanded, glancing from the top of the wall to where Daniel and Genevieve now stood. Daniel took hold of Genevieve's hand again and followed the kimono-clad woman toward the house.

"You can't come in that way—this is a private establishment, you know," the man called after them.

Ignoring the yelling man, Daniel climbed the few steps to the back door of the house. He had just reached for the knob when the door swung open, and he found himself face to face with the business end of a double-barreled shotgun.

Genevieve stiffened beside him, and he took a quick side step in front of her, placing his body between hers and the deadly weapon aimed at them.

From behind the gun came a deep, sorrowful sigh, and then the barrel was lowered.

"You'd best come inside, Mr. McCaffrey."

CHAPTER 12

The large, red-haired man, who introduced himself to Genevieve as Augustus, led them through a bustling, delicious-smelling kitchen—where none of the cooks or other servants batted an eye at their presence—and into a spacious, tastefully appointed drawing room. He and Daniel withdrew to a corner and spoke in hushed tones.

Genevieve looked around the room with interest. The walls were hung with a discreet botanical paper, dominated by green tones but with occasional lush, tropical pink flowers interspersed. A pair of lovebirds twittered in an elaborate gilded cage in one corner, and enormous vases of heavy pink roses were scattered on several surfaces. There was no fire in the grate, but the front windows were sealed shut despite the temperate night outside. Regardless, the room was not stuffy, and she soon spied the reason why: a fan with ingeniously twirling twin blades was affixed to the ceiling, which kept the air circulating.

"It's water powered," a voice remarked in a lilting Irish brogue. "Paid a pretty penny for it, but I can't be having the street-side windows open, now can I?" A lovely woman, perhaps a few years older than herself, with dark auburn hair and a shimmering green evening gown stepped forward and offered Genevieve her hand. "Welcome. I'm Kathleen Dugan, and this is my house. What sort of devilry has my cousin got himself into now?"

Genevieve shook Daniel's cousin's hand, fascinated. Their mad, desperate dash through the streets had gotten her so turned around that she hadn't realized at first where they had landed. *Of course.* They were at his cousin's brothel. She had once held vigil in a small café across the street from here, watching the front door for hours, waiting for Daniel to emerge. Back when she had thought he was a jewel thief.

This didn't look at all like what she had pictured. There were some paintings of nudes on the walls, to be sure, but they were Venuses and nymphs, the same as might be found in any art collection.

"It's Boyle, Miss Dugan," said Augustus. The set of Kathleen's mouth betrayed exactly how she felt about this information.

"That hooligan," she muttered. "He may not have put a gun to their heads, but he killed those girls who died in his establishment all the same. Poor souls." Kathleen shook her head as if shooing a fly. "But no need to worry—he and his thugs can't follow you in here. They don't dare, not with my benefactors."

Kathleen moved across the room to embrace Daniel. "I do wish you'd take more care, though," she scolded her cousin. "Boyle's all mixed up with Meade these days, and you've tangled with him enough."

Daniel sighed and ran a hand through his hair. "It wasn't intentional," he muttered.

Kathleen pursed her lips. "With you, it never is. Trouble seeks this one out, Miss Stewart. You'd best watch yourself if you want to continue associating with him, or trouble will find you too." She sighed also and planted her hands on her hips, assessing the pair. "You two look a fright. We're busy tonight, but I can rearrange a few things and find a room for you. I'll have some food sent in."

A different kind of alarm reared through Genevieve. "Stay here? Overnight?"

Kathleen's gaze cut to her sharply. "You don't want to be leaving at this time of night, now. Boyle won't come in, but I'm sure he's figured out you're here. It's known Danny and I are kin. He'll have men posted at both entrances. But come morning, a few of my trusty officer friends will come by, and they'll skulk away like the dogs they are. We'll bundle you in a carriage back home then."

Augustus, who had been peering through the slight crack in the curtains, caught Kathleen's eye and gave a curt nod.

"See, they're here already," Daniel's cousin said. "Now, make yourselves comfortable, and I'll have that room made up. Then I want to hear all about whatever mess you've gotten into."

"But . . ." Genevieve began as Kathleen and Augustus took their leave, then faltered. What would she say, exactly? That she was willing to risk her life, and Daniel's, to avoid spending the night in a brothel? She couldn't voice such a thing.

Kathleen turned back and seemed to have some sympathy for her. "Nobody ever need know you were here," she said gently before closing the door with equal softness.

Genevieve could feel herself color. "I didn't mean to be rude," she said to Daniel, who had watched the exchange with an inscrutable expression. "I've never been in a place like this before." She swallowed. For reasons she didn't want to fully explore, being in a brothel with Daniel was making her feel unaccountably nervous. "This is a lovely room."

Daniel peeled himself off the far wall, where he had been leaning, and settled himself into one of the many comfortable-looking armchairs. "It's where Kathleen receives new guests, and deems whether they're worthy of an appointment," he explained. He had lost his hat too, somewhere in the melee, and a bruise was beginning to form on his right cheekbone from the hit he'd taken in the barroom. "One of the more public rooms. And I agree— I've always liked it."

Genevieve sat as well. The fear that had overwhelmed her at Boyle's, followed by the exertion of their run, was slowly ebbing away, leaving her feeling shaky and exhausted. A maid entered, bearing a tray with sandwiches, water, and hot coffee, and Genevieve suddenly found herself famished.

They helped themselves to nourishment for a few moments. The comfort and sheer normalcy of simply eating and drinking was calming, and after a little bit Genevieve felt more grounded, more ready to accept where the evening had taken them.

"That didn't go very well," she finally said, putting down her plate and picking up her coffee.

"No."

"Was it a mistake to go?"

Daniel looked thoughtful. "I don't think so, no," he finally said. "I think we learned that John Boyle is at the heart of this, somehow. And that he is definitely in league with Meade. We need to know if that was Nora screaming upstairs."

"Don't you think it was?" Genevieve asked. *She* certainly did.

He tilted his head from side to side in response. "It could have been," he admitted. "Or it could be some trick of Boyle's, to throw us off whatever is really going on."

"Have us chase demons instead of him?" she said.

"Chase our own tails, more like," Daniel muttered, tilting back his head and stretching his long legs out in front of him. "Which is all we've been doing. Meanwhile, Detective Longstreet is still sniffing around Rupert, two men are dead, and Nora Westwood is still missing."

"Speaking of the police," Genevieve said, "what did Kathleen mean when she said her officers would come by in the morning? Or that her benefactors would keep Boyle away?"

"Miss Dugan's, as this is known"—Daniel gestured around the room with the hand not holding his coffee—"is very popular with certain high-level city officials. Boyle is only a few steps above a street thug, and the police are constantly raiding his tavern. But here, it's the opposite. In fact, there are certain police officers assigned to make sure Miss Dugan's remains quite undisturbed."

"Ah." Genevieve understood. It was the same as anything: wealth bought comfort and safety, even when one was engaging in illicit activity. She thought of the young men she had seen on the Bowery, hiding in the shadows, or some of the girls they had passed, many of whom looked to be barely teenagers.

Kathleen bustled back in. "You have everything you need? Good," she said to their nods. "Unfortunately, there is a suddenly pressing matter I must attend to, so I'll have to wait to hear your tale in the morning unless there's something that can't wait?" She cast a questioning look to her cousin, who shook his head.

"You know all you need to know for now. The entire story will keep," Daniel replied.

"Well, that's a small relief. I can't really bear one more item on my plate tonight. But I've got your room all arranged. Come with me."

"Kathleen, there's no need to attend to us yourself—" Daniel began, but his cousin cut him off with a wave.

"Nonsense, you're family. I'm not handing you off to the servants. Don't mind me, there's just an unpleasant business I must deal with, and it's got me out of sorts."

Genevieve followed Daniel's cue and unwrapped her body from the armchair, tiredness once again seeping into her limbs.

"Now we're going to pass by some of the places where guests are entertained, just to warn you," Kathleen said over her shoulder as they left the room.

The house was much larger than it appeared from the outside; indeed, it rivaled the size of some Fifth Avenue mansions Genevieve had seen. Kathleen led them past an airy, open drawing room, made cozy with large potted plants and small clustered seating areas, where Genevieve glimpsed several couples nuzzling in intimate corners, and others laughing over a shared drink. The men were very well dressed, though they typically had removed their jackets and unbuttoned their collars. The women, on the other hand, were in various stages of undress, in petticoats or bloomers, chemise straps slipping off their shoulders, garter bows visible.

"Where our guests can get to know a potential companion," Kathleen explained comfortably, gesturing toward the room as they passed. "And vice versa. One of the tenets of this house: my girls choose who they might like to entertain. And only one guest per night." A maid in a stiffly starched uniform passed them, bearing a tray of expensive champagne. "My application process is quite rigorous. Invited guests can pay a monthly or an annual fee, which comes with certain privileges." She nodded to the passing maid. "None of this pay-per-visit business at my house."

Genevieve took in the information, as well as the passing scenery, with wide eyes. The rooms were still well appointed and tasteful, but the art, she noticed, had taken on a decidedly more erotic subject matter as they moved from the more public to the more private areas of the establishment.

Kathleen led them two flights up a large staircase with a mahogany bannister, and finally to an unmarked door on the second floor.

The decor in these back halls, too, had a more distinctly amorous overtone. Further paintings with subjects that could only be described as salacious were interspersed on the walls, which were covered in a dark red brocade. Gas lamps in gilded sconces were lit low, giving the windowless corridor what would be a sensual, provocative mood even if it were high noon outside. Genevieve noticed they did not pass many doors along the way, and tentatively asked how many bedrooms the house contained.

Kathleen smiled at her over her shoulder as she unlocked the door. "Fourteen for guests only: seven on the second floor, seven here on the third. The girls who live here have private rooms on the upper floors, though some do choose to live in their own residences. My chambers are just down there." She pointed to the end of the long hallway. "Don't hesitate to knock on my door if you need me."

The door opened to a bedroom decorated not in the ruby red of the corridor, but a lush, deep pink, echoing the flowers in the drawing room in which they had eaten. The bed was the most enormous Genevieve had ever laid eyes on, it was easily as big as two put together, covered with a pink satin counterpane and giant, fluffy feather pillows.

"Water closet"—Kathleen pointed at a door—"and I think you should find everything you need in terms of soaps, lotions, or hair accessories. There's more in that dressing table over there. Just ring for help if you need it. Oh, and Miss Stewart," she began, but Genevieve interrupted.

"Please, do call me Genevieve," she said. "You're being so kind."

Warmth lit Kathleen's eyes. "If you like. Genevieve, then. I've left a nightdress for you, should you like it. I suspect you'd prefer not to sleep in your clothes."

Genevieve eyed the garment, neatly laid out on the bed, in surprise. It was a high-necked, white cotton affair, with long sleeves and an abundance of lace at the neck and cuffs. It was nothing like the flimsy, silky pieces she had seen the girls in downstairs.

"Sexual tastes vary widely, and playacting is often part of those tastes," Kathleen explained, giving a one-shouldered shrug. Genevieve bit back a smile; she had seen Daniel make that same gesture countless times. "I am sorry I don't have separate rooms for you both. Normally I'd have Danny sleep on the lounge in my quarters, but I was not expecting company and have a visitor from out of town just now," she explained rather primly.

Daniel looked startled. "What? Who? Why have I never heard of this person?"

"I'm a grown woman with a private life, same as you, Danny," Kathleen replied archly, though Genevieve noticed a slight blush stain the other woman's cheeks all the same.

With Kathleen gone, Genevieve blinked at Daniel from across the room. He sat in the delicate birchwood chair pulled up next to the small dressing table, and was removing his shoes. The act forcibly reminded her of the last time they had been alone in a bedroom, the year prior, when they had retreated to a hotel room during a fancy-dress ball. It had been her idea, one she had insisted on for both privacy and haste, as they had been on the trail of a killer. The memory of Daniel removing his boots on that cold winter night flashed in her mind.

But then they had remained in the adjacent sitting room as they laid out their plans, avoiding the bedchamber altogether.

She glanced longingly at the bed, wishing for nothing more than to remove her filthy clothes, change into the ridiculous nightdress, and sleep.

But where would Daniel sleep? On the floor? On the chaise lounge? It barely looked large enough to contain him sitting, let alone lying down. Neither option seemed fair.

"Might I?" Daniel was suddenly near her, gesturing toward the water closet. Genevieve nodded mutely and moved across the room to investigate the various sundries on the dressing table. The sound of water splashing came from behind the closed door.

Her heart began to accelerate slightly, and she knew it had nothing to do with the very real danger they faced. It was, instead, the unexpected intimacy of hearing a man to whom she was not related engaging in his ablutions. It was the sight of his shoes tucked beneath the matching birchwood dressing table, his jacket hanging over the back of the chair.

It was the thought of sleeping in the same room as this man. A man whose proposal of marriage she had rejected, but the moment of which she could recall with absolute detail.

Daniel emerged, his face scrubbed clean of soot from the passing elevated trains, making the blossoming bruise on his cheekbone even more apparent. Genevieve saw now that he had a slight cut there too.

"Your face," she said in dismay, reaching toward the wound by instinct, but stilling her hand halfway there.

Daniel offered his usual half smile. "It will heal." The hair around his temples and forehead was slightly damp from washing.

Genevieve snatched the nightgown off the bed. "I'll just duck in myself now," she said, darting into the bathroom. Once inside, she leaned her back against the closed door and took a few deep breaths. She could do this. She could share a room with Daniel for the night. They had put themselves in this situation, and now this was the consequence.

Suddenly annoyed with herself, Genevieve began to undress, angrily yanking at the buttons of her jacket, then at her blouse underneath. She was an adult, twenty-seven years old, who had been traveling to Europe annually since she was twelve. She was a journalist, one who had survived nearly being killed not once but twice last year, one who had successfully hunted down a murderer. She wasn't some young bud freshly out in society, scared of making a misstep. Her own parents would probably not even notice she was gone—they had long since stopped keeping track of her comings and goings. Why was the thought of sharing a room with a man, a man she considered a friend and who she knew would be a perfect gentleman, causing such palpitations?

Genevieve stared at her pile of discarded, dirty clothing on the bathroom floor, then at her own reflection. She knew exactly why the idea of spending the night in the same room as Daniel was so unsettling.

It all came back to that winter night the previous year. That night when she'd glimpsed, for the barest of moments, what a future with a man like Daniel could entail. A life of trust, of adventure, of . . . passion. Despite her advanced age, she had only been kissed by her former fiancé, Ted Beekman, who had thrown her over three days before the wedding. That had been seven years ago, and she'd kept herself away from romantic entanglements ever since.

Genevieve's undergarment-clad likeness stared back at her, reflected in the vast mirror affixed to the blue and white tiled wall, surrounded by a bathroom of utmost luxury. Her gaze snagged on the image of the enormous bathtub behind her. She turned to study it more closely, suddenly wanting nothing more in the world than a hot bath.

Yes, a bath would help. Surely her nerves were simply jangled from the events of the night—running from an angry former prizefighter who looked as though he could demolish her with his fists, being shot at on Houston Street, and taking refuge in a brothel, of all places.

The bathtub was a delight. It featured the modern convenience of hot running water, to which Genevieve added a liberal dose of the lemon-scented salts she found on a nearby shelf. Her own parents had added this type of plumbing to their house in the past few years, but the bathtub they had at home was not nearly this large. This one was grand enough that two people could easily fit into it—which, Genevieve realized with a start, was probably the intention. It was, gloriously, one of the first bathtubs into which she had comfortably fit as an adult.

She stayed in the hot, lemony water, eyes closed and immersed to her neck, until relaxation seeped into her back and shoulder muscles, and her limbs felt pleasantly like jelly. Only when the water began to cool did she regretfully pull herself out. The towels, like everything else she had encountered at Miss Dugan's, were of the highest quality, thick and plush.

Genevieve wondered briefly at the economics of such an establishment as she pulled on the white cotton nightgown, which unsurprisingly was a trifle short, and wound her hair high on her head. Just how much did Kathleen have to charge her "guests," as she termed them, to afford such high standards? Perhaps Daniel would know.

The thought of Daniel, somewhere on the other side of the door, stopped her bare feet in their tracks. She hadn't heard a peep from the room while bathing—perhaps he had fallen asleep?

She cautiously poked her head through the door. "Daniel?"

He was in his shirtsleeves and trousers only, shirt untucked, vest removed, his long form ridiculously stretched on the pink-and-white-striped chaise lounge, stockinged feet hanging over the edge.

"What on earth are you reading?" Genevieve asked as Daniel stuck his finger in a well-worn leather-bound volume.

"Moby Dick," he replied, holding the book up. "A favorite."

"Do you always carry a copy around with you?" She was holding her clothes close in front of her body, but forced herself to lay them across a matching upholstered armchair in a corner. The nightgown *was* buttoned to her neck after all, making it more chaste than every ballgown she owned.

Except for the fact that it stopped mid-calf.

"Of course not—it was here." He gestured toward a credenza with glass doors, and she did see several similar-looking books lining its shelves. "I thought the Shakespearean sonnets a nice touch but wasn't in the mood for poetry." Daniel shot a lazy grin her way.

Genevieve smiled back hesitantly as he stood up. "You take the bed," Daniel said. "I'm fine here."

Guilt washed over her at the sight of his bruised face. He looked exhausted. "No, you were hit. And that thing is far too short for you. There's no way you'll get a wink of sleep on it. You must have the bed. I'll sleep on the chaise."

"Absolutely not. You won't fit on it either."

This was true. "I can sleep in this chair, then," she countered, removing her dirty clothes from the armchair and depositing them on the end of the chaise.

Daniel dragged the chaise over to the end of the armchair. "I can take the chair and rest my legs on the chaise." He deposited himself on the chair and propped his feet up to demonstrate, folding his arms and leaning his head back. "See? Perfect," he said with closed eyes.

It looked excruciating. *Insufferable man*. Genevieve dragged the chaise away, causing Daniel's legs to flop down.

"Get in the bed."

"No. I can't let you sleep on the floor or in an uncomfortable chair. I shall be fine. *You* get in the bed."

"We'll share the bed." Genevieve could feel herself coloring even as she said it.

It would be hard to describe Daniel's expression as anything other than shocked.

"We couldn't possibly," he said in a stiff voice.

"Nonsense," Genevieve replied, pulling back the coverlet. She hoped her brisk tone hid the butterflies that had suddenly erupted in her stomach. "You've been struck, you're hurt, you're tired, and so am I. Neither of us fits on any of this other furniture, and the floor is out of the question. This bed is enormous. There's no reason not to share it." She climbed in, and tugged back the quilt on the opposite side.

"Genevieve, if anyone were to find out . . ." Daniel began in a warning tone.

She rolled her eyes at him. "We've already been down that road when gossip circulated that we shared a hotel room last year."

"*True* gossip," he reminded her. "We *were* in a hotel room together last year. And you were very nearly a social pariah. I'm not risking that again."

A laugh burst forth from her before she could stop it. The ridiculousness of either of them being concerned about her reputation when they were already in a brothel together was suddenly overwhelming. "If anyone found out I'm here at all, I'd be a pariah," Genevieve reminded Daniel. "Whether or not either of us sleeps on the floor is, at this point, immaterial. Now get in."

Daniel simply gaped at her for a few moments, then slowly did as he was bid. Once he was settled, Genevieve turned down the gas lamp on the bedside table, then lay still, listening to the sound of Daniel's breath in the darkness. Though they were not touching, the warmth of his body seeped through the sheets, and it felt as though every nerve ending she possessed was on high alert, thrumming at his proximity.

Which was, again, ridiculous. She had stood close to Daniel, indeed been held by him, on many other occasions. But somehow *not* being in physical contact, yet sharing a bed in the dark, felt like the most intimate encounter she had ever shared with anyone.

Genevieve did not think sleep would be possible, but the regular sound of Daniel's breath must have lulled her there at some point, for when she woke, light was straining to enter the room between the cracks in the curtains.

Daniel was nowhere to be seen, but the pillow on which he'd slept still bore his imprint and was warm under her tentative fingers.

A knock sounded at the door. "Genevieve?" It was Kathleen.

"Come in," she called, stepping out of bed.

Daniel's cousin entered, dressed in a high-necked, raspberry-colored day dress. "Oh good, you're awake. You'd best come downstairs." Worry was plain on the lovely woman's face.

Genevieve grabbed her clothes from where they'd fallen off the chaise during her and Daniel's arguing the night before. Apprehension began to creep in, jolting her fully awake. "What has happened? Is Daniel alright?"

"He's fine—he's already down. You have a visitor, I'm afraid."

The apprehension turned to alarm as Genevieve recalled Knockout Eddie's hefty forearms, the gun in his hand.

"John Boyle?" she gasped.

"Worse," Kathleen replied grimly. "It's the police."

Chapter 13

The bright green and orange lovebirds were a dazzling pop of color against the cooler, more muted greens of Kathleen's public front room. They were busy this morning, those birds, chirping at each other and nuzzling their beaks into their partners' necks.

Longstreet scowled at the birds, and Daniel suspected if he could order them quiet, he would.

"It's really very simple, Mr. McCaffrey." The detective was once again encased in tweed. Even though the windows of the front room remained closed, as always, Daniel could see through them that it was shaping up to be another glorious June day. "I know you've been asking around about Marcus Dalrymple's death. I know you were at the Metropolitan Theater when Paul Riley took his own life. I know you know more than you've let on. If you tell me what you know, things could be easier for those you profess to care about."

Daniel flicked an imaginary speck of dust off his shoulder, maintaining a facade of bored indifference, masking his very real confusion. What on earth was Longstreet after? The detective must have been tipped off to their presence at

Kathleen's by John Boyle, which felt off to Daniel. Everything he knew about Aloysius Longstreet was fairly one-note: the man was purported to be as straitlaced as they came. He didn't have the reputation for being in anybody's pocket, so far as Daniel knew, so why did the detective seem to be here on the bidding of a thug like Boyle?

But anyone, he supposed, could be swayed by the right sum. As Longstreet had on both their previous recent meetings, he seemed to be taking in his surroundings with the utmost disdain, mustache trembling.

For this meeting, Daniel had chosen not to wear his jacket, playing the part of the dissolute playboy in his rolled-up shirtsleeves and mussed hair, which seemed to infuriate Longstreet even more than the trappings at the Union League Club had.

"As I said at our last meeting, I neither understand nor appreciate your meaning."

"But I think you do," Longstreet countered, his brown eyes glinting under the bowler hat he'd refused to surrender to the maid who had shown him in.

Daniel paused, frankly unsure of what to say. He knew the detective believed Rupert to be caught up in Marcus's death, but was Longstreet insinuating Rupert was somehow responsible for Paul Riley's suicide as well?

It didn't make any sense.

"I really do not," Daniel said, his voice firm. "Now, I am sure you appreciate my cousin has a business to run, and her guests are not accustomed to seeing officers on the premises." Longstreet was accompanied by a uniformed policeman, who was standing near the doorway with his arms folded.

"Miss Dugan has friends in high places," the detective remarked sourly. "But so do I."

At that moment, the door behind the uniformed officer opened, and Kathleen came in, leading Genevieve, who stopped short at the sight of Detective Longstreet.

"Miss Stewart," the detective said. "Perhaps you are willing to be more cooperative than your . . . friend," he continued with a distasteful look at Daniel.

Genevieve entered the room cautiously, moving to stand closer to him. She was dressed in her shirtwaist and skirt from the day before, both of which, like his clothing, were somewhat wrinkled and dirty. Kathleen must have sent someone to help with her hair, though, which was neatly pinned.

"Cooperative about what?" Genevieve inquired, folding her hands in front of her waist. She was standing tall, shoulders back and chin raised, gazing at the detective as though she were at a society luncheon rather than a brothel. Daniel suppressed the urge to smile; he knew that look well.

Genevieve didn't scare easily.

"About answering my questions," Longstreet said.

She inclined her head, as if to say, "Go ahead."

Longstreet's mustache bristled.

"Why are you asking about Marcus Dalrymple's death?" he asked.

"Whatever do you mean?" Genevieve returned in a mild tone.

"You are meddling in police business," Longstreet warned. "I won't have it."

Genevieve gave the detective a puzzled look. "I'm confused. I haven't even spoken to the poor young man's parents. Have you, Mr. McCaffrey?"

Daniel shook his head. "It would be most insensitive, wouldn't it? After the loss they've suffered."

"The services were quite private," Genevieve added. "Why, we at *The Globe* only ran a simple obituary, out of respect for the family. We did not want to add to their burden by discussing the unfortunate circumstances around Marcus's demise."

"Indeed," Daniel murmured.

Longstreet looked from one to the other, clearly furious. "So you won't cooperate either." He eyed Genevieve coldly. "I could make your life quite difficult, you know."

Daniel's fist automatically clenched, and he forced himself to release it before Longstreet noticed. He managed, but god, what he wouldn't have given to knock the supercilious little man across the room.

"Undoubtedly you could," Genevieve returned coolly. "And even if you did, I still wouldn't be able to help you, as I have no idea what you're talking about. You cannot get blood from a stone, Detective."

Longstreet's jaw visibly clenched. "I'll give you one week," he warned, "and after that, I shall be forced to take other measures." With that cryptic warning, he marched out, the officer trailing behind him. Daniel could hear the detective speaking in clipped tones to Augustus as he departed.

Kathleen breathed a sigh of relief once the door to the parlor was shut. "What a horrible wee man. He needs a few hours with one of my girls, he does. Not that I'd have any waste their talents on him—you can tell he's the sort that barely allows himself to feel pleasure."

Daniel huffed. "I believe he derives a great deal of pleasure from seeing justice prevail, though I also believe his concept of the principle is more than a little skewed. I've seen him harass innocent men he was convinced were guilty out of pure zeal." He glanced at Genevieve, finding her white-lipped and stony-faced as she stared at the closed door. "Are you all right?" he asked.

Genevieve also heaved a sigh, though hers was more of anger than relief. "Fine," she said in a clipped tone. "I was seen. There's nothing to be done for it now."

"He already knew you were here, dearie," Kathleen reminded Genevieve gently. "I don't know how, but he came knocking on my door early, demanding to see the two of you. I had to stash him in here quickly. I can't risk any guests seeing a police officer about. Bad for business."

"It must have been Boyle," Daniel said, shoving his hands in his pockets. He wandered to the window and peered through the shutters, checking the corner to make sure Boyle's thugs had departed. It was the logical explanation, but it still didn't sit right.

"I thought you said last night the police protected your establishment, Kathleen. Why would a detective come here and harass potential, um . . . visitors?' Genevieve asked.

"There are certain, shall we say, well-placed gentlemen who do not wish to see Kathleen's business disturbed," Daniel explained. "They are friendly with other well-placed gentlemen, who make sure some members of the police force are also invested in the establishment operating smoothly. Longstreet, though, seems to be an outlier."

He watched as Genevieve digested this information, knowing she was thinking of the backdoor dealings and handshake agreements that constituted the cogs and wheels that made the city run.

The front bell rang, a gentle, sonorous tone, but it still made Kathleen throw her hands up in frustration. "Why all these visitors on a Sunday morning?" she cried. "This is normally our quiet time. And I need to be getting to church."

Augustus's head poked in through the door. "It's McCaffrey's men, miss," he said.

"Show them in, show them in." Kathleen bustled to the door as three men entered, greeting them each with a small peck on the cheek. "Now I must be off or I'll be late. Danny, you know Augustus here will arrange anything you need. Now, I'd offer you breakfast, but my guess is you'd both prefer to be on your way. If you stay much longer, you may run into someone you know."

The knot of tension that had been living in Daniel's shoulders finally unraveled a tiny bit at the sight of his secretary, Asher, followed by Paddy and Billy. All four had been members of the Bayard Toughs gang when they were young, and while Asher now worked for Daniel, Daniel considered the former boxer more a friend than strictly an employee. His relationship with Paddy and Billy was harder to define. They were both still active gang members, a life Daniel and Asher had left some years ago. But Daniel trusted them, for the most part, and they respected him just enough to help him out when he asked.

"Asher will take us home," Daniel said. "Paddy and Billy, would you keep a look out, make sure we aren't followed?"

Genevieve went a trifle pale. "Do you really expect Boyle would try to harm us in broad daylight?"

"I wouldn't put anything past him, but even more so, I wouldn't put anything past Tommy Meade." It was a grim reminder not only to her but to himself as well. Tommy was somehow involved in whatever was happening.

He instructed Asher and the other men to wait while he and Genevieve returned upstairs to gather the few things still in the pink room. He found his jacket and tie while Genevieve retrieved her pistol, placing it firmly back in her pocket. Daniel kept his gaze averted from the sight of the vast bed, still rumpled from their night's sleep. Its presence stirred him uncomfortably.

It had been an excruciating, exhilarating form of tor-
ture, lying next to Genevieve in her ridiculous, voluminous nightgown.

He had lain awake long after she slept, enjoying her
mere proximity, the tiny sighs she made in her sleep, the
lemony scent of her bath salts overwhelming his senses.

"I've got all my things. Are you ready?" Genevieve
interrupted his reverie, standing near the door. She looked
anxious to leave.

"I am," he responded, shoving from his mind the
thoughts of their night in a bed together.

They were both quiet on the carriage ride to Washington
Square Park, where Genevieve lived at her parents' home,
watching the city go about its various Sunday-morning
rituals as they rumbled their way uptown, Asher at the
reins.

"Will it be trouble for you, coming home at this hour?"
Daniel finally asked.

"Hmm?" Genevieve didn't pull her eyes away from
the passing sights out her window. "No," she said over her
shoulder. "I'll tell my parents I went to the office early.
They're rather used to me keeping odd hours." This part
was true, but she quaked a bit inwardly at the thought of
her parents ever finding out where she had really been all
night. Genevieve shoved the thought aside, as it couldn't be
helped. "But, Daniel, what now?"

He knew what she meant. What was the next step in
what had become their investigation? In finding Nora, in
solving the puzzle of Marcus's and Paul's deaths.

"I'll need to think on it," Daniel admitted. He could see
several possible courses of action ahead for them, but none
were terribly desirable. "Let's get home, freshen up, and
perhaps meet later. Or tomorrow?"

They were pulling up to the front of the red brick Stewart family townhome on the Square's north side.

"Come to luncheon today," Genevieve said, suddenly turning toward him. "Here, at the house. We can go for a walk afterward."

"With your family?" Daniel asked. He couldn't keep the surprise from his voice.

A small smile nudged her lips. "Yes, they'll be there. You should come. You probably take Sunday luncheon alone, mostly."

"Mostly I do." Well, that wasn't entirely true. He sometimes ate with Asher. It would thrill both his housekeeper and his cook if he invited more people over, but Daniel had little patience for the effort that went into hosting. Rupert had been a frequent guest before his engagement, causing his housekeeper, Mrs. Kelly, to sniff, "Two bachelors does not a dinner party make."

"I would like that," Daniel replied, accepting Genevieve's invitation. She seemed pleased, and in truth Daniel was pleased himself.

"Good. One o'clock?"

At Daniel's nod, she departed, helped down from the carriage by Asher. He waited until she was up the broad stone steps and safely inside before glancing down the street to ascertain that Paddy, who had been following them in his own conveyance, was ready to give the all clear. At Paddy's signal, Asher grunted and raised a brow at him.

"Let's go," Daniel said. He allowed the exhaustion he hadn't wanted to show Genevieve to overtake him. Their time at Boyle's had been brief, but intense, and he had barely slept.

Try as he might, memories of the night at Kathleen's kept resurfacing. Daniel wondered, not for the first time, what

Genevieve's experience of sharing a bed with him had been like. He, after all, had slept in the same bed with a woman before. Many times. But he guessed it was a new phenomenon for her. Had she been similarly affected by his presence?

Was this luncheon invitation an olive branch after their year apart? A way of welcoming him further into her life? He wasn't sure, but he was eager to find out.

★　★　★

"Mr. McCaffrey! I cannot believe we haven't formally met—it does seem odd. Doesn't it seem odd, Wilbur?"

"We were introduced to Mr. McCaffrey at the Hall's garden party last summer, dear," Wilbur Stewart, Genevieve's father, reminded his wife. He smiled gamely at Daniel and shook his hand, his brown eyes kind and welcoming.

Anna Stewart, Genevieve's mother, dismissed this with a flap of her hand. "That was in Newport, which hardly counts. I mean, of course, I cannot believe we haven't had you to the house before. Genevieve has been sorely neglectful on that count, and I should have gone ahead and issued an invitation myself. Now do come in and make yourself comfortable."

Daniel remembered meeting the Stewarts at Florence and Bertie Hall's party the previous summer, it was where Genevieve's brother Charles Stewart had come close to giving him a thrashing. They were just as he recalled: Anna, a statuesque woman with graying, dark blonde hair, perpetually in the midst of delivering a passionate lecture to whomever was nearby, and Wilbur, while outwardly quieter than his wife, a brilliant lawyer who seemed to possess compassion and intelligence in equal measure.

He liked them. It was easy to see how Genevieve had formed into the person she was, with parents such as these.

"Hello, McCaffrey." Genevieve's brother Charles met them on the way to the dining room, offering a decidedly cooler reception. They shook hands, but Charles was giving him an unfriendly, assessing look. Daniel could hardly blame the man. If his sister had been in the kind of danger Genevieve had put herself in the previous year, he would be wary of the man involved as well.

Anna had them all seated at an oval mahogany table. The dining room was small by most New York society standards, as the table probably sat no more than twelve comfortably, but it was still an elegant room, brighter than current trends tended to dictate, going against the present preference for heavy paneling.

Easy conversation was kept up as the soup was being served, much of it centered around the eldest Stewart brother, Gavin, who was returning from Egypt in a few weeks' time.

"He's been there for almost three years," Genevieve remarked, taking a sip of water. She looked lovely, as always, today in a lightweight, dark pink dress with pretty bands of embroidery crossing the bodice.

The same shade of pink, he realized with a start, that had dominated the room in which they had spent the night.

"I'm sure you're all looking forward to his return," Daniel said, feeling unusually flustered at the sight of that pink.

"Aha!" Wilbur cried, holding a finger aloft in triumph. A finger on his other hand marked a place in a large, red-bound volume. Daniel blinked. Even though he was only one guest and this was not a formal occasion, it was still quite unusual for one's host to have a book at the dining table. "The hieroglyph Gavin drew in his last letter is of Anubis, not Seth, as I originally thought." He gazed around the dining table in glee.

"You can ask him all about it soon, dear," Anna said mildly, signaling for the soup course to be cleared.

"Gavin often leaves me little riddles in his letters," Wilbur confided to Daniel as he accepted his fish course with obvious pleasure. "What a joy to see trout on the plate! Our upstate anglers must be doing quite well. Anyway, Mr. McCaffrey, these riddles often take quite a bit of time to untangle. Often I make an effort to send one back. It's become quite a game."

"And one soon to end, Papa," Genevieve said, grinning at her father.

"I must confess, it will be good to have all three of my children home again." Wilbur beamed.

"Mr. McCaffrey, can I interest you in attending the next meeting of our local chapter of the National Council of Women of the United States?" Anna inquired, spearing a piece of asparagus. "It's next Tuesday and could be quite illuminating for you."

"I'm sure it would be," Daniel replied, doing his best to follow the twists and turns in conversation. "Though would I be welcome, not being a woman?"

"A trifling matter." Anna dismissed the point. "You *are* for universal suffrage, are you not?"

"Most assuredly," he said.

"Then there it is." Now Anna was beaming as well. Daniel was not quite sure what had just transpired: Had he agreed to attend a meeting about granting women the vote?

"Let Mr. McCaffrey be, Mother," Charles said, reaching past Genevieve for the salt. She swatted his arm with her napkin.

"I would have passed that," she complained.

"Any plans to head to Newport this summer?" Charles directed the question to Daniel.

"Yes, I will, now that Rupert and Esmie are not going abroad." He refrained from mentioning that he wasn't sure Longstreet would allow their friends to leave the city. "I've been invited to stay with them. I haven't decided whether to build a house of my own out there. I've been thinking about spending summers upstate instead."

This launched the table into a lively discussion of the various places to spend one's summer, of Long Island versus Newport, of the benefits of beaches versus lakes. It all felt very comfortable and familial in a way Daniel had rarely experienced. His own family had been scattered before his twelfth birthday, dead or gone, leaving only him and his older sister, Maggie, who had died by her own hand the summer before Daniel started university. Other than spending some stilted holidays at Rupert's family's house during their school years, he had not spent significant time with a family in over twenty years.

It felt good, and for several minutes he allowed himself to be carried by the ebbs and flows of the Stewarts' ever-changing conversations, interjecting a few times but mostly listening, riding on their tides.

"And Eliza? How is she liking Long Island?" Charles asked Genevieve. Daniel's ears perked; he recalled Genevieve's friend Eliza Lindsay, an artist, from the year prior.

"She has been trying her hand at painting but still prefers sculpture," Genevieve reported. "But she enjoys it. Mr. Chase is an excellent teacher, by all accounts, and most encouraging. She believes he'll start a formal school there soon."

"And any word on Callie?" Charles asked, his voice gentle.

Genevieve visibly swallowed, shaking her head. "She has asked to be left alone, and I am honoring her wishes. I believe she will come back when she is ready." Daniel could hear the sadness in Genevieve's voice and felt a pang in his heart.

"I have heard that your friend Esmie Bradley has been seen on a bicycle, of all things," Anna interjected in an obvious attempt to change the subject. "Frankly, I can't begin to fathom it. She was never terribly coordinated, was she?"

"Mother, Esmie is Countess Umberland now."

Anna waved this away. The Stewarts had been famously feuding with the Bradley clan for years but now seemed to have gotten beyond it. The Bradley matriarch's murder did rather shift things, he supposed.

The same maid who had invited him in now appeared at the dining room door. "Miss Stewart has a visitor, ma'am," she said to Anna.

The entire table turned to stare.

"A visitor? On a Sunday?" Genevieve looked puzzled, then half stood out of her seat. "Is it Miss Maple?" she asked. Daniel ached to hear the hope in her voice. Genevieve had told him how her dear friend Callie Maple refused to speak with her or indeed to even inform Genevieve of her whereabouts.

"It's a young man," the maid clarified. "He's quite insistent."

"Careful, Mr. McCaffrey." Anna gave him a sidelong glance. "You may have some competition."

Genevieve shot her mother an irritated look. "Mother, Mr. McCaffrey is a friend. And Nellie, there's nobody I wish to see at present. Tell him to leave his card and give him my at-home hours."

"He says to tell you he's here on account of Nora, miss," the maid, Nellie, said.

Daniel's heart skipped a beat, and he instantly locked eyes with Genevieve. As one, they rose from their seats and bolted from the table.

CHAPTER 14

The young man Nellie had shown into the front parlor was disarmingly handsome. His delicate jaw and full mouth could have been painted by Botticelli, and his face was topped by a head of golden curls. He was holding his cap in his hands, but not in a deferential manner. His shoulders were back and his face was determined.

"I am sorry to bother you, Miss Stewart. I figured this would be the time you were most likely to be at home." The man's accent and clothing betrayed his working-class status. He shot a troubled glance at Daniel. "Who's this?"

"That is a question you should answer first," Genevieve said. She maintained a calm demeanor, but her heart was racing with excitement. She was almost positive she knew who this young man was, but wanted him to confirm it.

The man swallowed. "My name is Oscar," he said.

"Oscar who?" Daniel interjected.

The visitor's beautiful face took on a petulant cast. "Just Oscar," he said in a flat tone.

"Well, just Oscar, I don't like strangers chasing me down in my own home. I particularly don't like strangers who refuse to reveal their identity," Genevieve warned. She was in no mood for games.

The young man eyed Daniel warily.

"You told Miss Stewart's maid you wished to speak about Nora," Daniel said. "Of which Nora do you speak?"

Genevieve understood Daniel's tactic, that he was waiting to make sure this young man had Nora Westwood's best interests at heart before they revealed too much, but she had little patience for this type of cat-and-mouse game either.

"Tell us who you are and what you want, or leave my house," she ordered, resisting the childish urge to stamp her foot.

The visitor's petulant look turned mulish, and he seemed to be weighing his options. Genevieve was on the verge of asking Daniel to see the young man to the door when he spoke.

"Miss Nora Westwood," he said. "I heard you were looking for her."

She and Daniel exchanged a glance. Oscar still hadn't given his last name, but her suspicions were likely correct, and she could tell Daniel was thinking the same thing as her: this had to be Nora's secret suitor.

"What do you mean?" Daniel asked in a cautious tone. "Is Miss Westwood missing?"

"Why do you think I am seeking her?" Genevieve added.

Oscar gave Daniel another distrustful look but answered Genevieve. "Word gets out," he said.

"Do you know where she is?" Daniel interjected.

Oscar's eyes shifted between the two of them. "I know where she *was*," he admitted. "But not where she is now. And I am afraid for her." His jaw clenched, and Genevieve could tell this was something Oscar didn't like to admit.

"Who is Nora to you?" Genevieve asked gently.

His pale blue eyes snapped to hers. "She is the girl I will marry." She had been right, then. This was the young man Frank Westwood blamed for his daughter's disappearance.

"Her father believes Nora has run off with you," Daniel said.

Oscar shook his head. "No. We were planning it," he added, his expression defiant. "But we had not done so yet." He swallowed visibly, then took a deep breath. "I can't risk her, you understand. I can't say too much. If they even knew I was here . . ." He cast a glance at one of the windows that looked toward the street, and Genevieve understood that Oscar was deeply afraid.

"If *who* knew you here? The more you can tell us, the more we can help," Genevieve urged. She took a step forward as Daniel, arms crossed and expression wary, took a slight step back. That was good; Daniel's presence seemed to spook the young man.

"I can't say more," Oscar repeated, his tone becoming desperate. "But the answers are at the Garcia mansion," he said, his voice dropping to a whisper. "I can't go back there. I could get killed or get Nora killed. But that's where I last saw her."

Daniel spoke again. "We were there recently," he said, "but Nora was not."

"No, she's not. I tried to go back, tried to find her. The rumors . . . the demon. They're true. I saw it." Oscar swallowed again, his face pale. He was on the verge of tears. "I went back for her, but she was gone, and I saw it."

Genevieve and Daniel exchanged a puzzled, worried look. The young man wasn't raving, as Marcus and Paul had been. He seemed in his right mind—and calm. Calm, but terrified.

"Find her, please. Before it's too late," Oscar said in a strained voice. "And please don't let anyone know you've seen me."

"Oscar, who is behind—" Genevieve began, but the young man cut her off.

"Check the dungeons," he said in his low, terrified voice before jamming his cap on his head, turning on his heel, and rushing out of the room. They heard the sound of the front door closing behind him.

Genevieve and Daniel stared at each other. He seemed as flabbergasted as she felt.

"Well, I suppose we know what our next step is," Genevieve said. She had no desire to return to the decrepit mansion, but it seemed they had no choice.

"We should gather some additional information first," Daniel said, his voice grim. For a moment Genevieve was puzzled—where would they find out more about the Garcia mansion? Then it clicked.

Genevieve was instantly appalled. "No," she said.

"It's one of the options I have been considering but hoping we wouldn't have to use." Daniel sighed and looked out the front window. "No sign of Oscar, not that I expected one. He's long gone. Maybe Rupert and Esmie learned something useful, and we can figure out this Oscar fellow's full identity."

"Don't change the subject, Daniel—there's no way she would speak to us," Genevieve protested. "Besides, Sarah Huffington tried to have me killed."

Daniel turned back from the window, his expression bleak. "You don't have to go," he said.

"If you're going, I'm going." Genevieve felt her mouth set into an unattractive line, but she didn't care. She wasn't afraid of Sarah Huffington—the woman's power had mostly come from her wealth, her social status, and that of her late husband. Sarah still held a measure of her own money, but her place in society had plummeted after her involvement in the plot to profit off of tenement construction was revealed. While Sarah no longer had the power to harm Genevieve, part of Genevieve still wondered if Sarah had killed her husband, Andrew, herself.

Even declawed, Genevieve felt certain Sarah could still find ways to bite.

"She's the only person we know of, other than our recent visitor, who has spent time in that mansion. We have to at least try to find out if she knows anything useful. Something about these purported demons, maybe."

"Did you explore the basement when we were there?" Genevieve asked.

"No," he said, running his hand through his hair. Genevieve resisted the suddenly powerful urge to reach over and smooth it down, to tame the corkscrews his anxiety had created. "No, we ran out of time. You were missing, and the storm broke."

"We weren't prepared," she admitted. "Fine, I'll see if we can get an audience with Sarah. She may accept if I present myself in light of my position at the paper."

Genevieve began to mentally scheme the various ways she could persuade Sarah Huffington to allow them an audience. Daniel was right, attempting to ferret out anything the other woman knew was the logical next course of action. But disquietude began to creep into her midsection, fluttering there and robbing her appetite for the rest of her lunch.

How did one prepare to face one's attempted murderer?

★   ★   ★

"Oh, she's furious, all right," Rupert said as they walked to Sarah Huffington's townhouse. It was on Madison Avenue in the high fifties, a perfectly fine address, but a huge comedown from the vast, elegant mansion she and Andrew had shared on Fifth Avenue.

That had been lost, of course, in the aftermath of the scandal, and Sarah had been forced to relocate to more modest quarters.

"Esmie has barely said two words to me in three days, she's so upset we're visiting Sarah," he continued. For once, Rupert's flippant demeanor had vanished. He seemed truly glum over Esmie's anger with him. "And neither of us has said a word about this visit to Amos. As upset as Esmie is, she wants me alive, I think. If Amos knew I was going to visit Sarah Huffington, he might rip me from limb to limb right underneath those painted cherubs."

"Can you blame him? Or Esmie?" Genevieve asked. To be honest, though, she more snapped the question than asked it. Her nerves were jangled and raw, alternately causing her heart to flutter, her shoulders to bunch, then her throat to tighten, and had been that way ever since she had received Sarah's positive response to her request for a meeting. Genevieve had been surprised that her gambit had worked, asking if Sarah wanted to be included in a story about society widows' plans for their Newport summers. She had made sure, though, to add that her editor was hoping Sarah would agree, thinking perhaps Sarah's vanity wouldn't allow her to refuse.

And Genevieve had been right. It probably gave Sarah a vicious little thrill to think that Genevieve's editor had asked her to speak with Sarah, knowing full well the discomfort Genevieve would feel.

Sarah had always enjoyed the discomfort of others.

"Of course not," Rupert said, looking at Genevieve in genuine surprise. "I know Sarah and I used to be friends, but I don't want to see the woman either. She did attempt to have me framed for murder after all," he finished in a hissed whisper.

"I think we can agree that not one of us is interested in spending time with Mrs. Huffington," Daniel interjected. "But, Rupert, you were friends with her once. You know her, including her weaknesses. I feel if she'll talk to any among us, it will be you. I can't shake the feeling that time is of the essence, and anything we discover could be helpful."

The group fell into a grim, thoughtful silence as they approached the home's front steps. Genevieve wondered if Sarah would simply turn her back and have all three of them escorted out once she realized the interview had been a ruse.

A housekeeper showed them into a drawing room, where Genevieve awkwardly positioned herself close to a shuttered fireplace. Daniel and Rupert seemed to be having trouble deciding where to stand, as well.

The furniture was all covered with white drapes. Every surface had been removed of knickknacks, and the walls were bare.

A maid bustled through, her arms piled high with linens. She barely glanced their way before exiting through an opposite door.

"Are we in the correct home?" Rupert mock-whispered.

The question was answered almost instantly, as Sarah Huffington's distinct, amused drawl was heard in the adjoining hallway.

"You'll have to forgive me, Miss Stewart. As you can see, I'm quite unable to offer tea . . ." The voice trailed off as the woman herself entered the drawing room and caught sight of her unexpected visitors. For a moment, pure shock, tinged with a touch of fear, crossed Sarah's face. She quickly composed herself, though, and affected a look of utmost disdain.

"Well, well, well. Look what the cat dragged in." Her upper lip curled in condescension. Sarah was as beautiful and fashionable as ever, her red curls piled high atop her head, an artful fringe framing her smooth forehead. She was still wearing half mourning over a year past her husband's death, but managed to look resplendent in a white dress with wide strips of black lace crossing the bodice and running vertically down the skirt. In her arms she held a shaggy-eared miniature dachshund, who offered a small yip in their direction before settling farther into Sarah's grasp, eyeing them balefully.

"As you can see, Miss Stewart, my plans to head to Newport are well underway." Gripping the dog with one arm, Sarah languidly gestured around the room. "Your message came just in time, in fact. I leave this afternoon. Though the presence of the gentlemen makes me quite certain there is no article. Tut-tut, Miss Stewart, how sly." Sarah raised a brow in Genevieve's direction. "There may be hope for you yet."

Genevieve had never cared for Sarah, not even when they had both been pupils together at Mrs. Gibson's school. Sarah was two years her junior but had gained a well-earned reputation as a malicious gossip with a blistering tongue even then. She had terrorized the younger girls and enjoyed pitting her classmates against each other, and had behaved in the exact same manner once she reached adulthood.

"Hello, Sarah," Rupert said. He matched their hostess's look of haughtiness with one of his own. "I apologize for our little deception, but we didn't think you'd see Daniel or myself if we asked."

Sarah eyed Rupert in an assessing manner. The two had once been bosom friends, but Rupert had exposed half of Sarah's secrets to the world in a letter to the newspaper. As Robin Hood, he had also stolen her diamond engagement ring. Genevieve waited, breath held. Sarah had a choice here. She could admit to having known Rupert was Robin Hood, thereby admitting her culpability in Esmie's mother's death, or she could feign ignorance and maintain her claims of innocence, that she'd had no prior knowledge of her husband's nefarious plots.

"Water under the bridge," Sarah finally said. Genevieve allowed herself a quiet exhale; so Sarah was choosing neutrality, admitting neither innocence nor guilt. Though her words were not antagonistic, the other woman's tone was cold as ice. "What have you gotten yourselves involved in now?" she asked, gray eyes glittering.

"We were hoping you could tell us about your time at the Garcia mansion," Genevieve said. She folded her hands politely at her waist but kept her chin held high. She had no doubt as to Sarah's involvement with the group the year before, the one that had tried to have her killed. No doubt at all.

Actual surprise registered, for the second time in under five minutes, on Sarah's face. "The Garcia mansion?" she asked in what seemed like real confusion. "That old house uptown the boys like to say is haunted?"

"That's the one," Daniel replied. "A young girl is missing. She was last seen at the mansion." In the days they had been waiting for Sarah's reply, the three had discussed exactly what to share with her if she happened to allow the visit. Genevieve had argued they keep the details to the bare minimum but stay as close to the truth as possible.

Sarah raised a lazy brow at Daniel. "A girl? I did hear your courtship with Miss Stewart here ended some time ago, Daniel. Pity." She shot Genevieve a patronizing glance. "Though I'm not surprised, frankly. I never did think someone like you would be able to hold the attention of a man like Daniel for long."

An old heat, an old shame, flushed through Genevieve's system, though she refused to allow herself to rise to Sarah's bait. "Don't believe everything you read in the papers," she softly said instead.

"So it does have claws," Sarah said, now raising both brows. "Well done, Miss Stewart."

"The Garcia mansion, Sarah," Rupert prompted. "You told me once that you visited the place when you were first out in society. What was it like?"

"Like? It was a moldy old place about to fall down around our heads, that's all it was *like*," Sarah said in her amusement-tinged voice. But Genevieve detected an undercurrent of something else: Apprehension? Anger? It was hard to tell.

"What parts did you explore?" Daniel asked.

Sarah circled a hand in the air. "We went all through the place, as I recall. The boys were all vying to impress me with their bravery." She didn't quite roll her eyes, but her tone implied her contempt at the past young men's endeavors. "What was there to be brave about? It was an old abandoned house, nothing more."

Again that ripple of something in Sarah's voice. Genevieve tried to place it.

"You were quite young to be traipsing about alone with young men," Genevieve said instead, wanting to keep Sarah talking. "Especially to an abandoned house in a remote location."

Sarah's tinkling laugh echoed through the emptied room. "Concerned for my virtue that was, Miss Stewart?

Of course, you always were such a rule follower." She smirked at Genevieve. "And look where it got you: jilted at such a young age. You never did bounce back from that, did you?" This time Genevieve couldn't control the heat and felt it infuse her cheeks, betraying that Sarah's barbs had found their mark. Sarah noticed and laughed harder. "Despite my currently widowed status, I think we can all agree I made a brilliant match—despite my youthful shenanigans—did I not?"

Genevieve saw Daniel's eyes narrow, and she gave him a quick shake of the head. Sarah didn't need any further ammunition with which to needle them.

"Did you make your way to the basement, perhaps? We have reason to believe this young woman was last seen in the basement," Rupert said. Genevieve knew he was choosing his words carefully.

Another spasm of some emotion quickly crossed Sarah's face, there and gone so quickly Genevieve almost thought she imagined it. Genevieve shot a quick look at Daniel, who gave a single, tiny nod, without looking back.

Daniel had seen it too.

What was in that basement?

"I draw the line at digging through the muck in basements," Sarah drawled, holding the dachshund tighter. The dog gave another yip, this time in protest of being squeezed. Genevieve could see Sarah relax her hold. "Every girl has to draw the line somewhere, does she not, Miss Stewart?"

Without waiting for an answer, Sarah opened the door of the drawing room that led back to the house's foyer. "As fascinating as this little trip down memory lane has been, I must ask you to leave now. As you can see, we still have quite a bit to pack up. Perhaps I'll see you in Newport, Miss Stewart, and you can observe the widow in summertime in her natural habitat." Sarah's lip curled again, deliberately signaling exactly how she felt about Genevieve's job. "You are in a position of some power now, you know. You could exploit it in any number of ways."

"And what makes you think I don't, Mrs. Huffington?" Genevieve replied, finding ice in her own voice.

"Because I've read what you write," Sarah said. "Such a shame, an opportunity like that wasted on the likes of you." She cut her eyes toward Daniel. "Yet another one."

"Now see here, Sarah," Rupert began in an angry voice.

"Never mind, Rupert," Genevieve said to stop him, even though her heart was beating fast and she could feel her flush deepening. "She's not worth it."

Genevieve led the way to the door, holding her head high, and could feel the two men gathering in her wake. "You may not want to look too hard for this missing girl of yours," Sarah said as they passed. "It is altogether possible she does not care to be found."

Genevieve stopped short, as did Daniel and Rupert. Daniel, who was closest to Sarah, looked at her sharply. "What do you mean?"

Sarah's eyes widened in mock innocence. "Just as I said. Some things lost prefer to stay lost." Genevieve swallowed, thinking of Callie. Sarah stroked the dog's head. "And if I were you, I'd draw the line at mucking about in basements, as well."

With that, Sarah closed the door to the parlor, leaving them standing in the foyer. The housekeeper appeared from a different room and showed them to the door.

Back on the street, Genevieve opened her parasol against the bright June sunshine. She thought back to the look that had crossed Sarah's beautiful, austere face when she had mentioned the Garcia mansion, the slight tremor she had heard in the woman's voice. It dawned on her, all at once, what emotion had been expressed, and a chill passed through her limbs. No wonder she had had a hard time recognizing it; the feeling Sarah seemed to be suppressing was utterly incongruous with her constant semblance of self-assurance.

It had been horror. Complete, abject, and unmistakable horror.

CHAPTER 15

Genevieve thrummed her fingers on her desk, idly staring at the article she was meant to be writing on who else had departed for their summer homes this week, when a shadow suddenly loomed above her.

"Tell me it's not true, Genevieve."

Confusion lanced through her. "Tell you what isn't true, Luther?" The man looked positively distraught, and Genevieve racked her brain to think what he could be causing him such distress.

Her friend perched on the edge of her desk and lowered his voice. "I didn't want to believe it, but I'd like to hear the truth from you." In addition to his obvious dismay, Genevieve detected another emotion dancing across his features: betrayal.

Genevieve's bafflement deepened, now mixed with some alarm. What could have transpired to cause Luther to react so?

"Your whereabouts last Saturday night." Luther said the words so quietly, Genevieve had to strain to hear him. "I heard a rumor about them that was unconscionable."

Understanding dropped, swift and cruel. She wasn't able to control her expression in time and watched as Luther's face changed and shuttered.

"I was willing to think that last year's rumors about the two of you in a hotel were a misunderstanding," he said slowly. "So many guests swore Mr. McCaffrey had been in the gaming room. But this . . ." Luther's eyes searched hers, desperate for Genevieve to contradict him. "It's true, then? A . . . brothel?" The last word was issued in a hissed whisper.

A frustrated sigh escaped Genevieve before she could stop it. There was no denying it now. "Would it help if I told you we are trying to save someone's life, and that establishment was our only safe haven? And that, despite the damning circumstances, there is nothing between Mr. McCaffrey and myself but friendship?" Even as she said the words, her heart gave a discernable pang in protest, which she ignored. Now was not the time to explore any further feelings she had toward Daniel.

Wariness and distrust now occupied Luther's normally aimable countenance. "I don't know that any explanation could help me understand, Genevieve." He was looking at her as though she were a new species, one he'd never encountered before but found highly suspicious.

Genevieve pursed her lips in annoyance. On the one hand, she was sympathetic to Luther's emotions. She understood it was a tough position for him. But his feelings often segued into an inappropriate protectiveness that irked her. Luther had no claim on how she spent her time, or with whom.

"From whom did you hear this?" Genevieve asked, still keeping her voice quiet. She wasn't going to defend her or Daniel's actions any further.

"I overheard a police officer discussing it at a crime scene I was covering," Luther admitted. "The officer was shocked to see a lady in such a place, and there was much ribald talk and laughter at the thought. He knew your name, Genevieve. Yours and McCaffrey's both." A tinge of Luther's old friendly concern shone through, but it was quickly replaced by his new wariness.

He stood, wearing his dejection like a suit that needed cleaning. "I'll see you around, Genevieve," Luther said. Then he walked away as if for good.

Genevieve blew out a breath. This didn't bode well. If officers were gossiping, soon that gossip would spread. But more importantly, she suspected Detective Longstreet ran a ship so tight it didn't dare squeak. If the officers under his purview felt free to make conversation, it was possible Longstreet was about to make good on his threat to expose them.

The detective had given her and Daniel a week to tell him what they knew, and that week ended tomorrow. But they still hadn't ferreted out what Longstreet wanted to hear. That somehow the deaths of two young men and the disappearance of a young woman seemed connected? That they suspected foul play in all three? That a criminal tavern owner might be in league with a notorious, murderous gangster, but to what end they still hadn't deciphered?

She and Daniel had discussed it at length, and together they had decided not to work with the detective. For now. Daniel didn't trust him, and Genevieve's own experiences with the police in the recent past had not been favorable.

Genevieve began to gather her things, article unfinished. It was an odd time to be a society reporter, as society was in a transitional moment: half of New York's elite had already left town, setting up their summer cottages, and the half that was left was in the midst of preparing to leave. Parties and functions in both New York and Newport were minimal, as households were being packed and unpacked.

The article was not urgent, and her editor, Mr. Horace, had given her until Monday.

In the meantime, she had a pressing appointment at one of her least favorite places in the city, a place she had spent an undue amount of time when she and Daniel had last engaged in an investigation: the municipal archives.

This time, however, she wasn't going to endure the tedium of archival research alone.

★ ★ ★

"Shh," hissed the clerk in a furious whisper.

Daniel and Genevieve ducked their heads guiltily. They had turned in their slip and were waiting for the clerk to deliver the materials requested. In fact, they had been waiting for over thirty minutes, which seemed to Daniel an unreasonable amount of time to pull one set of documents, especially as there was nobody else in the research room. During their wait, Genevieve had been filling Daniel in on what she had learned at her office through her coworker, Luther.

Luther. Daniel thought the name with distaste. Genevieve had made it perfectly clear she didn't return Luther's obvious affection, but the man still irked him.

Which was unreasonable, he knew. And yet.

"What do you think this means for Longstreet?" Genevieve was asking, making sure to keep her voice low enough not to rile the clerk.

"I'm afraid your instincts are correct; it can't signify anything good for us." Daniel worried mostly for Rupert. The detective seemed to have an unreasonable fixation on his friend.

The clerk laid a large, rolled-up set of documents in front of them.

"Let me know if you want to submit another slip," she instructed, before returning to her desk.

Daniel nodded his thanks as Genevieve began to unroll the large papers.

"Whether or not Longstreet had somehow orchestrated Luther overhearing the officers talking is regardless," Daniel murmured as he moved to help Genevieve separate and flatten the sheets of paper, each of which wanted to curl after being rolled for at least three decades. "I believe we should interpret the information as a warning shot from Longstreet all the same." He paused in his endeavors with the papers to give Genevieve a weighted look. "We are running out of time."

Genevieve blinked at Daniel for a moment, but took his words with her usual aplomb. She drew her shoulders back and applied her attention to the three drawings now spread before them on the long table of the archives research room.

"Then we'd best get to work," she replied firmly.

Daniel's usual admiration for her tenacity swelled.

She was, without a doubt, the most remarkable woman of his acquaintance.

"What do you make of this?" Genevieve tapped her finger on the plans, and he turned his attention from her clear profile to the mass of lines and shapes laid neatly on the table.

The plans to the Garcia mansion, which of course had originally been built as the Cummings mansion, were beautiful in their own way. The original owner had named the mansion Everwood, which Daniel thought fitting given the dense forest one had to traverse to reach the house. It was a precise, careful drawing, beautifully watercolored, with each of the many rooms, doorways, and passages carefully labeled.

"Where is the lower level?" he asked, scrutinizing the complex plans.

Genevieve pulled one of the sheets on top. "This one."

They bent their heads together, searching for some clue to the mysterious dungeons Oscar had mentioned. "Some of these are clear enough, but some of these more technical aspects escape me," Daniel said. "I see doorways here . . . and here, and a basic plan for a cellar—but what of this door?" He pointed to an egress demarcated in the cellar plan itself. "Am I reading that correctly as a door? This is not my field." Daniel ran a hand through his hair in frustration.

"Let's ask Charles," Genevieve suggested. "He'll be able to interpret this."

"Excellent idea," he agreed, relieved. "Perhaps it's easiest if I draw a copy, rather than try to lure him here. I don't relish the idea of attempting to call these plans up again." The clerk glared at them, surely ready to deliver her terrifying hissed *shh* again, and Daniel quickly applied himself to the task at hand, as though he were an errant schoolboy.

He caught Genevieve's eye as she smothered a giggle, and couldn't help but feel the corner of his own mouth twitch up in return.

★　★　★

"Wait until you try this," Rupert said enthusiastically, dipping a spoon into a dish at the center of the table and spooning a portion onto his wife's plate. Esmie gave her husband a cold stare in return, and Rupert deflated in his chair a little.

"It smells good," Genevieve said gamely, helping herself to a portion of rice. She seemed to be trying to lighten the mood, which Daniel appreciated. Esmie was still visibly angry about their visit to Sarah Huffington and was making her feelings on the matter quite clear.

Their waiter poured them each a cup of tea from a larger pot, also in the center of the table.

Genevieve picked up her cup and inhaled, trying to forge ahead with their evening. "What blend is this? It doesn't smell familiar."

"Oolong," said Daniel. "I've had it every time I've come here, and it is also quite good."

He was used to the scents and rituals of a meal in Chinatown, as was Rupert. The Mott Street restaurant they had chosen was one he and Rupert frequented often, but neither of the women had eaten Chinese food before.

The restaurant, simply called Yee's, was tucked in between a grocer's and a shop that seemed to sell medicinal herbs. He and Rupert had been coming here for almost a decade, and it was one of the first places they would visit when Daniel returned to town. Several other restaurants had opened in the neighborhood in the past few years, and although they'd sampled the new places' wares, he and Rupert always found themselves back at Yee's.

"I'm glad you both were fine with eating here," Daniel said, helping himself to some of the steaming dish once the ladies had been served. "They call this chop suey, and Rupert and I have grown very fond of it over the years. Do you have enough rice?" he asked Genevieve.

"I do, thank you. And you know me—I'm always ready for something new." She took a cautious bite of her food, and he and Rupert watched with anticipation until a wide smile broke across her face. "Delicious," Genevieve pronounced.

The lanterns suspended from the pressed tin ceiling gave the room a warm, comforting glow, enveloping the friends in a cheerful light that reflected off the patterned, gilded edges of their round table. They were not the only Caucasians in the restaurant, as at least two other tables were occupied with non-Chinese diners: a couple in a corner, holding hands and staring into each other's eyes over their cups of tea, and a trio of men who, from the cut of their suits and the length of their hair, appeared to be members of the more bohemian set. They were earnestly arguing over something, and finally one removed a book from his satchel and began pointing to a passage excitedly.

"We could have gotten a private room at Delmonico's, but I thought it better if we went somewhere where we were unlikely to run into anyone we know," Rupert said between mouthfuls of rice.

"It is better," Esmie said, after having grudgingly taken a bite. "I'm still unhappy with all of you, but I do understand the visit couldn't be helped." She hesitated, then helped herself to more chop suey. "Rupert, what other delicious restaurants do you frequent that you have been hiding from me?"

A delighted smile lit Rupert's whole face, his relief at being somewhat back in Esmie's good graces apparent. "Oh, so many. Maybe being stuck here all summer isn't so bad after all." Daniel smiled at them in return, happy to see Esmie had softened somewhat.

"Esmie was a huge triumph at the garden party," Rupert boasted, giving his wife an admiring look. "You should have seen her. She could have been a spy, she was so believable."

Esmie blushed lightly. "It's easy to get others to talk about themselves," she said. "That's all most people want to do anyway."

Rupert grinned wider. "See? She already knows the tricks of the trade."

"Tell us what you learned, Esmie," Genevieve said, taking a sip of her tea. Daniel noticed she kept her voice low, even though the restaurant was far from crowded.

Esmie leaned forward, speaking in a quieter tone as well. "I noticed some time ago that Nora Westwood and Darcy Sanford were close friends, and we were in luck that the Sanfords are intimate with the Pettigrews, who were our hosts last Saturday. This was probably one of the last fêtes the city will see this summer. It does seem most families will be gone by next week." Esmie gave Genevieve a regretful look. "You probably should have been there for your work."

Genevieve pursed her lips slightly. "Perhaps. But I couldn't be in two places at once, could I?"

"This Darcy, had she heard of Nora's secret boyfriend?" Daniel prodded Esmie, nudging the conversation back on track.

"She had," Esmie confirmed, taking another bite of her food. She delicately wiped the corners of her mouth before continuing. "I told her I had already heard from Annabelle Graves, whom I had been seated next to at the luncheon to celebrate Frances Owlman's daughter's christening three weeks prior." Daniel blinked. There was no way he would be able to keep track of who was whom in this story, but it was better to let Esmie tell the tale in her own way. "I had been seated next to Miss Graves at the luncheon, but we did not, of course, discuss Nora Westwood nor the secret sweetheart. I believe we mostly talked of my upcoming honeymoon and the places Rupert and I were scheduled to visit. She thought my becoming a countess was the most romantic of situations."

Genevieve and Rupert appeared to be similarly engrossed by Esmie's story.

"This was indeed delicious, as Genevieve said," Esmie continued, setting down her fork. "Do they serve sweets here?" She looked about hopefully, and their waiter hurried over.

"Esmie." Rupert flapped his hand in a wild circle, urging her to continue. "Keep going—tell them the rest."

"Thank you." Esmie accepted a menu from the waiter, but put it aside for the moment. "Of course, Miss Sanford had not been present at the luncheon, and Miss Graves has already departed town, so the chance of being caught in my falsehood is, I believe, quite small." Esmie nodded in a satisfied way and turned her attention back to the choices for dessert. "Oh, only chocolate or vanilla cake? I can have that anywhere. I was hoping for something more authentic."

"On the way home, we can stop at a shop I know for Italian pastries not far from here," Daniel offered.

"Perfect."

"Esmiiiiie," Rupert groaned, burying his face in his hands. "Tell them!"

"Since she thought I already knew the tale," Esmie continued, handing the menu back to the waiter, "Darcy was pleased to speak with me about it, only she did swear me to utmost secrecy. I do believe my new status as a countess makes these young girls trust me quite a lot."

Genevieve nodded. "It does seem that way."

"I asked Darcy where Nora had met her young man, knowing that opportunities for star-crossed lovers to, well, cross paths, can be rare for a debutante. Oh, that must be it, don't you think? They assume Rupert and I are somewhat star crossed as well, given the difficult circumstances around our last year?"

"Yes," Genevieve said thoughtfully. "That makes sense to me."

Daniel caught Rupert's eye, and the two exchanged a baffled look. Was this how all women's conversations went when men were not around? Meanderings into personal matters when one was trying to stay on topic?

"Well, Darcy confided that Nora had met her young man at the flower shop she frequents. The young man in question works there."

Genevieve gave a happy gasp, and Esmie sat back in her chair with a contented air.

"I was right, wasn't I? She's a natural at this." Rupert excitedly beamed at Esmie again.

Daniel understood the implications immediately. There were only a few select flower shops the Astor 400 deigned to patronize, and as Nora Westwood was a young woman of means and, according to her father, expensive tastes, she would undoubtedly have met him at one of those establishments. It would be easy enough to find out which one employed a man named Oscar.

The group toasted Esmie with their tea before happily ambling to the pastry shop Daniel had mentioned. They piled back into Rupert's carriage, in which they had arrived, and began traversing uptown. Rupert instructed his driver first to Washington Square, to drop off Genevieve, who lived the farthest south.

Daniel found himself quiet, for the most part, on the drive up, enjoying the coolness of the evening breeze through the window after the heat of the summer day, feeling comfortably full and sated from his dinner and happy to be in the company of his friends.

The carriage pulled up in front of Genevieve's townhome, and Rupert set the box of pastries resting on his lap aside to help her disembark. Genevieve embraced Esmie and gave Daniel a warm smile that, along with the rest of the evening, enveloped his heart in gladness. She was in the midst of stepping out of the carriage, holding Rupert's hand, when she abruptly stumbled out of sight. Her yelp of surprise and what sounded like pain mingled with the sudden harsh yelling of male voices.

Daniel hurled himself from the carriage and straight into a fractious melee.

Rupert was trying to wrest his left arm from the grip of a uniformed officer while his right arm was swinging toward the livid countenance of none other than Detective Longstreet. Genevieve was on the ground, scrambling backward like a crab to get out of the way of the sudden rushing of feet as several other officers emerged from behind nearby hedges and trees in the darkened park to assist in restraining Rupert.

"Stop! What is the meaning of this?" Daniel plunged into the fray, yanking Rupert out of the way of an officer's nightstick before holding up his hands, palms out. The four officers halted but kept their hands on their nightsticks at the ready. "Detective, what is happening here?"

"The earl"—Longstreet sneered the title—"is resisting arrest. And he attempted to assault an officer—me."

"I didn't realize you were police," Rupert panted. "Someone pulled me from behind, causing Miss Stewart to fall, so I swung out."

"Arrest? For what charge?" Daniel demanded, lowering his hands.

"The charge of murder," Longstreet clipped out, hooking his thumbs in his front jacket pockets. The detective's eyes gleamed in the light of the gas streetlamps.

"Murder?" Esmie gasped, half out of the carriage. "You can't be serious."

Genevieve had made her way to her feet and was by Daniel's side in an instant. Daniel felt another presence behind him and glanced over his shoulder to find Genevieve's parents and brother Charles there as well. Indeed, several of the Stewarts' neighbors had emerged from their homes and were standing on their stoops, watching the scene on the sidewalk unfold with wide, horrified eyes.

Longstreet turned his hard gaze to Esmie. "But I am, madam. Your husband is under arrest for the murder of Marcus Dalrymple. Mr. Milton? Or—excuse me—Lord Umberland," Longstreet added in a sarcastic tone, "you shall come with us."

Two of the officers held Rupert's upper arms, and his friend looked toward Daniel with a wild expression. "Daniel?" he asked.

"You haven't a choice at the moment," Daniel said. "Where are you taking him? I am Lord Umberland's attorney, and I want to know where I can reach my client."

"We're taking him downtown for booking," Longstreet said as the officers led Rupert to the corner. A police wagon was waiting there, another officer ready to drive. Incredulity was slowly morphing into rage as Daniel realized how many men Longstreet had brought with him. The detective must have had men tailing their group and had been planning this all night.

"Downtown?" Daniel questioned sharply. "Lord Umberland resides uptown. Should he not be taken to the nineteenth?"

"The crime was committed downtown, and the courts where he must appear are in The Tombs. Come, Mr. McCaffrey, you're not such a poor solicitor as that—you know how these things work," Longstreet taunted. Ashen faced, Esmie tried to follow her husband, but another officer held up a restraining hand.

"I'm sorry, miss," he said with a regretful look.

It was an unwritten practice that upper-class detainees such as Rupert were not typically held in The Tombs, a notorious, foul police and detention complex near Daniel's childhood neighborhood of Five Points. The rage festered and grew within Daniel, and only the feel of Genevieve's restraining hand on his shoulder kept him tethered to the earth. Without that gentle pressure, he had no doubt he would have launched himself at the detective.

Based on the smug, knowing look in Longstreet's eyes, this may have been exactly what the detective was hoping would happen. Daniel inhaled deeply through his nostrils.

"Stay safe, Rupert," he called. Anna held Esmie as the latter began to cry quietly while the officers loaded Rupert into the wagon. Rupert's pale, shocked face was visible for the barest of moments before the officers slammed shut the wagon door and drove away.

CHAPTER 16

Genevieve watched as Esmie, who was already very pale, went positively white.

"Daniel," Genevieve called, putting as much alarm into her voice as she dared while slipping a supportive arm behind Esmie's shoulders. Just in time, as it turned out, as the other woman's knees buckled within an instant. She could have held Esmie on her own—Esmie was a slight little thing, and Genevieve was considerably stronger—but she didn't like the feral expression on Daniel's face as he stared after the retreating wagon.

Best to give him another task on which to focus.

Daniel hustled to her side, and together they assisted Esmie up the broad steps of the Stewart family townhome and inside, Anna hovering anxiously. Charles bounded away to reassure Rupert's stupefied driver, who had leapt from his seat at the first sign of trouble, ready to offer aid had it been needed, and now stood with his mouth hanging open in astonishment.

Once inside, her mother began issuing orders to the staff with the decisiveness of a general, bringing a relieved smile to Genevieve's lips. Her mother's forcefulness could be exhausting sometimes, but Genevieve would be the first to admit that her mother got things done, and quickly.

Soon, Esmie was ensconced in a blanket with a mug of steaming coffee in her hands—coffee tended to be the hot beverage of choice for the Stewarts, though tea was always available for those who wished it. Rupert's driver had been dispatched back to Amos, but not before Wilbur had telephoned Amos himself with the news. Esmie's father had tried to insist she return immediately, but Esmie took the telephone and told Amos in a surprisingly strong voice that she had things to sort out where she was and would be home shortly. Trays of food were brought in just in case anyone felt like eating, but nobody did.

"I would be happy to help out in any way I can," Genevieve overheard her father say quietly to Daniel as she poured herself more coffee from the sideboard.

"It may come to that," he replied in a grim voice.

"I think it would behoove us all to learn more about this detective," Anna exclaimed, settling in next to Esmie on the settee. "You said you thought he may have a grudge against poor Rupert. I may call him Rupert, may I not, dear?" she addressed this to Esmie, who nodded, looking surprised. "Whyever would he?" Anna continued.

Genevieve caught Daniel's eye and gave him a small shake of her head, reminding him that her parents did not know Rupert was Robin Hood, the notorious jewel thief all New York believed had been killed last year. Daniel shot her a wry look in return, with an almost eye roll. *I know,* the look plainly said.

"From my experience with him, Detective Longstreet has long held two main prejudices. The first is against the upper classes. He seems to hold in great disdain those who have great wealth, particularly inherited wealth, and Rupert being a titled aristocrat is particularly galling for him. I, of course, am included in this contempt." Daniel paused and took a sip of coffee. "On the other side of the spectrum, he also despises those from impoverished circumstances, particularly those from Five Points." He gave an ironic smile at that. "Yes, I'm doubly cursed for a man like Longstreet."

"The detective has made a name for himself with his Rogues' Gallery, has he not?" Wilbur asked from the far side of the room.

"He has," Daniel acknowledged. "A photographic gallery of all known criminals in my former neighborhood, posted on police headquarters walls. His methods of interrogation are known to be quite brutal, I regret to say." Genevieve cast a quick look at Esmie, who had been looking somewhat revived but had gone pale again over this last fact. She glared at Daniel. "For known offenders," he hastily amended. "Despite his dislike of the Astor 400, I cannot imagine he would use such tactics against a man of Rupert's status."

"But you don't know that," Esmie said in a low voice. "You also didn't think they would take him to The Tombs, and yet there he is."

Daniel dipped his head in acknowledgment of her claim. "You're right, and I'm sorry. I don't know what they will do to Rupert. But I shall be there first thing tomorrow to assure myself of his safety."

Genevieve's anxiety had been climbing during Daniel's explanation of Detective Longstreet, and at this it bubbled over into anger. "We can't leave him there all night," she cried. "You're both attorneys," she said to Daniel and her father. "Can't you do anything?"

"Mr. McCaffrey is correct, my dear," Wilbur said gravely. "We cannot do anything this evening. But we can go in the morning."

"I'm going too," Genevieve announced.

"As am I," added Esmie.

"We can't all go," Daniel said. "That would do Rupert more harm than good. Wilbur, perhaps it's better if you work behind the scenes. And Esmie, speak to your father. Amos surely has connections in the justice department of this town."

"He does, I'm sure," Esmie agreed, nodding. Genevieve was relieved to see small patches of color were returning to Esmie's cheeks.

"But what does all this have to do with Rupert?" Charles asked. He had been quiet, but Genevieve had no doubt he had absorbed every word.

She and Daniel exchanged a glance. "Because they found Marcus Dalrymple dead in Rupert and Esmie's stateroom, the detective seems to think Rupert was somehow involved," Genevieve explained.

"Longstreet has seemed convinced of this from the moment it happened," Daniel added. "And that man is like a dog with a bone. Once he has an idea someone is guilty, he tries to figure out a way to make it stick. He has a habit of rounding up any known criminals in Five Points on a Saturday morning, lining them up, and trying to pin any crimes from the previous night on them. I've never seen him go after someone of Rupert's standing before, though."

Esmie appeared to be becoming agitated again, pressing her hand to her mouth.

"It's getting quite late, dear," Anna said, wrapping an arm around Esmie's thin shoulders. "Let Charles take you home in our carriage."

"Might father go instead?" Genevieve jumped in. "Mr. McCaffrey and I need to speak with Charles."

"I'd be happy to," Wilbur said. "Come dear, let's get you home."

Once Wilbur and Esmie had departed, with a plan to reconvene with Esmie at seven thirty the following morning, Anna excused herself to retire for the evening.

Charles regarded them with a mildly amused, quizzical look. "What's all this about?"

"Come with me," Genevieve said, retrieving her satchel and leading both men into the dining room. She relit the gas lamps mounted on the wall on either side of the fireplace, illuminating the room with a warm glow, and pulled out the copies Daniel had drawn of the Garcia mansion's plans, laying them out on the dining room table.

Charles's brows raised as he regarded the detailed drawings. "You've been busy."

"We've been asked to help find a missing person," Genevieve explained carefully. "We have reason to believe that person was possibly held in this house, in a subbasement, perhaps, but we can't find any such level on these plans. Or maybe we're not reading them correctly."

If anything, her brother's brows raised higher. "Can you divulge more?"

She exchanged another glance with Daniel, who shook his head minutely at her. "Not at this time," Genevieve admitted. She hated lying, even by omission, to her family, but there didn't seem to be another choice.

Charles exhaled a deep breath and leaned in close to the plans, tracing areas with his finger and occasionally muttering something under his breath. At one point he glanced up and caught Daniel's eye. "These are good copies. Nicely done."

An automatic sisterly annoyance flared in Genevieve. "How do you know I didn't make those drawings?"

He huffed a small laugh. "You never could draw worth a damn." Turning his attention back to the plans, Charles paused on a section that detailed the cellar.

"This is odd," he murmured, tapping his finger. Genevieve and Daniel clustered around him.

"What is it?" she asked.

"See that line?" Charles pointed. "It indicates a door, but it's not labeled, and the door doesn't appear to lead anywhere. It could simply be a storage room within the cellar that the original architect didn't indicate, but if there were an entrance to a lower level, this is all I see that could fit the bill." He looked up from his musings. "Does that help?"

"Yes," Genevieve said. She put an arm around her brother and briefly hugged him close. "Yes, that helps."

★ ★ ★

The Tombs was a low, squat building, fronted with massive pillars, so large it ran the length of an entire block of downtown. Its design was popularly thought to have been modeled after an Egyptian tomb, though Charles told Daniel this was probably untrue, even though it was designed in the general Egyptian Revival style. Daniel knew only the basics of architecture but had always thought the moniker rather descriptive. Though The Tombs had previously held the city's courts, and some police were stationed there, it was most well-known and feared for its role as a municipal jail.

The building also held a gallows. Many who went in never came out.

Daniel had frequented the interior of those cells many times, both visiting his fellow gang members when he was a young man and sneaking out of Jacob Van Joost's mansion in his teenage years to run wild on the streets of Five Points, and later, in his adulthood, as an attorney, visiting clients, many of whom also hailed from Five Points. It was a dank, festering place, having been built on a filled-in swamp. Charles also told him that soon after its construction, the building began to sink into its watery foundation. As a result, the very walls seemed to weep with deterioration, leaking through ever-growing cracks with filthy waters that seeped up into the building. The prison was notorious for its foul stench, and it was dark, overcrowded, and horrendously corrupt.

"Brace yourselves," Daniel said in a low voice to Genevieve and Esmie. "The Tombs is a harsh place."

Genevieve looked at him askance but nodded once firmly. Esmie said nothing but grabbed Genevieve's arm and regarded the large, imposing entrance with wide eyes.

They marched up the monumental stone staircase and through the heavy, carved pillars that guarded the front entrance. They were joined by a multitude of other visitors, older women in dark dresses carrying baskets to deliver to loved ones inside; police officers; a young, dark-haired woman holding a small child by the hand. A thin man with small, shifty eyes in a brown plaid suit approached their group.

"Perhaps I can offer my services," he began in a smooth, oily voice. His entire manner reminded Daniel of a rat, sniffing around for fresh garbage. "Fine folks such as yourselves have no business sullying your hands here. Is there someone you wish to visit? I would be happy to meet with them and offer my representation." The man tried to reach past Daniel to offer Esmie his card, but Daniel swatted the man's arm away with, if he was being honest, a trifle more force than was necessary.

"Ow," cried Plaid Suit, snatching his arm back.

"We do not require any assistance," Daniel clipped out in his iciest tone, staring at the man—surely a lawyer or bail bondsman of some kind, preying on those too confused and desperate to know any better—until Plaid Suit sulkily turned away, glaring back at Daniel once before hunching his shoulders and scuttering off.

"Predators," Daniel explained, guiding the women through the front door.

Immediately both women covered their noses, Esmie with a handkerchief and Genevieve with her gloved hand.

"What is that smell?" Esmie asked faintly.

"Sewage," he replied. The less he expounded, the better. The only light came from a vast skylight above. "This way." He gestured up the staircase, but they were stopped by a guard before they could get very far.

"Who you here to see?" the guard asked in a bored tone.

"My husband, Rupert Milton, the Earl of Umberland," Esmie answered. She drew herself up tall and thrust her shoulders back, a stance, Daniel realized with a start, that she had probably absorbed from Genevieve.

"An earl, huh?" The guard did not seem impressed.

"He would likely be on the second floor," Daniel interjected. "The charge is murder."

"A murdering earl, then," the guard responded blandly. Nothing, it seemed, could faze him, and he wanted them to know it. "Come with me. Let's find His Highness."

Daniel and the ladies followed the guard up a set of stairs and to the second floor, which split into two main passages on either side of an open section that looked down to the ground floor. Heavy black iron doors lined each side like grim sentinels, revealing nothing of what lay behind their facades.

The incurious guard spoke to another, this second guard's face mainly covered with a truly impressive set of sideburns, but in tones so low Daniel couldn't overhear them. The second guard pointed down the hall.

Their group allowed themselves to be led past the long row of thick, imposing doors. Daniel knew what they concealed, knew what Rupert's cell would contain. A tiny, barred opening, far too high to see out of and that would have revealed a view to nothing even if one could see, served as the cell's only window. A mean, narrow plank counted as a bed, and there would be a small table holding a wash basin, and a chamber pot shoved into a corner, all in a room so narrow Rupert could probably stretch his arms out and touch the walls with the tips of his fingers.

The guard stopped before one of the interchangeable, endless iron doors and withdrew a heavy key. "Visitors, Your Highness."

As the door opened, Daniel was unsurprised to find Rupert's cell exactly as he knew it would be, but the ladies' quickly stifled gasps revealed their shock. Daniel mentally cursed himself; he should have better prepared them.

Rupert quickly stood from where he had been sitting on the bed and rushed toward them. Genevieve glanced to the guard, worried, but Daniel nodded, letting her know interaction with the detained was permitted. As Esmie and Rupert wordlessly clutched one another, Genevieve began unpacking one of the baskets they'd brought, laying out blankets, a small pillow, some fresh clothes, and plenty of food.

Releasing Esmie, Rupert saw the piles and blanched. "What's all this? How long am I going to be in here? I assumed you were here to take me home."

"We have the arraignment first," Daniel reminded him as gently as he could. "It's not until Monday morning."

Rupert let out an exasperated hiss and folded his arms. "Two more nights? Very well, if I must, I must. At least I have provisions now." He cast a surly look at the guard and began poking at the food they had brought him. "Oh, currant scones. How delightful." Esmie blinked in surprise, but Daniel felt an enormous relief. Rupert had always been shockingly resilient.

"I'd ask you to sit, but as you can see there's not really any place appropriate," Rupert said around a mouthful of scone. He shoved the lidded chamber pot under his bunk with his foot. "Apologies."

Esmie bustled in and began arranging the blankets Genevieve had set on the bare cot. Her face, though somewhat ashen, had recomposed since her first look at the spartan cell.

Rupert settled himself on the newly made-up bed, and gestured for Esmie to join him. "Have you learned anything?" he asked as Esmie passed him a second scone. Daniel unearthed the jar of tea they'd placed in a second basket and poured some for Rupert into a tin mug they had also brought. He took a deep breath; telling his friend the rest would not be easy.

For Daniel had, in fact, learned more. Early that morning, he had called in a favor from a friend at the coroner's office.

"According to the autopsy, the cause of Marcus Dalrymple's death was poison," he said.

The second scone was paused halfway to Rupert's mouth. "Poison?" He lowered his voice to a furious whisper. "They think I *poisoned* him, like some Medici?"

"That seems to be precisely what they think," Genevieve said. Daniel had filled in both of the women on the way to The Tombs that morning. "It has been determined the poison used was nightshade."

Rupert's eyebrows raised. "Well that is very Medici-like, isn't it? *Atropa belladonna.* And how do they suppose I administered said poison to the boy? Let alone acquired it; it's not as if I have a garden of deadly herbs hidden in the middle of Fifth Avenue."

"I don't know those details yet," Daniel admitted. "I'm sure we'll find at least some out tomorrow, and of course we'll know everything the detective suspects if the case goes to trial."

"Trial?" Rupert interjected, sloshing his mug of tea. "They can't possibly have a shred of evidence. I did grow up on a country estate, yes, but I really know nothing about plants."

"Perhaps they won't argue that you grew the nightshade, Rupert, but that you acquired it somehow," Genevieve suggested.

"I suppose," he said, sighing. "One can acquire any-thing in this town—I know that well enough."

"From what I understand, the symptoms of nightshade poisoning are consistent with how both Marcus and Paul acted," Esmie added. Daniel looked at her in surprise, and she gave a slightly embarrassed shrug. "I've read a lot of novels."

"How so?" Genevieve asked. "I'm no use here. I know nothing about poisons."

"The vomiting and the hallucinations, from what I've read," Esmie said.

"Also the incontinence," Daniel added.

Genevieve wore a puzzled frown. "So the scream-ing about demons and the crazy behavior were from hallucinations?"

Daniel shrugged. "Perhaps." He could hear the bewil-derment in his own voice, and it accurately reflected his feelings. This whole situation was like the minotaur's laby-rinth. As soon as he thought they were making progress, they would hit a dead end and have to scramble backward lest they be devoured.

"But how could both men have the same hallucination? Isn't that akin to two people having the same dream?" she asked. "And the woman's voice at Boyle's Tavern too. Three separate people having the same hallucinations . . . I'm no doctor, but that doesn't seem feasible."

"You're not wrong," Daniel said, troubled. The feeling of walking in a fog, hands outstretched and unable to see four feet ahead, intensified.

"But there are other constants," Esmie pointed out. "You just said one, Genevieve. Boyle's Tavern."

"And the Garcia mansion is the other," Rupert added.

Daniel blew out a breath. Yes, there were threads to hang on to. Threads that needed following. Threads like Ariadne's, which, if traced for long enough, could possibly lead them out of the labyrinth.

"What if we told Longstreet some of this?" Genevieve asked. "If he's as big a zealot for justice as you think, Daniel, perhaps what we know—however scant—will spur him in a direction other than Rupert?"

Daniel looked around the moldy, cracked walls of the cell. They had been inside The Tombs long enough that he, for one, was beginning to become accustomed to the stench of raw sewage from far too many detained men, women, and boys. The place was horribly overcrowded, but Daniel bet Longstreet had been the one to insist Rupert receive a private cell. The detective knew optics, and Rupert was a well-liked figure in society.

"Unfortunately, I don't think that conversation would help Rupert," he finally said. "And if word got back to Boyle somehow that we had been speaking with the police about him, it could most certainly be detrimental for Nora.

I do think she is being held by him at the Tavern, though I've no idea why, and a raid there would likely result in her death." Daniel's stomach churned at the thought. "Boyle would be able to pass off her death as another suicide by a desperate young woman, as Nora ran away with an unsuitable lover and was, in essence, ruined. He could spin any tale he liked."

"Right, no police," Genevieve agreed quietly, glancing at the robust figure of the guard in the door. Daniel had also been speaking just above a whisper; Sideburns had rejoined the guard who had brought them here, and the two were guffawing in the hallway. They didn't appear to be eavesdropping on the conversation within the cell, but he wasn't taking any chances.

"Boyle's is still too risky," Daniel continued. "But Genevieve and I have a new lead within the Garcia mansion, thanks to Charles. We'll explore that tomorrow if you can begin to ask around the appropriate flower shops for Nora's beau, Esmie?"

"Yes," Esmie said, seeming relieved to have a task. "Yes, I can do that."

"Good. Rupert, can you stand it here two more nights?" Daniel frowned at his friend in concern.

"Needs must, as my mother always says," Rupert said, finding a ginger cookie and eating it in one bite. "At least I'll be well fed for the duration. What time will I see you Monday, Daniel?"

"The arraignment is at ten o'clock, so I'll be here at nine."

"Nine o'clock, then."

Genevieve and Esmie emptied the last few necessities out of the baskets and set them where they could while Daniel clasped Rupert's shoulder.

He looked into his friend's dark brown eyes. Daniel could detect apprehension dancing in their depths, although Rupert was putting on a brave, slightly nonchalant face, as he was wont to do.

"We'll find answers," he promised, before releasing Rupert into the arms of his bride. Daniel took one more look around the clammy, rotting cell. He met Genevieve's eyes over Rupert's shoulder. She gave him one fierce, resolute nod.

"We will," Daniel vowed. He prayed it was a promise he could keep.

Chapter 17

Genevieve was prepared for the automatic gate's motion this time, but its foreboding creak still sent an involuntary shiver up her spine. Perhaps it was because they passed through the tall, spiked metal bars just as the warm June sun was slipping toward the horizon. After leaving Rupert in his barren cell at The Tombs, it had taken her and Daniel the better part of the weekend to prepare for this visit. They had felt so unprepared last time, they both wanted to make sure they had all the supplies they might need. They set off with multiple kerosene lamps, additional food, warmer clothes in case the temperature dropped, and other sundries such as a sturdy length of rope and an assortment of tools. Daniel had thought a small shovel might be prudent too.

Her derringer, of course, was in her pocket. She suspected Daniel had a weapon or two at his disposal as well. After a lengthy discussion, they had both decided it would be best to visit the house under the cover of nightfall. The estates there were so large that neighbors were far flung, but Daniel, especially, had not wanted to risk their being seen.

The sun was almost fully disappeared into the water by the time they walked again under the dense, heavy canopy of trees, before emerging once more onto the broad expanse of lawn that led to the empty facade of the Garcia mansion. Its many windows seemed to gaze at them dispassionately, becoming less and less decipherable in the darkening night, morphing into something unwelcoming and unrecognizable.

A blaze of illumination from the lamp suddenly lit Daniel's face, a welcome sight against the deepening shadows. "Light yours too," he urged.

Genevieve did as he suggested, and immediately her shoulders relaxed a fraction. Even though the area their lamps lit was not large, the small, glowing lights cast just enough warmth to dispel the encroaching gloom. The house looked like just a house again.

She steeled her shoulders and set her jaw. "Let's go."

Daniel led the way to the door in the kitchen that took them to the cellar stairs. Their lamps created small patches of brightness in the narrow staircase, illuminating the walls and the few steps in front of them, but not much more than that. The moldy, damp smell that had permeated her senses on their last visit only intensified as they continued down the stairs.

"I'm surprised a house this close to the water has a cellar," Genevieve murmured. Even though she was speaking quietly, her voice sounded unnaturally loud in the tight space. She had no reason to suspect anyone else was in the house, but it felt appropriate to talk softly. "You'd think it would flood."

"Perhaps being up on the rise helps," Daniel said. He was also speaking barely above a whisper.

The door at the bottom of the stairs leading into the cellar stuck slightly from the damp but gave after Daniel applied his shoulder with a modicum of force.

Genevieve held her lamp high as they entered the cellar itself, trying to see as much as possible. There wasn't much to it. Bare stone walls dripped with condensation onto a packed dirt floor. The smell of the sea had intensified but now mixed with the strong odor of earth and, underneath it all, the unmistakable tang of decay.

Swallowing hard, Genevieve moved deeper into the space, shining her light into dark corners. By unspoken agreement, she and Daniel moved in opposite directions, trying to cover more ground. The cellar, like the rest of the house, was massive. She found a stack of rotting wooden crates and a shelf containing a few empty, dusty glass jars, but not much else.

"Genevieve," came Daniel's urgent whisper from across the room.

She hurried across the cellar, lamp in front of her, toward the glow of Daniel's light. He gestured toward a half door set into a recess that had been hewn out of the thick rock comprising the house's foundation.

"Is that it? The door Charles saw on the plans?"

Daniel pulled out a small piece of paper onto which Charles had copied the cellar plans, highlighting with a circle where the door he'd seen could be found. He held the drawing up to the lamp light. "It must be," he said. "I haven't found any other egress in these walls, have you?"

Genevieve shook her head. "Nothing. And I would never suspect that a door such as this would lead anywhere. It looks more like it would be the entrance to a small root storage area or the like."

"Only one way to find out," Daniel said. He set his lamp on the floor and gave the iron door handle a firm tug. Like the main door to the cellar, the half door resisted at first but then flew open so easily that Daniel stumbled back. Kneeling down, he picked up his lamp and crawled halfway inside.

"What is it? What do you see?" Genevieve hissed at Daniel's rear. He pulled himself out and looked up at her in wonder.

"This is it."

Genevieve's heart sped up as she handed Daniel her lantern and crawled through the small opening. Smooth dirt changed to rough brick under her palms as she passed under the low entrance, and she gazed up, shocked at where the tiny door led.

Daniel took her hand and helped her stand. The walls were still stone, but they formed a roughly hexagonal-shaped chamber, large enough to fit perhaps a dozen adults, that itself served as the entrance to yet another staircase, also formed of brick, curving down to unknown depths.

She and Daniel exchanged wide-eyed glances. "The dungeons?" she whispered.

A muscle in Daniel's jaw worked. "I suppose we'll find out. Stay close to me."

He needn't have reminded her. Fear was beginning to send chills down her arms, and it was reassuring to hover behind Daniel's broad, strong back as they began their descent. "But be careful with that lamp—don't singe me," he said over his shoulder.

They followed the light of Daniel's lamp down the spiral stairs, passing through one turn and then another, the sound of dripping water accompanying their every cautious step. Genevieve stayed close to the warmth emanating from Daniel as the utter blackness both behind and before them seemed to accentuate the clamminess of their environment.

They had to be fairly deep underground at this point.

"I can see the bottom," Daniel whispered. Genevieve peered over his shoulder and she, too, saw where the steps ended, leading into some type of passageway, big enough to walk through but still fairly narrow.

How deep it went was impossible to tell.

Genevieve followed Daniel's careful tread as they slowly descended the last few steps. She readjusted the strap of the supply bag she had slung across her body, and patted the derringer in her pocket for reassurance.

She had expected the staircase to end in a room of some sort, a dungeon from the type of Gothic horror novel Esmie liked to read, replete with chains dangling from the walls. But instead, they were in a narrow hallway that seemed to stretch on endlessly.

Genevieve raised her lamp higher and tried in vain to make out what lay beyond the sphere of illumination. Curiosity was edging out her uneasiness at this place as she wracked her brain to recall the facts she had relayed to Daniel about the man who had built the house, Frederick Cummings. Why would anyone go to such lengths to have a secret lower level beneath his house? What had he been hiding?

Daniel gave a thoughtful frown when she posed the questions to him. "You said Cummings was a Confederate sympathizer, did you not? He must have been dealing in some type of illegal trade."

One cautious step after another, Genevieve began to advance down the tunnel, Daniel by her side, both lanterns held aloft. They had only traversed a few feet when, on either side of the tunnel, large, semicircular openings appeared. Genevieve thrust her lamp into one.

Her breath caught.

They had found the dungeons.

★　★　★

Light from his kerosene lantern bounced off the heavy brick walls of the subcellar, casting more light than Daniel had anticipated, particularly once he ducked into one of the small rooms lining the passageway.

He was unsurprised to see Genevieve also had to stoop under the semicircular opening to make her way into the chamber, as she was nearly as tall as he, but once they were in the center of the space they were both able to stand fully.

"I wonder how many of these there are," Genevieve mused, bending down to shine her lamp into the far corners of the room. Like its opening, the room was shaped like a half dome. There wasn't much to see, just a bare, packed dirt floor and dripping brick walls.

"We'd better check them all," Daniel replied.

They each took one side of the tunnel, and made their way into every chamber. Daniel shone his light high and low, scrutinizing the corners of each one he entered, but found nothing.

"How far does this passage go?" Genevieve asked as they both emerged from their third respective chamber. She peered back the way they had come. Daniel followed her gaze, but there was nothing to see. The staircase they had descended was already shrouded in thick darkness. "This must lead back toward the woods and the main road, don't you think? Otherwise, we'd almost be at the water by now."

Daniel hesitated, as he had been pondering this exact question from the moment they had stepped foot into the tunnel, and he was reasonably sure he knew precisely where they were. He had refrained from saying anything yet, so as not to alarm her.

But Genevieve, apparently, knew him better than that. Something must have given on his face, for she narrowed her eyes at him. "Out with it, McCaffrey."

"I believe we are heading toward the water, not away from it," he admitted. "In fact, I think we may be close to being under the river right now."

Genevieve's gaze instantly shot to the low ceiling, clearly startled. "Really?"

"Indeed."

"An underground tunnel that leads under the water," she marveled. "How very piratical. Esmie is going to be quite envious—she loves a good pirate story." Genevieve turned her large amber eyes to his. "Well, it can't lead any-where, then, can it? I'd been thinking eventually we might pop up in the woods somewhere."

Daniel wasn't so sure about that either, but this time kept his mouth shut. The entire mansion made him uneasy, and this underwater tunnel only added to his disquiet. He wasn't afraid of it not holding; it had stood for at least thirty years, and the construction seemed sound. Whoever built it knew what they had been doing. But as to where and how it would end? And to what purpose it had been and was possibly still being used?

There wasn't an explanation that boded well.

"Let's keep going," he said, anxious to explore the rest and leave as soon as possible. Genevieve nodded, and they each ducked into the next chamber in the row.

Daniel was in the midst of examining the floors with care when Genevieve's excited cry came from across the passageway.

"I found something—come!" she yelled.

He darted through the low opening and into the cham-ber across the hall. Daniel's heart began to speed up, and the disquiet that had been dogging him intensified.

What appeared to be a makeshift bed was lumped into a corner of the room. It consisted of a pile of unclean blankets, mostly, but one was rolled into what might have served as a pillow. Daniel set down his lantern and crouched, poking gingerly through the blankets. Genevieve knelt down next to him and began to help, and together they unfurled the pillow with care, holding the unrolled blanket wide as if they were about to lay it down for a picnic.

"What's that?" Genevieve said, gesturing with her chin.

It was difficult to see in the dim light, but something was glinting in the center of the spread-out blanket.

"Lay it down, carefully," Daniel instructed. He reached onto the blanket and held up a small gold ring.

Genevieve crowded close to Daniel to get a better look. "I was sure it would be another one of Boyle's medallions," she said, examining the ring closely.

"Let's get into the light," he suggested, and they huddled next to one of the lanterns they had set on the floor.

Daniel felt Genevieve's breath intermingling with his as they leaned in close to the ring. It was yellow gold, with a floral design inset into an opening in the center, each petal filled with green enamel. It was a lovely thing, but to Daniel's eye it didn't look particularly valuable.

"No diamonds or precious gems," Genevieve said, apparently thinking the same thing.

"But that gold seems a high quality."

Her eyes flickered toward his in the lamplight, then back to the ring. "Oscar told us to check the dungeons," she said quietly, looking around the cold, damp space. "This was the last place he saw Nora. There are no bars on these chambers, though."

"But where would one go? If the door leading to the cellar were locked, you'd be trapped down here." Daniel felt Genevieve shiver slightly, and in truth, it was hard not to follow suit. Genevieve had given him the photograph of

Nora some time ago so he could show it to some of his associates and have them keep an eye out for the girl. Though it was safely tucked into his inner breast pocket, Daniel didn't need to remove the picture to see Nora's laughing face. He tried to picture that playful-looking girl held within these bare walls, but it was such a sobering image, his mind skittered away from holding it too long.

"Unless there's a door at the other end," Genevieve said thoughtfully.

Daniel felt his mouth quirk in a slight smile; he ought to have known she would figure out that was a possibility. "Yes, but if that is the case, surely it would also be locked."

"And it would lead where? The middle of the river?"

He tilted his head at her. "We'll find out, won't we? Let's keep moving."

They unfolded the remaining two blankets, running their hands and lantern over the length of each carefully, and searched the remainder of the chamber but found nothing else.

Two more chambers each, all of which revealed nothing, then about a twelve-foot stretch of tunnel unmarked with any half-circle openings. This they walked in silence. Daniel suspected they were quite deep under the river at this point—the air, such as it was, felt heavier, and the smell of saltwater was as strong as if they were within the water itself. Which, he realized, they rather were.

"Here's another," Genevieve said, her voice echoing. The semicircular openings had resumed, he had one on his side as well. Daniel shone his light into the chamber, and all at once several aspects of this mystery became enormously apparent.

He still didn't know why Nora Westwood was likely being held captive. He also didn't know the specifics as to why Marcus and probably Paul had been poisoned to death.

But, with one sweep of his lamp, he absolutely knew what John Boyle's, and by extension Tommy Meade's, interests were in the Garcia mansion.

Piled within the chamber were gleaming stacks of firearms. Daniel reached his lamp in as far as he could, trying to estimate how many there could be, and found himself challenged. At least one hundred, possibly more. They were not handguns either, but military-grade .45 caliber rifles.

A chill that had nothing to do with the clammy conditions of the tunnel ran down his spine. Daniel was well used to firearms and weapons, but the sight of so many in one place made him feel slightly sick. He'd never seen such an accumulation.

"Daniel?" Genevieve's voice sounded very small.

She was two additional empty chambers down the tunnel from him, leaning halfway into the opening. The illumination from her lamp spilled out of the recessed area and into the passageway, lighting her lower half before she stepped fully into the chamber.

Genevieve's lamplight gleamed off a pile of Gatling guns. It was at least as large a pile as the rifles he had found, though as these were larger—and surely more expensive— weapons, they were probably fewer in number. Daniel quickly moved into the next chamber and found some stands for the Gatlings, in pieces, and in the chamber across the hall from that one, there were what appeared to be boxes and boxes of ammunition. In a third, more rifles.

Genevieve had emerged from the chamber with the Gatlings. Her face was pale in the orange light shining from her lamp. "Is someone planning on going to war?" she asked in a voice that shook slightly.

"Someone," Daniel agreed. He looked up and down the tunnel, as far as the light from their lamps allowed. How much farther did the tunnel go? How many more chambers hid weapons?

"Boyle?" she asked, disbelief evident in her voice. "But to what purpose?"

"Not Boyle. He's not using these guns. He's selling them. They're gunrunners, Genevieve."

Her mouth dropped open as understanding dawned across her face. "And Marcus? Paul? They were in on it?"

Daniel shook his head, not in the negative, but in confusion. "We don't know. Perhaps. How on earth they would get involved in a scheme like this is beyond me. But the location makes perfect sense, doesn't it? An abandoned house with no neighbors visible, right on the water. Anyone could sail up the river, anchor, row a boat to shore to load their stash, then sail away via the Sound and be in the open Atlantic within hours if they timed it right. Sailing to anywhere in the world."

"Cummings must have used these tunnels for smuggling too, then," Genevieve mused.

Daniel raised his brows. "Absolutely. He had them constructed specifically. And surely chose this plot of land specifically as well."

"I wonder—" Genevieve began, but before she could finish her sentence, a loud bang and a blinding flash of light erupted from the end of tunnel from which they'd come. The tunnel shook slightly, and a light shower of dirt rained on Daniel's face.

Genevieve let out a small shriek, and Daniel heard himself emit a surprised yell as his heart dropped to his stomach. He shielded his eyes against the glare, then blinked as the light slowly dissipated, willing his sight to adjust. It was impossible, though, for his vision to acclimate quickly enough, as the image of that flash echoed behind his eyelids again and again.

A low grating laugh echoed down the tunnel. The hair on the back of Daniel's neck stood up.

"Daniel?" Genevieve whispered, her voice laced with fear.

Only seconds had passed since the sound of the blast, the noise of whatever had produced the light, but Daniel's eyes were beginning to return to normal. He blinked again, certain he was seeing things.

What looked to be a pair of red, glowing eyes was visible at the far end of the passage, surely near the staircase. As they began to advance, Daniel grabbed Genevieve's hand and backed up a few steps.

The laugh sounded again.

Genevieve dropped his hand. He glanced at her in surprise but then saw she had retrieved her small pistol from her pocket and was pointing it down the tunnel toward the eyes.

Bits of masonry flew and pebbled the side of his face as the unmistakable sound of a gunshot exploded through the narrow confines of the tunnel.

"Genevieve, don't shoot—" he began but stopped abruptly as his brain registered the searing pain on his upper left arm at the same time as Genevieve's gasp.

Blood was steadily blossoming on the sleeve of his jacket.

Genevieve instantly grabbed the lantern out of his hand and doused it, before doing the same with her own. They were plunged into complete and utter darkness, save those slowly, steadily advancing red eyes.

"Run," she hissed, and his stuttering brain dutifully obeyed, as he whirled on his feet and stumbled down the dark brick tunnel, toward a near certain dead end.

But there was no helping it. There was no other way out of the tunnel. They were trapped.

CHAPTER 18

There was no sound save Genevieve's own gasping breath, joined with that of Daniel's. She listened in vain for rushing footsteps behind them but frustratingly heard nothing. As they ran, she reached her arm back and fired indiscriminately, once, but heard her shot ricochet off a wall. She shoved the derringer back into her pocket so as not to waste ammunition. An answering shot responded, cracking against the bricks above her and showering small bits of debris onto her head.

That was too close. She focused on running, arms outstretched. Surely they would reach the end of the tunnel soon, and they would have to turn and make a stand.

Daniel, who was a few steps ahead of her, ran into the tunnel's end, unable to stop moving quickly in time to avoid what sounded like a painful stumble. Genevieve was able to halt her steps a bit sooner, but rough rock dug into her hands as she, too, tripped on something solid on the ground, lost her balance, and pitched forward.

"There are steps," Daniel gasped, and she heard him scrambling up like a cat, followed by another painful sounding smack.

"It's a door, in the ceiling," Daniel yelled.

A blessed rush of cool, fresh air blew into Genevieve's face as Daniel heaved open the heavy wooden door, and she wasted no time scurrying through and into the night, finding herself climbing a rugged, rocky surface.

The sound of metal clanging on metal echoed dimly, and she risked a look back. The bright moonlight showed Daniel a few feet behind her. He stopped also, and gestured for her to stay where she was. He pulled a gun out of his waistband and began cautiously advancing toward the small, rectangular wooden door set into the rock.

Genevieve withdrew her gun again, too, and lay on her belly, ignoring the jagged stones poking her. She propped herself on her elbows, derringer in her right hand, left hand supporting her right forearm. She trained her gaze on the trapdoor and waited, heart pounding, breath still coming in heavy pants.

Daniel's form was silhouetted in the moonlight, one arm reaching for the trapdoor, the other with his gun readied. Genevieve took in a deep breath and held it as he slowly reached down and pulled the handle.

Nothing happened.

The door had been locked from within.

Genevieve let out her breath in huff, and for a moment allowed her body to sag against the hard rock. Daniel slowly climbed up to where she lay and sat down heavily, clutching his upper left arm, but keeping a wary eye on the area of the trapdoor.

Slowly pressing herself up to stand, Genevieve took in their surroundings in full for the first time since they had emerged from the tunnel.

They were on an island, in what she assumed was the middle of the East River, though they were so far north they might technically be in Long Island Sound. Even though the moon was bright, she couldn't see lights or land in any direction, and though intellectually she knew they could not possibly be that far from the mainland, she had to fight back the panicky feeling of being trapped.

Because, in actuality, they *were* trapped. The island was little more than a long, narrow pile of rocks with a few scraggly trees. Genevieve guessed it was no more than a quarter-mile long. While she couldn't quite make out the tip of each end of the island in the dark, she could clearly see the moon reflecting on water on all sides of them.

A shuffling noise and stifled groan drew her attention back to Daniel. He was attempting to remove his jacket.

"Stop—let me," Genevieve commanded. Her heart contracted when Daniel winced as she gingerly pulled the jacket off his left arm. Kneeling beside him, Genevieve carefully rolled up his sleeve, trying desperately not to hurt him.

She found herself incanting a silent prayer: *Please don't let it be serious, please don't let it be serious.*

The whole of Daniel's upper arm was covered with blood, so it was impossible to tell the severity of the wound. She had lost their lanterns in the tunnel after dousing them and running, but still had her satchel slung over her shoulder, and she pulled out a canteen of water. "I need to rinse this to see how bad it is," she said. He nodded wordlessly.

She felt Daniel stiffen slightly as she carefully poured water on his arm and had to blink back quick tears. The knowledge of his pain sent excruciating lances through her, surprising in their vehemence. Genevieve shoved aside her reactions as best she could; there would be time to examine them later.

Please don't let it be serious.

The water cleaned the area but caused fresh blood to surge, the sight constricting her heart again. Genevieve quickly tore off a length of her petticoat—luckily a light summer one, easy to rip. She found a clean section of the cloth and pressed it onto the wound.

Old tattoos, revealing his gang affiliation, decorated the band of flesh she cautiously cleaned. She had seen them before, once. When he had rolled up his shirtsleeves for a fight in a snowstorm, a storm that eventually morphed into the worst blizzard the city had ever seen. Genevieve had only glimpsed the tattoos then but now was able to study the strange markings more closely as she dabbed away blood. The inked Celtic dragons and crosses intermingled with the wound, which, once cleared of blood, appeared to be long but shallow.

"I think you've just been grazed," she said, unable to keep the relief from her voice.

Daniel twisted his neck in an attempt to examine his own arm. "That's what I thought too."

Genevieve tore off more petticoat and tied the length around Daniel's arm. She glanced worriedly toward the door. "Do you think they'll come back? Or do they intend to leave us stranded here?"

"I'm not sure," he said, wincing again as she tied the cloth. He examined her makeshift bandage. "Thank you."

Daniel stood and moved toward the trapdoor again. Keeping his weapon trained on it, he gave the handle another slight tug. Still locked.

"Whoever it is knows we're armed," he said slowly, gazing around the small island. "They know we could take them out as they try to emerge. They also must know this island, and that there's nowhere to hide. Maybe they're waiting for daylight, to come by boat."

Fear prickled Genevieve's middle. None of the possible scenarios for them seemed very hopeful.

"Do you know which way is shore?" she asked.

Daniel frowned but pointed in the direction of the trap door. "If I have my bearings correct, that way is the mainland. That way," he pointed his thumb over his shoulder, in the opposite direction, "should be Riker's Island. We're at a relatively narrow section of the river." He put his hands on his hips and gazed in the direction where he'd indicated the mainland lay.

"How narrow?" Genevieve asked, but her mind was already made up. She began undoing the tiny pearl-shaped buttons at the neck of her dress.

"Perhaps a half mile?" Daniel guessed. When he turned her way, she was wriggling the rest of her dress down her body, the night air cool and refreshing on her bare limbs. The moon perfectly illuminated his expression of shock, instantly followed by one of resolute denial. "Absolutely not."

Genevieve cocked her head at him. "I don't recall asking your permission." She untied the strings of her thin, ripped petticoat, and let it fall to the ground. Next she unlaced her shoes, then slipped off her stockings. It was exhilarating to be so undressed in the outdoors, to have her skin kissed with saltiness.

Daniel gaped at her, and Genevieve gave him a sweet smile in return. Her heart was pounding again, and not just from fear. She was dressed only in her chemise and bloomers, with a light corset above. She'd never been this undressed in front of a male to whom she was not related before—and even then not since childhood. Even her bathing costumes provided more coverage. Daniel seemed to catch himself and snapped his attention back to the unseen distant shore.

Genevieve swallowed hard.

Best to put that feeling aside for now. Right now, the only thing that mattered was getting to shore and to safety. With slightly trembling fingers, she unlaced her corset and dropped it on top of the petticoat. She eyed the pile of pale, lacy garments. They could stay.

"They'll come back," she said, retrieving her dress and tying it in a bundle around her waist. It was a light summer frock, obviously not one of her best as she'd worn it for skulking, but she would need something to wear once back on shore. It shouldn't weigh her down too much. "One way or another. They know this island and that tunnel, and we do not. We're sitting ducks out here, despite our weapons." Genevieve frowned at her shoes, then tied the laces around the bundle of dress at her waist.

"Our best chance at success is to swim for shore, if you really think it's only a half mile or so." She risked a look back at Daniel.

A frisson that had nothing to do with being in severe danger for her life, nor with being nearly naked on an island in the middle of the East River, coursed down her arms.

Daniel was nearly bare to the waist, wearing nothing on top save a thin, sleeveless white flannel undershirt. His arm tattoos stood starkly against his pale skin, and a light smattering of hair was visible on his chest above the curved neckline of his undergarment. He was beginning to undo the buttons of his trousers.

"Your arm," Genevieve protested. "You can't risk a swim. I shall go and get help." She gulped and averted her eyes just as his trousers fell.

"I can manage," floated Daniel's voice. "You said yourself it was only a graze. The salt water will help disinfect the wound."

"But we don't know how far it is, and if you tire . . . Really, I should be the one to go and bring reinforcements."

"Whom?" His voice was wry in the night air. "The police? And you know how far north we are—there's nothing here. You can't risk going back to the house for my carriage to drive back to town, and it's going to be a long walk until we can find a cab or a carriage to rent. By the time you get to town and get back, they'll have come back, and I'll be dead."

Genevieve bit her lip, undecided. Regardless, it was silly to keep facing the water and the moon, having this conversation over her shoulder. She wasn't fresh out of the schoolroom; she could speak directly to a man in his underthings, for heaven's sake.

Turning, she steeled herself. Daniel was wearing a pair of knee-length, white flannel drawers, not terribly unlike what she had on, only more fitted and with less lace. He was awkwardly folding his clothes and stuffing them into the sack he had been carrying for their explorations.

"Here, let me," Genevieve rushed over, her desire to save him from unnecessarily inflicting further injury to his arm winning out over her modesty. She took the clothes and began the task again, withdrawing their water canteens and a packet of sandwiches Daniel's cook had prepared.

"We should probably eat first, keep our strength up." She handed Daniel a sandwich and sat on the rocky ground, taking one for herself as well.

Daniel cast a worried glance in the direction of the trapdoor but acquiesced, accepting the sandwich. "I think they'll wait." He gestured with his sandwich toward the door. "They would have come out by now if they were planning to have a go at us right away." He chewed thoughtfully for a few moments, then swallowed. "I think reinforcements are coming."

Another shiver of fear, this one *not* related to the near-naked states of both herself and the handsome man to her left.

"Then we'd best eat quickly."

Five minutes eating, then another ten arguing over which items to carry and which to leave behind. Any additional food they left, knowing it would be ruined. The canteens, both half full, they kept. They kept the bare minimum of clothing they would need for the long and perhaps treacherous walk through the wilds of the Bronx until they found some means of conveyance. After a heated debate (Daniel for, Genevieve against), they left the shovel. They jettisoned as well a small pickaxe, extra clothing they had brought, and—after what appeared to be an agonized but brief internal debate—Daniel left one of his guns.

"It will be a while before it works again after getting wet, and I need to shed weight in this bag. But I do hate to leave it behind," he groused.

The rope they kept, by mutual and undiscussed agreement. Genevieve eyed the dark water and tried not to think too hard about the ways in which a rope could be useful.

All the while, the moon was rising. The continued passing of time made Genevieve increasingly jittery. Half of her mind was focused on the task of sorting their belongings, and the other half was solely focused on the trapdoor, fully expecting it to fly open, shots blasting, at any moment.

They finally seemed ready to take to the water. Daniel cast her an inquiring look, and she nodded. Together, they gingerly walked to the shoreline. Small, sharp rocks and pieces of shell jabbed the soles of Genevieve's tender feet, and her bare toes curled in protest at the first tickle of cold saltwater.

"Daniel?" Genevieve asked, once they were ankle deep. "We haven't yet discussed it, but what about . . . the demon?"

Even in the moonlight, she could make out his sharp expression. "Do you think it was a demon?"

"No," she said at once, "but I think it's what Marcus and Paul were calling a demon. And perhaps Nora, if that was her screaming upstairs at Boyle's."

Daniel nodded. "Yes, those are my thoughts. The so-called demon will have to wait until we get to shore, though. We'd best get on with it."

Genevieve bit her lip and waded farther into the water, drawing in a quick breath as the cold of it enveloped her belly and chest. It was still only June, and the heat of the summer hadn't warmed the water the way it might by August. And though perhaps on a hot day the lingering chill would feel refreshing, in the middle of the night there was no relief from the water's unrelenting iciness.

"Once we start moving, we'll warm up," Daniel promised, a visible shiver wracking his body.

Bouncing on her toes, Genevieve ventured deeper and deeper, until her feet were no longer brushing the river's sandy bottom. Swimming was more difficult than she'd anticipated, not only because of the heavy wad of clothing and shoes tied to her waist and the bag still slung on her shoulder, but also because the water was growing increasingly choppy the farther from the island they swam.

She swam harder than she ever had before, keeping Daniel's white, flashing arms and bobbing head to her left. At one point she glanced over her shoulder and could just make out a faint outline of the trees that marked the island they'd left, but what felt like minutes later, she looked again and they were gone. There was nothing but water in every direction, stretching endlessly into the dark.

Were they heading in the correct direction?

A sharp yelp escaped her as something brushed her legs. Daniel stopped, treading water.

"Are you well?" he asked.

Genevieve spit out a mouthful of foul-tasting water, enjoying for a moment not fighting the water, but allowing herself to be gently carried in it, rising and falling with the swells. "Probably just a fish."

"Can you keep going? We can't float like this for too long, or the current will take us past the house and farther toward the Sound. We need to be heading south, not north."

"How can you tell which way is north?"

A light splash sounded as Daniel raised a hand from the dark water to point up. "The stars. I know it's hard, but we can't risk getting swept in the wrong direction. Keep following me."

He sounded tired. Genevieve nodded and gestured for him to keep moving. She was getting tired too, her limbs starting to ache from their efforts.

Onward they swam, and still she followed Daniel. She had no idea how long they had been in the river, toes and fingers numb, when finally shapes began to emerge from the darkness of the water. Darker shapes, coalescing into a long, inky band.

"Is that—?" She gasped, unable to fully form the words. Was it land?

"Yes," came the raspy reply. Genevieve swam closer to Daniel, alarmed at his tone. It was impossible to make out his expression, but he kept swimming with a steady, even stroke. After what seemed an eternity, the shoreline not appearing to come any closer, Daniel's movements abruptly changed.

"You should be able to stand," he said. Now she could clearly hear how his voice was laced with unmistakable exhaustion, how his breath was coming in shuddering heaves. Gritty sand scraped her toes, then the soles of her feet, and together they fought against the current and their heavy bundles until they eventually emerged, water streaming down their limbs, onto a rocky shore.

Genevieve collapsed, gasping, and stretched out on the sand. She had no room for any thought except gratitude that she was no longer in the water, no longer forcing her arms and legs to fight against its inexorable pull. Next to her, Daniel did the same. Their wet undergarments clung to them, but she had no modesty left.

Once she was no longer panting, Genevieve shakily sat up, shoved off her shoulder bag, and pushed the heavy roll of wet fabric from her waist. She unwound the dress and untied her shoes, wringing out the heavy mass before laying the dress out, hoping it would dry at least a little.

Daniel hadn't moved. She crawled over the rough sand and leaned over him with worry, dripping. "Are you all right?" He was resting one hand on his heart and the other lay on the ground beside him, inert. His breath was coming in short, even huffs, and his eyes were closed.

Genevieve hurriedly wrested Daniel's canteen out from the bag still attached to his body. "Drink," she commanded, slipping a palm under his head to lift it and holding the bottle to his lips.

One eye cracked open a hair. "You would have made the most horrible nurse," he said. His voice sounded like sandpaper. "Terrible bedside manner."

"Then let's celebrate my choosing the correct profession. Drink."

Daniel took a dutiful sip, and then another. She placed his head back on the sand—more gently than he deserved, really—and unearthed her own canteen. The water felt fresh and cool in her mouth and slipping down her throat. After a moment, Daniel pushed himself up onto his elbows.

"Look," she directed him, pointing at the horizon.

The palest strip of gray was visible in the far distance, illuminating the place where sky met water. As they watched, Daniel slowly pressed himself to fully sitting, and took another glug of water. The strip of gray lightened, eventually turning a delicate blue. The stars on the horizon began to disappear, and Genevieve blinked as the first rays of bright sun lit the sky.

CHAPTER 19

Daniel was content to sit in silence, for now, and watch the sun slowly climb, the sky morphing from pale blue streaked with pink clouds to a deeper shade, though one still infused with the haziness unique to early morning. He had spent twenty minutes or so, early in the sun's ascent, studying the positions of the stars as they gently disappeared from view. He had been attempting to get his bearings, and now felt confident of which way they should begin walking once they were ready.

But they were still far from ready. The sun was doing a decent job of warming their skin, though he suspected Genevieve felt as sticky and salty as he did. He could feel his hair drying into near corkscrews, and smiled at the deep, unruly waves that had overtaken Genevieve's honey-colored mass. They both still sat in their underthings, not speaking, just companionably looking toward the horizon line, occasionally taking a sip of water. Genevieve poked at her dress every once in a while, testing its dryness.

"Where are we?" she asked. Her voice sounded hoarse, like she hadn't used it in weeks. "Do you know?"

Daniel nodded, though even the small gesture felt exhausting. "I believe so. Well, not specifically, but I have a general idea of our vicinity and an idea of which way to go."

"Do we need a . . . story? As to why we look like we do?" she asked. "Did our boat capsize?"

It was surprising to find himself smiling. "I don't think so. Once our clothes are back on, we'll look passable enough. And we have money to pay for cab fare."

"We just have to find one," Genevieve pointed out. She pushed herself to her feet and groaned slightly. "I want to sleep for days."

"As do I," Daniel agreed. He followed her lead and pressed himself up to stand as well. "But we do need to hurry. Rupert's arraignment is in a few hours."

Genevieve's hand flew to her mouth. "I had completely forgotten. Oh no. Can we get there in time?"

Daniel began to pull on his pants, which were incongruously both slightly damp and slightly stiff, an unpleasant combination, over his equally damp and salty underwear.

Everything itched, but there was nothing to be done for it. He tried to shrug on his shirt, but Genevieve stepped closer to help, taking the garment from him and gently easing it over his shoulders, and he didn't refuse.

In truth, the wound on his arm ached fiercely, but he could attend to it in time. Their priority now was to get to Rupert.

Genevieve pulled her dress over her head, wrinkling her nose in distaste at the feel of the fabric. "It's still somewhat wet."

"Everything will dry as we walk."

It was his turn to help Genevieve as she struggled with some of the small buttons at the back of her high neck. "Thank you," she said. "They're much easier to undo than to rebutton."

For the briefest of moments, Daniel's fingers stilled in their task. A wish, forceful and abrupt, blossomed in his mind. That Genevieve was saying those words to him in another context, in another place. Not on a deserted, rocky shore on the East River, not after they had been shot at, trapped on an island, and forced to swim for their lives in the dead of night. But somewhere clean and calm, with both of them flushed and sated and happy.

For the barest of moments, he allowed his hands to rest on her shoulders after he finished with the recalcitrant buttons. Her shoulders rose with a deep intake of breath, and then she, too, stilled. They stood like that, facing the sunrise, for a few shared breaths, before Daniel removed his hands and busied himself with gathering the remaining items they had scattered around the rocky ground, repacking his bag so they could begin their walk.

Genevieve remained motionless for another few moments. Daniel kept his attention on his task, but he could feel the weight of her brown eyes following his every motion. She drew in a breath as if to speak, but seemed to decide against it, instead sitting down and wriggling her bare feet into her damp boots.

"Ready?" Daniel asked once she'd stood. Genevieve twisted her heavy mass of hair up and secured it somehow in that mysterious way women had, then slung her bag over her shoulder and nodded.

"Can you manage that?" She gestured toward his bag. "Or shall I take it?"

"It's fine," he said. "Let's get started. It must be almost seven—we've only got a few hours to get downtown."

Daniel led Genevieve southeast, following the shoreline of the East River, sticking to the mostly rocky and sandy turf, the land still undeveloped. They trudged on, not talking much, until the coast began to curve north again, and the waterway they'd been keeping to their left narrowed considerably.

Genevieve stopped and pointed, hand shielding her eyes from the sun. "Is that Randall's Island?"

"It is. I was lucky my siblings and I weren't sent there, after our parents died." The island housed several institutions for the city's unwanted: an asylum for the mentally impaired, a hospital for children, an almshouse for the impoverished. A potter's field. Daniel felt a grimace cross his face. "Particularly me. The so-called House of Refuge there is for teenage boys, but in reality is little more than a workhouse. Many of the Irish boys I used to associate with wound up there."

"There were some reforms a few years ago, weren't there?" Genevieve squinted at the island.

"They stopped using children as city laborers, true. But the conditions are still abhorrent. The boys routinely revolt."

He did not have time, at this particular moment, to consider the specific twists and turns of fate that had prevented him from being one of the unfortunate souls trapped on that island, but he knew in his soul it had been a very close call. After his parents died, and his younger siblings were essentially kidnapped and sent somewhere—he still knew not where—on the orphan trains, he and his older sister had been alone. He had been savage in his grief, running absolutely wild with his fellow Bayard Tough gang members, engaging in all kinds of petty crimes. Sooner or later the authorities would have caught him, and he would have been another nameless teenager in the bowels of the dirty, massive building he couldn't see from here but that he knew lay just on the other side of the island.

Daniel turned his back on Randall's Island. *Another day,* he vowed internally. Another day, he would attempt to see some justice for the boys there.

He looked north. "We'll keep to the water," Daniel said, pointing. "This becomes the Harlem River, here, and if we stick to its shores, we should hit the New Harlem Bridge up ahead. We can walk across that into Manhattan."

Genevieve cast a worried look at the sky. "Do you think we'll make it to The Tombs in time?"

Anxiety over missing Rupert's arraignment had been gnawing at Daniel's insides during their entire walk. It had to be close to eight in the morning at this point. He bobbed his head in an indecisive gesture. "If we can find a cab quickly. And we should be able to find something as soon as we cross the bridge. Maybe even at the foot of the bridge on this side."

On they walked, trampling through grass, staying close to the water's edge. They were forced to forge two small creeks along the way, and once waved to a man and a woman setting into the river with a rowboat. More and more buildings populated the opposite shore, and sailboats and additional rowboats occasionally floated past them.

Genevieve's stomach growled loudly, breaking the peaceful silence. She cleared her throat loudly to cover the sound.

"What about the train, Daniel? Can't we pick up the 3rd Avenue Elevated somewhere nearby?"

Daniel stopped and thought. "I'm not sure where the closest stop is," he confessed. "I know we'll reach the Bridge right before where the Elevated crosses the river. See? There it is." The handsome, arched structure was not far off now. "We'll take whichever we come across first—train or cab."

Genevieve's stomach gurgled again in response, and Daniel hid a smile. He was ravenous himself, but his insides were less vocal about it.

Eventually they reached the foot of the Harlem River Bridge and were relieved to find a few businesses dotted there. Glancing up the avenue, Daniel could see more stretching deeper into this part of town, which was growing quite a lot.

"I don't see the El," Genevieve said, sounding disappointed. "We could ask someone."

"Let's do so, in that bakery over there." Daniel smiled again at Genevieve's reaction, enjoying watching her face light up as though it were Christmas morning.

The girl in the bakery was able to direct them to the Elevated, and they decided it would be quicker to get downtown via train rather than cab, and avoid any risks of getting caught in traffic. A clock mounted on the tower of a local bank building revealed it was now a few minutes after eight thirty, and the knot Daniel had been carrying in his chest began to loosen a hair; as long as there were no problems with the train, they should make it to The Tombs before ten.

Settling into his seat, Daniel watched as the city rushed by in a blur. Over the Harlem River and into Manhattan, down Lenox Avenue, the train sped past buildings and people and painted advertisements. He passed Genevieve a bottle of milk he'd purchased at the bakery and opened one for himself. The cool, sweet liquid tasted like heaven, and he tried not to guzzle it all at once.

Genevieve's face passed through alternating bands of sunlight and shadow as the train slowly wended its way downtown. Daniel was content to surreptitiously watch as she broke open a steaming bread roll from the bakery and inhaled its fragrant scent.

"Normally, I wouldn't eat on a train like this, but desperate times," she murmured to him, glancing around to make sure she was unobserved. The few other passengers in their car did not seem to be paying them any mind; they were too absorbed in their own worlds to pay much attention to the bedraggled man and woman having their breakfast.

Salt from the river combined with sweat from their walk had crystalized slightly on Genevieve's face, and wild tangles of hair were falling from her makeshift coiffure. Daniel's hand twitched, it was near impossible to resist the urge to tuck a particularly stray lock behind her ear, but even as he thought of doing so, she raised her hand and shoved the unruly piece back into place. The rhythm of the train was soporific, but he knew he wouldn't—couldn't—sleep. He had to see this through to the end, see Rupert out on bail, see Genevieve home safe.

Safe.

For the first time since the previous night, when they had ventured out of the tangle of woods and onto the lawn of the Garcia mansion, Daniel allowed his guard to drop. Not all the way. He wasn't sure he was even capable of such a thing. But enough, for now, to relax slightly in his seat, feel some of the tension in his shoulders release, and enjoy his own bread and milk, and the body warmth emanating from the dirty, beautiful woman on the seat next to him.

For now, it was enough.

★   ★   ★

Genevieve picked her skirt up slightly as they ran, breathless, up the front steps of The Tombs and dashed between the massive stone pillars.

Esmie was waiting by the front door, an expression of acute worry on her face, which quickly transformed into one of profound relief when she saw them.

"Thank goodness you're here. The arraignment is in five minutes." Esmie led them both down the corridor and toward the appropriate courtroom. "You both look awful," she said, looking them up and down. "What happened?"

"Later," Daniel said, thrusting his bag at Genevieve. She took it, then joined Esmie on a hard wooden bench where Amos was already waiting.

Esmie's father turned his heavy-lidded gaze on Genevieve. "Took you two long enough," he said in a mild voice. "I nearly called on your father to represent Rupert, Miss Stewart."

"He would have been happy to help," Genevieve replied, pressing a hand to her heart in an attempt to catch her breath. She wasn't sure where she had found the stores of energy to run. Tiredness seeped into her very bones; it took a great deal of effort not to lie down on the wooden length of the bench and give in to sleep.

The arraignment passed in a blur, but Genevieve managed to take in the important moments: Rupert pled not guilty, and bail was set. Amos lumbered out of the courtroom to pay the bail, and shortly, Rupert would be released.

"We have to get you home," Daniel said. They were standing by the front doors again, waiting for Rupert and Amos. Daniel was peering at her with a worried expression. "You look as though you're about to drop."

Genevieve *felt* as though she were about to drop. "I'll get a cab," she agreed.

"I don't want you going alone," Daniel said. Esmie looked at him sharply.

"There's nothing more to be done here," Esmie said, taking Genevieve's elbow and guiding her down the steps of The Tombs. "Father and I will take Rupert home, you take care of Genevieve. When you're both rested, send a note. I have news."

Genevieve perked up slightly. "About Oscar, the secret beau?"

Esmie looked pleased with herself. "The very one. I've found him. But neither of you look like you can accomplish anything else until you've both slept, and . . . um . . . bathed," she said apologetically.

Genevieve didn't blame her. She knew she needed more to eat, a bath, and a long rest, in precisely that order.

"I don't need an escort," she tried to protest as Daniel climbed into the cab with her.

"Genevieve, they know who we are," he said quietly. "Which means they know where you live. Where I live."

She was too tired to argue. And, in truth, she didn't want to. Genevieve was tired of being shot at, tired of being chased. She just wanted to sleep.

In the lulling motion of the carriage, she allowed herself the intimacy she had so wanted to take on the train, one that had danced in the corners of her mind ever since they had shared a bed at Kathleen's brothel. She leaned against Daniel's body, resting on his uninjured arm. That strong arm slipped around her, and she let her head get heavy on his shoulder. Peace made her limbs relax, and it was impossible to keep her eyes open, secure under the comforting weight of his embrace.

★ ★ ★

It was an ordinary flower shop. Or at least it appeared to be from the outside. Genevieve felt she might have even ordered from it at one point, but couldn't recall. It was a bit far uptown for her, and the Stewarts were loyal to a shop closer to them, a few blocks up Fifth Avenue from Washington Square. But even their favorite retailer didn't always have the blossoms her mother sometimes wanted, and they'd been known to shop elsewhere.

A wagon lumbered to a stop in front of the shop, and a man in a white jacket began carrying fragrant buckets of delphinium, freesia, and peonies around the corner, presumably toward a back door where bulk deliveries were deposited. Daniel jerked his head after the delivery man, and they followed him.

Peeking around the edge of the building, Genevieve felt a surge of triumph as she saw Oscar emerge from the rear of the building, inspect the flowers, and pay the deliveryman. Esmie's sleuthing had worked! They both ducked around the corner as the delivery man returned to his vehicle, giving them a curious glance as he passed. Genevieve felt a trifle ridiculous, flattened against the wall as if she were a child playing hide-and-seek, hoping not to be found, but she gave the man a polite nod.

As soon as he was out of sight, Genevieve risked a look around the corner again, but their quarry had retreated back into the building.

"Let's do it," said Daniel.

Genevieve took a deep, steadying breath. She arranged her expression into that of a society lady with one thing and one thing only on her mind: flowers. She was dressed the part too, in a delicate pink walking dress with slightly puffed lace sleeves that ended at the elbow, and a scalloped overskirt revealing matching lace underneath. An equally delicate straw hat with pink ribbons and pale green blossoms accentuated the ensemble, as did her light green kid gloves.

A bell attached to the door gave a pleasant tinkle as Genevieve entered the shop. Wide glass vases of flowers lined shelves along the walls, and a center table held an attractive display of roses. An older woman was deep in conversation with an equally aged man—perhaps he was the shop's owner. Oscar was nowhere in sight.

The older man in his white jacket caught Genevieve's eye over the other patron's shoulder and gave her a reassuring nod. "Someone will be with you in one moment, madam," he said. Genevieve gave a short nod back and turned her attention to a vase of yellow day lilies, studying them as though she were pondering a purchase.

She felt a presence behind her left shoulder. "Can I help you, madam? The lilies are quite lovely today."

Genevieve turned. Oscar's face paled at the sight of her, and his eyes instantly darted to the shop's entrance.

"Perhaps," Genevieve replied. She subtly moved her body to block the route to the door, gesturing toward the roses in the center table. They were a deep, luscious pink, the same color, she realized, as the room at Kathleen's she had shared with Daniel. "I've been asked to locate a specific bloom for someone," she said, keeping her eyes on the blossoms, "but I cannot seem to find it." She slid her own eyes back to Oscar.

The young man visibly swallowed. He, too, gestured toward the roses, picking up on her pantomime for his employer. "That's a shame," he said. "Did you check the most likely place?"

The older man slipped into the back room, and the customer with whom he had been working let out an aggrieved sigh. The older woman, dressed all in black, harrumphed and peered crossly at a small display of cornflowers.

"Oh, I did," Genevieve said, laying a careful finger on one of those vibrant petals. Its smooth surface was silky beneath her touch. "With my associate. We looked high and low, but that particular bloom was nowhere in sight. There were other . . . things, present, though. Not blooms, I'm afraid. Quite the opposite." Genevieve paused and searched her mind. What was an appropriate euphemism for the stacks and stacks of firearms they had seen? She couldn't think of anything. "There were many, many of them," she settled for, giving Oscar a significant look.

He froze for the briefest of moments, then nodded to indicate he understood, and swallowed again. "Those other items belong to someone else."

"I understand." Genevieve casually turned toward a bright selection of Gerbera daisies, forcing Oscar to follow. "I do think lilies are bit too funereal for what I have in mind. These are far more cheerful. However, my associate and I would still like to find the bloom we were asked to seek. Perhaps more information about these other items could help."

A look of utter terror washed over the young man's face. "I have no information about those," he said in a low voice. The older man came out from the back room with a bundle of some flower Genevieve couldn't identify in his arms, and the woman in black sighed again, this time in satisfaction. "I think the person in question has told you all they know about where to find the right flower," Oscar continued.

Genevieve tipped her head to one side and met Oscar's eyes directly with her own. "I don't think so."

The bell above the door tinkled again, and a nervous-looking man entered, glancing around the shop in dismay. The woman in black bustled past Genevieve to the door, a cone of paper containing some bright yellow blossoms in her arms. The older man moved to help the young one, speaking in gentle tones.

"If you will excuse me, madam, I will check in back to see if we have more of what you seek." Oscar's voice was overly loud and, to Genevieve's ear, jittery. He scurried toward the back room, holding himself stiffly.

Genevieve instantly left the shop, bell tinkling behind her, and rushed around the corner. Sure enough, she found Oscar in the alley, standing still as a statue and staring at Daniel with wide eyes.

There was nobody else in the alley, as only deliveries came this way, and if one were to casually pass by, the scene might resemble two men engaged in what was perhaps a tense conversation. One had to look quite hard to see the bright morning sunlight glinting off the barrel of Daniel's gun, which was pointed straight at the other man's heart.

CHAPTER 20

Daniel was not happy about holding a firearm on Oscar, but he couldn't risk the young man running away. His arm was still healing, and he didn't relish the idea of tackling Oscar on the street should he try to flee.

So the revolver it was.

Oscar's jaw trembled. Daniel didn't blame him. He doubted the young florist had had a gun aimed in his direction in the past. It was an unnerving experience.

"You weren't fully honest with us, Oscar," he said in a quiet voice as Genevieve approached. "Tell us everything you know."

The young man's eyes fearfully darted left and right, as though he were assessing his chances of escaping via either end of the alley.

"Don't even think about it," Genevieve said. She had pulled her own gun from her reticule. Oscar's mouth dropped open. He also had likely never seen a woman hold a firearm before.

"We don't want to hurt you, Oscar. But we do want to find Nora and bring her home safely, the same as you do.

We can't do that if we don't have all the facts." The seconds ticked by as indecision danced over Oscar's face.

Daniel pulled the gold ring from his pocket and held it close to the other man's face. "Does this look familiar?"

Desolation and grief knotted the young man's visage. He grabbed at the ring with shaking hands, dropping it in his haste and clawing at the pavement until it was safe in his clutch again.

"Where . . .?" Oscar gasped.

"Where you sent us," Genevieve said. "The dungeons."

He looked at them with wild eyes. "So she was there." Oscar slumped, burying his handsome face in his hands. "May I sit?"

Daniel exchanged a look with Genevieve. She shrugged slightly.

"Yes," Daniel said, keeping his pistol trained on the other man as a precaution.

"You wanted us to find those guns," Genevieve continued. "Why? Where were they meant to lead us?"

Oscar sat on the one step that led from the shop's back door. "I gave this to her, you know. She said she couldn't wear it because we were a secret. *I* was a secret. But she accepted it. We were going to be married." His voice was little more than a broken whisper as he ran his finger repeatedly around the circle of gold in his palm. "She said she didn't need a diamond. This was all I could afford."

It was hard not to feel for the boy, but Daniel also knew they didn't have time for Oscar to go to pieces, not if they were going to find his fiancée. "The guns, Oscar," he gently prodded.

"I only saw the guns the one time, when I went to the mansion with Nora."

"Nora and . . .?" Daniel asked. He wanted to hear Oscar say it.

"And Paul Riley. And Marcus Dalrymple."

Daniel waited.

"And?" he finally prompted.

Oscar sighed, deeply and unhappily. "And several other men were there. The ones in charge . . . one was called Boyle. The other they called Meade." He looked up at them, the misery clearly written on his face. "And I've just signed my own death warrant."

Daniel exchanged a worried look with Genevieve. "Nobody has to know what you've told us," she said in a gentle tone.

"They'll find out," Oscar said. His tone was flat and hopeless. "They always do. I think it's the demon that tells them, somehow. Don't you?" The look he gave them was almost child-like in its wonder.

"They won't find out because we won't tell them," Daniel said firmly, leaving aside the matter of demons for now. "What else?"

Oscar shrugged, a gesture of despair. "I was the odd man out. The other three—Nora, Paul, and Marcus—they knew these men. They'd been to that place before. Paul and Marcus, they were helping organize the guns. Nora took me, said she wanted to get me involved, that it was important, but when I saw those piles and those men . . . I knew it wasn't anything I wanted any part of. I tried to get Nora to leave with me, but she just laughed. Said I was being a coward." A flash of defiance crossed his face. "I'm no coward. But I'm not stupid. My father makes a good living with this shop, and I will too. I don't need any part of whatever is going on with those guns. But Nora . . . she said I had to agree, now that I had seen. I took her arm and tried to get her to leave, but two of the men, they grabbed me and dragged me out. I was screaming for Nora, and I could see her. Her mouth, wide open. She was holding Riley's arm and looked like she might faint. And then one of them hit me on the head, I guess. Because I don't remember anything else, and I woke up here." Oscar wearily gestured around the alley. "With a giant lump on my skull, and Nora nowhere to be found."

Daniel looked at Genevieve again, troubled, and found her expression matched his. Surely she was thinking what he was: *Why had Boyle and Meade let Oscar live after what he had seen?*

"How did someone like Nora come to be involved in gunrunning? And the other boys, Marcus and Paul? Do you have any idea?" Daniel asked.

Oscar blinked at him. "They were all childhood friends, you know. That's what she told me. And that her father wished she and Riley would marry, but she didn't want him. She wanted *me*."

"The guns, Oscar," Genevieve prodded.

"It was Riley," he said, his voice miserable. "That's all I know. And now he's dead. Can't you find her? She's nowhere. I was afraid if I went to her father, he'd tell the police, and I'm afraid if I go to the police, Nora will get killed. If she's not dead already." Oscar looked at them helplessly. "I can't eat. I can't sleep. All I do is worry about where she is, *how* she is." He closed his eyes against the bright morning sun and dropped his head back into his hands. "You can shoot me if you like, but save her. Find Nora."

★ ★ ★

A shadow fell over Genevieve's desk. It was lunchtime, and she had just been gathering a few things, about to step out of the building. Her mind was so completely on the vexing problem of what to do next about the guns in the Garcia mansion, and how to help Nora Westwood, that she nearly jumped out of her skin at the sudden shift in light.

"Genevieve." Arthur Horace was standing over her with a stern expression.

"Mr. Horace." Genevieve was surprised to her see her editor at her desk. Usually when he wanted to speak with her, he called her into his office. "Is something amiss?"

"There is. Why are you not in Newport yet?" Arthur's thick gray eyebrows danced on his forehead in consternation.

Genevieve was truly baffled. They had already discussed that she wouldn't be heading to Newport until later in the season. "Don't you recall, Mr. Horace? I'm not going until my brother returns from Egypt. Then my family will open our cottage."

Arthur set his mouth and shook his head. "That won't work any longer, I'm afraid. You're missing some crucial events by not being there. Surely you can go and stay with a friend, or you can go ahead of your family and open your house early. Our society pages aren't *the* most vital aspect of our paper, I know, but they are *an* aspect that many expect, and the stories have been sorely lacking lately."

Heat rose in Genevieve's face. It was never pleasant to be dressed down at work, but it was particularly unlike Arthur to do it in the open space where most of the staff had their desks. As it was lunchtime, the large, high-ceilinged room wasn't as crowded as it could be, but she still noticed a few pairs of eyes sliding their way, and saw a smirk or two.

Her editor caught the amused glance one of Genevieve's male colleagues was giving them, and narrowed his eyes. The reporter, a youngish man called Harry who was new to the paper, hastily turned his attention back to his typewriter. Arthur pulled a wooden chair over from a nearby empty desk and sat heavily. He looked at her with expectation.

Genevieve hesitated, unsure of what to say. She had been so preoccupied lately, she knew she was not doing her job well. Frankly, she had hoped the lull in social activity as the season switched for the summer would afford her some leeway at work, but apparently she had misjudged.

"The *Times* is already running regular reports on the happenings in Newport, as is the *World*," Arthur continued. "We need to stay competitive. I know this isn't your first choice of a job, but I am happy to send you back to the ladies' home column if you prefer." Her editor's tone was genial enough, but Genevieve knew a warning when she heard one. The message was clear: get serious, or get demoted. Her insides tightened; there was no way she could go back to writing about soap flakes.

"Are you sure you're not involving yourself in other matters, Genevieve?" he asked. "Say, having to do with your friend Rupert Milton's recent arrest?" Arthur's eyebrows rose, and while he looked at her with deceptively mild curiosity, Genevieve wasn't fooled. Her editor was sharp as a tack and missed nothing. She swallowed but didn't respond.

Arthur nodded. "I know these things take time to wrap up." He didn't specify which "things" he meant. "You have a week, and then I need you in Newport. You have to be there for the Fourth of July."

Genevieve knew that was as good an offer as she would get. She had worked long and hard for her career, and even if the society column wasn't the kind of investigative reporting she really wanted to do, it was better than trying to conjure up ways to use baking powder.

"I'll make it work," she promised.

"Good," Arthur replied. "And I'd like to see an anticipatory piece on Edith Chapman's Fourth of July costume ball for later this week. You know as well as I do that it's the official start of the Newport season. Really, Genevieve, these are the kinds of things you should be telling me, not the other way around." His gaze remained stern behind his glasses.

The heat returned to her face, and Genevieve nodded meekly. "I apologize. Yes, of course. I'll do better."

"Make it colorful," Arthur instructed. "Perhaps a history of the event. You should have some firsthand knowledge of the party, do you not?"

"I do usually attend, yes." Prior to becoming the society columnist at the *Globe*, Genevieve hadn't participated as much in the rituals around the social seasons of New York's elite, particularly after having been jilted by her former fiancé at the age of twenty. But it was true—she did typically attend the Chapmans' summer fête. Indeed, it was one of her favorite parties of the year: the costumes not as fussy or elaborate as the winter fancy dress balls, consisting often just of extra flowers in one's hair, and it was held outdoors on a grand lawn overlooking the ocean.

"That's settled, then." Arthur's expression softened. "Perhaps best to leave the other matter aside. The earl has plenty of allies to help him fend off whatever may come his way. And if there are other . . . distractions in your life, perhaps it is time to get those straightened out too."

Arthur didn't wait for an answer this time, but tapped her desk twice with his fingers before weaving between the desks back to his own office, summoning one of his junior editors on the way. Genevieve stared blankly at her desk's surface for a moment, gathering her thoughts.

Her editor was surely referring to the rumor of her and Daniel having spent the night in a brothel, and she was unsurprised word of it had reached him. Arthur had his fingers in every pot in the city, it seemed, and somehow knew about news as it was happening. Despite her outward bravado around the incident, she had been relieved the gossip hadn't seemed to circulate more, particularly to her parents. She supposed that since Longstreet had gone ahead and arrested Rupert, he hadn't felt the need to threaten them with further exposure.

Genevieve thrummed her fingers on her desk. She wasn't totally convinced by her own logic but didn't have the mental energy to pick at the possible motives of Detective Longstreet at present, not when she now only had a week left before she had to leave town.

Not when she and Daniel were still undecided about which next step to take in finding Nora Westwood.

After their encounter with Oscar, they had spent the day arguing about what to do next. Genevieve still wondered if the police were the best bet at this point, which Daniel remained firmly against. He maintained that a police raid at Boyle's, if indeed Nora were still alive and being kept there, would only endanger the girl more.

What they needed to do, Daniel argued, was figure out to whom Boyle and Meade were selling these weapons, and why Marcus and Paul had been killed, when, according to Oscar, the young men had been helping the gangsters. Once they had those answers, they should know what happened to Nora, know why the young men had been poisoned, and then they could give the information to Longstreet and exonerate Rupert.

Daniel reported he was having some of his associates ask around, see what they could ferret out. Genevieve knew this meant Daniel's former gang associates. Or current? It was hard to say, and on that aspect of his life she didn't press much.

The memory of the black ink markings encircling Daniel's upper arms flashed in her mind.

Genevieve sighed, forcibly pushing aside the thought of Daniel's bare arms. She had also suggested they confront Meade himself, another idea Daniel had flatly rejected.

"Absolutely not," Daniel had said. "It is far too dangerous, even in public, even in daylight. Let me see what else my associates and I can discover."

And so she waited, which was completely, utterly, and infuriatingly galling. Her brain itched for action, that they *do* something. She took a deep breath and reminded herself again that for the moment there was nothing to do.

Her stomach grumbled. Genevieve ignored it. Lunch would have to wait now that she needed to conduct some research about the Chapmans' party. Grumbling herself, Genevieve made her way to the paper's archives, to search through the files of her predecessor.

An hour later, she had combed through the past ten years' worth of articles written about the fête and was reasonably satisfied she had enough information to write a compelling piece about the different themes the Chapmans had chosen, the flowers selected, and the various attendees. She wanted to look at one more year, 1878, and then she would allow herself to break for lunch. Surely a decade's history was plenty.

Genevieve skimmed Jackson Waglie's article on the 1878 Chapman party, taking quick notes about who was in attendance, what the weather was like (unseasonably cool that year), and the theme (tropical islands), when a passage leapt from the page.

The unfortunate confluence of this week's inopportune cold snap with Mrs. Chapman's chosen tropical motif did not deter guests from gamely braving the cool ocean breezes in their island attire. Both Mr. Pablo Garcia, a native of those realms, and New York's own Mr. Frank Westwood, came outfitted as Robinson Crusoe. The two gentlemen, who recently partnered in a shipping venture to Garcia's native Cuba, shared a laugh about which was more suitably ragged.

Her breath caught in her throat and her mind raced. How could they have been so blind? She had wondered about the construction of the underground chambers and tunnel by the house's builder, Frederick Cummings, but failed to wonder what the house's next owner, Pablo Garcia, might have done with them. And if Garcia and Westwood had been in business together, right before Garcia abruptly relocated back to Cuba . . .

Westwood knew more than he was saying—she was sure of it.

Genevieve quickly shuffled the papers back into their respective files. All thoughts of lunch had flown from her mind. She had to get to Daniel, and quickly.

Hurrying through the newsroom, Genevieve grabbed her belongs from her desk and shoved them, along with her notes, into a leather satchel. Should she call Daniel first, let him know she was coming? It seemed too risky. Most of the paper's employees had returned from lunch, and the newsroom was crowded again. Besides, someone else was using the office's one telephone. Better to dash to his house, where he kept his office, and hope he was there, or figure out where to find him. She was rushing toward the elevator, her mind leaping to and fro between various possibilities of what Garcia and Westwood's association could mean, when a sight quite literally stopped her in her tracks.

The clamor of the newsroom didn't halt. Secretaries still nosily banged away on typewriters; reporters still rushed to various editors' desks; and journalists still popped up and down from their desks as they hurried to confirm a detail or complete an assignment. But Genevieve noticed none of this. Her entire focus had distilled to one item as a wave of shock rushed to her head and her heart began to race.

On her colleague Luther Franklin's desk lay a photograph. It was undoubtedly from the police, for it showed a grisly crime scene.

Lying on the ground was a man's twisted body. The form lay in a pool of dark liquid that was unmistakably blood, and there was so very much of it. But it was the man's face that had arrested Genevieve in her tracks, that caused her shock to slowly turn to fear.

Oscar was dead. The face that had been so perfect in life was distorted, a grimace of fear and horror permanently etched on his features. More of the dark liquid matted his pale curls, stained his graceful hands.

The image flipped over. She blinked at the back of the piece of paper.

"Genevieve, don't look at that." Luther frowned at the upside-down photograph on his desk, then at her. "I shouldn't have left it there—I'm sorry."

"When did that happen?" she asked, trying and failing to keep a tremor from her voice. "And where?"

Luther looked at her with concern. "Last night," he said gently. "I was at the scene first thing this morning. Dagmar sent this over around lunchtime." Dagmar was a police photographer who sometimes shared images with the press.

A shudder passed through Genevieve. *Last night*. She and Daniel had questioned Oscar just yesterday morning.

He had predicted his own death. Because he had talked to them. And it had come true.

"Where? Where did it happen?" Her lips felt numb. Genevieve was surprised she could form words.

Luther's brow furrowed. "The Gas House District," he said. "Seems a new gang is emerging over that way. This poor fellow must have gotten caught up in something. Name of Oscar Becker, a flower seller. Oh, Genevieve," Luther said, his tone changing to alarm as she sat down with a heavy *thunk* in his desk chair. "Did you know him? Go to his father's shop?"

Genevieve couldn't keep her hands from trembling. *How had they known?* How had they known so fast that Oscar had talked to her and Daniel?

"Yes," she managed to say. "Yes, I knew him."

Luther appeared stricken. "Ah, dang. I'm sorry. I can't believe I left this photograph on my desk. Can I get you anything? Some water?" He hovered over her anxiously, his hands floating above her shoulders, though he did not quite dare to rest them there.

The sound of her own blood pounding in her ears was thunderous. Genevieve held up a hand. "No, nothing. I'll be fine," she lied.

"Genevieve," Luther said, sounding helpless. He looked around for somewhere to sit, as Genevieve was in his chair, and settled for perching on the edge of his own desk. Luther leaned in and kept his voice quiet.

"Genevieve," he said again, and the sadness in his voice was startling, "I need to apologize."

"You have. It's not your fault—there are always crime scene photographs around here. You had no way of knowing that young man was my . . . florist," she said. Talking was slightly more manageable. Oh god, she needed to get to Daniel.

"Not about that, though I am sorry. Look, I heard McCaffrey's friend the earl was arrested. I know he's your friend too. And I know it was for Marcus Dalrymple's death," Genevieve blinked at him, her mind still processing the murder of Oscar Becker but now trying to comprehend what Luther was saying. "But I don't think the earl—Rupert—killed anyone. From what I hear, Longstreet has it in for Rupert. It's how he operates—decides someone is guilty and doesn't ask too many questions after that, but just goes after them. I think McCaffrey knows that too." Luther admitted this last in a grudging tone.

"There are some odd connections between Marcus Dalrymple and Paul Riley's deaths," Luther continued. He stared at Genevieve for a moment, seeming to want some sort of confirmation to what he was saying. She nodded, still not trusting herself to speak much. "Was what you said, about being in that . . . place, with McCaffrey, about trying to protect someone innocent—does that have something to do with all this? With these odd deaths?"

Genevieve nodded again. She wasn't prepared to say, even nonverbally, anything further.

Luther blew out a long breath. He looked at her with such tenderness it made Genevieve's heart contract with a pang. She thought, not for the first time, about how her life would be different if she loved Luther back. If she could be content with his patient devotion, his normally endless good cheer.

But she wasn't in love with him and never would be. Over the years, Luther had confided how much he wanted a wife, someone to dote on, someone to be waiting at home for him after a day of chasing dead bodies. She could never be content with the type of staid, quiet life he desired.

"Whatever you're doing, I sure hope you're being careful, toots." Luther's voice was full of regret but also of resignation. As if he, too, had visualized their life together and also found it lacking.

Careful. The word almost made her laugh, a viciously inappropriate gallows humor. How could she tell him? How could she tell Luther that she was deathly afraid, terrified nowhere was safe?

That she'd seen something she wasn't supposed to see. That three people, at least, who had also seen it were now dead.

And she strongly suspected she and Daniel were next.

CHAPTER 21

The head butler at the Union League Club was normally the very picture of composure, remaining unruffled in the most extreme of circumstances. In fact, Daniel had seen Nichols stay as calm as undisturbed water in the face of incidents such as when two elderly members began raining blows on each other's heads, one with a finely polished mahogany walking stick, over a dispute about the proper way to prepare a gin cocktail; and on the memorable occasion when a rogue squirrel, which had somehow made its way through an open window, was discovered calmly perched on the edge of a cut crystal bowl of nuts, munching happily, and had eluded capture for days.

But, Daniel supposed, there was a first time for everything, and his actions today seemed to have broken the facade of Nichols's impenetrable veneer.

"Mr. McCaffrey!" The butler chased after them as they marched down the main hall. "I must ask that you stop at once, Mr. McCaffrey. Stop and leave with your guest this instant or you risk your membership." Nichols's tone was becoming more and more frantic. Daniel glanced over his shoulder and saw the normally placid butler red in the face, a lock of gray hair falling over his damp brow.

Daniel hadn't expected to retain his status as a member of the Club after the action he was undertaking, but had already decided he didn't care. Once Genevieve had revealed to him what she had read in the eleven-year-old article about a Newport summer party, several pieces of the vexing puzzle they had been chasing for weeks neatly fell into place.

Neatly and infuriatingly.

They had been lied to.

That fact was apparent immediately. What he wasn't quite sure of yet, but was determined to find out, was just how deep the lies went. He already had Billy and Paddy, who were still active Bayard Toughs, on the case of figuring out to whom Boyle and Meade could be selling guns. It had been hard for them to get information, as the Toughs were rivals with Meade's Oyster Knife gang, but eventually they found someone willing to talk. Daniel didn't ask how.

The answer, however, seemed so unbelievable he wasn't sure he could credit their source.

"Cuban revolutionaries, Danny." Even Paddy had looked doubtful as he relayed the information. Billy, who had been slouching against a wall in Daniel's library, shrugged.

"That's what the man said," Billy confirmed.

"Since when does Tommy Meade care about political causes? Outside of New York, of course," Daniel had wondered aloud.

Paddy and Billy accepted drinks from Daniel's secretary Asher, Billy knocking back the excellent Scottish whiskey in one giant gulp and looking hopefully toward Asher for another.

It hadn't added up at the time. Tommy Meade and John Boyle were hard-boiled New York gangsters. Even though Tommy had made a bid for respectability with his mayoral campaign the previous year, the two were thoroughly local operators. There was plenty to occupy them in this town, plenty of people here to sell firearms to.

But Daniel remembered the gleaming, giant piles in the mansion's basement. It was way more firearms than any one local gang needed.

Soon after Paddy and Billy had left, Billy sulking that after his second drink he hadn't been offered a third, Genevieve had arrived, breathless.

And it all clicked.

Genevieve in tow, Daniel had stormed uptown to Westwood's house. He knew his fury was bordering on dangerous but couldn't seem to keep himself in check. His mind kept replaying the way shots had whizzed by Genevieve's head in the underground tunnel, how she had gasped as she swam for her life in the murky waters of the East River. When the stammering butler who answered the door revealed that Mr. Westwood was at his club, Daniel had nearly run the twenty or so blocks down Fifth Avenue to West 39th Street.

He would find Westwood, and he would have answers. For himself and for Genevieve.

Even if that meant bringing Genevieve to the Union League Club, where women were strictly forbidden.

"Mr. McCaffrey!" It sounded as though Nichols was nearly out of breath. Various members popped their heads out of reading rooms and card rooms. One bearded man's jaw dropped so abruptly his pipe fell out of his mouth and singed the patterned burgundy rug at his feet.

"Jensen, attend to that," snapped Nichols, pointing one of the underbutlers, who had begun following his boss, to the smoldering patch of carpet. "If you do not stop, I shall call the authorities and have you forcibly removed," the butler threatened.

Daniel didn't care. He was singularly focused on finding Westwood, and he knew just where to look. He ran up the wide, central flight of stairs, taking them two at a time, not glancing back again. He could hear Genevieve's breath, though, and knew she was keeping pace just fine.

She always did.

The maps room was a large, square space, decorated in the same way as the rest of the Club, with dark wood-paneled walls and elaborate carvings on the ceiling beams, and armchairs covered in dark blue, red, or tobacco-colored leather. The entire building reeked of traditional masculinity, and perhaps no specific place more so than the maps room. Framed charts and maps from the fifteenth century to the present decorated the walls, and the bookshelves were lined with atlases and travel guides. Rolled maps were also stacked within cases. The room itself was a monument to Western culture's colonial dominance over the world.

Daniel had never liked it much, as he was inherently suspicious of overt self-aggrandizement.

It was Frank Westwood's favorite spot in the Club.

Sure enough, as Daniel burst into the maps room, he found Frank, sitting in one of the deep club chairs. A drink that looked untouched sat on a side table, as did a neatly folded newspaper. His skin looked ashen, and there were deep purple bags under his eyes.

At the sight of Daniel and Genevieve, Frank rose. Nichols rushed into the room after them, panting.

"Please, Nichols, allow Miss Stewart to stay. Just for an hour. As a special favor to me." Perhaps it was Frank's haggard appearance, or perhaps because now two esteemed members were asking to allow Genevieve's presence, but for whatever reason, Nichols thinned his lips and relented.

"One hour. And she must leave by the back door. And you, Mr. McCaffrey, will be hearing from the board." The butler hesitated, his deeply ingrained sense of duty impossible to ignore. "What may I get you?" he asked politely. "Mr. McCaffrey, Miss?"

Daniel shook his head. They needed privacy for this discussion, and there was a pitcher of water already on a sideboard in the room. "If you could please make sure we are undisturbed, Nichols, that would be all. And I do apologize for breaking protocol. I would not have done so were the situation not of the utmost urgency."

Nichols's gaze lingered on Genevieve for the barest of moments, studying the first woman to ever enter the Union League Club through the front door rather than the servant's entrance. But once again, his years of training and innate manners conquered his curiosity, and he bowed his head once before departing.

They were alone with Frank. Daniel's breath had returned to its normal pace, though his heart was still racing and his blood was still up.

Frank picked up his drink and took a sip, then put it down, waiting. He wore the heavy, braced look of someone who fully expected to receive the imminent blow of bad news.

"You weren't honest with us," Daniel began in a low voice, one that sounded ominous even to his own ears. "You lied and endangered both me and Miss Stewart."

For a full minute, Frank said nothing. Daniel waited, letting the uncomfortable silence stretch. He wasn't going to lead Westwood any further, he wanted to hear what the man had to say.

It was Frank who finally broke the quiet. "Have you news of my daughter?" His voice was low also, but not with fury. It was weighted, instead, with sadness, with resignation.

"Nothing definitive. We may know where she is, or at least where she was." Genevieve's voice was gentle, far gentler than Daniel thought Frank deserved. "But we haven't been able to get into this place to find her. We are working on it."

Frank Westwood sagged in place for a moment. "I need to sit," he murmured, reoccupying the chair he had been in when they arrived. Daniel had noticed that its leather seemed to bear the imprint of Frank's body; he guessed the man had been spending a lot of time in this particular chair lately.

A heavy sigh wrenched itself from Frank's lips, and he steepled his fingers for a minute, resting his forehead on their tips.

"You're right," Frank said when he finally raised his head. "I was not truthful with you. I thought if I told you the truth, you would contact the authorities. And perhaps you should have. Perhaps I should have, right at the start."

"The start of what?" Daniel ground out. He had an idea but again wanted to hear it from Frank.

The older man swallowed visibly. "Nora didn't run away. At least, that's not what I have been led to believe. She was kidnapped."

"And you're being blackmailed," Genevieve guessed, her voice still soft. "Someone is demanding use of your fleet of ships to sail their arms to Cuba, or she dies."

Frank blinked wearily. "Yes. I unwittingly became involved in such a scheme in the late 1870s, with a man named Pablo Garcia. I already knew him slightly through social circles—he was quite wealthy, you know, and had ingratiated himself to a few important families and was being invited to select events. He told me he was entering into a partnership with a producer of condensed milk, a dairy farm upstate, to export to his homeland of Cuba. I regularly send ships to and from my plantations in Jamaica, and Cuba would be a fairly easy stop, particularly given the generous profits I was to receive. It all appeared on the up and up—there were contracts and deeds; I even toured the dairy farm. We started the venture, made maybe two trips successfully. But then"—Frank paused and rubbed a hand over his face, remembering—"I surprised the crew of a ship that was about to depart—I like to do impromptu visits, make sure everything is in order. I was a Navy man in my youth—did you know that?"

Daniel shook his head but kept quiet.

"And . . . I saw them. Caught Garcia's men red-handed. Using my ships to illegally transport weapons, right there among the condensed milk and some other goods." Frank shook his head helplessly. "Garcia was a revolutionary. A leader in the Cuban fight for independence. He hated me, hated everything I, and my business, stood for. Which is nonsense, of course. None of my plantations are even on Cuba."

Genevieve's eyes flicked to Daniel's, but he gave his head a tiny shake. *Let him talk.* A man like Frank Westwood would not understand why a country like Cuba, colonized and profited upon by Europeans and their descendants, would crave independence.

Frank's face grew hard. "I threatened to expose him, go straight to the federal government if I must, if he didn't leave the country at once."

"Why didn't you?" Daniel asked. He took a cue from Genevieve and kept his voice quieter this time.

A spasm of discomfort briefly crossed the older man's visage. "Because my ships had already been involved. Twice. Like it or not, I was complicit as well. But I have enough clout in this town that I was able to get my point across. Garcia left—took his family and hightailed it back to Cuba—and it was unnecessary to contact the authorities."

Daniel could well imagine the threats and intimidation that must have rained down on Pablo Garcia from all corners of the Astor 400 as their ranks closed to protect one of their own. And not just against Garcia, but surely against the man's wife and children as well.

"The fight for independence ended two years later, and I will admit I breathed a sigh of relief," Frank continued. "Not only because the island was still safely in Spain's hands, but I thought surely, after—what, twelve years of fighting?—surely the revolutionaries had learned that Spain is a mighty power, too mighty to overthrow. I thought the matter was done. But apparently I was wrong. Garcia must still be holding a grudge, and he's teamed up with somebody here in an attempt to coerce me to transport these weapons."

"Why didn't you tell us the truth?" Genevieve asked. "Did you think we wouldn't help you?"

Frank shrugged uncomfortably. "Again, I was afraid of my own exposure, afraid you would insist on the police. But I didn't lie about everything. He's involved, you know—Nora's suitor, whoever he is. He must be. All I told you on that front was true: we did argue, I was planning on sending Nora away with her aunt, and at first I had thought she'd run away. Then I received the letter."

"And then you contacted us," Daniel confirmed.

"Yes."

"And sent us chasing dangerous gunrunners," Daniel continued, "with absolutely no warning." His tone caused Frank to shrink in his chair a bit.

"I didn't think—" Frank tried to interject, but Daniel's anger at this man, at his stupidity and selfishness and disregard for the well-being of anyone save himself, bubbled over and exploded.

"No, you didn't think. You endangered Miss Stewart, myself, and your own daughter to protect your sorry skin. Nora's young man is dead," he bit out. Frank flinched. "We were almost killed as well. I have no guarantee that your daughter is alive."

The older man tried for a moment of bluster, then wilted. He appeared to have aged twenty years since their first meeting with him on that fine June morning three weeks prior. "Can you still find her?" he asked in a voice laced with defeat.

Daniel exchanged another look with Genevieve. She answered for them. "We can try."

"If it were just you, I'd let you twist in the wind," Daniel said flatly. "But Nora is innocent in all this. It seems Riley talked her into it somehow." He had his own theories about how Tommy Meade and John Boyle might have enticed some young society men into helping with illegal arms sales, but he wasn't willing to share those ideas with Frank Westwood. "Convinced her and Marcus Dalrymple to help support the gunrunners. You failed to mention Marcus was Nora's childhood friend."

"Why would I? What has that boy got to do with this?" Frank looked confused.

"I'm sure you have heard that he has died as well," Genevieve said. "And they were all seen together at the old Garcia mansion."

"The one way up north?"

"Yes. There are underground tunnels that lead to an island in the river where ships can pick up goods," Genevieve confirmed. "We think the original owner constructed them for illegal exports during the Civil War, and somehow Garcia found out about their existence, and that is why he bought the house."

"But Garcia didn't have the ships to transport the guns, so that's where you came in," Daniel continued. "The house is rumored to be haunted, and young people have been going there on dares for some time," Daniel said. He was still fuming but kept his tone even. "We don't know how Riley crossed paths with the gunrunners, but he became involved, and involved Nora as well."

"That wild girl." Frank shifted in his seat and stared out the window moodily for a moment. "I should have sent her to live with her aunt years ago. Away from New York. As soon as her mother died."

"Can you show us the letter demanding your compliance?" Genevieve asked.

"I burned it," Frank said, turning back to them, his face becoming defiant once more.

Daniel was torn between the urge to groan and the desire to punch Frank senseless. One piece of evidence they might have used, and it was gone.

"What did it say?" he ground out.

"That they have Nora and that she is safe. For now. That I will"—Frank paused, seeming to search his memory— "let me see, 'make your fleet available for the efforts of Cuban independence, as you did before.' I believe that was the exact language. Or else they could not guarantee Nora's safety. I was to wait to receive further instructions."

"And?" Daniel prompted. "Did you burn those missives as well?"

"Nothing more ever came."

Genevieve caught his eye again, and he nodded. Another piece of the puzzle clicked into place. Something had disrupted Meade and Boyle's plans to move forward with their scheme, and they had begun killing the people who knew about the weapons instead, starting with Marcus Dalrymple.

Which put Nora's life—and their own—into even more jeopardy.

Chapter 22

"You can't possibly be serious." Rupert set his crystal whiskey glass down with a thud, causing some of the amber liquid to splash onto a nice little birch side table. Asher thumped over and wiped the liquid up, sending Rupert a dirty look.

"Sorry," Rupert said, pulling a handkerchief from his pocket and mopping at the spill. "But, Daniel, this is your plan? To somehow break into Boyle's Suicide Tavern? I thought you said the bouncer there tried to kill you."

"He did," Daniel confirmed soberly, swirling the liquid in his own glass and staring into its depths. Genevieve recognized the gesture, it was one he did when he was deep in thought.

"Well then, to go back is madness, surely," Rupert protested. "As your associates here seem familiar with the establishment, maybe it would be better if they undertook the task." He nodded toward Paddy and Billy, who were standing by the entrance to the library in Daniel's house, Paddy with his hands shoved deep in his pockets and Billy slouched against a wall of books.

Warning bells flared in Genevieve's mind. She didn't know Daniel's friends Paddy and Billy well, but she could tell by the set of Paddy's jaw that he deeply disliked Rupert's suggestion.

Daniel chuffed a small laugh in response and glanced at the men by the door, whom he'd known since childhood, raising a brow in their direction. Paddy's jaw softened, and he offered a slight smile in return but shook his head once.

"It's not their fight. And they've already done plenty." Daniel tipped his head toward Paddy and Billy as a gesture of thanks.

"You know where to find us if you need us," Paddy replied. "The Dog's Tail, on Bleeker. Be careful, Danny. Knockout Eddie is out for your blood."

Asher cracked his knuckles so loudly it caused Genevieve to start. "I can handle Eddie," he muttered. He appeared ready to challenge Knockout Eddie then and there, a terrifying look on his scarred visage.

"We need more stealth than that," Daniel said. "And Eddie will recognize you, know I'm nearby. The only way to rescue Nora is to sneak in."

Genevieve shifted uncomfortably in her seat. Daniel had called this council of war to plot how they would liberate Nora Westwood from Boyle's, but they weren't sure if she was there. Or if she was even alive.

Unfortunately, Daniel's plan seemed their only option.

"What about Tommy Meade?" Esmie asked the question quietly. She had been quiet all evening, in fact, and was staying close to Rupert. Genevieve had to remind herself the couple had only been married for a few weeks, though in that time so much had transpired the wedding almost felt like it had happened in another lifetime.

"He won't be there," Paddy said. "Meade doesn't go to Boyle's, never has. But especially not now he's trying to be respectable again." Billy rolled his eyes at this, then nudged Paddy with his elbow and tilted his head at the door.

"We gotta go," Paddy continued. He fixed a beady eye on Daniel. "Remember what I said. Stay out of Eddie's sight and John Boyle's too. You as well," he said to Asher, who grumbled in response.

The two Toughs slipped out the door, followed by Asher, still grumbling. Genevieve drummed her fingers on the side of her glass, restless. Something about this plan didn't sit right with her—something other than the obvious danger, that is—but she couldn't put her finger on what.

Rupert's resigned sigh echoed her own feelings. She had wracked her brain to come up with alternative scenarios to what they were planning, and had come up empty-handed.

"They did find out some useful information," Genevieve said, trying to convince herself this scheme would somehow work. By "they" she meant Paddy and Billy, who had spent several evenings at Boyle's, unobtrusively observing the comings and goings of various staff members, looking for a way to break in. They had been the best suited for the task, as Rupert would stick out like a sore thumb, and Daniel was obviously known to Eddie now. Billy complained of a sore head from the quality of the whiskey, which, coming from Billy, as Daniel pointed out, meant it was truly substandard fare.

Their patience and sore heads had paid off. Paddy had discovered a back door, which, like the one at the flower shop owned by Oscar's father, was used mostly for deliveries. It was locked at all times, they said, and only opened from the inside if a delivery was waiting. But it was a way in, one that was not guarded by a bouncer and that provided access to a set of back stairs. The back stairs, of course, that led to rooms for rent, mostly used for women and their clients, where they hoped they could find Nora Westwood.

If she was still alive.

"How do you plan on getting through the door?" Rupert asked. "Breaking it down?"

Genevieve had been wondering about this herself.

At Daniel's hesitation, Rupert snorted. "I'll come along, pick the lock for you."

"Too dangerous," Daniel countered instantly. "You're out on bail for a murder charge. If you were to get caught, it would be disastrous."

"How many officers are likely to be patrolling the back alley of Boyle's Suicide Tavern?" asked Rupert, crossing his arms and leaning back in his chair. He shook a lock of blond hair out of his eyes. "We know they're paying off the cops to avoid raids, and we know those raids that do happen are for show and are known about in advance. They had a raid three nights ago, Billy said. There's no way another will happen so soon."

Daniel still looked doubtful, though, and crossed his arms in return. "And what if this is the one lock you can't break?"

Rupert rolled his eyes. "I've yet to meet the lock I can't pick. I broke into some of the most well-secured mansions on Fifth Avenue."

"We could use another pair of eyes," Genevieve urged. "Esmie, are you okay with this idea?"

Esmie looked as troubled as Genevieve felt, but acquiesced. "If you think it would be helpful," she said. Genevieve noticed, though, that Esmie closed her fingers around Rupert's forearm in a tight grip.

"I don't like it," Daniel said.

"Well, I do," Genevieve countered, even in the face of Esmie's obvious discomfort with the idea. She glared at Daniel, readying herself to remind him again that they were partners in this endeavor.

It wasn't that she didn't trust Daniel to see the task accomplished. It was the foggy sensation of *wrongness* that surrounded the task itself. There were too many variables, too many unknowns. It would reassure her greatly to have another person along, one they knew they could trust. Though she knew it frightened Esmie, she would rather see Daniel safe.

"Fine," Daniel grumbled, clearly disliking the idea but seeming to sense he was outnumbered. "Rupert, you shall pick the lock, and you and Genevieve can wait in the alley while I see if I can find Nora and fetch her out to the carriage Asher will have waiting at the corner. Perhaps it's better you're not waiting alone," he said thoughtfully, looking at Genevieve.

The feeling of wrongness intensified. "And I don't like you going in there alone."

"We've been over this," Daniel said. "One of us sneaking around the upstairs at Boyle's is far less risky than two of us."

"And if Nora has been traumatized during her ordeal, she may well not want to put her faith in a strange man. Another woman's presence may comfort her."

"There will be no comfort for her if she gets killed."

"Nor if *you* do. Then you'll be dead and she'll still be held captive."

"Better me than you," Daniel barked.

Stunned, Genevieve could feel her mouth opening and closing like a codfish's.

"Genevieve, on this I agree with Daniel. If he runs into one of Boyle's men, he is better equipped to deal with it," Rupert said in the long quiet that followed.

"I know you can handle yourself in a fight, Genevieve." Daniel sounded so weary. Something tight squeezed in her chest at the sound of it. "But Boyle's has a way of swallowing up women and spitting them out disfigured or dead. It has come by its name honestly; women die there."

"I wish we could take more time, find another way," Genevieve said. "This feels too haphazard." She herself felt jangled, nervous energy ricocheting around her body like a fast-moving tennis ball.

"We're out of time," Daniel reminded her. His tone was gentle, but she could hear the determination in his voice. And he was right: they were out of both time and options. Nora's only hope was that they find her, and Boyle's was their only lead. They had already agreed that if Nora wasn't there, it was time to turn the case over to the authorities. Genevieve would be leaving town in a few days, and although they had picked apart some of the sticky strands of webbing that linked these deaths, there were still unanswered questions. Why had Meade and Boyle not followed through with their plans to force Westwood to use his ships for their gunrunning? Or were those plans simply delayed? Why poison Marcus and Paul, and then shoot Oscar? And what of Nora? She had apparently embraced the gunrunners' schemes, but why? Had Paul convinced her the Cuban revolution was a good cause, or was she simply as wild as her father claimed, excited to be caught up in something secret and forbidden?

There was still so much that didn't add up.

Neither she nor Daniel knew if they would ever get these answers. Tommy's men and Boyle's men would never talk. Marcus and Paul and Oscar had carried any further secrets to the grave.

This plan, hare-brained as it seemed, was their last hope.

★ ★ ★

"Hurry, Rupert," Daniel hissed. The particular sensation that came with being watched was plaguing him, that tingling feeling that gathered at the nape of his neck and radiated upward through his skull, though he couldn't see anyone else lingering in the dark alley behind Boyle's Suicide Tavern.

Which, of course, was no proof no one was there.

"You can't rush genius," Rupert replied softly, and Daniel could see him grinning in the very dim light of the kerosene lantern they had brought. He was carefully working two long metal picks inside the lock, his ear pressed close. "Quit distracting me, I need to hear what she says."

"She?" asked Genevieve. She glanced over her shoulder, her puzzled expression illuminated by the lamplight. She had her back to Rupert, her gaze trained on the far end of where the alley opened to Houston Street, ready to give warning if someone approached.

"I call all locks 'she,'" Rupert responded. He tossed a quick wink to Genevieve before he bent back to his work. She rolled her eyes at Daniel before she, too, resumed her own work of keeping watch.

Though he lacked Rupert's skill, Daniel had a rudimentary knowledge of lock picking, as did any kid who'd grown up on the streets. He knew that to do it properly took time.

He also knew they didn't *have* time.

Daniel had kept the lamp lit low, and held it near Rupert's working hands—just close enough for his friend to see what he was doing. Scant light also shone through a few windows in the upper floors of some of the other buildings that faced the alley—probably lamps like the one he held, or possibly candles, their glow weakly penetrating the thin scraps of fabric that served as curtains for the impoverished who lived here. But even if they were overheard, he was sure any neighbors of Boyle's would be disinclined to stick their head out at one in the morning to see what was happening below. Such an act, if viewed by one of the thugs Boyle employed, could have deadly consequences.

Otherwise, it was black as pitch in the alley, the new moon and obscured stars offering little assistance. Each end of the narrow passage was completely shrouded save the meager light coming from the streetlamps on Houston Street. If he glanced that way, Daniel could see the occasional figure moving past the alley's opening, distant and otherworldly as wraiths. If any of these late-night pedestrians spied the small glow of his lamp down the alley, they, too, kept to their own business and hurried along.

The other end of the alley, which opened to East 1st Street, might as well have been the moon, it seemed so far away and dark.

Anyone could be in the shadows, hovering just outside their sparse pool of light. Anyone or anything. The prickling feeling of being observed intensified, and he wished Rupert would speed it up.

As if on cue, his friend whispered to himself, "Almost there." Then, "Come on," Rupert coaxed, moving his instruments delicately. "Come on." A bead of sweat rolled down the side of his face, but he didn't stop to wipe it. Instead, a satisfied smile spread across his features, and his eyes shone in the darkness.

"We're in," Rupert whispered.

Relief eased the tension in Daniel's shoulders, short-lived but welcome. One hurdle crossed. Picking the lock, though challenging, had been the easier part of the plan. Now he had to maneuver through the back rooms of one the most dangerous hellholes in the city, ferret out a kidnapped society girl, and abscond with her before they were seen and killed.

That feeling of unease, of being watched, tickled his scalp again.

"Nicely done, Rupert," said Genevieve, as her friend stood up and brushed the dirt from his pants.

"Very," said Daniel, and he meant it. Rupert had been his best friend for over twenty years, and the man still managed to surprise him. "I apologize for distracting you."

"You mean for doubting me," Rupert countered. "I hope you've learned your lesson and never do so again."

On the surface, it was a flippant comment typical for Rupert, but Daniel could hear the undercurrent of fear in his friend's voice. He laid his hand on Rupert's shoulder for a moment, signaling his thanks.

"Take this." Daniel handed Genevieve the lamp.

Her brow furrowed. "No, you'll need it."

"I can't draw attention to myself, and neither should you. Douse it and wait here. Remember, Asher is just that way," he said, pointing to the end of the alley that culminated in Houston. "He's got the carriage waiting. If anything happens, get out of here at once."

Even in the dim light, he saw the color drain from Genevieve's face, the worry flash across Rupert's.

"The same applies to you," Genevieve said, quiet but firm. "If there is trouble you can't handle, just leave. Save yourself. We'll go to the police."

Daniel hesitated, knowing that if things were to play out as Genevieve described, it could mean death for Nora Westwood.

"Please," Genevieve added. She still held the lamp, and he witnessed, for just one moment, an expression of mixed longing, desperation, and disquietude flitter across her beautiful features before she drew back her shoulders and fixed a look of stoicism on her face instead.

His chest flared in response, and he found himself nodding, agreeing, yes, he would leave if there was danger. Daniel had no immunity to that look, stood helpless before it.

There was no time to ponder its implications at present. He reached over and doused the lamp, plunging the alley into now almost complete darkness. Heart pounding, Daniel turned toward the door and took a deep breath.

"Do it," he whispered to Rupert, who had his hand on the knob. Daniel could just make out the outline of Rupert's head nodding once, and then the knob silently turned under his friend's hand, and the door opened a few inches.

The interior space revealed was almost as black as the alley. Daniel couldn't quite make heads or tails of it, though he was almost instantly engulfed in sound, as the raucous noise of the bar floated through the various rooms and out the back door to where they stood. He took a cautious step in, hands forward as though he were blind, feeling his way.

A light briefly flared, and his heart dropped to his stomach before he realized Genevieve had relit the lamp in the alley.

"It's not going to do you any good if you can't see a foot ahead of you," she whispered furiously. Genevieve stuck her arm with the lantern into the space, and forms instantly sprang into view: it was a short but wide corridor, with crates full of bottles and what could be foodstuffs stacked along one side. There were doors on either end, and the noise of the bar was coming from the left.

From the right? All was quiet.

"Turn that back off," Daniel whispered back. "I've got my bearings now."

The light went out immediately. Daniel glanced over his shoulder quickly, reassuring himself of their forms in the dark, before gently closing the door behind him.

This next part, whatever it entailed, had to be done alone.

Dankness overwhelmed his senses, and Daniel was forcibly reminded of the tunnel beneath the river at the Garcia mansion, though he knew the two were not a reasonable comparison. Still, the unease was the same as he softly made his way down another dark and narrow passage toward an uncertain end.

He had entered the lion's den, though perhaps snake pit was a more apt metaphor.

In a few cautious steps, Daniel reached the door at the end of the corridor. Barely allowing himself to breathe, he pressed his ear close to it.

There was no sound.

Daniel gave the knob an experimental twist, prepared to encounter resistance, but it turned easily in his hand.

What was on the other side? What lay within the quiet?

Inch by inch, he eased the door open, grateful the hinges seemed well oiled. Risking a look, he found a narrow set of stairs that took a sharp right about ten steps up. These must be the back stairs Paddy had found.

Or was there more than one set? Would these stairs lead to Boyle's private office rather than the rooms for rent?

A surge of voices from the main room of the tavern carried faintly through the walls, rose, and then dropped to its previous volume.

Uneasiness continued to prickle all over Daniel's body: his arms, his shoulder blades, and neck.

Was this *too* easy?

Daniel could see no way forward but up. A small amount of ambient light shone through a window at the landing, just enough that he could make out the general shape of the steps. He pulled his gun from his pocket, its weight in his hand reassuring, and slowly began to ascend, pausing after each step to listen. Other than the occasional creak of a floorboard, there were still no sounds except the din from the barroom wafting through the tavern's thin walls, but even that noise was lessening the farther he climbed.

At the landing where the stairs turned, Daniel paused, pressing his back to a wall. He carefully peered around the corner, confronted by nothing more threatening than stairs that culminated in yet another door, brighter light shining through an inch-high crack at its base. He paused and considered. If this staircase was primarily used by the ladies, they wouldn't bring clients up this way; it was too narrow and too dirty, even for a place like Boyle's, and didn't seem to connect to the main barroom where they would acquire said clients. This was more likely a back staircase, where one could walk down a full chamber pot. Given that, the chances of the stairs leading to an office seemed less likely.

But not impossible. Daniel kept his gun at the ready and cautiously made his way up the final few steps.

He eased the door at the top of the steps open with the same care he had with the lower one: ear pressed to it, making no sound, and opening it infinitesimal degree by infinitesimal degree.

Taking a look, Daniel couldn't stop the small breath of relief that escaped him. He had guessed correctly.

The door opened to a hallway lined with more doors, all closed. It was empty, the walls on either side lined with faded floral wallpaper, and two gas lamps mounted on tarnished brass holders at either end of the corridor. The rowdy sounds of carousing in the tavern were louder now, floating up from an open doorway on one end of the hall that led, he assumed, to the barroom itself. It was from this hall, carrying down that staircase, that he and Genevieve had heard a woman's voice screaming about demons.

Silently praying a woman wouldn't suddenly appear, laughing, at the top of the stairs with a client in tow, only to abruptly stop with wide eyes at the sight of him, Daniel slid into the corridor and carefully closed the door behind him. His jaw worked as he glanced left and right.

None of the doors were guarded. If Nora was here, how was he to know which room was hers? Assuming at least some were occupied by women plying their trade, he couldn't very well start knocking on doors without causing the type of outcry he needed to avoid.

A click and a creak alerted him to the opening of one of the doors, and Daniel quickly shoved his gun out of sight. A plump, red-headed woman in a shift so thin it left little to the imagination emerged into the hallway, stopping short when she spied Daniel.

"Lost your way, love?" she asked in a slightly wry tone.

Daniel pulled Nora's photograph from his inner jacket pocket along with a twenty-dollar bill and gestured for the woman to come closer.

She did, warily, glancing between his face and the money in his hand.

He silently showed her the picture.

The red-head stifled a gasp and started to shake her head. Daniel held up the twenty and mouthed the word "please." The woman hesitated, indecision clearly written on her face. For a few seconds they stood in that hallway, both breathing heavily, caught between the redhead's obvious fear and her equally obvious desire for the money, probably more than she'd ever seen in one place in her lifetime.

It was a lifeline to her, a way out of Boyle's, and they both knew it.

Desire won. The woman snatched the money from Daniel's hand and gestured with her chin to the third door on the left.

"I've never seen you," Daniel whispered. She nodded, still wary, and darted back into the door through which she'd emerged.

Daniel tucked the photograph back into his pocket and moved to the door the woman had indicated. There was nothing special about it, nothing to indicate a young society woman was being held there against her will. He braced himself for what he might find, hoping against hope Boyle and Meade had needed Frank's ships so badly they had kept Nora unharmed.

Slowly, silently, he turned the knob, simultaneously withdrawing his gun again. He slipped into the room as quickly and quietly as he could.

For the past few weeks, Daniel had stared at Nora's photograph for what probably added up to hours. For the longest time, he hadn't been able to put his finger on what had drawn him to this unknown young woman's face, why he was so deeply concerned about her safety. Soon after Frank had revealed that Nora had been kidnapped, as opposed to running away of her own volition, Daniel had been once again studying the lines of Nora's jaw, the set of her shoulders, the distinct laughter in her eyes, and it had hit him, all at once.

She reminded him of his sister Maggie. Or at least of the Maggie he had grown up with, the laughing, lively girl with the bright eyes who had turned the head of every young man in their neighborhood, and many of the older heads as well. He'd watched as Maggie's light dimmed, as she traded her youth and vibrancy for his safety, by becoming the mistress of their employer, Jacob Van Joost, largely to secure Daniel's own future.

It had worked, more successfully than Maggie ever could have imagined. Daniel had not only received the education his sister had so desperately craved for him but had also eventually inherited the entire Van Joost fortune.

The cost for that had been Maggie's life, ended at her own hands, and Jacob's guilt.

Daniel himself didn't believe the trade-off had been worth it, but it hadn't been his choice to make.

He had realized that was what was driving him forward in their search for Nora, in their search for answers. He couldn't bear to witness another girl lose that vibrancy, lose the spark that made her whole. He didn't want to see the light dim from Nora Westwood's eyes, and would do anything in his power to prevent that.

When their eyes finally met, Daniel nearly crumpled with relief. Nora was not only alive, but she appeared unharmed and intact. She was sitting cross-legged on a bed, a fashion journal in her lap, and her gaze, startled at first by his entrance, quickly shifted to the one he recognized from her photograph: playful, impish, and just a little too knowing for a girl her age.

"Hello, Mr. McCaffrey."

CHAPTER 23

Daniel blinked in surprise. Later, he cursed himself for not recognizing the moment for what it was. For the blinders that Maggie's choices and death had thrust on him, to his own detriment, and that he couldn't seem to remove, no matter how hard he tried.

But that was later. In the moment, joy exploded in his chest, mingled with gratitude. They weren't too late.

"Miss Westwood. Nora. Come with me, I'm getting you out of here," he whispered urgently. And though she seemed unharmed, he felt compelled to ask. "Are you well?"

Nora made no move to leave her perch on the bed, but tilted her head at him curiously, the beginnings of a coy smile tilting up the corners of her mouth. "I am quite well, thank you."

"We heard you screaming," Daniel said. Taking in the room, the feeling of being watched intensified: a tingling up his spine, radiating down his arms. Something here felt off. "That *was* you, was it not? About demons. You're quite sure you're well?"

Mirth lit Nora's pretty face as her light laugh tinkled within the room, sending a further shiver across his back.

"You heard that, then? You and Miss Stewart? Oh, good. I wasn't sure."

It dawned on him: the room was in excellent condition. New, glossy wallpaper decorated a space that should have been as threadbare as the hallway. Books and fashion journals were piled high on a side table next to the bed, which itself was covered in a thick, silken quilt. From his youth in Five Points, Daniel was well familiar with what the inside of a dive bar tended to look like, including the upstairs rooms.

And this was . . . not it. The smell of cheap liquor still wafted up from the barroom downstairs, as did the noise, but there were clean, fluffy pillows piled on the bed, a gilded mirror hanging above a small dressing table littered with expensive-looking powders and perfumes, and a birch-veneered wardrobe. One of its doors was partially open, and he could see several equally expensive-looking dresses bunched within.

Wariness settled over his body like a cloak.

"Come, let us leave now," Daniel tried again, though his relief was already being replaced with a sinking feeling in his chest.

Nora unfolded her legs and tossed her magazine aside, scooching to the end of the bed, but she didn't stand. Instead, she dangled her legs and leaned back on her hands, her eyes dancing merrily at him.

Something else struck Daniel: Why was Nora awake at one in the morning? And dressed? Not in nightclothes, but in a summer day dress, white linen sprigged with tiny pink flowers. As clean and tidy as the rest of the room. When she had first said his name, Daniel had automatically assumed she simply recognized him. It wasn't vanity—he was a well-known figure, especially among New York's elite.

He realized a second too late she didn't know his name because she recognized him. She knew his name because she had been expecting him.

Nora Westwood hadn't been kidnapped. She was, improbable as it seemed, involved in the entire scheme. The gunrunning. Marcus's, Paul's, and Oscar's deaths.

Nora wasn't the victim. Nora was the perpetrator.

Daniel whirled on his feet, fully intending to dash from the room and down the back stairs, but instead ran straight into the wiry chest of Tommy Meade.

He raised his gun, but Tommy was ready. A bright ball of pain exploded in Daniel's left temple, and he felt his feet stagger beneath him as he fell to his knees, stars covering his field of vision. Struggling to stay conscious, Daniel allowed his hands to drop so he was on all fours.

Another burst of pain, this one in his right hand, as his gun was kicked away. Then the sensation of his face hitting the carpet as rough hands yanked back his arms, and coarse rope encircled his wrists, binding his hands tight.

Daniel rolled to his side and focused on his breath, willing the pain to subside so he could think clearly. Through the haze covering his vision, he saw Tommy wrap an arm around Nora's shoulders and pull her close, whisper in her ear. She released that tinkling laugh again, smirking down at him on the floor.

Nora had a secret boyfriend after all, and one her father truly wouldn't approve of. It just wasn't Oscar. It had been Tommy all along.

More pieces of the puzzle were fitting together.

Tommy. His childhood nemesis looked the same as ever, whip-thin but, Daniel was sure, banded with the same corded muscle he'd always had. Tommy's dark eyes glinted down at Daniel, a thin mustache gracing his upper lip.

Daniel had heard women thought Tommy was attractive, but he knew the blackness of the other man's soul too well to be able to see it.

"You were two-timing poor Oscar?" Daniel didn't like how raspy his voice sounded. Of course she had been, but he wanted to hear what Nora would say.

She raised an amused brow at him. "Poor Oscar, indeed. What a sap. He actually believed a boy like him could win the affections of a girl like me." Nora wrapped her arm around Tommy's waist and pulled him close, nuzzling his neck with her nose. "And with a gaudy little trinket like the ring he offered, no less."

"You left the ring at the mansion deliberately."

Nora shrugged lightly. "I had no use for it."

"And Paul? Marcus? Were they in love with you too?" Daniel asked. The more he could keep her talking, the more information he had, the better his chances at survival.

Though the odds weren't looking to be in his favor, at this point. Bands of pain still radiated from the spot where Tommy had struck him with the butt of his gun, and he felt a stream of liquid—blood, he assumed—making its way down the side of his face.

Nora tilted her head and pursed her lips in an exaggerated gesture of thought. "Let me see . . . Paul. Yes, yes, I think he was. He and my father had concocted some scheme of the two of us marrying, uniting our family fortunes." She added an eye roll. "Paul loved how adventurous I was—until he didn't. And he would have wanted me to stay home and be a good, boring society wife, let Miss Stewart report on my new spring wardrobe." She turned her attention back to Tommy, who still remained quiet. Daniel's vision had cleared to the point where he could see a small half smile on Tommy's face, and the sight of it made his stomach contract slightly.

He knew from long experience that smiling Tommy was much more dangerous than angry Tommy.

"But let's not be too cross with Paul," Nora continued, running a hand down Tommy's shirtfront. "It was because of him that I met Tommy."

"And how did an upstanding young man like Paul Riley get involved in running guns for Cuban revolutionaries?" Daniel rasped. He had to keep her talking.

Nora rolled her eyes. "Oh, Paul. He thought he and his friends were so rebellious, drinking here. Daring each other to rent a room and survive the night. He got to talking to one of John's men one night, I guess, and decided to take his rebellion even further, become a revolutionary. Then thought he could impress me with his daring ways." She giggled again and drummed her fingers lightly on Tommy's chest.

Another puzzle piece.

"You letting yourself get bossed around by the uptown set now, Tommy?" Daniel asked with just the right amount of mocking in his tone. He knew he was courting trouble, and sure enough, Tommy casually walked over and kicked him square in the stomach.

There was nothing to do but gasp for breath. It was the same spot, newly healed, where Genevieve had kicked him.

"And Marcus?" Daniel said between gasps. His breath was coming more easily, though his midsection throbbed. He surreptitiously tested the ropes binding his wrists, pulling a bit. His efforts did nothing but dig the material deeper into his flesh.

"Oh, Marcus. Marcus was not in love with me. Marcus, I believe, was in love with Paul. Had been since we were children."

"Not Esmie Bradley?" Daniel managed. The pain in his stomach was not abating.

"Not like that, silly." Nora had the tone one used when explaining simple matters to a small child. "Marcus couldn't *propose* to Paul, now could he? Followed him around like a lapdog, instead. Followed us to the mansion. Followed us to Boyle's here." She laughed again, the tinny sound scraping the interior of Daniel's brain. It was hard to keep from wincing.

"But he did love your friend the countess, as a friend." Nora fixed Daniel with an arch look. "I was at their wedding, you know. You were quite the hero on the front steps. Marcus was bereft, as it left no path for traditional marriage for him, though he understood Esmie's choice. He was very protective of Esmie. And, by extension, her husband."

"And by extension you, Danny boy." Tommy spoke at last, crouching down so he was closer to Daniel's eye level, shaking his head sadly. "It was a good plan. Garcia and I had been in touch during my run for mayor. The campaign *you* ruined." Tommy's mouth twisted slightly, and Daniel braced himself, waiting for a blow that, in the end, never came. "He wrote to ask if I would consider supporting Cuban independence if I won. I don't give a damn about Cuban independence, but then . . ." Tommy smiled again, and Daniel's insides clenched. "But then he started talking about the need for weapons. It didn't take long for Garcia to spill the whole tale, and once I learned about the tunnels, and about Westwood being compromised, well, how could I pass on such an opportunity? And imagine my luck: a young man like Paul Riley becoming interested in our noble cause." He dropped a perverse wink, and Daniel understood instantly. Boyle's men had been instructed to keep an eye out for privileged young men at the bar. Ones who might have money.

Ones who might have a connection to Nora Westwood that could be exploited.

Tommy stood and casually sauntered back to Nora, wrapping his arm around her tiny waist again. "How fortunate he was friends with Nora Westwood herself. For a while, it was all working beautifully. But then you came along, Danny." Tommy's face hardened. "You always have been a thorn in my side, you know. Still, you haven't ruined my plans completely this time—just set them back."

Daniel's brow furrowed, and he immediately smoothed it again. It was never good to show your hand to Tommy, plus the motion made his head hurt more. "How did I ruin your plans?"

"It was because of you Marcus had to die," Nora said, sitting on the bed again and smoothing the coverlet under her hand. "He overheard Tommy and some men talking about, oh, plans for you." Her laughter tinkled again.

Tommy smiled down at her, then turned that smile on Daniel. "Payback for last year," he said gently. "I've been waiting a long time. You really didn't think I was going to let that go, did you?"

"Marcus was afraid his precious Esmie or her new husband would get caught in the cross fire," Nora added. "He was going to warn her and try to talk Paul out of helping Tommy with the guns. Marcus said they were *bad men*." She shot an amused look at Tommy and covered her hand with her mouth, laughing again.

Tommy shrugged. "He wasn't wrong, there. But that was a stroke of luck for us. Kept the police looking at your friend the earl for a bit. Someone else I have plans for, by the way."

"Why poison?" Daniel asked, ignoring the alarm that coursed through him at the thought of his oldest friend being targeted by Meade. He had to keep his focus on getting out of this alive. He tugged at the ropes again, but they didn't budge. The butt of his gun gleamed from underneath the wardrobe, where it had landed after the kick.

"That was my idea," Nora said brightly.

Tommy gave her an even broader smile. "And a brilliant one it was, love." He turned back to Daniel. "Well, those lads couldn't stay involved forever, and they knew too much to live. You saw our demon. I had some theater fellows install a few tricks like that throughout the house, once we settled on using Duck Island for the guns last year. Give these young folks who thought the place was haunted a real scare, convince them not to come back. One of our boys wears a costume. We had it outfitted with those red lights, and he chases the kids out of the house. It wouldn't stand up to daylight, but down there, you know how dark it is. You're familiar with Duck Island, now, though it was an unpleasant surprise for me to get all the way north and find you gone. I was so hoping you'd drowned, Danny, I really was. Would have saved me so much trouble."

Nora tittered again.

"My boys told the society lads about the demon, acting like they believed it themselves. Those lads scoffed at first, but at the suggestion of my pet here, Eddie started giving them small doses of the poison when they'd come drinking, until one night they had a bigger dose than normal, and we came back to the mansion, left them there in the tunnels. In the dark. With our demon. Boy, you should have heard the screams." Tommy chuckled.

Daniel could see it. Nightshade caused hallucinations, and on being shown a fabricated ghost they'd been told was a demon, the poison took hold of that information and clung to it, expanded it, until both young men were out of their minds with fear. It must have been terrifying. "They were going to die, and the poison couldn't be traced back to you. I take it Marcus did sleep here, then," Daniel said. "He came by his medallion honestly."

Tommy looked surprised. "That he did, I guess. One evening when the nightshade was too strong."

"And I screamed about demons when one of the gang told me you and Miss Stewart were in the bar again, talking to Eddie," Nora added eagerly, like a proud child. "I knew it would cause a ruckus. Such fun," she said, shaking her head with apparent fondness at the memory. Daniel stared at her, once again appalled at his own blindness.

It would, it seemed, potentially be the literal death of him.

"Did Paul also overhear what you were planning for me? Is that why he, too, had to die?" Daniel asked. He could hear the dullness in his own voice. Such senseless deaths.

"No, Paul decided I was a damsel in need of rescuing." Nora rolled her eyes. "He went to my father after I came here to be with Tommy. Paul thought I'd run away with Oscar. Which is exactly what I wanted everyone to believe," she said, for a moment looking like a cat with the cream. "But father told him he had you and Miss Stewart looking for me. Paul let it slip to one of Tommy's gang." She shrugged, a pretty shoulder lifting its summer fabric nonchalantly. "He was too risky. He wanted to tell you and Miss Stewart everything."

Another puzzle solved. That was how Riley had been on the roof of the Metropolitan Theater the same night as he and Genevieve. Riley had been following them, waiting to tell them about the gunrunning. But the nightshade had taken hold of him first.

"But you needed Oscar," Daniel guessed. Unless a miracle happened, he was a dead man. The bonds that held him weren't loosening. The gun was too far to reach, and there was nothing he could do with it without use of his hands anyway. But he would die knowing the truth. "You needed the illusion of him, so you kept him alive."

"My friends wouldn't fathom someone like Tommy. But Oscar? The pretty boy from the flower shop?" Nora clasped her hands under her chin and blinked her eyes rapidly, mimicking besottedness, before a cynical smile took over her visage. "They swooned over our star-crossed love. And he was another pair of hands, so I tried to convince him to work with Tommy too."

"And then, again, you got involved, Danny," sighed Tommy. "You just keep getting people killed, you know."

Daniel ignored the jab. "Not enough time for the belladonna charade that time, so you had Oscar shot," he said dully.

"This conversation is doing nothing but reminding me how much trouble you've caused me, Danny," Tommy said. "And I'm done with it."

The creak of the door caused Daniel's heart to leap with unconscionable hope. He craned his neck to look up from his uncomfortable position on the floor, his brain insisting on picturing Genevieve with her derringer pointed straight at Tommy's heart. But it was the stony, intractable figure of John Boyle, staring at Daniel on the floor.

Boyle shifted his gaze to Tommy and Nora, distaste glazing his features. "Don't kill him here," Boyle said shortly. "He's got powerful friends. Bad enough I'm harboring this one," he said, his chin jutting toward Nora.

Daniel refrained from pointing out that Boyle had already shot at both himself and Genevieve less than two weeks ago. "Still surprised you're in bed with the Oyster Knife gang, Boyle," he said. "You're picking a fight with the Bayard Toughs, you know. Usually you keep yourself out of these disputes."

"It's just business, McCaffrey. Meade approached me with the opportunity, and it was too lucrative to turn down. Nothing personal." He turned his indifferent face back to Tommy. "Get him out of here."

The door closed firmly, and Daniel's hopes sank with it. His heart began to pound, beating blood steadily to his pulsing head, as Nora's grating laugh again filled the room. She began to busy herself with something at her dressing table while Tommy checked Daniel's bonds. Daniel's fingers tingled as the ropes tightened painfully, cutting off his circulation.

Nora leaned down and looked him in the eye. He could count every one of the faint freckles on her pretty face, she was so close.

A wave of regret passed through Daniel. Not for himself, but for Nora. He hadn't been in time after all. Tommy would use her to get her father to comply with his scheme, keep her as long as she amused him, but eventually he would chew her up and spit her out. She wouldn't be able to rejoin society, not fully, and her life as she knew it would in essence be over. Her spark would diminish and die. Her actual death might or might not follow, but even if she lived, she would never be the same.

"He's using you," Daniel said. He could hear the desperation in his voice, knew the satisfaction it gave Meade, but he was past caring. "I've known Tommy my whole life. He doesn't love you; he doesn't love anyone but himself. They recruited Riley just to get to you, to your father's ships. You don't have to do this," he said, knowing full well it was a lost cause but urgently needing to try. His energy was ebbing. "You can still leave," Daniel said to her. "Your father wants you home."

She cocked her head at him. "Why would I want to do that? This is the most fun I've ever had. I've seen you in person, you know, but never this close. You're just as handsome as the gossip pages claim. Oh well." Nora shrugged again.

Daniel's heart went from pounding to racing as a white cloth came toward his face, filling his field of vision completely. He gave the ropes at his wrists one final, desperate tug—but then knew no more.

★ ★ ★

The wait felt interminable.

Genevieve was deeply glad of Rupert's presence. They both had their backs pressed against the dirty brick wall of one the neighboring buildings of Boyle's Suicide Tavern, staring at the general spot in the darkness that contained the door through which Daniel had disappeared. The darkness was almost total, the only light a weak shaft that shone from an upstairs window.

Rupert's breathing was shallow and steady in the dark, mimicking her own. As they waited, Genevieve's mind raced with a thousand possibilities as to what could be happening inside. Daniel finding Nora, a battered wreck of her former self. Daniel finding Nora, miraculously whole. Daniel not finding Nora. Nora dead. Daniel dead.

Over and over her brain spun images and scenarios, most of them resulting in a dreadful conclusion. There were so many more chances for this to go wrong than to go right.

Enough. If she didn't get herself under control, she was going to be hysterical soon. Genevieve forced herself to focus on her breath, slowly counting her inhalations, feeling the air fill and expand her lungs, and then counting down as she exhaled.

The sudden rough clatter of hooves was so startling she literally jumped, her chest nearly exploding. The emergence of rushing dark shapes combined with a familiar noise meant a carriage was speeding down the narrow alley toward them, coming from Houston Street.

Genevieve watched its progress stupidly, her brain not quite able to make sense of what she was seeing. Was it Asher? He was supposed to wait.

Rupert hissed a breath and pulled her into a nearby doorway, the back door to a tenement, just shallow enough to contain the two of them. Genevieve shrank back, swallowing down her fear, as the horse and its vehicle thundered by.

It wasn't Daniel's familiar chestnut mare pulling the carriage. It wasn't Asher.

The horse whinnied as it was pulled to an abrupt stop a little way beyond where they hid. Whoever the driver was, he didn't appear to have seen her and Rupert, tucked deep into the shadows of the doorway.

Genevieve risked a peek around the corner of the recessed space. Rupert's palm pressed against her arm, a warning, but it was unnecessary. She knew not to be seen.

Light suddenly spilled into the alley, and Genevieve jerked her head back. She could hear low male voices, but they were speaking too quietly for her to make out the words. She risked another look.

The door to the back of Boyle's was open, the light illuminating the alley coming from within. A silhouetted man stood between the carriage and the open door, looking down the alley toward East 1st Street.

"Hurry," she heard him say to someone inside the door, before he stepped back.

Two other figures shuffled out, crossing the short distance to the carriage, carrying between them the limp form of a third man. The first man clambered into the carriage to help load the—dead? Unconscious?—body into its confines.

As they heaved their burden, the carried man's head lolled to one side, and for a brief moment his face was illuminated.

It was Daniel, his mouth slack, his eyes closed.

Genevieve didn't recognize the noise that emerged from her mouth, unbidden. It was a cross between a gasp of shock and a moan of pure terror, a verbalization of the horror that suddenly consumed every fiber of her body.

Now Rupert's hand was holding her back in earnest.

The men were talking among themselves, less quietly now, and didn't seem to have heard her. In a flash, the carriage door was closed, and the vehicle raced down the alley again, heading away from her toward the darkness of East 1st Street. One man went back inside Boyle's and shut the door with an air of finality, plunging the alley back into blackness.

It had happened in what seemed like seconds. Genevieve's mind was singularly focused, pushing out all other thought: she had to get to that carriage, to Daniel.

With a heave, she shoved Rupert farther into the doorway, breaking free of his grasp, barely registering the cracking sound of his head colliding with hard wood or his pained cry. The carriage was just at the end of the alley, the horse turning left to head back to the Bowery. She knew she could catch it if she ran fast enough.

Her legs pumped, her hands held her skirt high, and she sprinted, faster than she'd run before, but it was no use. She had only closed half the distance to the carriage when it completed its turn and disappeared into the night.

Too out of breath to scream for it to stop, a sob choked her throat instead as her mind hammered a single, insistent syllable: *No. No. No. No no no no.*

CHAPTER 24

The insistent tugging on her arm snapped Genevieve's consciousness back to the alley. At some point she had dropped to her knees, staring into the darkness that had swallowed the carriage containing Daniel.

Daniel? Or Daniel's dead body?

Another low moan escaped her.

"Genevieve, stand up. We have to get out of here." She could barely make out Rupert's features in the meager light from the upstairs window, but she could see enough to know he was also terrified, and half crazed with grief and worry. "Come on, we have to get to Asher. He'll know where they've taken Daniel."

Yes. Her brain grabbed onto the plan greedily, and to Rupert's reference to Daniel in the present tense. *Yes, he's alive. Now get up and find him—he's alive.*

The slight glow that emanated from the streetlamps dotting Houston Street brightened as they ran closer to the mouth of the alley. Asher was waiting under one of those lamps, and his face drained of color as he saw Genevieve and Rupert round the corner alone.

Rupert quickly explained the situation as Genevieve flung herself into the carriage.

"Where do we go, Asher? Where would they take him?" She poked her head out the window, resisting the urge to bang the side of the vehicle with her hand.

Daniel's friend's broad, scarred visage typically concealed all emotion, and Genevieve watched as it shuttered even more, an act of self-preservation as Asher blocked out thoughts of the worst.

"Too many possibilities," he grunted. "We don't have time to chase them all down. Get in," he directed Rupert before flinging himself into the driver's seat.

Rupert had barely closed the door when the carriage took off at an alarming speed, tossing Genevieve into Rupert's lap. She was glad of their haste, though, once she and Rupert untangled their limbs. The city flashed by as they raced to an unknown destination, and Genevieve silently urged, *Hurry, hurry, hurry.*

Or maybe not so silently. Rupert took hold of her hand as Asher rounded a corner at breakneck speed, and they both braced themselves this time to avoid colliding into each other.

"We'll find him," Rupert said, squeezing her hand. "Asher's going as fast as he can."

The carriage came to an abrupt halt a few blocks later. They were still downtown. Not far from Boyle's.

Genevieve tumbled out of the carriage, Rupert in her wake. Asher jumped off the driver's seat and tied the horse, then gestured for them to follow him through a door under a sign featuring the painted rear end of a dog.

The Dog's Tail, Genevieve remembered. Where Paddy had said he would be.

It had to be close to two in the morning, but the saloon was full. Genevieve stopped just inside the door, behind Asher's broad back as he scanned the crowd, sure for a moment they were in the wrong place.

The crowd was of mixed race. Black and white patrons, men and women, laughed together at tables and sat knee to knee on stools jammed at the bar, and she saw a pretty woman with skin as smooth as mahogany drop a quick, loving kiss on a blond man's mouth before shaking her head at him and picking up a glass of beer to sip.

Her parents had Black friends, of course. Other wealthy intellectuals, including one family in particular, the Gloucesters, whom they had befriended during their years active in the abolitionist movement before the war. Genevieve had dined at the grand Gloucester mansion in Brooklyn Heights countless times, and the Gloucesters had been equally welcome guests at the Stewart home on Washington Square's north side. And of course New York was an incredibly diverse city, with the languages spoken on the streets often changing, block to block, along with the color of people's faces.

But this . . . she had never encountered this. Never this causal mixing of so many black and white and brown faces in the same social space.

It made her wonder what other spaces she had been sheltered from.

"There," Asher said, pointing.

He elbowed his way past people who took one look at his giant physique and battered face and instantly scuttled aside, Genevieve and Rupert trailing in his wake.

As the crowd parted, Genevieve saw the familiar figures of Paddy and Billy at the bar. Billy spied their approach first, dread washing over his features as he frantically elbowed

Paddy in the ribs. Paddy turned, and at the sight of them set his mouth into a thin line.

"What happened?" he asked when they were close enough.

"They took him," was all she could manage.

A shadow of emotion rippled across Paddy's features like a fast-moving cloud, there and gone. "Meade?"

Genevieve shook her head. "I don't know—it was dark. I only saw Daniel. He was . . ."

"Unconscious," Rupert supplied in a low, grim voice. He shot a look at the man on Billy's right, who casually sipped at a glass of clear liquid—water? Liquor?—and appeared to be nonchalantly looking anywhere but toward them. He could clearly hear them and was trying to say with his body language, equally clearly, that he was minding his own business.

"If Meade wasn't there, he'll be wherever they go," Asher growled. "Where's he taking people these days?"

Paddy pursed his lips and glanced at Billy. Genevieve looked between the two of them, the knowledge settling on her that Asher was referring to where Tommy Meade took people to die. Blackness swam at the edges of her vision for a moment.

"Not the Eagle Head," said Billy in a low voice. "They don't use that no more, not after last year." He slid a quick look to and then away from Genevieve. Billy was referring to when Genevieve had been the one taken by Meade and stashed at the Eagle Head Tavern in Five Points.

"The Gas House," the man to Billy's right said quietly, keeping his dark brown eyes on his glass.

Billy looked stumped, Paddy thoughtful. "The Gas House District," Paddy repeated slowly. He had lowered his tone so much that Genevieve had to lean in to hear him over the noise of the bar. He sent a sharp gaze to the man who had spoken. "Thought that was that new outfit."

The man shrugged slightly. "Could be. Could also be the Oyster Knife boys taking advantage, doing some dirty work round there, hoping it won't look like them."

"You heard this?" Asher leaned closer too.

The brown-skinned man shrugged again. He kept his face forward, but slid his gaze to Asher. "I heard it," he said in a firm but quiet voice before turning his head away pointedly.

Genevieve's pulse quickened, remembering what Luther had said about Oscar's death.

"Yes," she said urgently. "A young man caught up in this was shot there only a few days ago."

Asher nodded once, then gestured with his chin toward the door. "Let's go."

They departed much the same way they had arrived, with the crowd parting before them as though Asher were Moses, only this time Paddy and Billy joined them.

By the time they reached the area known as the Gas House District, jammed into Daniel's carriage, she and Rupert and Paddy and Billy had formulated a plan. Genevieve wrapped her arms around herself and wished for a shawl as she stepped out of the carriage, as the river, a block away, whipped a strong breeze in their direction. Despite the wind, a thick, noxious smell hung over the street, so intense it had a nearly physical presence, heavy in her nostrils and instantly clinging to her hair and clothes.

They were at the corner of East 18th Street and First Avenue, huddled in a small group as Paddy relayed their plans to Asher, who had been driving. The big man nodded, then gestured to Genevieve and Rupert.

They joined him as Paddy and Billy silently slipped down 18th Street toward the water.

Genevieve watched their retreating backs, prickles of fear dancing up her spine.

"Come," Asher whispered. They followed him north, up First Avenue, through darkened streets as quiet as a graveyard. It was too early for day laborers to be up and about, and too late for all but the most hardened of tavern dwellers, that uniquely silent hour in New York when the majority of the city slept.

Genevieve shivered again as the wind picked up strands of her hair and sent them aloft. There was no sound but their own soft footsteps.

Asher led them to 21st Street but paused on the corner at the sound of a horse's muted whinny, gesturing for them to stand back as he peered around the corner.

He came away, face stony.

"You two find Daniel," Asher whispered in a gruff voice. "Try in there," he said, jerking his head in the direction of a warren of brick buildings containing the gasworks. Six enormous, cylindrical gasometers loomed over the whole complex, their squat, shadowy forms dominating the length of the block.

Asher sidled around the corner, sticking close to the murky sides of the tenements.

Risking a quick look east as she and Rupert scuttled across the street, Genevieve spied Knockout Eddie standing guard by the carriage and the same white and brown spotted horse that had carried Daniel away.

A thrill of triumph coursed through her. They were close.

Just as they reached the corner, hurrying to duck behind the cover of a coal shed, Eddie saw them. Genevieve only had time to gasp, grappling at Rupert's arm with suddenly numb fingers, as Eddie raised his gun. Before he could shoot, though, he was flattened to the ground by Asher, who had managed to sneak unseen behind Eddie's carriage. Eddie's gun skated across the street, and after a moment of hesitation, Genevieve jogged a few steps and snatched it up. Asher flipped Eddie onto his back and punched his old rival, hard, but Eddie heaved Asher off and sprang to his feet. Genevieve's hand with Eddie's gun flew up, but she couldn't get a good shot.

"Go," Asher commanded without looking their way.

The meaty sound of fists landing on flesh, accompanied by the occasional low grunt, resounded in Genevieve's ears as she and Rupert ran past what appeared to be a watchman's booth, ominously empty, and into the heart of the looming structure.

★ ★ ★

His head hurt, and the metallic tang of blood filled his mouth. The effort it took to open his eyes made Daniel strongly consider the possibility of simply leaving them closed. It was so much safer in the dark, quiet world he had been inhabiting, so much more pleasant than this one, which seemed filled with nothing but pain.

His arms hurt too, and as he experimentally tried to shift them, a stinging so intense shot through his wrists that his whole body gave an involuntary flinch.

The events of the night—he assumed it was still the same night—all came flooding back: the malicious laughter of Nora Westwood, John Boyle's contemptuous distaste, and the gleam of vicious satisfaction in Meade's eye as Nora had come toward him with her handkerchief of chloroform.

It was the same look Meade sported now as he once again crouched before Daniel.

"You're awake," Meade said, unceremoniously hauling Daniel up into a seated position. Daniel bit his inner lip to retain consciousness as the world swam briefly, then came back into focus. "Took you long enough."

Where was he? Not upstairs at Boyle's any longer. Daniel blinked a few times, taking in the massive round brick structures surrounding him.

The gasworks. Of course. Where Oscar Becker had been killed.

By the height of the moon, he judged it was perhaps three in the morning. Not that long, then, since he had been at Boyle's. Too early for any workers to be arriving. His hands were still bound, and waves of pain continued to radiate throughout his skull, where he had been struck earlier; the head blow was also making him slightly nauseous. Blood soaked the front of his shirt, presumably from the same injury.

He and Tommy were alone, hidden among the four giant gas tanks.

"You should leave Nora Westwood alone," Daniel managed. His voice was raspy. "She doesn't seem your type, anyway."

Tommy's lips thinned momentarily. "Always the hero," he said softly, before a lazy, malignant smile formed on his lips. "Nora's a sly one. She'll make her way even after our business is finished. Though I rather like her. Maybe I'll keep her around. You, on the other hand, . . ." Tommy shook his head in mock sadness. "This has been a long time coming, Danny."

Tommy lifted a gun and pointed it straight at Daniel's forehead.

There was nothing left to do. He wasn't going to plead for his life, not to Tommy Meade. In a way, Tommy was right. This moment *had* been a long time coming. Some-way, somehow, he had known since he was young that sooner or later one of them would kill the other. It was a dance they had been practicing for decades, and it appeared to be almost over.

Daniel looked past the cold, cruel barrel of the gun and met Tommy's eye. Some emotion, undefinable, passed over Tommy's features. Was it a tiny amount of regret? At the prospect of killing someone he'd known since his youth, or perhaps that their yearslong feud would finally be over and he would have to define himself differently now? Or was Tommy pausing to savor the moment, relishing the immi-nent end of their conflict, the end of how Daniel seemed to inadvertently always make him feel small?

Daniel didn't know and didn't waste any further effort trying to unpack the madness that was Tommy Meade.

Instead, he prayed Genevieve and Rupert had escaped unharmed. He also sent a quick prayer to his mother, his father, and his older sister, promising to see them soon.

The *click* of Tommy removing the safety reverberated between the giant, silent cylinders.

Images from his life flooded his brain, flicking quickly like a kineograph, there and gone in a fraction of second, yet he saw them all clearly: his long-lost younger siblings playing in the dirt in Five Points; the cool rush of air on his wet skin as he jumped into the Hudson River on that horrible, fateful day they disappeared; his parents waltzing in their tenement kitchen; Jacob Van Joost telling him to be good overseas; Rupert, at age fifteen, holding aloft a fish he'd caught in the pond of his family's Suffolk estate, grinning like an idiot; and on and on and on. The rapid flipbook slowed as it approached the present, and distilled to pictures of Genevieve, always and only her. He willed his head to stop, to pick just *one*, one he could clearly envision in his mind's eye and hold onto as the light faded.

His brain obliged. One image rose to the surface of his memory, caught there, and held. A recent one. In it, Genevieve wasn't looking at him. She was staring at the sunrise, an oddly peaceful expression on her exhausted, salt-covered face. Her clear, lovely profile was lit orange by the early light, her glorious hair unbound, tangled, matted, and wild, after their swim in the East River.

It was perfect. A moment that captured Genevieve's incredible strength combined with her heartbreaking vulnerability.

A moment that encapsulated exactly how much he loved her.

A perfect image with which to die.

★　★　★

Genevieve held her breath as she crept past a long, low brick building, heading toward the massive gas tanks that overlooked the bulk of the complex. She paused when the building ended, unsure of where to go.

"Should we check inside here?" whispered Rupert. He was following behind her and had stopped as well, trying in vain to see the darkened interior through a murky window.

After a moment's thought, Genevieve shook her head. "I feel like they'll be outside somewhere," she whispered back. "Easier to get in, get out."

Rupert silently nodded his assent. He gestured with his head for her to advance toward the giant tanks. They both had guns drawn, Genevieve carrying her familiar derringer, after pocketing the revolver that had been Knockout Eddie's, Rupert holding his own weapon.

She glanced over her shoulder quickly, but the paved area between the brick buildings leading back to the street was empty. Asher and Eddie's fight must be ongoing.

Moving as silently as she could, Genevieve lightly ran toward the nearest tank. Four of them were within a fenced square, one occupying each corner. They were so huge she couldn't see what, if anything, was in the center of the square.

"Psst," Rupert hissed. He had slipped toward the center of the fence so quietly Genevieve hadn't noticed he wasn't behind her anymore. Rupert cocked his head at a gate that stood slightly ajar.

Taking a deep breath, Genevieve followed Rupert into the enclosed area. The tanks nearly touched here, and there was no way to go but around them. She gestured that Rupert should go left and she would go right. He gave a quick nod and crept away on completely silent feet.

Genevieve edged her body around the warm curve of the gas tank slowly, straining her ears. Was that a scuff she heard? Or a low voice? It was impossible to tell if either had emanated from the street or from farther within the complex. Following the shape of the tank, she rounded toward the street and then away from it, back into the center of the square.

The sound of a male voice, though quiet, was now unmistakable. She had reached almost the opposite side of the tank from where she had begun, and the distance between her and the tank to her right was several feet.

Pressing herself as flat as she could, Genevieve risked a look around the bend of the tank to the center of the square.

Her breath caught, but her heart leapt.

Daniel. His face and shirtfront were covered in blood, and he looked as though he could barely keep his eyes open. But he was sitting up, hands bound behind him.

And he was alive.

Alive, but facing Tommy, whose gun was pointed at Daniel's head.

Genevieve raised her own derringer.

She caught sight of Rupert, across the square from her, pressed against his own tank. There was just enough light from the streetlamps on the other side of the fence to make out his horrified expression. Wide-eyed, he pointed to his own gun, then shook his head violently, gesturing an explosion with his hands.

Genevieve understood. A stray bullet could potentially rupture a tank and cause an explosion so enormous, none of them would survive it.

The entire block wouldn't survive it.

Tommy's shot was nearly point blank, and he was standing, gun pointing down toward Daniel. From where she stood, however, Genevieve's shot would have to cover over a hundred feet.

Her gun was intended for short-range use and would be useless here. She slipped it into her right pocket and removed Eddie's revolver from her left, its weight unfamiliar and heavy in her hand.

No matter. A gun was a gun. Genevieve lifted the revolver in her right hand and gripped hard, her palms suddenly slick with sweat, as she supported it with her left hand. She slowly crept along the bow of the tank, keeping Tommy's head in her sight at all times.

Rupert's horrified face, the sound of her own heart pounding, even Daniel's battered, bloody visage, all fell away. Her vision narrowed to focus solely on Tommy, on the cock of his head, the ruthless expression on his face.

The click of his safety being turned off was louder than any explosion.

Genevieve tightened her finger on the trigger.

★　★　★

The crack of the shot echoed through the still night. Daniel winced, fully expecting a burst of pain followed by the silence of oblivion. He held Genevieve's image as tightly as he could in his mind, but reality was insistent.

Instead of Genevieve's serene face, Tommy's surprised one filled his sight. It wasn't until Tommy crumpled, nearly folding in on himself as he fell, that Daniel saw the left side of Tommy's head was missing.

His vision began to swim again. The gas tanks, the tight wrought-iron fence beyond, the blinking stars, all began to blur and waver, as though he was regarding everything around him from under a clear, calm lake.

Genevieve's face abruptly floated to the forefront of the mirage, and he could hear her voice calling his name, again as if from underwater. Daniel tried to smile. He'd gotten his wish after all, that she would be the last thing he saw. Then darkness did come, and this time it stayed.

CHAPTER 25

The morning light streaming through the dining room windows was as peaceful as always. Genevieve stared at the piece of toast in her hand, not quite remembering how it had gotten there. It was spread with a thick layer of raspberry jam, causing her to frown. Genevieve disliked raspberry jam, less because of the taste and more because of the bothersome seeds. She placed the toast on her plate and picked up her coffee cup instead.

This had been happening often these past few days. She'd lose track of entire minutes, finding herself blinking in the midst of an ordinary task: writing a letter to Eliza, perhaps, or choosing a hat, when suddenly she'd become aware that she had no recollection of how or when she had gotten to that moment in time.

Ever since she had killed Tommy Meade.

Genevieve's mother was regarding her with a furrowed brow. "Are you quite all right, dear?" she asked in a gentle tone.

"Yes," Genevieve replied distractedly, pushing her plate away.

She hadn't wanted to eat much lately either, which was quite unlike her.

It wasn't that Genevieve was a stranger to death, or even to violent death. The previous year, when she and Daniel had stopped a series of murders, she had been exposed to all kinds of horrific demises. A fellow reporter had even perished in front of her very eyes, falling from an icy rooftop in his attempt to kill her. But until Meade, she had never been directly responsible for the loss of another human's life.

She didn't regret it, though. Tommy Meade was dead, and Daniel was alive. It was a trade she would make again and again without a moment's hesitation.

The minutes following when she had pulled the trigger replayed in her mind, as they did so often. She hoped in time they would eventually dim and perhaps disappear altogether, but she also recognized this was perhaps a fool's hope. Genevieve suspected, instead, that the sequence of events would be etched into her consciousness forever and would remain as crisp as they were now until the day she died.

How she and Rupert had run the moment Tommy dropped like a stone, and the complete terror she felt when, mere seconds later, Daniel had followed suit, slumping to one side, saved from hitting the pavement only by Rupert's quick hands. How her first horrified thought had been that maybe her bullet had passed through Tommy and somehow found Daniel, or that Tommy had managed to pull his own trigger after all. The sound of Asher's fast and heavy footsteps as he followed the sound of the shot and found them; frantically untying Daniel's hands and checking his wounds; her utter relief when it became apparent Daniel wasn't shot, quickly followed by a renewed surge of fear on realizing his life was still in danger due to severe blood loss.

Rupert and Asher had carried Daniel out of the gasworks just as the sky was shifting from the utter blackness of night to the slightly brighter, grayish cast of the predawn hours. By the time they had reached the nearest hospital, the stars were just starting to fade.

It had taken some quick work by the doctors and nurses, but Daniel had survived. And two days later, he'd woken, bandaged and bruised and still slightly woozy, but alive, with a prognosis to make a full recovery.

Genevieve visited Daniel daily, as did Rupert.

And one day Detective Aloysius Longstreet joined them. Not by invitation.

He crowded the doorway of Daniel's hospital room, accompanied by two officers. Rupert, who was on the far side of Daniel's bed, folded his arms and glared, and Genevieve moved to stand protectively in front of Daniel's bed. She didn't trust Longstreet as far as she could push him, an act she was quite prepared to undertake.

Longstreet gestured for one of the two officers with him to remain outside the room, and closed the door behind him. He didn't approach their group but stayed close to the door, taking in the private hospital room in one swift glance with his usual expression of disdain.

"I've arrested Edward Murray for the murders of Marcus Dalrymple, Paul Riley, and Oscar Becker," Longstreet said without preamble. His dull blue gaze flicked to Rupert. "You've been released from all charges."

Genevieve exchanged surprised glances with Daniel and Rupert. Edward Murray, she assumed, was Knockout Eddie, whom Asher had left unconscious and bleeding in the middle of 21st Street.

"Why Knockout Eddie?" Daniel asked. "What changed your mind?" He took a sip of water from the glass on the bedside table and fixed the detective with a hard look.

Longstreet's mustache twitched. "Marcus Dalrymple's death was suspicious from the start. We suspected poison immediately and have known that some of the downtown establishments have been experimenting with various poisons as a way to confuse their patrons and rob them of their funds."

Daniel's brow furrowed. "The dives along the Bowery have been doing so for decades," he pointed out.

"Precisely so," Longstreet said. "But we also know that members of *society*," he near sneered the word, "have of late been frequenting some of these establishments more than usual, particularly Boyle's. We had also heard rumors of gang-related gunrunning." Longstreet hooked his thumbs into his belt loops and stopped, seeming not to have anything further to say.

Genevieve waited a few beats, her temper rising with every passing moment. "That's it? That's all you have to say?" Questions tumbled in her mind. The police had known about the gunrunning and done nothing to stop it? How did they know of Marcus and the other young men's involvement?

Longstreet's nostrils flared and his gaze tightened. "What I am about to say is off the record. If any of you bring it up, in any context, outside of this hospital room, I shall deny it." He paused again, looking at each of them in turn. When neither she, Rupert, nor Daniel responded, Longstreet continued.

"We knew of Frank Westwood's prior involvement with gunrunning. We had heard rumors of young men of society being involved with the latest plots, but they were only rumors. After I saw you at the scene of Dalrymple's death, and then visiting Frank Westwood the next morning, I had a suspicion perhaps the two were connected. What if Marcus had been one of those involved? But I had no proof, nor any idea how it connected."

"You had us followed," Daniel said, his voice weary. He looked out his window for a moment, then back at Longstreet. "I was distracted that morning," he murmured. "Unlike me."

Something like amusement lit in Longstreet's eyes. "We're also rather good at not being seen," he said. "I didn't know about Miss Westwood's disappearance, and I didn't know what you were doing for Mr. Westwood."

"So you threatened us," Genevieve said, the realization dropping with sharp clarity. "We were so flummoxed as to why you were hounding us. And *Rupert*," she cried. "You jailed him for nothing."

Rupert had not uttered a word, just continued to fix Longstreet with a cold, hard stare. Genevieve noticed her friend's jaw tighten.

"I am not entirely sure Lord Umberland is innocent in all matters," Longstreet said delicately. "The matter of which I speak does seem to be settled, though I would hardly call it nothing." Longstreet fixed Rupert with a hard look, making his intent clear: the late Commissioner Simons had confided in Longstreet. The detective suspected Rupert was indeed the jewel thief of the previous year.

"Yes, I did have you followed, and yes, I did threaten you. And I regretted having to use such tactics," Longstreet said. He didn't, in fact, look or sound regretful in the least. "But they were necessary."

"So much for being a paragon of justice," Daniel said in an icy voice. "That is your reputation, is it not? I wonder what the press would make of this illegitimate arrest." His eyes flicked meaningfully to Genevieve, who raised her chin and did her best to look threatening.

Longstreet's eyes moved between the three of them, his expression carefully neutral. "No doubt they would find the story compelling. As equally compelling as that of a young lady of great wealth shooting and killing one of the city's leading gangsters." He paused again. "The department would be willing to overlook any illegalities in the death of Mr. Meade, and avoid the public arrest of any persons responsible, if Lord Umberland is willing to understand our mistake," Longstreet finished carefully.

Outrage flooded Genevieve, so palpable that, for a moment, she was sure she would levitate. It was on the tip of her tongue to tell Longstreet that Rupert would agree to no such thing, and furthermore use some very colorful language she had learned from her brothers as a girl, when Rupert gave a single nod.

She couldn't help the gasp that escaped her, and she whirled toward her friend, ready to argue. There was no way she was going to go along with the travesty of Rupert's false arrest to save herself.

The feel of a quiet hand on her arm quelled her. Daniel had rested his palm there, gently. He met her eye and gave a brief shake of his head, then quickly cut his eyes to Longstreet and back. *I'll tell you later,* the look said, *after he's gone.*

Genevieve switched her gaze to Rupert, silently imploring him to change his mind. He shook his head at her. "Let it go, Genevieve," he said quietly. The look of pure loathing Rupert shot toward Longstreet expressed his feelings more than words ever could.

If Rupert was willing to forgo challenging his false arrest, the reason must be very good indeed.

As the younger sister to two older brothers, Genevieve knew when she was outnumbered. She also knew that even if she couldn't obtain her main objective, there were other ways to avoid leaving a fight empty-handed.

"There is one condition," she said to Longstreet, drawing herself tall. "You'll serve as a quoted, public source in the story on the deaths of the young men and the gunrunning that will appear in *The New York Globe*."

Over his mustache, Longstreet's eyes narrowed. "The story you will be writing, I take it?"

"That's right," she replied, folding her hands in front of her and lifting her chin again. Out of the corner of her eye, she saw a familiar half smile quirk on one side of Daniel's mouth.

"It's a fair trade, Aloysius," he said quietly. "You know Miss Stewart shot Tommy Meade in self-defense. And a damn good shot it was too."

"Nearly blew up the whole block," muttered the detective.

"You don't know much about me, detective," replied Genevieve. "Least of all about my skill in firearms. But you probably also don't know my well-earned reputation for . . . tenacity."

Daniel's grin widened before he affected a more sober expression.

Longstreet tried to stare her down, but Genevieve held her ground. "Fine," he finally growled. "But your story better corroborate that of the New York City Police Department."

"I've no doubt it will. Now if you'll excuse us, Mr. McCaffrey needs to rest. He is still recovering."

As soon as Longstreet departed after a final, baleful glare at them all, Genevieve had rounded on the two men.

"Rupert, I cannot believe you would let that go! As Daniel said, my shooting Meade was obviously self-defense. You know my family is used to scandal. I don't care if I get arrested—What?" Both Daniel and Rupert were sporting near identical worried expressions.

"Longstreet hasn't been my only unwelcome visitor," Daniel admitted. He and Rupert exchanged a glance.

"What?" Genevieve repeated. The unwelcome but now familiar sensation of fear began to claw at her heart. She hadn't been lying to Longstreet about Daniel needing to rest. He looked exhausted, and she feared whatever he was about to say was among the reasons why.

"Boyle was here," he said. Genevieve suddenly felt cold despite the warm breeze coming through the open window.

"He came in the middle of the night," Daniel continued. "Slipped right in. I was awake, luckily."

"What did he say?" Genevieve asked, her fear climbing into her throat. The thought of someone like John Boyle visiting Daniel when he was vulnerable and weak in his hospital bed made her sick to her stomach.

"He reminded me it was all just business, and asked that I have no hard feelings. Said Eddie would take the fall for everything, now that Tommy was gone."

Genevieve's mind raced as her fear shifted to outrage. "But Boyle ought to be exposed. Wouldn't Longstreet want the real man in charge? The real killer? Even if Eddie administered the drinks with nightshade or pulled the trigger on Oscar, it was all at Boyle's or Meade's behest, was it not?"

"Longstreet doesn't have any evidence against Boyle," Daniel replied. He sounded even more exhausted than earlier. "But he knows Eddie was involved, and Eddie is willing to take the fall, and that's good enough for Longstreet right now. Eddie would die before selling Boyle out, plain and simple. With Tommy dead, there's nobody to contradict him."

Rupert shifted Daniel a look. "Well, nobody *willing* to contradict him," Daniel amended.

"*I'm* willing," Genevieve protested.

Daniel fixed her gaze with his, and intermingled with the weariness and determination in his dark blue eyes, she read another emotion there, one that gave her pause: fear.

"They know where you live, Genevieve," he said quietly.

Genevieve could feel herself blanch, and she swallowed, her own fright returning as quickly as it had fled.

"You have a good story," Daniel continued. His blinks were lengthening, his eyelids appearing heavy. "A great one. Epic in scale: parental fallacy, corruption, revolution-aries, poison . . . You don't need Boyle in the mix, and you don't want to make an enemy of him. Let him be. Please."

Genevieve crossed her arms and sighed. She watched carriages pass on the street below, bright green leaves rus-tling in the sunshine, a robin hopping on a branch. She thought about the tenuous nature of justice, and the way Tommy's body had folded to the ground, almost gently, as her bullet had found its home.

"It all sounds like something the ancient Greeks could have written, when you put it that way," she finally said.

Daniel huffed a small laugh. "Greed is a time-honored theme. See? The society pages may have more to offer than you think."

The memory of Arthur's words, a full month ago now, dropped on her like a stone sinking in a pond: *"There's meat on those bones, Genevieve."*

It gave her a sudden chill, thinking of the secrets hidden behind the grand facades of Fifth Avenue.

"Fine," Genevieve finally agreed. "I'll leave Boyle out of it. But it's not just us, Daniel. What about Nora?"

"She's gone," Daniel replied. "I've had Paddy and Billy looking, and Asher too. Nobody has seen her."

They were all quiet and sober at that, Genevieve, at least, pondering the possibilities of what might have befallen a girl like Nora Westwood upon the death of her protector, Tommy Meade. She could have gone home to her father but had apparently chosen not to.

The city had swallowed her up, for now.

★   ★   ★

Daniel raised his fist to knock on the front door of the Stewart family townhouse but paused, struck by a sudden and uncharacteristic bout of uncertainty. There was nothing to blame in the quality of the morning, which was shaping up to be rather perfect. The more temperate days of June had only just edged into the early steam of July, but the day was new enough that the night's coolness still lingered slightly, aided by a soft summer breeze. The scent of flowers was heady, as was the sound of contented bees going about their business, all emanating from the small front garden of the Stewart home.

What if she doesn't want to see you? The thought reverberated. Genevieve's visits to him at the hospital had tapered after their encounter with Longstreet. Daniel knew she was busy writing her story and getting ready to depart for Newport—already almost a week past when her editor had wanted her to leave—but after the past month of being in each other's near constant company, he felt her absence as though he were missing a part of himself. On his last day at the hospital, two days ago, he had found himself looking hopefully toward the door every time he heard footsteps echoing down the hallway.

Was she simply swamped, as Esmie had claimed when she and Rupert had come to collect him home? Or had she decided that her association with him brought more harm than good into her life?

He hadn't failed to notice the shadows under her eyes on the days she had visited.

Go ahead—knock. Before he could change his mind, he rapped his fist on the door loudly.

The family was at breakfast, but when a maid led him to the dining room, they appeared delighted to see him. Anna rose and wrapped him in a warm, matronly embrace, inquiring after his health, and Wilbur shook his hand with a firm and cheerful grip. Genevieve rose but kept to her place. Daniel was pleased to see her smile, but also noted the continued presence of those circles under her eyes.

He could guess what caused them. A pang of guilt reverberated through him; she was suffering because she had killed a man, an act she had only undertaken to save his life.

"I hope you don't mind, dear, but Wilbur and I were just on our way out," Anna explained. She pulled back a chair and gestured for him to sit. "We're part of a committee that wants to make the arch on the square a permanent fixture. Wouldn't that be something? But sit, please, and eat something. You look near skin and bones. Didn't they feed you at that hospital?"

"Come, Anna," Wilbur urged. "Charles will be waiting." He gently guided his wife out of the room, Anna still chattering, smiling gently at Daniel as they departed.

Daniel took in the detritus of the breakfast table: a rack of toast, an untouched piece of which lay in front of Genevieve, the dirty dishes left by Anna and Wilbur, just being cleared by the same maid who had shown him in. He accepted a cup of coffee and waited to speak until they were alone.

"How is the piece coming?" he finally asked, adding some cream to his coffee and stirring.

Genevieve twisted the corner of her napkin but smiled again. "It's finished. I gave it to Arthur last night. I'll be heading to the paper later this morning to receive his verdict."

"I'm sure he will love it," Daniel said.

"I hope so. I think it's rather good."

"How are you otherwise?" he asked, keeping his voice soft.

She looked at him with surprise. "Fine," she shrugged. Genevieve picked up her coffee cup but set it down again, untouched.

"Really, Genevieve. How *are* you?" Genevieve kept her gaze on her cup, but blinked several times in succession. "I know what it feels like to take a life," he said. "I'm so sorry you had to do that. But I wanted to thank you. It is because of you I'm still alive."

Her gaze flew up, intense and focused on his. "There is no need of thanks." She opened her mouth as if to say more, but shut it again. He waited, his heart in his throat.

"How are *you* feeling?" Genevieve finally said, turning the question back on him.

Daniel decided to let the matter of her killing Meade be. She would come to terms with it in her own time, and when she was ready to talk, he would be there.

"Mostly back to myself," he said. "I tire easily, which is galling. Seems unmanly."

This elicited a short peal of laughter, as he'd hoped. "Your stamina will return shortly, I've no doubt," Genevieve responded in a wry tone. She picked up her own coffee cup and gave him a fond look over its rim.

Fond. Was that all he was to her? A friend of whom she thought fondly?

Or could there be more?

Daniel's mind returned, as it so often did, to the moment when he was staring down the cold, deadly barrel of Tommy's gun. Of how he had been quite certain he would die in that moment, and of how, there at the end, all he wanted to see in the world was Genevieve's face.

He also recalled her refusing his proposal of marriage. Even though it now seemed a lifetime ago, Daniel could replay the entire scene in his head.

Patience.

Perhaps there was still time. Perhaps he could try again.

After looking death in the eye at the gasworks, Daniel had a deepened appreciation for the value of time, for its preciousness. He didn't want to waste a second of it.

But he also didn't want to overwhelm Genevieve when she was already feeling vulnerable, or ruin their friendship, newly re-formed and fragile, with presumptions.

Patience.

He would bide his time. For a little while.

"Rupert and Esmie are leaving soon," Genevieve was saying. Her hands were more relaxed now. She leaned back in her seat. "They said you were considering joining them at the Bradley house in Newport for the summer. Do you think you might?" Her tone was casual, but did he detect an undercurrent of hope in it?

Or was he simply projecting his own hope onto what was just friendly conversation?

"Yes," Daniel replied.

He was instantly gratified when an unmistakable, brilliant smile of joy lit Genevieve's beautiful face.

"Yes," he repeated, his heart lifting. "I believe I will."

"Genevieve?" The female voice, quiet and tentative from the door, caused them both to turn. At the sight of the young woman, Daniel stood automatically, a bit confused; he hadn't heard the front bell ring.

Genevieve's face paled, and she pressed a suddenly trembling hand to her heart.

"Callie?" Genevieve stood also, so abruptly her chair overturned. She rushed to the doorway and wrapped her arms around her friend, sudden tears streaming down her face. "Callie!"

Callie embraced Genevieve in return, and Daniel watched the pair of friends, deeply moved. He knew how saddened Genevieve had been over Callie's disappearance.

"Come, sit," Genevieve urged, after their embrace ended. She wiped tears from her face and gave a small, joyful laugh. "I can't tell you how good it is to see you. Do you need food? Coffee? Let me ring for some." Genevieve reached for the bellpull, but Callie stopped her.

"Genevieve, wait," she said. "Wait." Daniel saw it then: the tension in Callie's brow, how her mouth was drawn and taut.

Something was wrong.

Genevieve seemed to see it, too. "What is it?" Her voice was suddenly full of dread. "Callie, what is going on?"

Callie's deep green eyes flicked from Genevieve to Daniel, and then back again. She took a deep breath. "I need your help," she said, finally. "Both of you."

Daniel's heart, which had been so happy moments ago, sank. He knew that look. Whatever help Callie needed, it was no trifling matter. And no matter what it was, he knew Genevieve would not refuse her.

He had a sudden, sinking suspicion that neither of them would get to Newport that summer after all.

ACKNOWLEDGMENTS

It was such a pleasure to inhabit the world of 1889 New York City while writing this book, and I relied on multiple sources in my attempt to make that historical period come alive for readers. Many of the locations and moments that appear in this story are inspired by actual places and events. *The Bowery Boys* podcast is a treasure trove of information about historic New York, and I owe them a huge debt of gratitude. Thanks to hosts Greg Young and Tom Meyers for their meticulous research, and if New York City history is of interest to you, I highly recommend the show. It is through their work that I first learned of the now-demolished Casanova Mansion in the Bronx. The moment I heard about the house I knew it had to play a major role in Genevieve and Daniel's next adventure. Originally called Whitlock's Folly after its original owner, the wealthy Southerner Benjamin Morris Whitlock, the mansion had an iron gate that opened automatically, as described in the book. It also contained underground tunnels with storage vaults that were indeed used by the second owner, Cuban sugar importer Inocencio Casanova, for the storage and shipment of guns and ammunition for the aid of Cuban revolutionaries. The tunnels led to a small island called Duck Island in the East River. The island is no longer there, but was located under present-day Tiffany Street in the Bronx.

Similarly, McGurk's Suicide Hall came to my attention through *The Bowery Boys*. This real place served as the inspiration for Boyle's Suicide Tavern in the book, and John Boyle and Knockout Eddie are based on the historical figures John McGurk and his former boxer turned bouncer, "Eat 'Em Up" Jack McManus. The slogan "Better Dead" was inscribed over the door, and the dive became notorious for a string of deaths by suicide of women who rented rooms on the upper floor. Similarly, Detective Aloysius Longstreet was inspired by the real-life figure of Detective Thomas F. Byrnes, who started the infamous "rouges gallery," or photographic gallery of criminals. I took a minor liberty with the timing of rooftop bars in New York: such establishments as the Metropolitan Theater, which Genevieve and Daniel visit, were not prevalent in the city until the following year, 1890. Otherwise, I have tried to be as historically accurate as possible. Bagels, Chinese food, the safety bicycle, were all available in 1889 New York. Other sources I consulted include *This Podcast Will Kill You* for the effects of belladonna, Maureen E. Montgomery's book *Displaying Women, Spectacles of Leisure in Edith Wharton's New York,* and the indispensable *Low Life, Lures and Snares of Old New York* by Luc Sante.

Though my name is on the cover, the process of transferring this book from my brain into readers' hands was a collective effort, as are all books. Great thanks to the entire team at Crooked Lane Press, in particular my editor, Faith Black Ross, as well as Melissa Rechter and Madeline Rathle. My agent Danielle Egan-Miller of Browne & Miller Literary Associates makes all things possible, and I am enormously grateful to her and everyone at Browne & Miller.

I wrote the majority of this book while under quarantine in 2020, and I couldn't have accomplished it without the support of my family and friends, either virtually or in person. Big thanks to Christine Gillespie, Celeste Donovan, and Juli Ann Patty for their patience and good advice during the ebbs and flows of my writing process. And, of course, my husband Marc gave me the time, space, encouragement and love necessary to keep going.